THE SILK BETRAYAL

THE
SILK
BETRAYAL

Daniel Ausema

GUARDBRIDGE BOOKS
ST ANDREWS, SCOTLAND

Published by Guardbridge Books,
St Andrews, Fife, United Kingdom.

Silk Betrayal, The

© 2017 by Daniel Ausema. All rights reserved.

No part of this book may be reproduced in any written, electronic, recording, or photocopying without written permission of the publisher or author.

This is a work of fiction. All characters and events portrayed in this book are fictitious, and any resemblance to real people or events is purely coincidental.

Cover art © Kit Foster, 2017

ISBN: hardback: 978-1-911486-20-6
paperback: 978-1-911486-21-3

The Silk Betrayal is dedicated to the stories and storytellers—of many times, peoples, places, and languages—that have shaped the ever-changing matrix of my imagination. Their magic gives form to the world we experience.

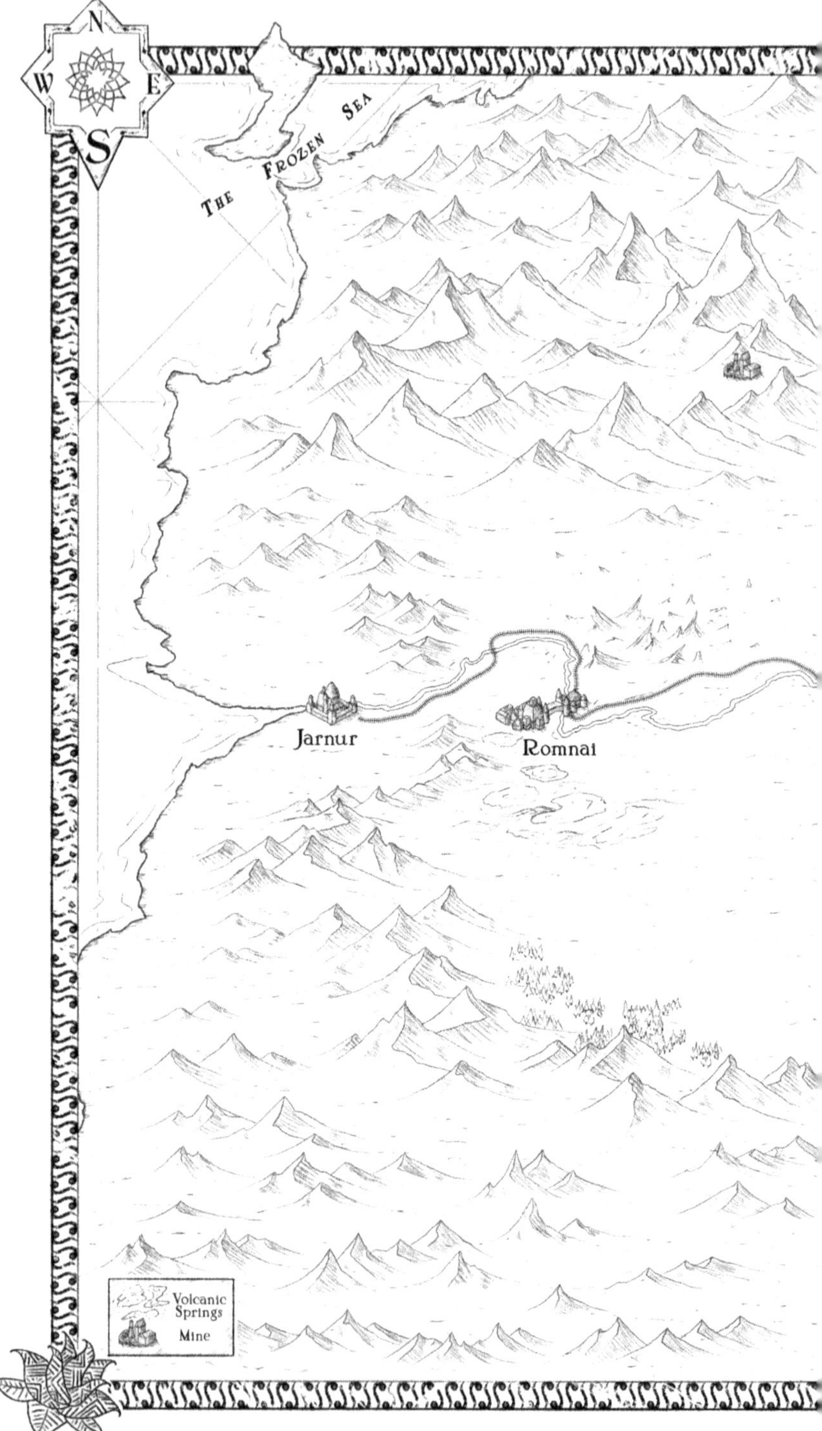

N
W
E
S
THE FROZEN SEA
Jarnur
Romnat
Volcanic
Springs
Mine

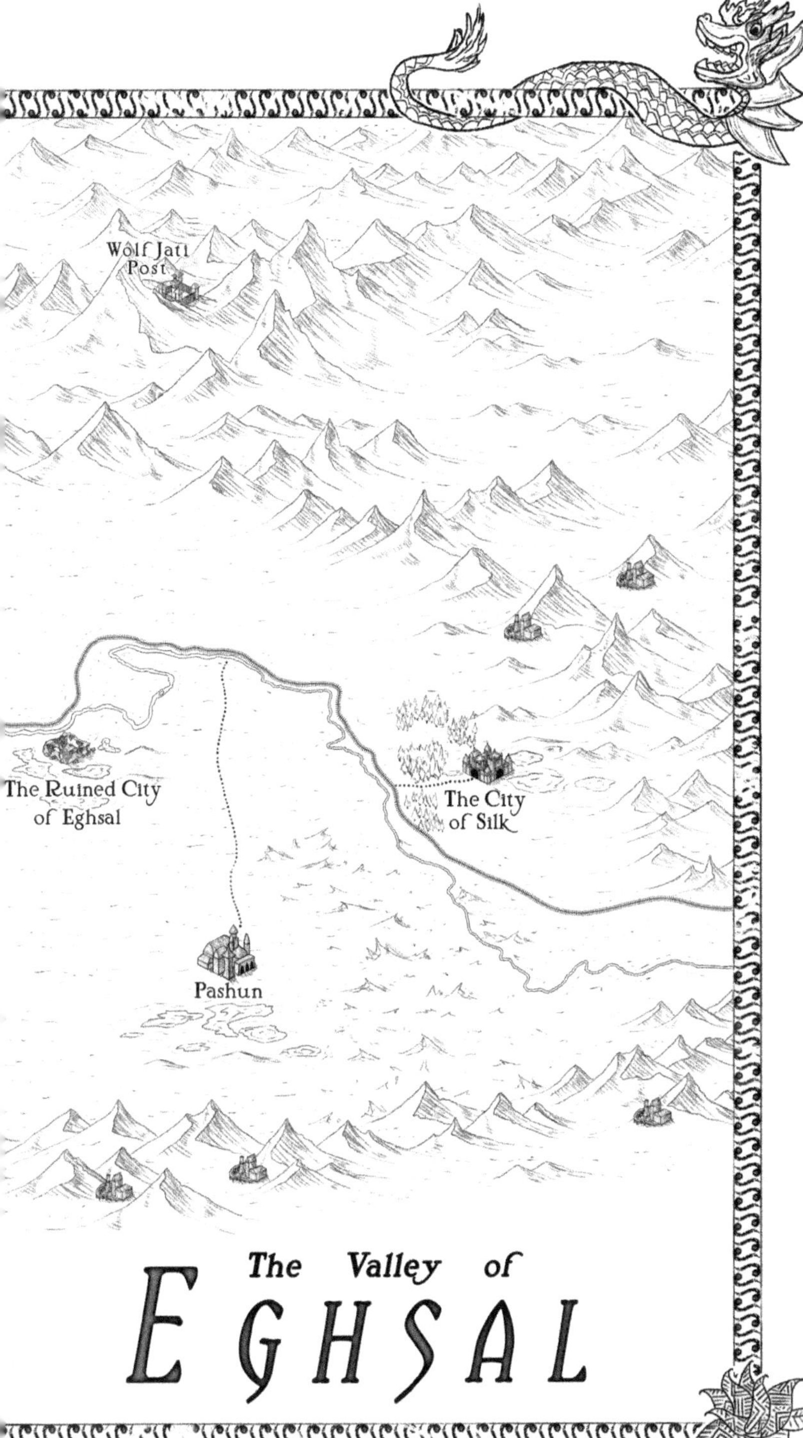

Wolf Jati Post
The Ruined City of Eghsal
The City of Silk
Pashun
The Valley of
EGHSAL
© Zach Bodenner 2017

Chapter 1

Two things stood out in the stillness of the high tundra plain—the gleaming metal of new train tracks and a huge trail of destruction that stretched along those rails. Pavresh moved cautiously among the debris. Scraps of metal lay scattered beside other detritus. Broken bales of raw cloth. The hard rinds of unripe squash split open, their seeds spilled on the ground. Raw ore, maybe even from his father's mine. Other upriver goods, unrecognizable with the force of the crash. At one point, shards of ice littered the ground where a car had been carrying glacial ice down to Romnai. Splintered wood covered the ground like a coarse snowfall. Stillness and violence combined in such a complete and uncanny way. Pavresh shivered at the terror of the scene.

Real snow also fell, a dusting that melted as it hit the ground and sizzled where it touched hot metal. Autumn had barely arrived, but out here snow could come any time of year.

At the worst of the destruction, where even the rails were melted and twisted into grotesque shapes, Pavresh saw the remains of the terrifying new steam engines. They still radiated heat. There were no cries of survivors, no calls for help. A cold like that of the high winds blew down his neck.

Beyond the crash center, the goods were downriver items, mostly fish that were already beginning to rot. Despite the smell, Pavresh stopped, thinking that his father had once known that smell every day, before being sent inland to leave the sea behind for good. Pavresh only knew the smell from the occasional fish brought to their remote home for special feasts. His sister, three years older than him, might possibly remember the sea itself, but he'd never asked her. And leaving as he had, it seemed doubtful he'd get a chance to speak with her or any of his family, even if he somehow met them. That thought didn't sit well on his mind, so he pushed it away.

Instead of fish, Pavresh and his younger brother had only known the smells of mineral-heavy water pumped from the deepest tunnels, of iron ore and copper, of the many people of lower castes forced to labor in the mines. The smell finally made him bring his hand up to his nose, a thin nose, its color he would have preferred to compare to the rich copper that came from their mines, but in truth, he thought it closer in shade to the rust that gathered on the rails running deep underground.

The devastation was shocking, far too much to let him dwell on the past. Pavresh tried to examine exactly how it made him feel. It wasn't the anger of being robbed or the outrage of a murder or the indignation of a *nefli*, a low-caste laborer, touching someone from a higher caste. It was betrayal. The technology that promised so much had betrayed those who had trusted it.

Which magic would that be? Pavresh closed his eyes and tried to recreate the same feeling. The betrayal. He imagined a brother's murder, a lover's unfaithfulness, a child's rejection. He added a touch of hope only to crush it. It still felt a little too human to fit the scene. He'd have to keep working on it as he finished his journey to Romnai, find some way to bring in the mechanical feel of it. Even so, it was close. He should be able to add it to performances soon.

His satisfaction vanished as he opened his eyes to the destruction and the uncaring river beyond. How could he think so calmly about using this tragedy for his magic? It seemed cold and calloused, not the person he considered himself at all. And yet…maybe that was a part of him. Ever since he'd begun to understand the magic, he'd seldom had a situation, no matter how terrifying or sad or joyful, when a part of him didn't wonder how he could take those feelings and use them.

This scene nearly silenced that part of him with its absolute destruction. But only nearly.

Nonetheless, he gave a shiver and swore aloud to the empty scene, "I will never ride one of these contraptions."

Nothing answered his shout. Not even the animals yet dared to come and scavenge. Pavresh walked between the two sets of rails once he was past the worst of the destruction. How had both a downriver and upriver train ended up on the same tracks? He walked as quickly as he could and tried not to imagine what it had been like for those aboard the train.

Really, the new steam-trains weren't all that different from the rail cars that brought ore from his father's mine. He'd ridden them often growing up, feeling like he was flying into the darkness. It was a mock sense of danger that thrilled him. A safe danger, like riding a boat down minor rapids or taking a horse through a course that only looked tricky. He'd never actually done either of those things, but he had recreated the feelings in his magic after listening to the stories of others.

And they weren't even all that different from the horse-drawn rail cars that had brought goods upriver here for centuries. But somehow it was those slight differences that pushed it from safe danger to true danger. As exciting as the false kind was, Pavresh had no desire for real danger. He desired magic, and through magic, perhaps some level of fame. Danger had nothing to do with such things.

Downriver now he could see people arriving from the city to salvage and scavenge what they could. They would search for survivors. Pavresh pursed his lips sadly. After what he'd seen of the crash, he knew it would be a futile search.

Not wanting to meet the people, he moved north, away

from the river, and set up his camp among a small cluster of tumbled boulders. The dusting of snow hadn't wet the dead wood all around.

Pavresh lit a fire and bowed briefly to it. Then he untied the tightly woven cord that wrapped three times around his thin waist and performed his kusti. It was a graceful movement, slow and calm and punctuated only occasionally by a quick snap of the cord over the fire and to each side. The rest of the time he held the cord loosely in his calloused hands and moved it high and low, behind his neck, behind his back. His legs held his lower body in a sequence of stances to complement the motions and allow his mind to free itself and become a part of the fire.

As he felt himself enter the fire and the fire enter him, Pavresh wrapped the cord around his waist, chanting the ancient Enshi prayers. The ritual knots came without thought.

He sat beside the fire, his face blank. Large flakes of snow struck him and melted into steam. Some time later, he came back to himself, ate a piece of dry bread with salted meat, gulped some water, and lay down to sleep. Two more nights sleeping out here in the wild, he thought, and then he'd reach the city.

* * *

Romnai, the capital city of his people, stood across the river from Pavresh. It had never been his home, never been his father's home. It probably hadn't even been his ancestors' home for centuries, if ever, but it still felt like a homecoming. Certainly one of those deep-seated feelings his magic could play with.

A wet snow fell on the buildings, and that seemed right, fitting despite the warm air close to the ground.

Dilapidated buildings stood on the near side of the river,

the old loading docks and stables from the days of horse-drawn rail carts. Further on, the bit of city on this side of the river grew wider, and the tracks curved through their midst to follow the river north. He hadn't come this close to the tracks since leaving the debris-strewn field. They looked so innocent, once again promising everything about the future and progress and perfection that the terrible crash had betrayed.

A single bridge crossed the river, an elaborate structure that arced high over the water. Pavresh approached, and the far side of the bridge disappeared behind the curving summit. A sign beside the bridge named it "The Bridge of the Forgotten South," called for the land of folk tales that the people of Eghsal claimed as their original home, centuries ago. A few carriages glided over the smooth bridge, but mostly it was laborers who crowded its span, especially the messengers and delivery men known as *wallas*.

Pavresh climbed slowly, relishing the way the city revealed itself to him. From the middle of the bridge, he could see clear across to the lava fields, hot springs and geysers that kept this northern valley warm. They disappeared, and the sprawling houses of the city's thirty princes with them, as he walked down to the bank. Steam from the fumarole field still dominated the sky straight ahead, a backdrop to everything he saw. Where it reached cooler air overhead, it turned to snow. Rougher buildings stood before him.

As he stepped into the narrow streets, three men came forward to block his path.

They weren't untouchables. He saw that right away, despite their ragged clothing and rough looks. Something in their expressions was too defiant and self-assured for that. Back in the mine his father ran, they'd sent untouchables to the deepest tunnels. Most had broader faces and features that seemed only half-formed. Many had lighter skin, perhaps from an ancestry that included the native mumblers. These men looked too sharp and alive to be untouchable.

Pavresh untied the knots on the kusti cord at his waist and waited.

"Fine clothes you have there," one man said. "A bit rustic though."

Pavresh glanced at his sturdy traveling cloak but said nothing.

"To fit in on these streets, you'll need a new set," another said as a knife appeared in his hands. "We'll just take yours."

Pavresh knew he couldn't wait any longer. He pulled the cord from his waist and snapped it. The man with the knife cried out in pain and dropped his weapon. Moving quickly into another stance, he swung the cord again, making all three men duck. Then he switched directions and flicked a frayed end across a face.

Before they could react, he took off running. Slush sprayed from his feet. Street twisted into street, and he was breathing heavily when at last he dared stop.

His immediate thought, even as he swiveled around for any sign of pursuit, was to recapture the feeling he'd had, the fear of the attack, the thrill of fighting back, the terror of the flight.

It was the strong sense of fighting back for justice that overwhelmed the other feelings. He would have to be careful using that one. It made him wish he had stayed and truly punished the men. He imagined wrapping the cord around a neck, of snapping it so fiercely it would cut flesh. The cord was a decent weapon; he could have done that, he thought as he refastened the traditional knots. But the rational part of him knew he wouldn't have won. He'd caught them by surprise was all. If he'd kept up the fight, they would have easily overcome him. A quick charge by any one of them would have brought them too close for him to use the cord. He might have been able to sting whoever charged, but its threat was no more than a bit of pain. And what good was fighting for justice only to lose?

A powerful emotion, undoubtedly, but a dangerous one.

Pavresh moved on, looking for the district he'd heard of and the building he'd been seeking.

Now, as he wove among the buildings, he noticed the untouchables begging along the streets, some lame or injured, but most whole, merely unlucky by birth. It was a *nefli* neighborhood, low-caste with older buildings crumbling at the corners and narrow streets lined with refuse. In many places, the buildings reached across the street to touch those on the other side.

Pavresh walked by both the untouchables and the *neflis* with the mid-caste *brenil* behavior he'd been raised with. Though originally a fisherman and later a mine overseer, his father was *brenil*, technically a part of the merchant jati for reasons even Pavresh didn't fully understand. Something dating back at least to his grandfather's grandfather.

Without thinking about it, Pavresh did something he never would have done back home—instead of looking past these people, he turned his eyes to them. He saw the fear and, beneath it, the glimmer of defiance of the untouchables, the weariness and pride of the *nefli*. And for the first time since he'd left his home at the edge of the mountains, Pavresh wondered exactly to what caste and what jati he belonged. By rights, he should follow his father in the merchant jati, a sub-caste of the *brenil*. His sister had married within that caste, and his brother also would remain in the merchant jati. It hadn't mattered to him out in the wilderness where there were no other people, but now it seemed to. What caste was a magic performer, an arcist like him? The answer, he realized, was none.

None? Might as well be a mumbler, some hold-over from the Mumbler Wars of his father's era, hiding for forty years within the city they had tried to conquer. He even raised his fingers to his face, as if to feel the paleness of the valley's original inhabitants.

For once, he didn't try to understand the terrifying yet liberating sense this question created in him. He stumbled to a wall and leaned against it. The world beneath his feet seemed to open up. People passing by gave him odd looks, but all he could think about was falling into an endless chasm where the world wasn't what he'd always believed. Where a world without castes had no form to hold the sacred fire, where it merely fell away into nothingness.

Finally, he was able to breathe normally. He grabbed his canvas water bottle and poured what remained in it over his face.

After a moment, he pushed the thought away, echoing the mental action with the physical act of pushing himself from the wall. For now, he would assume all would be well, that the magic itself as he learned more and trained would eventually give him the certainty he lacked. The vertigo remained, threatened to overwhelm him if he thought about it closely, but with effort, he could keep it at bay.

Soon he found the building, tucked between an inn and a tailor's shop. Not a fancy area, but less run-down than some he'd passed through. It was a house, narrow and connected to the buildings on either side. A steep roof of wooden shingles sent snow falling down in front of the door. A single window opened from among those shingles on the left side, and other windows marked the two floors below, all of them lit.

Pavresh paused in front of the door. A hero was inside, hero to many. The soldier who'd saved the city from the mumblers forty years ago, but even more—to Pavresh, anyway—the man who'd discovered arcist magic. Using the magic's power he'd inspired his unit and later the whole army to fight back with a ferocity the mumblers couldn't match. And then at the height of his fame, he'd walked away, broken jati to wander Eghsal, speaking to people of every caste so he could understand the magic better. Chaitan, the legend. When sickness had forced an end to his wandering, the man had come here, to this house in Romnai.

Taking a deep breath, Pavresh pulled on his magic. He wanted to give himself the right image, a bit of the rugged wanderer, but still young and cocky. So, something of the rising star, the precocious wonder child. It took time and effort to focus on the magic, as his questions about how he fit among the castes threatened to return. When he'd crafted the glamor as he wanted, he hesitated. These people would be used to arcistry, so he didn't want to lay it on thick. He imagined the snow, coming down more heavily now, muting the magic.

Simple and blunt, but hopefully effective. That much he could do, even with what little he'd learned from a *nefli* miner, but he wasn't satisfied with knowing the magic merely at a simple level. He would learn from the master.

Most of the scene inside scarcely registered with him. He saw many faceless people sipping tisane through metal straws. He saw a musician in a corner, but he didn't bother identifying what instrument she played. He saw a stage of sorts along one wall where a couple danced a routine.

All of that was nothing.

He felt arcist magic shifting with the music and dance, but that also was nothing.

What mattered was the ailing man propped on pillows against an inner wall. Pavresh walked up, his own magic delicately playing the image he'd created. A red blanket covered Chaitan, and his eyes were half-closed as if in pain.

Pavresh knelt on two knees and bowed his head the way a *nefli* would to a prince or other member of the *kortru* caste.

"Who are you?" The words were slurred with pain, but there was interest in Chaitan's face, not the annoyance that might have accompanied those words.

Before he could answer humbly with his name, Pavresh

remembered his persona, the arrogant wanderer. What came out then surprised even him.

"I'm your heir."

Chaitan opened his eyes wider to look at him.

"I've been a wanderer. A mountain walker. A village bum. A train rider. A fisherman and a miner." With each claim, whether true or a lie, he altered his magic subtly. "I'm an arcist. Your heir."

"Well," Chaitan settled back into his pillows and closed his eyes, "I'm tired tonight, my heir. Tomorrow you may perform for me, and we shall see."

As Pavresh bowed his head in response, he was struck with an image, an arcist event: the Passing of the King and Choosing of the Heir. The force of the image nearly knocked him over as he withdrew from the old man.

He couldn't decide, as he looked for some place to settle himself, whether that had been an encouragement for him or a warning. Or even a bit of ironic mockery.

Chapter 2

"You look like another pilgrim. Have you reached your holy shrine?"

The words had the ring of the sea, and Pavresh looked up to see a fisherman, at least by dress, though he didn't smell of fish. He was dark-skinned and short, but with striking features—eyes like bronze that had begun to harden and smooth, sharp cheeks. He held a hollowed-out gourd in one hand, identical to the one Pavresh was sipping hot tisane from.

"I'm not sure yet. I..." *Play the part*, he reminded himself. "I've traveled all over the valley," he lied. "Maybe this is the place. Or maybe I'll move on to wilder places." He shrugged and sipped from the metal straw.

"I'm always ready to explore new lands, too. I'm Ekana." The fisherman held out his hand. "Welcome, and I hope you find what you want." He touched Pavresh's gourd with his own then sat beside him on the low, cushioned bench.

"Thank you. I'm Pavresh. What's this about pilgrims, shrines?"

Ekana laughed and rubbed his cheek with a finger. "Oh, just the way they talk here, as if everything they dream of is sacred and holy."

"And it's not?"

"Sure. And no. Some just take it so seriously, I guess. They believe their own boasts too much."

Pavresh nodded. He could see that happening. "You came here also. You're not a pilgrim?"

With a shrug, Ekana answered, "In my own way, I guess.

Isn't everyone? I like to be where new things are happening. I might be as happy working on creating the new steamships, but they don't accept a fisherman like they do here."

"So, are you an arcist, as well?"

"No. We perform with the arcists."

Pavresh looked around the room. No one was on stage now, and if anyone beside the stage was performing an arcist magic, it was too subtle to pick up. One woman sat beside the stage on a tall stool, playing an oddly shifting music on a large stringed instrument. She made the instrument seem to talk to itself.

"We?" He inclined his head toward the instrumentalist.

"No, not her. Indima and I dance together. Here, let me introduce you to her." He half stood up and leaned toward a clump of people sitting on the floor and talking in low voices. "Indima. Come, meet Pavresh."

A woman rose from the group, handing her gourd of tisane to a neighbor to set down, and Pavresh's mouth froze on the metal straw. She was beautiful. Smooth, bronze skin, a fine nose, light brown eyes flecked with darker colors. She was *kortru*, highest caste, he had no doubt. Her clothes were fine silks, which made them hundreds of years old, since the silkworms of the Forgotten South could not survive in the north.

Among the *kortru* jatis were the silk weavers, those people with the skill and knowledge and perhaps a bit of magic to preserve and reweave the precious silk that remained. They were respected above almost any other, the equals of the priests and princes. Pavresh was sure she must be one of them.

He fought the urge to play caste to her, to treat her as society demanded. But clearly that didn't matter in this house.

She smiled and held out her hand to him. Taking it, he realized that she had said something to him, but he hadn't noticed what. He swallowed the honey-sweetened tisane in his mouth, but his tongue stumbled. He added a touch more magic to his image, hoping to recover his poise. At last, he got out the words, "Pleased to meet you."

"And I you. Welcome to Chaitan's house." She gave no indication she'd noticed his distraction. "I don't think you're a musician. You didn't walk in with an instrument." Her eyes studied him. "Probably not a dancer either, though you're fit. A good dancer could work with you, if you're not clumsy."

Pavresh glanced at Ekana and back to Indima. What exactly was she saying to him? Pavresh swallowed hard and asked, "And, are you a good dancer?"

She laughed, and it was a beautiful sound to match her face. "The best. But no, I think you're a magician." She put her arm through Ekana's arm, and the motion spoke everything that words hadn't, that she'd seen how he looked at her, that she was flattered, that she was committed to her dance partner. "Would you like to perform while we dance?"

He almost refused, for his wounded pride, for the unfamiliarity of this place, for his own lack of practice performing. But then he remembered his persona. The young wanderer would have performed in public many times, for all kinds of people. Pulling on that role was a relief after the confusing introduction to the silk weaver. He nodded and moved toward the stage.

Ekana and Indima positioned themselves on opposite sides of the stage and waited for the musician to move into a new song. Pavresh watched them and listened to the music and tried to decide the primary arcist magic. In their first hesitant step toward each other, he knew it.

The Forbidden Love. The castes might not exist in the magic exactly, but he could often find ways to get at the idea. There was no way to see this pairing except through the eyes of the caste system. As they came closer, he added a touch of the thrill of false danger. When their hands first touched, it became true danger.

They moved about as the music developed, and he added other touches, hints of other emotions. One that crept in without him noticing was jealousy. The Rival. Once he recognized it, he kept it there, allowing it to swell and fade and return as the dancers turned and spun and leaped. The audience, he realized, should feel jealous, as if they were a third part of the picture.

This was why he'd come to Romnai. Not simply to develop his arcist skills, but to use them, to perform in this exciting new art form. The dancers and the musician and the arcist, improvising together a scene that was a sort of conversation. The audience would feel his magic, not overtly but an inner feeling that played on how they saw the dancing, how they heard the music, all without them realizing.

When they finished, the forbidden lovers crushed by the overbearing father or the self-righteous priest or whatever image the audience created to explain it, those sitting around set down their gourds and smoking pipes and applauded.

Pavresh's cheeks flushed with pleasure as he joined Ekana and Indima and the group of people she had been with when they had interrupted her.

"Nice work, Pavresh." Indima ran a hand down his upper arm. It sent chills up his neck. "You were good."

"Thanks. It was…fun. I've never performed with such skilled dancers. And musician." He turned back toward the stage and saw the woman move into another song as if unconcerned that they had stopped. This one seemed to be an argument, an inner debate as the instrument struggled with what to do.

"Namrani," Ekana said. "She's good, but she hardly seems to know we're here. Except when someone's on stage, then she catches every nuance."

Still smiling more childishly than his rugged wanderer persona ought to, Pavresh was introduced to those sitting there drinking tisane. Jaritta, at first glance, was another beautiful, high-caste woman, perhaps around thirty years old...but then he saw the old scars on one side of her face. She covered most of that side of her face with a loop of cloth from her dress. If that was caused by fire, and he guessed it was from the smooth skin of the scar, she would have been cast out, no matter what family she had belonged to. Her clothing didn't quite make her look untouchable, but it certainly wasn't silk or anything fine.

Iksheen called himself a poet. There was an angry look in his face as if the world he saw didn't match what was right. His clothes, a mixture of good quality and poor, his slightly unkempt hair, and the fine pipe he was smoking all seemed contrived specifically to frustrate any attempt to place him in any caste or jati. He didn't seem untouchable or outcast, simply outside the castes themselves. Neither below nor above them. He was young, like Pavresh, and his greeting was not enthusiastic.

Many of the other introductions went by him too fast. He promised himself he'd learn them all later. Most of them were young, from the late teens and up with Jaritta on the older end. But there was one older man—in his fifties, Pavresh guessed—Marankiya. As soon as Pavresh heard the name, he looked closer. It was not a common name, and he had to guess this was the man he'd heard of. Stories were told of him, or rather of the youth he'd been. When he was eight, he had already read all the sacred Aidras. When he was ten, he had studied the holy Tarmarayan epics. By the time he was twelve, he had memorized six thousand Peisharn verses and studied with the greatest religious leaders of the valley.

Great things were expected of him. Certainly, he would create the next religious text explaining the nature of fire and the gods and the way to free the soul, people believed. Only it never happened. The religious waited and waited, but Marankiya gave them nothing new. He wrote, but it never lived up to the expectations. He explained his understanding of the sacred fire and the gods, but it always lacked the profundity people had longed for. His fame soon fizzled except as a byword for one who didn't live up to expectations.

Pavresh wanted to talk more with Marankiya, to learn what he was doing there at Chaitan's house and to understand what exactly must go through his mind. What image could Pavresh possibly create with his magic to conjure up such promise and disappointment?

But the introductions continued, and Marankiya seemed to have attention only for his mug of something that wasn't tisane.

The center of the group, the most charismatic and vocal of them all, was Rashul. On the street, Pavresh would have pegged him for *brenil* caste like himself, perhaps the cheetah jati that served the families of the *kortru* caste as personal servants. But in this house Pavresh had already learned that he couldn't rely on appearances. Rashul had lighter hair than most people, though nothing like the strange yellows and reds of the pale mumblers. Yet his skin was very dark and smooth, his face handsome. He wore a farmer's clothes, but Pavresh was confident he was no farmer and had never been one. His words were cultured and hypnotic.

Rashul wasted little time greeting Pavresh before launching back into whatever discussion they'd been having.

"Haven't you ever wondered why we know so little of the Forgotten South? Six hundred years. That's not long enough to forget so much. And even the earliest history of our valley is incredibly vague. I say intentionally so. We know almost nothing of the first three hundred years here."

Several people grumbled an assent. Jaritta shifted into a thoughtful pose, her left hand resting against her scar, and asked, "So, you say there were no untouchables when we first came here?"

"Not only no untouchables." His voice was louder now and passionate. "No castes. We were all one caste, all one jati."

This created a stir, and Pavresh realized it must be a new idea he was sharing, or perhaps a new development of ideas he'd already been talking about.

"So, someone here just invented the whole system?" one of the listeners asked.

"Could be. Or maybe the Forgotten South had the same system, but the colonists were all one jati, driven away by the others. Maybe they were all untouchables or all princes, driven out by another jati that wanted to rule, or all priests who fled as heretics when the religion changed. I'm still trying to figure that out."

Pavresh wasn't sure what to think of this or the fervent talk that followed. He hadn't come to Romnai for political ideals or any desire to change society. He wasn't opposed to it, but he'd come for the magic. And for the performances. That was what woke his passions.

Yet, clearly these political ideas were important to the other performers. He would do well to listen and appear to agree. Perhaps his wandering persona would be more concerned with this than he was in reality. He'd have to think about that, see what exactly would lie hidden in the young wanderer. And there was real power in the ideas of justice they evoked, an arcist power that resonated in him, even if, at times, they took it too seriously, as Ekana had said.

The conspiracy about the past sounded unlikely. Rather, it seemed Rashul's attempt not to discover the truth of history but to reinvent the past. Pavresh fingered the kusti knot at his waist. Certainly, his suggestion that they were all priests didn't seem right, or they would all agree on religion. But the Enshi religion he believed in was not the same as the more common pantheonic religion of Tiespetre and all the other gods. Beyond venerating fire—Tiespetre's father according to the priests—they had little in common. But he wasn't about to tell even these people that he was Enshi.

The talk continued, and they refilled their gourds with tisane, and Namrani played her strange, conversational music that certainly didn't arise from the Aidras or the epics or any priest-approved source.

* * *

"Let's play kiwan."

The voice woke Pavresh up from the corner he'd crawled into to sleep, and not long enough ago judging by how tired he still felt and the way his cheeks pulled down on his eyes. Chaitan waited in front of him, supported by two figures who were blurry in his half-lidded sight. He climbed to his feet.

A few others were also sleeping in the room, but most of the people had left, including the musician, Namrani. He supposed even these most daring and accomplished performers must have tedious day jobs of some sort.

Pavresh rubbed his eyes, ran his hands through his dark hair, and followed the halting figure toward one wall. Chaitan and his two attendants—were they his children, perhaps?—formed a single blurred form moving slowly. Pavresh yawned and did his best to wake up.

The kiwan table stood near a window made of oiled paper, so muted sunlight fell onto the pattern of lines. Kiwan was usually played standing, but this table had been lowered for Chaitan's sake. His attendants lowered him onto a pile of cushions. Once he was situated, he gestured for Pavresh to seat himself on the bare floor, which put him too low to play, so he kneeled. The rim-wall that ran around the table was perfectly polished, the wood grain showing striking contrast both on the outside and on the inner curved ramp that led down to the table.

Pavresh scanned the squares and lines and raised wooden bumps that marked the board. It was the finest kiwan table he'd ever seen. Chaitan handed him two heavy bags.

"Check these. Make sure you're satisfied that both sets are fair. Choose whichever one you want."

Pavresh opened one bag and poured out the markers. They were all disks painted green, but beyond that, they showed a great variation. Some were metal, small and heavy, some wood and some clay and even a few that were a mixture of materials. They varied in size, and some had other ornamentation that would affect how they rolled and spun.

Keeping the green ones in front of him, he opened the other bag, ran his fingers casually through the blue markers there and handed the bag to Chaitan.

"Looks good to me."

"Then you go first." Chaitan shifted his back and shoulders, moving the pillows until one of his attendants leaned forward and adjusted them for him.

When he'd finished and appeared comfortable, Pavresh selected a medium clay piece and held it against the edge of the ramp. Chaitan gave the traditional nod, and Pavresh released the piece with some backspin and watched it roll down and settle on the edge of a black square.

Chaitan held his wooden piece, waited for the nod, and sent it directly into a corner.

Pavresh was selecting his next piece when Chaitan spoke. "Why are you here?"

He paused and looked at the sickly man across from him. "I want to learn the magic."

"Don't stop playing. Just talk while we play."

Pavresh dutifully sent a metal disk with topspin bouncing over the wooden bumps and into the center of the board.

"You know the magic already. You've been laying it on so thick since you came here I can barely breathe."

Chaitan's piece curled around the edge and settled along one side. Pavresh eased up on the magic and picked his next piece without answering. He could feel his cheeks warming with blood.

They continued in silence for some minutes, in some rounds sending new pieces onto the board, in other rounds moving those that were there, capturing each other's pieces and taking strategic positions.

Finally, Pavresh spoke again, meekly. "I know the magic, but I haven't had the experiences you've had. I haven't talked to all the people you've talked to. I guess I know the magic, but I want to understand it."

Chaitan nodded as he took a heavy piece, flicked it so it was spinning on its edge, and sent it careening into two of Pavresh's pieces, taking over the strategic spot between them. Pavresh had never seen such a move. He stared at the piece, trying to replay in his mind how Chaitan had done that.

"Good," Chaitan said, as if he hadn't done anything special. "It's good you understand that difference."

He gave Pavresh the ceremonial nod to continue play without adding anything else. Pavresh debated trying to duplicate the spinning move, but instead, he slid one of the pieces on the board into a better position.

"So, why don't you just go out and talk to people? Have experiences like mine. Easier than learning it at a remove from an old, dying man." Chaitan moved a piece into an attack position.

Pavresh studied the board in silence to decide how to protect his own pieces. No clear path ahead., He slid a new piece down to rest beside Chaitan's attacker.

"I guess because you've understood the stories you've heard. I want to understand them. I try to understand my own feelings, the events I witness, the people I meet. But you have, umm, a frame for them, I guess."

He looked at the board for a moment, then continued. "It's like I'm trying to play kiwan without the squares and lines on the board, just guessing where everything goes. I…I need your help to draw the pattern on the board so I can actually see what I'm playing."

Chaitan was looking at him now. Not just looking at him, but studying him, examining his face, his mind even, it seemed. He leaned closer, as if to see Pavresh, actually see him, for the first time. Pavresh realized he had completely dropped the arcist persona that he'd put on before entering the house. He was simply himself.

"Well, then." Chaitan was smiling now, though Pavresh noticed how uncomfortable he looked, even on his pillows. "Very insightful. And you admit you need help. Maybe you don't fit the image of overly confidant youth exactly after all. We'll see."

He picked up one of the oddly shaped disks and bounced it in his palm. "But for now, let's finish the game." The disk bounced down the ramp and twisted among the bumps and other pieces to land in a protected space on Pavresh's side of the board. To Pavresh, it looked like the advance troops of a conquering army, one he had little hope of defeating.

Telling himself—and the pieces that remained to him—that he was fighting a just war, a war to defend his own land, he planned his next moves and hoped his pieces would perform the best they could.

The game lasted much of the morning before Pavresh lost, but he was sure it could have ended much sooner if Chaitan had wanted.

When Pavresh's last piece was captured, Chaitan sat back with a sigh and closed his eyes. "I have enough people lounging around here with nothing to do."

Pavresh looked around the room at the few people moving about, most seemingly engaged in work for Chaitan himself, certainly not lounging around.

"Other arcists who fill the air with their overly dramatic performances. If you wish to be my heir, I'll teach you and tell you stories, but during the mornings, you need to be out of this house, talking to people and learning their stories and experiencing everything the city offers. In the evenings, you may perform if you wish. In between, we can talk and create this frame in your mind."

"Thank you, sir." Pavresh dipped his head as the old arcist's attendants led him away.

* * *

As he stepped into the street, Pavresh remembered his earlier encounter with the thugs. His kusti had saved him, and it was tied tightly about his waist now, but he didn't want to repeat that. He cast over himself the persona of an honest laborer with just a hint of the sly, good-natured thief. The combination, he hoped, should give him the appearance of one who belonged on the streets of the city. For good measure, he added a bit of the rough, old-fashioned soldier as well.

Within a few blocks, the streets became uneven, lined with garbage and old buildings in poor repair. Pavresh headed away from the river, toward the *kortru* houses and the lava beds. The buildings became finer and larger as he went. The streets everywhere were full of people, mostly wallas carrying their packages or messages, all in a rush.

The mass of people thinned out as he reached the hot baths and smaller manor houses along this stretch of lava fields. Replacing them were untouchables begging beside the street where the wealthy might pass. Pavresh walked by and stood beside the great, otherworldly jumble of rocks and steaming pools of acrid water. The heat was intense, like nothing he'd felt back home in the mines. Yet, he'd benefited from them even there, for it was only these lava beds and others like them that made living in that northern valley bearable. Without them, the river valley would be as cold as the mountain heights where they'd driven the pale-faced mumblers. The smell struck him, soon overpowering the other senses, like eggs lost in the hen-house.

A geyser broke the surface to his left, an awe-inspiring sight as the heated water tore through the air.

Here was the dwelling place of fire. Both his own religion and the more common pantheonic religion taught that. Water, yes. Stone, yes. But most importantly, fire, the source of the entire cosmos. Water and rock and even Pavresh himself were simply the smoke and ashes of that great cosmic fire.

Pavresh closed his eyes and imagined that warmth filling him. This was why arriving at the city had seemed a homecoming. It was the dwelling place of the almighty fire.

Chaitan had offered him a precious gift, and all he had to do was experience things like this, whatever the city had to offer. That and talk to people and learn their stories. No demands to change the world, as those gathered in Chaitan's house dreamed of, but merely to understand it. Pavresh turned and scanned those scattered about the wide boulevard, looking for someone who might be willing to talk.

Adding to the magic already there, he threw about himself the aura of the primitive storyteller, the wise keeper of tales. Then he stepped into the street in search of anyone with a story.

Which meant anyone at all.

Chapter 3

"This is not acceptable. I will not allow the trade rights to simply pass into your hands this way." The speaker, Prince Tarak, stood up, blocking Prince Jasfer's view through the windows of the cold, blue sky.

"No. You want to pull all the trade-lines into your own house, I suppose," Prince Vedu countered without standing.

The two men began yelling then, each trying to pull other princes in on their side. Jasfer blocked them out and shifted on his floor pillow so he could see the sky again. A clear sky was rare beside the steam beds, and the days were already shortening as the year died, so he could barely enjoy those few occurrences.

The shouting made it difficult to enjoy even so. Sometimes Jasfer wished they'd bring in a kiwan table and settle disputes that way. Not that he'd win arguments more often than he did as it was, but it would be more entertaining. Other times he felt like the whole room was a kiwan table, the Thirty Princes the pieces of the game. And he had to wonder what drunk deity would have ever chosen him as a piece of the game.

He tried to learn. He'd been brought up in it, the son of a ruling prince after all, and he had an exacting mentor in Apijet, who'd been his father's friend. He looked to his left where a row of columns lined the wall. At their base on a sprawling pile of pillows sat the older Prince Apijet, leaning forward and noting everything the two princes said. Everything they didn't say but their bodies did. That was the latest thing he'd been trying to teach Jasfer. The subtleties of power within a conversation.

And he understood it. He really did. When he tried, he could pick out everything Apijet wanted him to. But it was hard work and mind-numbingly dull most of the time. His mind wandered whenever he did it for long.

Settling himself into a better position, Jasfer took a sip of very strong and heavily sweetened tisane, hoping it would bring him focus.

The two princes seemed to have come to an agreement about trade in the eastern, inland end of the valley. Ice and furs and raw minerals. Jasfer had little interest in things out there, but he studied the men's body positions as they shook hands and returned to their floor pillows. Neither had come out badly. Neither was shamed or completely defeated. But Vedu had won the dispute. His body clearly showed his pleasure.

Jasfer tried then to follow lines around the room, picking out who else stood to gain from Vedu's win. This was what Apijet was so good at. He could glance around a room and know exactly who owed whom a favor and who secretly sided with which faction. Nearly anyone born to the princely jati of the *kortru* caste could have done what Jasfer did, inferring the winner easily enough. Certainly, most of the Thirty Princes could. But few could grasp the things Apijet knew.

With the princes returned to their seats and that business dealt with, a priest entered the room from the ornate door opposite the seat of the high prince, Prince Baram.

The priest bowed to the surrounding princes as an equal. He held up a lamp, the aromatic smoke from the oil wafting over Jasfer. Jasfer inclined his head to the sacred flame, the father and mother of the gods.

When the room was sufficiently infused with smoke, the priest spoke.

"In the name of Tiespetre, the only true son of the sacred

fire, I greet you."

"And we you," Jasfer intoned with the others, wondering what the priest wanted.

"And especially in the name of his half-brother Ryo, the son of both fire and flesh."

"Blessed Lawgiver," the princes answered. Jasfer stopped watching the priest to observe the other princes. Their faces and bodies should give him a clue to the priest's presence, or at least who had called the priest there.

"Ryo is the god of making things right, of law and marriage and healing. Blessed be his name."

The priest listed the other attributes and titles of the god of government and social customs, a droning noise behind the action that resolved out of the faces and postures of the princes. Tarak and Vedu, the two princes who'd been fighting earlier, seemed completely uninvolved in the monologue, although there was a hint in Tarak's body that he knew something. He seemed surprisingly self-assured after losing the confrontation over trade.

Jasfer followed that line and saw his second cousin, Samatrit. Jasfer's mother's mother had been a sister to Samatrit's grandmother. Jasfer and Samatrit had grown up hating each other. He frowned and imagined what he might do to annoy his cousin, and for a moment, he forgot the other princes. But he shook his mind into focus. Samatrit might know something, but he seemed peripheral to the main lines of power here.

"All is not right in the Valley of Eghsal," the priest was saying. "That is why the god has called me here to speak with you."

Did Jasfer notice a shift toward the middle-aged Prince Dartak? Dartak's house patronized fishing and other goods from the sea. Jasfer wasn't sure how that would tie in. He tried to see the line of power again, but now he could make out nothing. A cloud moved slowly across the light from the windows, making the flame of the priest seem more powerful.

"The city of our fathers is sick," the priest said. It seemed a ridiculous thing to say. The original city of Eghsal, founded six hundred years earlier, wasn't sick. It was dead, abandoned centuries ago when the lava beds shifted and threatened the city.

"Mumblers live there. Criminals and outcasts squat in houses that the gods hold holy. Ryo longs to make it healthy again, for it to be a true city of the glory of our people and the honor of the sacred fire. I call on you to retake the ancient city and make it live again."

Jasfer was too shocked to notice the reactions of others. Trying to drive out the squatters was pure folly. He didn't know anything about wars, so he could only guess that it would be a headache for the military to do, but what he knew was that it would be utterly pointless. It wasn't as if they could resettle it. No one but untouchables would want to go there, and the other three major cities had room enough for everyone. Finally, he glanced at his mentor, Apijet, to see the older man's reaction. What he saw was a perfectly composed face as the prince studied the other rulers.

The priest left, and whispers quickly spread among the princes. But it was too late for Jasfer to understand their body language. Before he could talk to the princes nearest him, the high prince stood. The falcon jati soldiers at either side of him, imposing women in distinctive bird-like headgear, emphasized his desire to speak by striking the floor once in unison with their short fighting sticks. High Prince Baram had a commanding presence, wide-shouldered and muscular, but he managed to always project his strength as something you wanted to join with, not something that was threatening. That sense often played into the lines of influence here, though subtly because he had to appear to be above such things. Even he looked surprised at the priest's announcement.

"I believe we need a short recess. We will discuss this and any other matters after a small lunch."

Cheetah jati servants immediately flowed into the room, carrying trays of thin meats and salted fish and sharp cheeses. The princes stood up to stretch and move about the room.

Jasfer found his way directly to Prince Apijet. Two other princes, Dhalip and Arbul, were already there talking with him. Jasfer greeted the older men and waited to speak. As they talked, they ate dried fruits from a low table standing nearby.

Dhalip was as old as his grandfather would be if he were still alive, and looked it. He leaned on a cane and squinted at the world. "I suppose it's a good thing," he was saying, his voice surprisingly firm, "for the priests to be involved with us. Or, for the people to believe the priests are involved, anyway. But I just don't see the purpose."

Arbul, only a little younger, but looking far more hale, nodded as if this were very wise and took a loud sip from his gourd of tisane. Apijet answered, "No, but there is a purpose. I wonder what my young friend Prince Jasfer thinks about it."

Jasfer inclined his head to his mentor and quickly finished chewing a slice of dried pear. "I'm not sure. Prince Dartak seemed interested in the priest's speech. And perhaps Tarak and even my cousin Samatrit, though I'm less sure of that. But what it could really be about, I just don't know."

Jasfer wanted to know his mentor's thoughts, but Arbul spoke first. "None of them would seem to have any interest in the city itself. Of course, I really don't see how it affects most of us directly." Arbul, like a few of the other princes, patronized the new railroad, and through it, trade in general throughout the valley, but the rails went along the north side of the river, opposite the ancient city. None of the princes stood to lose as much if the war—or whatever the priests had in mind—went badly as the growing merchant jati. Nor as much to gain. Jasfer wondered if the increasing power of the *brenil* caste had anything to do with the situation, but if there was a connection, it escaped him.

Apijet was still silent, so Jasfer answered. "No. I can't quite see where it's leading either." Jasfer looked over his shoulder at the other princes, trying to find a pattern to their conversations and movements. The light through the high windows had continued to dim, and now he thought it looked like snow coming down.

When no one else spoke for a moment, Dhalip stepped away to join another conversation, and Arbul left shortly after, wishing them a good day.

"What were your thoughts on all of this then, *tisrah?*" Jasfer asked, using the formal term of respect.

Apijet smiled briefly at the word, though it didn't mask the concern in his eyes. His fingers worried the piece of cheese in his hand. "Your assessment is good. And not much less than I could see. I tried to see what our high prince thought of this, but he was unreadable."

Jasfer turned to look at Prince Baram. He appeared unconcerned, dipping his fingers calmly in water to rinse them of fruit juices. Behind him was the door to the inner sanctum, always the source of speculation when something unknown happened. If a member of the princely jati could enter that room and hold it for a full night and day, then he would become the new high prince, and the thirty ruling princes would be chosen anew from the families.

If this somehow involved a coup, then it might extend beyond the ruling princes to the other families within the jati not currently represented. That would certainly make it worthy of concern.

"There was a hole in the lines of influence here," Apijet continued, "but I'm not sure if it was him or something else."

"Do you know of any non-ruling families who might be

trying to take power?"

Apijet looked at him quizzically. "Do you know of any who aren't?" He gave a slight laugh as a servant passed by with a platter of wine cups. Apijet took one, but Jasfer only shook his head and gripped his gourd more tightly. Since Baram had come to power nearly two decades earlier, rising more through shrewd agreements than force of soldiers, he hadn't yet had to endure a pretender in the inner sanctum, but rumors often erupted like a geyser, and Jasfer imagined that he expended a great deal of energy pacifying those of their jati who were not currently a part of the Thirty.

"No, it could be any of them," Apijet continued. "But I'm not sure how we can see that from the way things develop in here. The question will be, is anyone here likely to push himself forward into that position?"

One of the high prince's personal servants blew a note on his high-pitched flute, and the princes began heading for their places.

"Do you see anyone here doing that?" Jasfer asked.

His mentor bit the right side of his lip. "I could see some trying. But I don't see it yet, not coming from this priest's actions." He shook his head. "Keep it in mind."

He returned to his floor cushions, and Jasfer looked into his empty gourd. The leaves were still arranged properly to be able to brew some more tisane. He gestured for a servant with hot water to pour it inside. The man complied, giving him the mid-caste *brenil* bow that was appropriate for his jati as he added the honey. Jasfer glanced around at the other servants in all parts of the room. Most times they were invisible, beneath the notice of the princes. Jasfer hadn't bothered bringing his own servants, but many princes did, so they were a mix of those from the princes' households and those from who worked directly for the Assembly. He wondered if the lines of power might flow through them as well.

He took a seat on his own cushions with this uncomfortable thought chewing at his stomach. The sip of tisane he took to quiet it burned the inside of his mouth.

The mystery of the priest's demand made the conversations that followed much less boring. Jasfer listened and watched and tried to piece everything together.

The first arguments went both ways, but Jasfer knew that their importance was not in the words themselves. It would be unsurprising to learn a prince had argued strongly against the position he wanted, just to confuse and manipulate as needed. What he did instead was watch the eyes and hands and posture of everyone, this time including High Prince Baram and even the servants who moved about offering tisane and food.

The lines were still confused. As if a piece were missing, like his mentor had said, a hole in the pattern.

It was not long before Prince Dartak spoke, and then Jasfer listened carefully.

"The thought of sending soldiers into battle should chill us. It is right that we hesitate, that the high winds touch our bones. Ah, but it is a matter of belief. The priest speaks not his own words. Not the words of another prince. He speaks the words of Ryo, the god of customs and law. The god of healing. He has something he longs set right. I would not go against that." Dartak's voice carried with surprising force. Jasfer had always considered him intelligent, but never such a leader as he seemed now.

Jasfer's eyes darted all over the room, studying the expressions and body language of everyone, gauging their thoughts. He realized now that one of the servants near Prince Tarak was part of the pattern. Perhaps he was a spy of some sort, though whether spying on Tarak or working for him, Jasfer couldn't tell.

Dartak's voice rose into his closing words. "Let us argue how and when, for those are the tasks the fire gives us princes.

But let us not argue whether or not we go."

A smattering of applause followed this, started, Jasfer thought, by his own mentor. Apijet was playing the game as well, hoping to throw off whoever might be studying him. Perhaps he had feared that a longer wait would have simply gathered more power in Dartak's lap. Jasfer wondered who else was as skilled as Apijet at this game. Was there someone who knew the truth of what was afoot, one who studied his fellow princes to see where they would stand?

It was a frightening thought. He looked frantically around the room for some hint, a studious look, narrowed eyes, a false casualness.

His eyes immediately fell on his cousin, but Samatrit was watching the speaker with a look of mild interest that carried no hint of power. Jasfer looked around at the others with no other indication of anyone studying him. Would it be an old prince, wise and crafty? A young one, brilliant beyond his years? Surely someone who kept to the background. He decided he'd better be more circumspect in his own observations.

Other princes spoke for and against any attempts to reclaim the ancient city. To Jasfer, it still seemed silly. The city had been abandoned because it was too dangerous to live there. If a few mumblers moved in to claim the old buildings or set up their own shacks, why should they care? Of course, the army should keep an eye on them and make sure they weren't planning another attack. The people of Eghsal had endured sporadic fighting with the mumblers ever since they'd arrived in the north six centuries ago. But, strategically, the city didn't seem to offer much of a threat. And the risk of dying from an unexpected geyser or falling through a new crack in the street into boiling, sulfurous water was probably a good way to keep their numbers down.

That untouchables congregated there was probably more

of a concern to some of the princes and certainly the priests. They represented an offense to the gods, those who'd been cursed or born outside the laws of Ryo. But Jasfer himself had a sister who'd been cast out and made untouchable. She'd been young at the time, and he even younger, but he remembered her laughter in their manor beside the Romnai lava bed. And he remembered the terrible sadness that descended on their house when she slipped and burned her face and had to be named untouchable. They'd had to pretend they no longer knew her, no longer recognized the girl who walked quietly away in the cast-off dress of one of their servants.

That pain had led to his parents' early deaths. Shame was what they had to pretend, but in truth, it was simply the pain of losing their daughter. There was no way he could hate the untouchables after that, but it was quite tempting to hate the priests. And the gods? The sacred fire itself? No, strangely. Even when he wanted to, he couldn't hold them responsible. It was the people who worked in their names.

He wouldn't want her to go to the old city for fear of what it would do to her. He knew that was unlikely, since after his parents' deaths, he'd been able to sneak money and food to her and provide her with a decent place to live. It was as much as he dared, and probably more than he should have. But he wouldn't want to deny her the chance to live free of the castes if she wanted to. If she chose to go to the abandoned city, he'd wish her the best.

Jasfer looked up at the windows. It was definitely snowing now. Not surprising really. The constant steam, once it reached colder air away from the lava beds, turned to snow for much of the year. Soon the days would be so short they'd hardly see the sun. But the heat of the lava fields south of the city kept them fairly warm, and the snow would surely melt as soon as it touched the streets and buildings.

Prince Arbul had joined the empty arguments now, adding

little to the debate as he labored on about the railroad and trade and what effect clearing out the city might have. What influence Jasfer could see simply swirled and dissipated without telling him anything. High Prince Baram still sat silently, giving no hint of his thoughts. Others chimed in without affecting the lines of power.

After all the older princes had their turns, Samatrit rose to speak. He was Jasfer's elder by two years, had the same deep brown skin and narrow nose, but was built much sturdier. In that moment, he looked like a soldier.

"I would lead the force to take the city, if it pleases Your Highness." He bowed toward Prince Baram. "I would consider it an honor to do the work of the gods."

Forgetting his desire to disguise his observations, Jasfer whipped around to look at Apijet. This was not what he'd been expecting. Had his mentor suspected it? Apijet gave no clue to his thoughts, only sat there with one hand on his short, white beard.

Jasfer turned again, more slowly now, and scanned the other princes. Then he looked at his cousin. Nothing came clear. Was his cousin simply inspired by piety? Jasfer doubted it, though he would certainly use the right words to appear pious.

The high prince rose, accompanied again by the coordinated strike of the floor, and all eyes turned to him. Jasfer allowed his gaze to move slowly, taking in the way people faced Prince Baram. There was definite hostility in Prince Tarak's stance, and a few others hinted at displeasure. Neither his cousin nor Prince Dartak gave away anything.

"I have heard your arguments," he said. His voice had a slight hitch to it, not a lisp exactly, but an odd manner to certain words, but here it resonated with power nonetheless. "I have come to a decision, if the Thirty will agree with me." This was largely a formal statement. Technically, they could disagree and overrule the high prince, but it seldom happened. Jasfer kept his own face neutral, consciously relaxing his cheek muscles as he listened.

"Who are we to go against a god or question his servants?" There was a subtlety to the way he asked this, as if he really did question the priest's message, and Jasfer felt a sudden appreciation for Prince Baram, recognizing him as more than the silent figurehead Jasfer had imagined.

"As Prince Dartak argued so eloquently, the question now is only how." And again, the slight insinuation that tied the priest's demands with Dartak.

"We will make plans for clearing out the city, and I am grateful for Prince Samatrit's offer. It will certainly be a part of our consideration, but we will want time. Time to understand the exact will of Ryo. Time to study the ancient city and those who live there. Time to plan the best way to accomplish it."

And of course, Jasfer thought, *time to understand what exactly is behind this all.*

"I will set no date at this time," Prince Baram continued. "All of you are free to learn what you can of these matters, and we will discuss it again when next we meet."

The servant played the shrill notes to signal the end of the session, and the falcon jati soldiers encircled the high prince as he made his way from the room. The Thirty would meet again the next twelve-day unless someone called for a meeting sooner. From the edge of his vision, Jasfer looked at Prince Dartak and his cousin and thought he saw a hint of tensed jaws, even as they both smiled widely and spoke easily to those nearby.

Those were the two to watch. The eloquent speaker with ties to Jarnur and the ocean, and his cousin, whose interests were tied, if he remembered right, to the silk weavers and their careful preservation of ancient cloths. With Jarnur on the sea, as far west as they could go, and the center of the silk trade in their own private holding near the eastern edge of the valley, they would seem to have little in common. Jasfer was determined to discover what possible connection they might have.

He also was smiling now, greeting those princes near him, many of whom had been good friends of his father. In the two years since his father's death, Jasfer had never felt completely himself among them. It seemed that they either imagined him to be his father or they could only see the little boy they remembered years ago. Sometimes it was both. Only Apijet, who had been closer to his father than any, truly treated him as his own man.

As quickly as he could without seeming rude, he took his leave of the others and joined Apijet heading for the exit.

"I wish to discuss this," his mentor said. "There's something else I noticed, though… Well, come to my house so we can figure out what's going on." Other princes and their servants were nearby, and he seemed unwilling to say more until they were at his home.

The High Assembly stood in the center of a large square that was, in turn, surrounded by the fancy houses of the *kortru*. Most of the ruling princes owned manors beside the vast volcanic fields, a little farther away but still not far from the Assembly. Warm, steam-heavy air rolled from the lava beds into the city, turning the falling snow to slush before it hit the ground. Some princes climbed into their carriages or waited for their servants to ready the rigs, but Jasfer and Apijet walked to the Avenue of Geysers. Apijet was a patient man in Assembly, able to wait for the exactly right time to speak a word. But beyond those walls, he had little patience for those who constantly needed the help of servants. They said nothing as they rushed through the street, each holding a length of his robes over his head. Sprawling houses stood on both sides of the street, the largest straight ahead, built out over the lava beds themselves.

They reached the door to Apijet's house and tried to brush the wet snow from their faces and hair.

An untouchable stood beside the door, taking shelter from the weather.

"Go away," Apijet told the man. Then he turned to open his door, but the untouchable hadn't left.

"Are you the master of the house?"

He did not say, *tisrah*, did not bow as he ought, did not speak with the meekness and courtesy everyone was required to show to a member of the *kortru* caste.

"I am, and I demand you leave."

The man only stepped closer, and Jasfer thought of the times when he was young when the politics of the city had been uncertain and his father had gone everywhere with guards, trained members of the cheetah jati, or even, when things were at their worst, members of one of the soldier jatis. He wished they had such with them now.

Inside, Apijet would have his servants, including some quite capable of protecting them, but it had been many years since anyone bothered with guards for a simple trip between the manors and the High Assembly.

The untouchable did not attack, but he did stand far closer than caste rules allowed. "There's something for you to see. Here, beside your house." He leaned even closer then, and his breath struck Jasfer, a smell of sour squash. "I know what the priest announced today. This is tied to that."

No rumor could have escaped the assembly so soon. The man must know something. Apijet got his door open and called inside. Jasfer heard footsteps approaching, but his mentor didn't bother waiting. He walked around the side of the house, following the untouchable.

Jasfer was torn between following immediately and waiting for the servant. He stepped to the corner where he could be seen from the door and still see his mentor.

Something large was in the street there. He had an impression of rusted metal. A part of it near the back glowed red. It reminded Jasfer of the steam engines that powered the trains.

The footsteps had reached the door now, and Jasfer was already gesturing for whoever came through to follow. Apijet stepped toward the object just as the untouchable made some kind of motion with his arm. It looked like he was throwing something, or maybe pulling a lever.

Then the man was running, and Jasfer shouted a warning. Apijet turned his face toward Jasfer to say something, but the words were lost in an overwhelming clamor. Metal screamed, and Jasfer was forced back by a blast of heat. The object exploded, pieces flying everywhere.

He was on the wet ground. Turning, he crawled toward where he'd last seen his mentor. He found a form on the ground, but it didn't look right. The back of the robe was charred, the hair gone, the back of the head seared black.

He rolled the body over and crawled, dragging it away from the heat. Melting snow trickled down the back of his neck. There was no sign of life in his mentor's body.

Chapter 4

Bhadrik struggled up the snow-covered slope. His feet slipped down half of every step he climbed. It was only a little farther. Up this bit and around the skirt of the mountain, and they'd be back at main camp. Half a wolf-hour. His heartbeat already counted the time it would take. And then a little hot wine, or maybe something stronger. That would be good.

How long would he get to stay this time? All he knew was he didn't want to be sent on another pointless patrol for a very long time. The mumblers weren't massing up here. There was no planned attack. His superiors could leave him cooped up in camp all winter for all he cared. He could train, gamble, and sleep. And test himself against the fire. What more did a man need? Nothing if he was of the wolf jati.

Surjit and Turgar were falling behind him as Bhadrik reached the crest and easier walking, but he was too anxious to get back to slow down for them. The snow was picking up again, blowing fiercely as the wind shifted between the north and the west. Even his exertion scarcely warmed him, and they were far from the vast fields of steam springs and geysers that heated the valley below. They wouldn't really expect him to wait and freeze while they caught up.

Bhadrik would have waited earlier. Out in the middle of the patrol, deep in the mountains as they spied on mumbler villages, he would have stopped despite the cold. But they were so close to camp, he could already taste the warm food. He could already feel it in his mouth, its warmth spreading through him.

Twisted, stunted pines stood along his path. The snow broke in the lee of the trees, and Bhadrik kicked his way gleefully in and out of the piles of snow, imagining the welcome they'd receive. He felt a roar building up inside him. He wasn't cold anymore. Let the valley-dwellers worship their fire; he was the equal of any fire!

A sound up ahead froze him. He listened more carefully. People were walking. Armed people—he could hear their swords. The pale-faced mumblers carried primitive swords to battle along with their rough spears. Nicer swords when they could steal them from the Eghsals. He moved cautiously toward the sound. They seemed to be heading up the road toward the soldiers' camp.

Bhadrik made sure his short sword was ready to grab, then wrapped the ties of his sling around the fingers of his right hand. With his left hand, he grabbed a handful of lead bullets. The main road was just ahead, over a small rise. He crept up behind a boulder and peeked down.

Snow blew sideways over the road. No one in camp would be expecting an attack at a time like this. But there they were, in the thick furs of the mumblers, a band of warriors, hurrying up the road.

Placing the first bullet in the pouch of the sling, Bhadrik watched them. He could see their weapons and other gear, but only barely through the snow. He counted more than a dozen, not a big warband, but if they caught the camp by surprise, they could certainly kill many. Especially if the soldiers were as drunk as Bhadrik had hoped to be shortly.

He fingered the ends of the sling. He'd have to step out to throw the bullet. That was the one disadvantage the slings had. Valley bows could be fired without exposing the archer much, but the valley people could keep their bows, as well, along with their fire worship. Up here, bow strings became unreliable, and arrows flew erratically.

No noise reached him yet from behind. He glanced back to see if Surjit and Turgar were coming, but they weren't in sight. It would be better if they all attacked together, but if he waited, the mumblers might already be to the camp.

If he attacked now, alone, Bhadrik knew he might die. He could take out some with his sling before they knew what was happening. One or two more as they turned to charge him or ducked for cover. And then his sword would protect him for a while. Maybe long enough for his companions to reach him. Probably not. But to rival fire, as the mystery religion of the wolf jati taught them to do, he'd have to risk it. He'd have to sacrifice himself to save his comrades.

Narrowing his eyes to gauge the exact distance, Bhadrik stepped out and swung his arm over his head. A second bullet was already in the pouch when the first hit snow just behind the figures. He caught the end of the sling and kept his arm moving in the same motion. The second bullet flew a little higher.

A figure fell, and already he was swinging the third. He heard their shouts, muffled by the snow but echoing where bare rock showed.

Another figure fell, and something seemed wrong. The echoes…

He sent a fourth bullet, but now his concentration was off. The metal sailed over their heads.

The echoes sounded like words. Mumblers didn't speak. Not real words. They talked to each other, but it wasn't anything the Eghsals understood. Not civilized language, and that meant not words.

But these were words, almost recognizable. His fifth bullet didn't even come near to the figures, and after that, he stopped. The sling hung slack to the ground.

Two bodies lay on the ground, other figures huddling around them. The snow was lessening now, and one figure looked his way. That face down there, full of fear and anger and uncertainty, was not mumbler white. It was as brown as his own.

Bhadrik dropped the loose end of his sling and ran down the slope to the group, his hands out and open to show he meant no harm.

* * *

One man died, a low-caste servant hired to carry equipment. A personal servant to one of the priests lay groaning on a bed of furs. Bhadrik had carried the man himself, as gently and quickly as he could to the army camp. Now he was collapsed against a cold wall, too stunned to get himself the wine he so desperately craved.

Surjit and Turgar had both arrived in time to guide the rest of the company into camp, and now the priest who led the company was in another room, talking to Bhadrik's commander.

Another priest was in the same room as Bhadrik, the main mess, attended by his own men and the soldiers. Several furs draped his chair, and he was nodding off between bites of the stew he'd been given.

They hadn't locked Bhadrik up, which was good. If he'd even injured one of the priests, he would certainly be in a cell deep within the camp. He pulled himself to his feet and crossed the room, avoiding everyone's eyes.

The ceiling was low, and smoke hung about the room despite the chimney over the fire. It should have felt like home. These smoke-filled close quarters with his fellow soldiers were what he'd longed to return to after a long patrol. But he felt nothing, like having a frostbitten finger.

Finally, Commander Karuda approached Bhadrik. The priest glowered at him from behind the commander.

"Your punishment is not yet decided. At the request of the priests, we will be keeping you separate tonight. I know we can trust you, but to please our guests, your room will be locked." The commander's face showed no emotion, not annoyance at the demands of the priest, not anger at his subordinate, but also not the deference he likely should have shown the *kortru* priest.

Bhadrik could only lower his head in acceptance. His friend and fellow soldier, Deraj, stepped up from Karuda's side and walked Bhadrik through the swinging wooden door into the catacomb of individual rooms. The chill of the stone briefly shocked him from his stupor. The cold night ahead seemed suddenly menacing. Almost immediately the numbness returned, and he walked calmly into a narrow room lit by an iron brazier.

Deraj said something as he shut the door and locked it, but Bhadrik wasn't listening. He fell onto the mattress, filled with rough mountain grasses, and closed his eyes.

When sleep did not come, he kept his eyes closed and thought.

Thinking had never been Bhadrik's favorite thing. Better to do, to act, to fight. Now, though, he thought of every step he had taken through the snow that day. He thought of his first sight of the priest's party, struggling through the snow. How could he have thought them mumblers?

He thought of the lead bullets he'd slung, the bodies falling. He thought of the dead man, his arms now crossed as he lay on a wooden table outside the building.

It wasn't the first man he'd killed, of course. He'd been a soldier for more than ten years and had fought the mumblers through blinding snow, on treacherous mountain slopes, high beyond the edge of the trees, deep in hidden valleys. This was different. It was his own people. It was an accident. It lacked the honor demanded by the mystery religion of the wolf jati.

He hadn't fought any mumblers on this patrol. He and Surjit

and Turgar had climbed deep into the mountains. The mumblers formed their villages and rough camps in scattered locations along the edges of glaciers and hidden among the thick pines of narrow valleys. They found a new one, far to the east, as they circled back toward the valley. It was a series of caves and simple buildings near a dry run that could make easy access into the Valley of Eghsal.

They watched the camp for many days. Surely it was a sign of the mumblers preparing to attack. Women moved about, collecting snow to melt for water, tending the fires, milking their mountain goats. Children played, running within the caves, which must have been connected deep underground. The soldiers could hear their laughter from their own hidden camp among the boulders higher up. Men also were there, hunters who brought in the food for the women to prepare to last the winter.

Mumbler hunters were the same men who became mumbler warriors, but Bhadrik and his companions saw no sign of them preparing for war. They did not scout the run down toward the valley. They did not build the forge fires to make extra weapons. Their only training seemed to be the hunt.

Bhadrik tired of watching them and dreamed of the warm army camp, the mulled wine and spiced ale, the hot tisane.

At last, they'd left, and Bhadrik pushed them as fast as they would go.

Now here he was, but he had nothing to warm the coldness inside him. Even if they brought something, he didn't think he could drink it. He just wanted to go back and change what he'd done. Whatever punishment they gave him, he knew it would hurt his standing among the soldiers. He might never again join in the sacred rites of the army's mystery religion. He might never again strive to rival the fire, to equal and surpass it in ferocity and deadly beauty and chaos. He might never again be able to worship himself as a god.

More than the idea of the dead body, that thought sickened his stomach.

* * *

Deraj brought him food early in the morning, and a few hours later returned to escort him to the commander's room.

"Any thoughts on what he might say?"

Deraj shook his head. "No. They talked late last night, and the priest only now woke up."

"I hope he's had tisane to wake him up." It was meant as a joke, but neither of them laughed.

Bhadrik glimpsed some of the other soldiers through an open door and nodded to them solemnly. Hirsha, a young soldier he'd helped train, acknowledged him, but the others were distracted by something else. Or pretended to be.

They stopped before a heavy wooden door, and Deraj knocked. The wood swallowed most of the sound.

They heard words that might have been, "Come in," and Deraj pushed the door open. Commander Karuda stood while the priests sat comfortably in the room's only chairs. Karuda signaled for them to wait beside the wall as the senior priest continued speaking.

"You'll need to move down soon. I don't want any risk of the snows trapping you up here all winter."

"We can move out in a few days. A twelve-day at the most." The commander sounded so calm about this, as if moving their camp was the most natural thing. Bhadrik looked at Deraj to see his reaction to this, but if it was news, his dark face betrayed nothing.

"Watch, observe everything, and report what you see, but don't enter the city until you receive other orders."

Bhadrik looked carefully at the two priests, at the

commander, at Deraj to try to understand what they might be discussing. A city? Were they to besiege the capital? Or Jarnur or Pashun? That made no sense. The mumblers certainly had nothing that could be called a city. They said no more about it now as they turned to him by the wall.

"Bhadrik, please step forward." Karuda gestured with his sword-calloused fingers.

He approached and bowed toward the priests, careful to show the exact level of respect given their caste and his own. Like all soldiers, he was mid-caste, *brenil*, the same as the priests' personal servants. They would expect his reverence.

"You have killed a man and injured another."

Bhadrik allowed his head to drop lower. He could see the seated priests from their knees down, and beneath their sandaled feet, the smooth rock of the floor. Soldiers had walked on that floor for hundreds of years, he guessed. They'd left during the wars. The mumblers had risen up to fight fairly often throughout history, and a civil war once divided city from city for a few years, but always the soldiers came back. The thought of them leaving that place in a time of peace seemed wrong.

But was it really a time of peace?

That was an unsettling question to consider as the commander continued. "The killed man was only a *nefli*. The injured man was *brenil* but is recovering well. And you have been a good soldier for many years. Do you have anything to say to us?"

Bhadrik raised his head slightly, glancing at their calm faces before looking directly at the senior priest's chest. They didn't look angry, which might be a good thing.

"I apologize to you, *tisrae*," he said to the two priests, "for disrupting your journey here. I did not mean to harm your personal attendant, or kill the *nefli*. I saw a strange group approaching our camp through the snow, and we…" He paused. It was hard to speak like this. He wanted to simply ask them what in the name of their sacred fire were they doing visiting an army camp late in the year without soldiers guiding them. But he couldn't just say that, couldn't talk like he would with his comrades.

"We don't have visitors who aren't brought here by other soldiers. I...I thought I was protecting my comrades. I apologize profusely."

The priest's chest rose and fell in deep breaths. The clatter of voices came through the door from the soldiers' general room.

"Your mistake is understood, soldier." The chief priest paused to reposition his body on the soft furs. "Attacking a priest is punishable by death, but we grant you your life."

Bhadrik stood up straighter then. That was good. If the servant had died, they might not have let him live.

"But you are to be outcast."

Immediately he slumped as he pictured himself filthy and covered with sores, begging beside some building in one of the cities. In the valley, where he'd have to proclaim loudly the glories of the fire gods and all their silliness. No way. He didn't think he could handle that, the looks, the lies, the humiliation. Who was he to bow to such depths? He was a soldier of the wolf jati, an initiate of the mystery religion, a rival of the fire that birthed the gods.

He forced his shoulders square as the priest continued.

"For one year, you will be untouchable, beneath even the *nefli* who you killed. After that year, you may return to the army. Must return, for it is the gods' will that all soldiers, your entire jati, serve them and reclaim their glories."

It was a fair punishment, he thought. "You are merciful, *tisrah*. I thank you." Now, he bowed all the way to the ground, as an untouchable must. He hated the feel of the rock against his face, cool but not cool enough to be shocking. Tepid, like tisane left overlong in its gourd. There was no way he could stomach bowing like this for a full year to every city-dweller he passed.

He decided then that he wouldn't go to the cities. He would stay alone in the mountains as long as he could and then go to the ancient ruins where untouchables and criminals and mumblers scratched out their lives. There he would bow to no one. And in a year, he could return here to the camp and the army and the familiar life.

He was backing from the room without lifting his eyes when he realized that the army might not be here in a year.

Shifting his body to face the commander he asked, "Commander Karuda, how will I find this unit in a year if you have left here?"

There was silence at first, and it was the younger priest who answered. "Go to Romnai. There will certainly be people there who know what is needed. If you can find no one of your jati, ask at the temple. The priests will direct you where you need to go."

As he left the room, Bhadrik felt a twinge of uneasiness at the thought of the priests controlling the soldiers and armies that way.

* * *

Bhadrik had to leave his sword behind.

"It's my sword. I've had it since I was a child, too young to lift it." The sword was the right of the wolf jati. It was always a gift from their parents and their constant companion throughout their fighting. If a particular sword was lost or broken in battle, it was believed that the sword's spirit would pass to a new sword, but any other loss was a form of abandonment. He couldn't imagine leaving it behind.

"Yes, it was your sword," Deraj explained to him. "But you are not wolf jati now, not a soldier, you are untouchable. You have no right to carry a sword. I'm sorry."

"What if…" He brought his hands up to his hair, struggling to keep himself from shouting. "How will I get it back if no one's here anymore?"

Deraj was silent, as if he hadn't thought of this. They were friends, had fought together in the army for years. He would certainly understand how hard it would be for Bhadrik to leave his sword behind.

When he still didn't answer, Bhadrik asked, "Where will you be stationed? You can take it with you, and I'll come straight there to get it."

"I don't know, Bhadrik. I haven't learned that yet."

Deraj looked around the common room at the other soldiers, their eyes turned away from the scene.

"Here's what I'll do. I'll take the sword with us, and somehow I'll get it to Romnai, to the jati's neighborhood there." Within each of the cities, the soldiers had a section where their children were raised, where their women lived, and where the soldiers retired if they survived that long. "Go to the mysteriarch who leads the ceremonies, and he will return it to you."

Bhadrik nodded. It was probably a good plan. He couldn't think of anything better, anyway.

"But after your year is up. You have to swear on yourself that you won't try to get it back early."

"I swear," Bhadrik said loudly, holding a tight fist against his chest, "by my body that is the equal of fire." It was a powerful oath, based on the one thing initiates of the mystery religion worshiped: themselves. Even outcast from the jati, Bhadrik had no intention of breaking such a vow or going against the secret religion of the soldiers.

Bhadrik took a last look at his sword, a short, heavy blade with guards extending below the handle to protect its user's wrist and forearm. It was scarred like himself, beginning to show its age but still young and strong and capable.

Then Bhadrik gathered his other things, including his sling and a handful of bullets, webbed shoes for walking on snow, and provisions to last several days, and walked toward the door. Some sixty other soldiers filled the common room, all carefully ignoring him. He had to walk cautiously so as not to touch them as he passed. These were his friends, his comrades. If he touched one, the soldier would be obligated to beat him. That or be shamed. And he wouldn't be allowed to defend himself. He had no wish to cause either.

That walk seemed to last hours. At last, he stepped out into thick snowfall to begin his year as an outcast. On his very first step, his foot slipped on the icy snow, and he fell. The door shut behind him, as if even the building was embarrassed by him.

Bhadrik struggled to his feet and walked as quickly as he dared down the long road toward the valley.

Chapter 5

Jaritta listened in horror as Jasfer told his story. As soon as he finished, she rose from her thin floor pillow and hurried toward him, feeling once again like the big sister she'd been to him so many years ago.

"You're all right, though? It didn't hurt you?"

She pulled up a step away from him instead of hugging him, but even before she did, his flinch reminded her that she wasn't his sister, not as far as society believed. The awkwardness only lasted a moment. She'd had half her life to get used to the way others, even those most open to untouchables, reacted to her. The fear of being touched was a deeper instinct than mere convictions could unseat.

"I'm fine," he answered as she leaned back against the thin wooden wall of her rough room.

"That's horrible. Apijet..." She shook her head. Old crockery and a few chipped plates blurred through her vision as she did so. She hadn't seen her father's old friend for years, but the thought still seemed strange. Dead, just as her parents. It wasn't real to her that someone could be gone like that.

But then, she'd been gone to all of them ever since she was cast out.

"It is," Jasfer said at last. He sat on a pillow he'd brought with him with his head propped on his palms. "But why? Who did it?"

Jaritta stayed silent, knowing he was asking himself more than her. She wandered around the room, picking up what items she owned and rearranging them—the clay dishes, one glass bottle spider-webbed with cracks but still useful for keeping water, the few items of clothing she wasn't wearing. Even in such a small room, she scarcely owned enough to clutter the place, but it gave her something to do.

If only she could help him more. He needed someone to be his eyes when he wasn't there, talking to the people who didn't talk to princes. For a moment, she imagined herself doing it. Sneaking among the princes and through the half-abandoned corridors she still remembered exploring years ago with her little brother, listening to the words that weren't spoken openly, those that hid behind conversations without ever being spoken. Adding to that what she could learn among the many untouchables she'd come to know over the years. And then shaping those hints with her fingers until they made sense, until they pointed at the reason for Apijet's murder.

"He knew something. Or guessed it, anyway. We were going to talk about it at his house. But he only realized it just before we left. They couldn't have set it up that swiftly, could they?"

Jasfer's words reminded her what was at stake and how impossible her fantasy had been. She was untouchable and had no part to play in the actions of the princes.

"All they needed was time to send a servant out, right?" Jaritta asked. "If these people worried it was a possibility, they could have had it ready to go. Send a servant out to tell the untouchable—or person dressed as an untouchable—where to go."

"Maybe." Jasfer stood, shook out his pillow, though Jaritta didn't see any reason for that, and tucked it under his arm. "I wanted to let you know. I might have to be careful for a while about what I do. Everyone will be watching everyone else. I don't imagine anyone would think me a suspect, but if I'm a target, and they learn about you…"

"Thank you. You be careful, as well. And if I learn anything among the…untouchables, I'll let you know." Jasfer knew about the time she spent at Chaitan's house, but she didn't like to remind him of it. He didn't exactly approve of that crowd.

As he left, he placed a large handful of money on the counter, small coins so it wouldn't be suspicious in the hands of an untouchable.

Jaritta sat down, and her hand went automatically to the scar on her face.

Hearing him tell of the assassination, she wasn't sure she envied Jasfer and the rest of the princely jati. She didn't want to be a part of that intrigue and danger. She's rather listen to the exciting new music of Chaitan's musicians. She wanted the thrill of the secret dancing. And she wanted to be a part of something bigger, but didn't everyone? She wanted to feel like her actions had some effect on others, more than just the facelessness of the untouchables.

When Rashul spoke of his visions for the future of their valley, she longed for those utopian days, but here, away from his hypnotic voice, she wasn't sure of that. What if abolishing castes merely meant that everyone would face all the evils of every level of society and none of the benefits? People would struggle to earn their bread while constantly fearing that their neighbors, colleagues, and friends plotted to betray them. At least among the untouchables, she knew betrayal remained as unlikely as sudden riches.

She arranged her dress so a loop of cloth covered the left side of her face. It was rough cloth, a weave so thick even her servants long ago wouldn't have worn such. But fifteen years had made her used to rougher clothing. Wrapping a thick cloak around her, she stepped outside into a cool morning. The sun had not yet risen above the southern mountain peaks—it hardly ever seemed to this time of year, as winter approached. For once, no snow was falling.

Well, maybe her worries were overly cynical. Rashul seemed to have it all planned out, understanding things she could barely follow. And recently his plans had taken on more solidity, it seemed, although she didn't know any part of what shape they might take. More than just the words spoken beside Chaitan's fire, anyway. She would do what she could to support him. She'd given up on being accepted by her birth caste or even the other castes of Romnai, but at Chaitan's house, she found those who didn't care that she was outcast. Whatever she could do to repay that was practically a duty of honor. If an untouchable could have honor.

Jaritta headed briskly along a lesser street toward the rising cloud of steam on the southern edge of the city. Its twists in the poorer parts of the city became gentler curves as the houses became finer. At first the houses were mostly white-washed mud over a wooden frame, while a few were covered in garish, intricate patterns of various colors that didn't stand up well to the constant steam and nearly constant snow. Red paint peelings flaked down on her cloth-covered head as she passed the worst of these.

Nearer the lava beds, the painted houses disappeared, and more and more of the buildings were of fine white or gray stone. When she'd first been cast out, Jaritta hated coming here, afraid that people would recognize her. Or maybe that they wouldn't. Now, she didn't mind. It wasn't that she didn't think about her past anymore. She did, every time she walked by these fine homes, and often when she was in other places, also. She'd learned to not let it hurt her anymore. These days those who might recognize her were the beggars who haunted the streets, untouchables she'd come to know over the years as they shared their mutual woe.

A broad walkway ran next to the lava beds, here called the Avenue of Falling Steam, with a stone railing along the edge. Untouchables slouched against the railing, eyes downcast and hands out. That had been her when she was first outcast. Jaritta wished she had a coin to give them, but Jasfer could only help her so much. He did what he could, but there were still days, though rare, when she was forced again to beg.

Jaritta stood beside the stone railing and let the sulfurous steam flow over her, waking her up. Even now, fifteen years after she'd last had access to the private steam baths of her youth, it still took the volcanic air to truly wake her.

After a few minutes, she pushed herself away from the railing and strode along the steam beds. She refused to shuffle as untouchables were expected to, but she did lower her face whenever others came close. Public steam baths and *kortru* houses built over the warm rocks regularly blocked her view of the bubbling pools beyond. She saw no geysers this morning. The rock color shifted as she went, red and yellow and gray, and in some places, white deposits rimmed the rocks, creating fantastic sculptures like nothing humans made.

Seeing those weird formations made her want to recreate them herself, but she had never found the material to do so.

She turned away from the steam beds and headed north toward the river. Market sounds from the city's largest market carried the few blocks to Chaitan's street. By the time she reached the house, her muscles were pleasantly fatigued.

Chaitan was sitting in his chair at one side of the room, talking to someone Jaritta didn't know. Kapita, one of his attendants stood beside them, but his other attendant, Tanjali, sat alone beside the fire.

Jaritta approached with the half-smile that was the best her mouth could form.

Tanjali gave her a mock bow and gestured for her to sit. Tanjali had been born untouchable. Her parents were death workers, the only official jati that was also untouchable. Most of the untouchables Jaritta had come to know avoided the death workers, and their jati reciprocated, each looking askance at the other. Chaitan—who had been ignoring the caste system completely, at least since his illness set in—had hired her several years earlier, and only recently would she look people in the eye without flinching.

"Quiet morning?"

Tanjali nodded. "Nothing much happening. It's someone from the priest jati talking to Chaitan. They've been talking for an hour."

"You want to play kiwan?"

"Sure. We'll have to play on the worse board. Chaitan's deciding to be protective of the nice one."

The two went over to a corner and arranged their pieces. Jaritta didn't consider herself a great kiwan player. She could always see where she wanted her pieces, but they never rolled down how she expected. It meant that she was always choosing between wasting an extra turn to slide the piece where she wanted it, or simply dealing with what she had and sending another piece into the board.

The board quickly filled with their pieces, and Jaritta began a tentative attack.

Luckily for her, Tanjali wasn't a great kiwan player either. She seemed to have better control of the pieces, but her vision of the board wasn't as good.

Jaritta slid a heavy piece along the edge to a protected spot that Tanjali should have filled early in the game. It made sense, she supposed, that Tanjali didn't fully grasp the strategy. Jaritta had learned it as a child, practically a required skill for anyone of the princely jati. Death workers would have had little use for the game, although surely even they would have used kiwan to entertain themselves and their children.

Jaritta won the first game, and they played again, and the morning slipped on by.

After a few quick games, Tanjali stood and brought them some food to share. Soon afterward, Chaitan summoned her to help him, and Jaritta was left alone to sit near the fireplace.

The monotony nearly put her to sleep, and she was

contemplating getting up to wander somewhere when someone entered the house. The wind had picked up since she got there, and the person fumbled with the door. It was Pavresh, the new arcist who'd been learning from Chaitan for a couple of twelve-days.

He came toward her and sat on the pillows nearby, letting out a long breath.

Jaritta thought him a good-looking young man, but she wondered how much of that was just his magic. His skin had the slightest hint of red, his face smooth and young. Dress him in fine silks, and he could probably pass as *kortru*.

He turned his eyes on her then, and she found an intensity in their brown depths, as if a subtle pattern of many colors danced beneath the brown.

"Would you tell me your story?"

Jaritta cocked her head. "What do you mean?"

Pavresh brought the heels of his palms up to those stunning eyes and rubbed them. "I'm supposed to learn stories from people I meet. No one's on the streets in this wind. Or, they're there, but they don't want to stop and talk to me."

Jaritta laughed, and she thought it made her sound younger than she felt. Was that because of his magic?

"Sure, I can tell you."

Readjusting the pillows until they seemed comfortable enough to last awhile, she prepared to talk.

"Wait a moment." Pavresh jumped up and returned a moment later with two mugs. "There was no tisane prepared." He shrugged. "I hope water is fine."

"Sure. Fine. The tisane here is always too sweet for me anyway."

Pavresh made himself comfortable and faced her. Jaritta had to look down to begin her story. She resisted the impulse to touch the rough skin of her scar.

"I was born *kortru*, of course. Not a lot to say about that,

I imagine. It's like any other prince you might get to tell you their story."

"Tell me anyway."

"Well, it was just, everything was right. I had my parents. My servants from the cheetah jati. I didn't really think about things, you know. About castes and politics and the world beyond our house. My father was a respected member of the Thirty. Not widely liked, I don't think, but respected. Like all the princes, he was involved with merchants, earning some of his money that way. Each prince invests differently. I know now that his holdings were largely in mining."

She looked up, thinking she'd heard a reaction to this, but Pavresh only nodded for her to continue.

"I didn't know that at the time, of course. It didn't really concern me. I was more interested in who I would marry. I don't know if all girls that age are, but my friends and I—we would have been fourteen, I guess—were very curious.

"Other princes' families would come over for dinner, and I'd stare at the boys and wonder. Some were also involved in mining, some in trade by rail, some in other things. I guess I did learn a bit of that then, though it only interested me to give the boys my age nicknames. Would I marry the fishing boy? The train boy? Or might I step out of the jati and marry a priest boy or a silk weaver?

"For someone of my caste, I was too young to worry much about this, but I wondered and dreamed. It would be years before my parents actually arranged a marriage for me, but I was desperate to know. There was a rumor that if you went into a chapel or temple late at night and took down the sacred torch and danced with it, saying a certain rhyme, you'd see an image of who you were going to marry."

Jaritta pulled the cloth back from the left side of her face. "I tried in my family's private chapel. The fire rejected me. Or anyway that's what the priests proclaimed." Letting the cloth back down, Jaritta found she wasn't embarrassed anymore. Her privileged childhood, which others might have been proud of, shamed her, but her life as an untouchable did not.

"I was fifteen by then. Half as old as I am today."

"What'd you do? To be suddenly an outcast at that age must have been hard."

Jaritta looked around the room while she tried to find the words. Chaitan was napping now, with both attendants at his side like bodyguards. The visitor from earlier had left, but other people moved about. How could she possibly put it into words?

"It was difficult. Of course. I didn't dare go out where people would see me, even with my face covered. I felt abandoned, I guess, by my own people, but worse was the sense that I'd betrayed myself. I didn't hate the priests for casting me out. I hated myself.

"I was befriended by a boy my age, another untouchable. He was…a good friend for many years." Jaritta paused. It had been awhile since she'd last thought of Thamiba. "He ran off," she bit her lip briefly, "a couple of years ago, I suppose. To the old city. The abandoned one. We call it the Untouchable City."

"Why didn't you go?"

Jaritta leaned back against her pillows, enjoying the feel of stretching her neck. When she looked back at him again, she answered, "I couldn't leave Jasfer behind. He's my younger brother, and even when I was cast out, he never really abandoned me. My parents were afraid to have anything to do with me, fearing how the priests might punish them. But Jasfer was able to sneak the occasional bit of food or coin or discarded clothing."

She thought of the news he'd come to tell her that day about Apijet. How he was afraid he didn't understand exactly what was happening as well as his mentor would have, that he was missing some key information or insight. Her fingers moved, itching to help him, shaping some magic or vessel that could discover the truth.

"He still needs me, I think, and I won't abandon him."

The door opened, and Iksheen walked in, his hands clinging a small book.

"Thank you for talking with me," Jasfer said to her, a very formal-sounding phrase in his mouth, as if he always ended his time with people that way.

"What will you do with it?"

He shrugged. "Think on it. Remember it. Eventually understand it, I hope. Understand sort of the…" He moved his hands as if he couldn't quite find the words. "The underlying themes, I suppose."

Before he could say anything else, something came flying and landed on his head.

"Oh, I'm so sorry." Iksheen came hurrying over to grab the outer cloak he'd throw. "I didn't mean for it to hit you." Jaritta stopped him before he could take it.

It was a rough cloak, an outer wrap like an untouchable might wear, and suddenly Pavresh was transformed. She could hardly believe it was still him. Growing up in the *kortru* caste, Jaritta had learned early how to tell someone's caste at a glance. Even without identifying clothing, most people were obvious. Their faces, their bearing…both shouted their caste to those who knew how to look.

It wasn't perfect. Jaritta remembered one non-ruling prince, the brother of one of her father's friends, who had the face of a *nefli* dock-worker. But such exceptions were rare.

Now, looking at Pavresh with only the rough cloth to deceive her, she could have sworn he was untouchable. Yet an hour earlier, she had thought he could pass for *kortru*, given the right silks.

"Wait," she said to Iksheen as he pulled on the cloak. To Pavresh, she asked, "Forgive me, but what caste are you?"

The arcist's forehead wrinkled and he cocked his head. "*Brenil.* Why?"

"It's just…"

"Can I take my cloak back now?"

She glanced at the poet, who looked even more confused than Pavresh. "Yes. Take it back."

She stared at Pavresh as the cloak came away. And he changed again. His clothes could have been either low-caste or mid-, and in the right context she would have accepted him as either.

"Are you doing that with your magic?"

Now Pavresh looked even more surprised. "Doing what?"

"You're changing castes. You looked like an untouchable with Iksheen's old cloak."

"But Iksheen isn't untouchable."

"No, but his cloak could be." She glanced at Iksheen. His inner robe, while not silk, looked practically fine enough to be a *kortru* cloth. Another robe was wrapped around his legs, and this one was rougher but still not one an untouchable would likely wear. "He likes to play with expectations that way. But on you… Are you saying that you're not doing this through magic?"

Pavresh shook his head. "The castes don't exist within the arcist magic."

Jaritta thought about this and wondered if it affected the idea that was developing in her mind.

She turned to the poet. "Iksheen, I want you and Pavresh to switch robes a moment. Just let him try this one on." She touched the smooth weave of his inner robe.

Both men looked at her, puzzled.

"Please. I'll explain in a moment, but I don't want the way you think about it to affect how you walk in."

Pavresh looked at Iksheen and shrugged. Then they walked through a doorway into a more private part of the house. While

Jaritta waited impatiently for them to return, her fingers moving rapidly against her side, Namrani came in and began to play her haunting, conversational music. Jaritta loved the sounds of the instrument, but for once even it didn't calm her. She'd guessed he would look *kortru* earlier, but would he really?

Finally, Iksheen came back, now wearing Pavresh's common clothing. It looked so ordinary on him, without any contradictory clothing to set it off. Following him was a prince. Even expecting it, Jaritta had to blink to make sure it really was the arcist. He came and stood before her.

"Still no magic to this?"

He shook his head. Jaritta waved her hand back toward the hallway. "Change back to your usual clothes, and I'll explain." When she sat down on the pillows, she found the book Iksheen had carried in.

It was a poetry book. At first glance, it appeared to be religious poetry, the Peisharn verses or something similar, but then she read a bit more closely. The mysticism and fire-worship seemed slightly twisted away from usual.

"From Fire I came as a child / and Flames consume my life. / Now I smolder as hot Coals / and soon my life will be Ash."

Why did that seem not quite right to her? She read it again and realized that the priests only ever spoke of fire, not coals and ashes. The fire was eternal, the source of Tiespetre and the other gods. But this poet seemed to identify the fire, a finite fire, with himself. Having been touched by fire herself and made untouchable, Jaritta wasn't sure she would want to get so close to a sacred fire. Let it stay a step removed, beyond the gods.

Pavresh and Iksheen returned, and the poet took the book from her.

"What is that?" she asked him.

He held it protectively to his chest. "A book of poems. I wanted to show it to Rashul."

"I read the opening poem. It looked strange."

Iksheen opened the book as if to read the poem, but he looked up before he could have possibly read anything. "That's just the opening invocation. I'm not sure it's even by the poet who wrote the rest. But it's Enshi. They claim to worship the fire in all its stages: spark, flame, and ash."

Enshi. The priests warned them about this cult, but she'd never known anyone who belonged to it. It was much more common by the sea. She wondered if Ekana, who was originally a fisherman from Jarnur, was Enshi. If so, she'd never suspected it from anything the dancer said or did. Maybe she'd ask Indima the next time the couple was there to dance.

"Why would Rashul be interested in it?" Pavresh asked. The tone of his voice sounded a bit odd to Jaritta, slightly strained perhaps.

"Oh, he's not Enshi, if that's what you're thinking," Iksheen answered, setting the book carefully down next to him. Jaritta thought she sensed a bit of tension between these two, as if they were rivals in some way. "There's something in these poems, though, that argues like he does. Something that supports an end to castes and all." He shrugged. "But I can't really explain it without reading a bunch of them to you and explaining as I go. And I only want to do that once."

They didn't say anything for a minute until Iksheen added, "You were going to explain all that clothes-changing, Jaritta. What was that about?"

"Oh. Right." Jaritta tried to turn her mind back to that. "There's something about you, Pavresh. You could pass as any caste if you wanted to."

Pavresh shrugged. "Well, when you put me in costume, sure."

"No, it's not just that. Maybe you've never thought about it, but I can meet anyone and be fairly certain what caste they belong to just by looking at their face."

Pavresh and Iksheen seemed to consider this.

"It might be something we *kortru* were especially trained to recognize. But you, Pavresh, I look at you and assume you belong in whatever caste you're clothed in." She paused, feeling the idea fall into place. "Are you using your magic for that? Not castes, since they don't exist, but just to look like you belong?"

Pavresh shook his head, his face still looking a little stunned by this. "No. I can. I use it when I walk through rougher parts of the city. But I'm not using it here."

"That's even better. Just imagine how inconspicuous you'll be with the right clothing *and* your magic!"

"Inconspicuous? What would I need that for?"

Jaritta took a breath and glanced at Iksheen. It'd be fine. She'd known him for more than a year and knew he wouldn't betray them. He was far too naïve of anything beyond his own interests, beyond Rashul's cause. That left Pavresh. Could she trust him? Would Jasfer?

"I told you my story. What's yours?"

"I…I gather stories. I don't tell them."

Jaritta waited.

Pavresh licked his lips before he spoke. "I'm an arcist. That's the central story, the frame that I hang everything else on."

"An arcist can be anyone. I'm not asking *what you are* but *who you are.*"

Iksheen made a move to leave, then settled down to listen to their conversation. Pavresh glanced at him then continued. "My father ran a mine. Up north of the city." He took a large breath. "I suppose in an arcist theme, I was the overlooked one. The first male child, you'd think my father would have groomed me for my place in society following him, but he didn't. And that's about all. I learned enough of arcist magic to know I wanted to come here and learn more. Here I am."

Jaritta studied him. Did his eyes tell anything more? Did the fact he came from the mines, possibly the same mines that once her father and now her brother controlled, make him more trustworthy for this or less?

Her instinct said to trust him, and her mind already planned the ways he could help her mold the events of the city into something pleasing to her brother, to Chaitan and the people here, and to all the untouchables of Eghsal.

"My brother Jasfer told me some disturbing news today. A prince was assassinated. He…" She turned to look away for a moment. She'd never felt close to Apijet, but telling it to someone else made it more real, another connection to her old life severed. Another reminder of her parents' deaths—and death was the ultimate casting-out, making people truly untouchable, not just in name.

"He was a mentor for my brother and a friend of our father's. He…Jasfer that is, fears something is going on that he can't quite follow. Some of the other princes may be planning something, and he wants to know what it is."

"And you think I…" He left it unfinished, letting her be the one to say it.

"A spy." She nodded then pinched her lips together, wondering what he'd say. Before he could answer, she added, "Mostly you'd just be with him, posing as a servant, noticing things he didn't and talking to the other servants. It's not like he expects someone to go sneaking into the houses of the other princes or anything."

"I suppose…" Pavresh looked over toward Chaitan's empty chair. "I could meet with your brother. I wouldn't want it to take up too much of my time. I'm still learning so much from Chaitan, and I have to collect stories every day."

"I'm sure you'll have plenty of stories to gather from the princes and their servants." This wasn't something Jasfer had actually asked for. A thought flitted across her mind that he might not agree with her thinking. "I don't know how much time it'll be, but we'll have to see what my brother says. Maybe he'll decide he doesn't need a spy, but I think you'd be a great help to him."

Pavresh gave an exaggerated shrug, his palms out flat and pointing at the ceiling. It looked like a statue's pose, and Jaritta's mind flew back to the odd white material that gathered in the lava beds.

While her mind composed an abstract figure into roughly the same shape as Pavresh's pose, he said, "I'm here to experience the city. I suspect Chaitan would have taken the job instantly thirty years ago."

Jaritta only nodded without opening her eyes as her hands molded the minerals as if they were clay. As she did, the substance flickered between the formations in the lava bed and something else, something more human, as if it were people, society itself that she was shaping.

Chapter 6

Indima laughed with the other women as she pulled another garment from the pile. She studied the silk carefully, looking for any tears or stains.

Sitting beside her, Malya examined another piece of silk. "Have you heard that Juhi just returned from the Silk City?"

Indima rubbed at a small spot that marred the fragile yellow, thinking about the distant city on the eastern end of the valley where everyone belonged to the silk jati or were their cheetah jati servants. She pulled it closer. "So, who's she going to marry?"

Malya laughed. The few dozen silk-weaving families of Romnai always seemed to send their daughters to the Silk City when it was time for them to marry. "No one yet. She's got her eye on one of the princes, I hear."

"Ah. So she says. It's probably an old priest though. Barely walks straight, but oh, he's good with fire in the dark!" Both women laughed, and Indima turned toward one of the younger girls working there. "Take this one and use the green scrub. Gently. I don't want this yellow to fade."

When she turned back, Malya gave her a grin. "You're supposed to be the innocent one, Indima."

"Oh, I am. It's just I hear so many stories about your activities that I learn a thing or two."

Malya's giggle was almost a squeal as she hit Indima across the arm. "Don't be making up stories now. I don't want the fine young men in the prince jati to hear lies about me." She bent down to look at her cloth more closely, then turned back to her friend. "And believe me, there are some pretty men in that group. Have you noticed?"

"Oh, I imagine there are some pretty fine men in most jatis." Realizing what she'd said and what Malya might make of it, Indima rushed on. "Prince, priest, or silk weavers."

Her own laugh sounded forced as she tried to fall back into the easy banter with Malya, but the little slip scared her. She hated not being able to admit her relationship with Ekana. It felt disloyal to pretend he meant nothing to her, as if when she wasn't with him she believed all the ridiculous ideas that separated caste from caste. But if her people once suspected her involvement with radicals and agitators, they'd send her to the Silk City immediately. And unlike Juhi, she wouldn't come back.

Thoughts of dancing and Chaitan's place brought to her mind a scarred face hidden behind cloth. Jaritta, untouchable now, but born to a family of the ruling princes. What was her brother's name?

"What do you know about Prince Jasfer Talai?"

"He's young. And not promised to anyone. Why?"

Indima shrugged. She couldn't really give the true reason. "I'd just heard someone talking about him recently."

Malya pretended to speak in an aside to Charu, who'd just come over to join them. "She means she saw him and thinks he's handsome." All three laughed.

"I don't know much about him," Charu said. "He seems sort of quiet. Hangs around with some of the older princes. Other than that…" She shrugged. "You'd think some family would at least be courting him."

Indima answered. "No parents to arrange it for him, right?"

"Oh, that could be." Malya gave her silk to one of the girls without any instructions. "I seem to remember hearing something about their family. A long time ago."

Charu snapped her fingers. "They had a daughter, as well.

But she was burned, remember? I must have been eleven years old or so."

"Oh, I was barely born then," Malya shouted.

"I'm not that much older than you, girl. You were six. Maybe even seven."

"Yeah, I remember something about that," Indima said. "She was made untouchable, right?"

"I guess so." Charu turned back to sorting the silks, and the women fell quiet for a few minutes, breaking the silence only to instruct the younger girls on how to treat each piece of cloth. Indima found one robe with a tear in it and had to concentrate on fixing it herself. It was too tricky to trust to the young ones.

Silk could not be made here in Eghsal. The worms that made silk could not survive the cold. It was strange to hold in her hands something so precious it had been preserved for over six hundred years, carried here from the Forgotten South. The blue dye on this piece was more recent, of course. Indima selected a matching silk thread to mend the tiny tear. It was the silk weavers' skill and experimentation with preserving the precious cloth that had earned the jati its place in the upper caste. By tradition, the women of the jati cared for and fitted the silks for the women, while the men did the same for those silks worn by the city's most powerful men. It was a far more menial form of labor than the other high caste jatis performed, yet one held in the highest honor by all members of Eghsal.

Some claimed it had to be magic, and Indima wasn't completely sure they were wrong. In the sacred city of their jati, the most skilled weavers could work wonders with damaged cloth. And most precious of all, a single room held a hundred or so bolts of cloth that had never been worn, still preserved by methods even she didn't know, for all these centuries.

"Sulfur take it," Malya swore, holding up another robe. "How do they get these so dirty?"

The other women shook their heads in commiseration as they worked on their own piles of clothing. Whether what they did in the silk city was magic or not, Indima knew that what she did was no magic. It was a careful skill. Deep training and knowledge of special cleaners and unique knots. She finished repairing the blue robe and handed it to a child.

As she was reaching for the next piece of cloth, Charu spoke. "Oh, Juhi had other news from the city, I forgot."

"Oh?" asked Malya.

"She got to see the experiment rooms."

Indima leaned toward the other woman to listen.

"They're working with cotton there now. Some special kind of cotton they're growing between the lava beds and the mountains. They're really excited about it."

Malya waved this away with one hand. "My father says that every twelve years or so, they have a new, promising lead. A new kind of cotton, a new way to spin wool, a lighter form of hemp. But it never pans out. Silk's here to stay, ladies."

Indima's father had always been the opposite. Her mother, really, as well. They'd sit in their spacious house while the servants prepared an evening snack and talk excitedly about the latest experiments. Her father's dream, especially, was to discover some native worm or spider that could spin silk as fine as the silkworms of the Forgotten South.

"Probably," Charu conceded, but then she continued more forcefully. "But Juhi was pretty impressed with what she saw. They have great big rooms with low, glass ceilings, and they fertilize the soil with something special, and the cotton ends up very fine."

Malya shrugged. "Sure. Cotton's the closest we'll ever get. But it doesn't move like silk. It'll never shine like silk."

"Who knows?" Indima interrupted before they could continue. Knowing Malya, she realized that the discussion would never get to something new. "Probably not. But it's good they're trying."

She pulled her cloth closer and tried to think of a new topic to suggest. Malya beat her to it.

"I've chosen my dress for Kwona's Festival."

Even the girls running back and forth on their errands joined in then as they discussed the festival of the mare goddess, the rebellious daughter of the pantheon of gods. Her frequent affairs and seductions made for great stories, though parents were always careful how they celebrated her festival. They wanted to appease the goddess with feasts and sacred dancing, but they didn't want their own daughters to be seduced into following her. The festival was more than half a year away, but that fact didn't slow their preparations.

It wasn't the greatest topic to keep Indima's mind from her lover, but the day soon passed in a sequence of empty words and endless silks.

* * *

"You'll be coming to my house tonight, Indima?" Malya asked as they headed out of the silk-house. "My parents are holding a little party for my brother. I think they'll announce that they've arranged a wedding with that pretty priest girl."

It was snowing, like it seemed to almost every day this time of year as winter approached. The steam from the lava beds could barely rise before it turned to snow. Fortunately the streets were still too warm to hold the snow un-melted.

Indima felt like the snow was a lot heavier, pushing her heart and stomach down. She couldn't go to her friend's house. She'd agreed to meet Ekana tonight. "I have to dance tonight."

"Again? Where do you do that anyway?"

She cocked her head at Malya. "Where's the only place for dancing here? The temples, of course."

Malya looked at her like she didn't quite believe it, and

Indima struggled to keep her own face innocent. She did still go to the temples now and then to practice the sacred dances, and even with so little practice, she had no trouble performing on sacred days.

"Oh. I see."

"So what do you think of the priest girl?"

"She's young." Malya giggled and then covered her mouth, as if giggling made her seem young. "She's nice at least. It'll be like having a sister, I guess. For a little while anyway, until my parents marry me off. Then maybe I'll have other sisters. Or no one."

Indima was a bit surprised by the sad note in her friend's voice, but she decided to ignore it. She made herself laugh and said, "I thought I was like having a sister already."

Malya smiled back. "Yeah, that's true. That's how it's always felt."

They parted soon after that, and Indima promised to stop by if she wasn't too tired from her dancing. That would mean less time with Ekana when she would supposedly be dancing, but she thought she'd better do it. Just to be safe.

She wasn't afraid to walk alone through this part of Romnai. She passed untouchables begging, but otherwise, the streets were full of high-caste *kortru* with their cheetah jati servants returning to their elaborate mansions. The untouchables in the streets were distasteful—even after all her time spent at Chaitan's, she couldn't get past that—but they weren't dangerous. Not here anyway.

A group of princes walked by, and Indima wondered if one of them was Jaritta's brother. She wasn't sure if they were from the Thirty or not. They walked briskly past, talking loudly.

Indima turned down a side street, away from the rolling steam of the lava beds. Immediately, more snow reached her covered head, but still none stuck to the ground. She pulled the loop of cloth that covered her hair tighter, lowered her head, and increased her pace. The street soon opened onto a wider one angling away from the richest houses. It passed a small market, one frequented by the wealthy, and then wound off among newer parts of the city on its western side.

Her house was in the district she'd just passed. Her parents' house, that is, but her own for now as well. She was in no hurry to be married off. One of the advantages of being *kortru*, she supposed. If she'd been a *nefli* laborer, she'd certainly be married by now and the mother of a pair of children. Even a daughter of the *brenil* merchant, servant, or soldier jatis would probably be married off before twenty.

If she could only marry Ekana, she'd run straight to him, tie the silken knots of marriage, and be happy. She liked to tell herself that they'd come up with something. They could run away to the ancient city of Eghsal and live among the ruins. Or they'd go to the sea, and his family would welcome her, and her own jati wouldn't chase her down and bring her back.

But a part of her knew that just wasn't true. If she was lucky, she'd be married to a man who frequently traveled between Romnai and the Silk City, leaving her alone in the capital. Or she'd marry an old man who would soon leave her a widow. But even then, Ekana couldn't stay forever in Romnai. He was a fisherman. Eventually, he'd have to return to Jarnur and steady work.

Even the hope Rashul gave, the dream of her people without castes or jatis with everyone free to marry and work and travel as they wished, seemed not only unlikely but insufficient to keep them together. He could try to change society, but he couldn't force individuals to change.

The streets narrowed. She was well past her family's house and entering the neighborhood where *kortru* and *brenil* houses met. The dark and the snow made all the buildings look a light gray.

A stairway led along one building, away from the street.

At the top were several doors. Indima pulled open the third door, stepped into the warm room, and ran to Ekana's chest. Her arms gripped him desperately, and he held her against him with a strength that felt every bit as graceful as his most beautiful dance steps.

After a long silence, he spoke. "You're crying, Indima. What's wrong?"

Indima squeezed him once then pulled back enough to look up. Looking at his beautiful, dark face, she couldn't say anything. How could she say what she'd been thinking? She leaned back into his chest and let the tears ease to a stop.

"Sorry," she said at last. "I'm just glad to see you."

"Don't be sorry." Ekana laughed. "I'll take this kind of welcome anytime." He held her close until she stepped away. She brushed her hand against his cheek.

"How has your day been?"

Ekana shrugged and turned away briefly. "Fine, I suppose. It doesn't feel right to live off Chaitan's generosity. I went to the docks again, but everyone tells me that sea fishermen don't make good river fishermen. And those who experiment with the steam ships won't even talk to me."

Indima could feel his frustration. She wanted to go down to the docks herself, take whatever *nefli* was in charge of the place and push him in the water. Or better yet, make him bow and call her *tisrah* and demand that he hire Ekana.

It wouldn't work, of course. She'd have to explain why she was there, if not to the *nefli*, then to her family and jati when word came around. Indima walked over to the narrow bed in the room and punched the mattress.

"I hope Rashul succeeds." She was shouting, but she didn't care. "Even if it means my family falls into poverty."

Ekana stepped over and grabbed her arms. "Shhh," he said, with a genuinely worried look on his face. "There could be people in the rooms next to this. They might hear…"

"Even if it means violent, like Iksheen says it will. I just want an end to the stupid system—

Indima wasn't planning to stop even there, but suddenly Ekana's mouth was on hers, and she kissed him back. She put her arms around behind him and melted into him, like the snow melted into the city outside.

They stood there for several minutes. Indima let the kissing become her whole world, erasing the day, her fears, her doubts. They would succeed. Somehow, they'd figure it out, whether it was Rashul's grand plans for change or simply on their own. This was too right for any doubt.

They were still kissing when the door burst open.

Indima spun around, still loosely in Ekana's arms. She couldn't see anyone in the door yet, but how stupid that she hadn't locked it! She'd been so desperate for Ekana's chest and firm arms she hadn't been thinking.

Ekana reached out to push the door shut, but someone stood in the doorway. Indima squinted, but the room's light did not fall fully on him. Others came in behind, and the first walked in. A priest.

Indima was confused. She didn't recognize the man, only his robes. Why would he be here? Behind him were men she recognized. Silk weavers. Men from her jati.

She sank from Ekana's arms to the floor and covered her face with her hands. This couldn't be happening. How had they known? They must have followed her.

Ekana was still frozen in place. Surely, they'd seen them in each other's arms, even if the room itself wasn't compromising enough. There was no back way out, no way for him to pretend innocence or fight back. Indima wondered what the men would do to him.

She looked up then. The priest...she recognized him now. His daughter was the one who would be marrying Malya's brother. And the weavers behind him included Malya's father.

Somehow, Malya had betrayed her.

Emotion came rushing back. She stood in anger.

"What are you doing here?"

The priest barred her way as she approached the weavers. "That question we can ask of you."

"And I won't answer." She turned and looked at her lover's stunned face. "I pretend nothing and admit nothing."

"What is his name?" Malya's father asked.

Indima said nothing, and he turned to Ekana, lifting his head so he looked down his nose at the fisherman. "Tell us your name, *nefli*."

Ekana merely bowed gracefully, a bow that was practically a dance move in itself, and Indima's heart ached for him. "You honor me, *tisrah*."

But he didn't say his name, and Indima felt a flush of pride. If Ekana could stand up to these high-caste figures, maybe there was hope for Rashul's dreams. Even if there was none for her and Ekana. Already she felt that hope disappearing.

"His name doesn't matter," she said to the men of her jati, trying to keep her voice firm. "I will come with you, but only with all of you."

The priest stepped back onto the balcony, and Indima followed. Looking back once, she whispered, "I love you. Once we're clear, run!"

He followed behind her, and she saw him glance the other way on the balcony, but there was no way down.

Indima began descending the stairs, then stopped. The men of her jati had spread out below, as if to intercept Ekana when he ran.

"Unless you want to try to carry me down these steps, I need all of you standing beside that corner of the building." She pointed to the farthest point from the base of the stairway.

They didn't move at first, but she knew they didn't want the dishonor of having to carry her kicking and pinching and shouting down the stairs. Once they were all together, she continued, and Ekana followed.

She'd never known a stairway to be so long.

The priest was finally down and standing with the others. He was a dancer, she realized, one of the priests who performed the male-only sacred dances. He would have known that she wasn't dancing tonight. Indima cursed herself for her foolishness. A part of her mind ran back through the day's events, trying to find some way she could have prevented this. If only she'd… But it didn't matter. Even though she couldn't quite believe it had happened, she couldn't change the past.

Her foot came down on the street and slipped. The snow was actually sticking to the street, enough to make it slick. As soon as she had her balance, Indima walked toward the group of men, doing her best to stay in their way of chasing Ekana.

His hand brushed her shoulder as he took off running. The weavers clearly wanted to chase him, but they weren't ready to start chasing her, too, or to deal with her refusing to move.

They started up the street, the men packed so close around her she could smell them. None of them smelled as good as Ekana, despite their personal steam baths and expensive perfumes.

The sight of Ekana running away seemed to make them forget to worry about preserving their dignity. A hand grabbed her arm. An arm wrapped around her body, picked her up. She screamed, but Malya's father gripped her tightly. As soon as he had her, most of the other men took off running the other way.

"No. No!" If she could shame them, make them fools in front of the *nefli* passersby… She beat her hands against his back, but Malya's father kept walking, taking her home in complete disgrace while the other men of her jati chased the man she loved.

All strength went out of her, and she collapsed against her captor's back as snow landed on her neck.

Too soon they were to her parents' house where she ignored everyone to curl up on a large pile of pillows.

Several times she heard references to the Silk City. If she cried, she didn't remember the tears.

Chapter 7

Pavresh followed the servant into a room of fine pillows and polished wood. The prince did not look up immediately from the papers he had arranged on a low table beside his pile of cushions. This had been the man his father reported to, at least in recent years. Prince Jasfer Talai, and before him, his father.

Pavresh had created a very different picture in his mind, a powerful man, muscular but also with a look of wise slyness, a cautious schemer. The prince had a cautious look on his face as the pen in his hand hesitated over the words. But that caution didn't come with the look of subtle intelligence he'd expected. The look, he realized, that his mind put to any ruling prince he heard of without seeing. Not that Prince Jasfer looked stupid, by any means…merely straightforward. His intelligence, keen though it might be, lay entirely on the surface.

It was an initial reaction, nothing more, and he'd have to remember that. Even the most straightforward-seeming among these princes could hide a deviousness he'd scarcely be able to imagine.

Prince Jasfer set down his pen and looked up. "My sister has told me of you. What can you say to convince me to trust you?"

Pavresh used a touch of magic to make himself seem the trustworthy servant, but he didn't want to overdo it. "Nothing, *tisrah*, I suppose. But…"

"Good. Remember that. Nothing anyone can say or do should ever convince you to trust. Not here among the princes. Betrayal is the ore we mine."

Pavresh opened his mouth several times but wasn't sure

what to say. Eventually, he nodded.

"How long have you been in the city?"

Pavresh had the sense that the prince already knew the answer. "About two months, *tisrah.*"

The prince made a gesture, and a servant entered from a back hallway. He looked strong in the way Pavresh had expected the prince to, not like a dock-worker, but almost like a soldier. He gave Pavresh a brief bow, as to an equal.

"Yatim has looked into things and believes we can accept you for this role. Do you agree?"

"I...yes. I will do what I can for you."

The prince stared at Pavresh without talking, studying something—his eyes? his cheekbones?—then stood and walked toward the door. "Good. I want you to be invisible."

He gestured for Pavresh to walk beside him and spoke in more detail of what he wanted.

* * *

When Prince Jasfer led the way into the grand entryway of the High Assembly, his shadow spun around from a long, street-torch-cast shadow before him to a short, lamp-cast one behind that Pavresh found himself walking on. He slowed down, afraid following so close would make him look as nervous as he felt. Yatim caught up and walked beside him, two steps behind the prince. It wasn't so much the prospect of meeting the most powerful men in the valley—although he had to admit that that was part of it—it was the whole idea of spying. The recent assassination, of course, only increased the tension he felt.

They passed through high hallways lined with ancient and priceless pottery. The floor they walked on was a spotless pattern of white, black, and gray tiles. It seemed random at first, but then Pavresh realized that the lines and squares represented a kiwan board, repeated over and over with subtle variations. It was a reminder that the princes and their servants played an impossibly complex game of kiwan every day. How could he possibly be of any use among such experts?

Jasfer and Yatim both had pulled ahead while he looked at the floor, so Pavresh sped up, pacing quickly toward the chamber where the princes were gathering. They had to slow down at the entrance as several princes and their servants all arrived at once. There was little chatter among the princes, creating a somber mood, a sense still of shock from the assassination of Apijet. Pavresh took the moment to check his magic. Castes might not exist in arcist magic, but the helpful servant did, which didn't speak well for Rashul's hope to completely change society. Maybe it could be a helpful friend, he supposed. He wanted to add something to discourage attackers, a dutiful soldier, perhaps, or even the wild, unpredictable soldier of the mountains. But he feared that might be too much and draw attention to himself.

He fingered the sacred knots on his kusti as they walked into the hall. There was nothing special about the cord as a weapon, nothing magical, and not even the most useful against anyone prepared for it. It was little more than a lightweight whip, useful mostly because it was inconspicuous, but Pavresh found it comforting. The careful pattern of knots brought his mind to the edge of the fire, not into the flames where he might lose himself, but beside them where he found peace. If an assassin attacked, he was ready to do what little he could.

It was unlikely to come to that. Yatim, acting now as bodyguard, should be the one to handle anything like that and soldiers of various jatis guarded the Assembly.

The room opened before them. Windows high in every side must often let in the sunlight, but this time of year, the sun scarcely peeked over the mountains south of the city before it disappeared again. Glass-chimneyed oil lamps lit the room, revealing masses of pillows scattered about the floor. To the right was a door covered in an intricate metallic overlay, a stylized representation of flames. The chapel and the home of the highest priests of the pantheonic religion.

Pavresh looked the other way and saw High Prince Baram seated before another door. This one was smaller, though only slightly, and the decoration was in the form of carved wood. It must be the special inner chamber where someone could overthrow the princes.

Yatim touched him on the shoulder. "You're looking around too much. You don't look like a servant."

Pavresh glanced at the big man and nodded. "You're right. I'll…" He looked quickly around at the other servants moving about. "I'll try to blend in."

Yatim was already in front of him, following Jasfer to one of the piles of pillows. Pavresh still wanted to observe everything around him, but he forced himself to be more surreptitious. He looked at the servants first to get a sense of how they carried themselves. They moved like people sure of themselves and their place in society, but they never looked a prince directly in the face. To each other, they nodded and smiled and shared a few words, but all quietly so as not to disturb their masters.

Jasfer sat, the pillows propping up his back and shoulders, and Pavresh waited beside him.

"I'd like some tisane, well-sweetened." The prince's eyes never came near Pavresh.

"Yes, *tisrah*," he said, wondering where to get the drink. He looked at Yatim, and the other servant pointed toward a serving hallway angling back between the main entrance and the chapel.

Pavresh hurried away, doing his best to walk as the other servants did. Even so, he was afraid that anyone paying attention would be sure to notice how stiffly he moved, how uncertain he was.

People walked every way as more princes entered with their retinues, some with as many as three fighting servants in addition to one or two for serving. Others had only one who must double as bodyguard and server, although the chamber itself seemed to have its own servers as well who moved about with trays of nuts and cakes. Pavresh fell into the rhythm of weaving his way among them all and reached the hallway.

He wanted to explore it. Chamber servants moved down the hallway toward wherever the foods were prepared. But before they'd come, Jasfer had told him that the most important thing for now was that no one notice him as out of the ordinary. He had to blend in so well that people might talk even as he passed nearby.

The gourds of tisane stood lined up on the table, fancy metal straws sticking from the openings. One servant was positioned behind the table with his only job to carefully shake and turn the gourds until the herbs inside were angled just right before adding hot water. Pavresh grabbed a gourd and looked for the honey. There was none. Other servants stepped in, jostling him so the tisane splashed on his hands. It burned. In surprise, he brought one hand up to his mouth and sucked on his burned finger. Then he set the gourd down and waved both hands to cool them off.

It was a moment later when he noticed the sweetness in his mouth. The other servants were giving him strange looks. Noticing him, just what he didn't want. He grabbed the gourd again, nodding briefly at a few of the servants, and hurried away from the hallway.

Jasfer said nothing as he took the drink, and Pavresh couldn't tell if it was a part of the spying act, or how he always treated servants.

A chime rang, a series of notes that was clearly the signal to begin. Pavresh looked around and saw a priest ringing the small bells from a position beside the high prince. A full dozen women in bird headpieces stood to either side of them, looking around the gathered people with a predatory look that matched their uniforms. Then, remembering his role, Pavresh snapped his gaze away and acted as nonchalant as he could.

Prince Baram spoke. "It is a strange day for us all, and I thank you for coming. Today we will discuss the tragic assassination of our colleague Prince Apijet." The high prince was an impressive man, large without being overly fat. His voice had a slight hitch to it that kept it from being as stirring as it might have, but it filled the room.

He glanced at the priest beside him as he continued. "That is all we will discuss. Plans and debates about restoring the lost city of Eghsal shall wait." Pavresh thought the priest looked disappointed by this, and he tried to look around to see if any of the princes were as well, but he didn't know the names of anyone and had no idea where to look.

An older prince was the first to speak. He stood up next to his pillows and spoke quietly. "Prince Apijet was a good man. He had served this valley and his family nearly as long as I've been a prince."

Pavresh leaned over next to Yatim and whispered. "Could you tell me who the speakers are as they speak? I don't know any names."

Yatim answered, scarcely moving his lips, "Prince Dhalip. An old friend of Apijet's and of Jasfer's father."

Pavresh made a show of arranging the pillows around Jasfer as Dhalip continued.

"When he first started ruling, our country was at war. It was through his wisdom and that of men like him that we won that war over the mumblers. Now as our nation considers sending the soldier jati to fight once more, he will be missed. I can only hope Tiespetre blesses us with another prince of his character to join the Thirty."

Pavresh glanced at the high prince. Baram's eyes narrowed,

and he looked like he might interrupt, but he didn't seem to want to interrupt this elder member of the princely court. And without any prodding, Dhalip said no more of the plans for war and only spoke of Apijet, his quiet nature, his friendship, his subtle understanding of the workings of people's minds.

Others followed, carefully skirting any talk of the current situation. They recalled little experiences, lessons Apijet had taught them, key ideas he'd thought of to guide the decisions of the body, and many other gems of his life. Jasfer told of the prince coming to his family's house when he was young and quizzing him on things only a much older child should be expected to know.

"But that was Prince Apijet. He didn't care what others expected of you or what you'd settle for expecting of yourself. He always expected great things of those around him, and if he saw you weren't reaching them, he'd only push harder, sometimes taking another tack, but never giving up or letting you assume you'd done all you could."

Pavresh recognized that the late prince would have been a perfect master to teach him about spying, and probably many things that could help him dig deeper into the arcist magic. He also would have been a huge obstacle to anyone trying to manipulate the body of princes in some foolish direction.

What he couldn't figure out was who might be wanting that.

He decided to return to the table in the hallway for refreshments. If the other servants milling about knew anything to help him, he didn't learn it. What he overheard was only talk of the immediate duties. When he returned with a small tray of sweet cakes, another prince was talking.

"Dartak," Yatim said from the corner of his mouth. "Watch him."

"He was a good man. I'm sure you know that we did not always agree, but we always respected each other."

This was a voice to impress. Dartak was middle-aged and

losing much of his hair, but there was something about him that demanded respect.

"It would be unjust to forget him quickly or move so fast into other matters, and I applaud the high prince for his decision to hold off our plans to retake the ancient city."

Applause followed this statement, and Prince Baram graciously accepted it, but his face had a guarded look.

"Prince Apijet was among the first to applaud the discussions about retaking the city," Dartak continued, and Baram raised a hand as if to warn him. "And the best way to honor that is to honor the man, the memories we have, the wisdom he gave, and to leave his dreams and ours of the future for another day."

Dartak continued, artfully alluding to the lost city repeatedly, but always obliquely so Prince Baram never had cause to order him quiet. The man was a gifted speaker, Pavresh had to admit that. He was at home with words. Pavresh wondered exactly why Yatim had warned him to watch the man. He seemed determined to see success in the retaking of the city, but he didn't strike Pavresh as malicious. If he were to recreate it in arcist magic, he'd say Dartak was an Honest Elder Statesman. A Charismatic Leader, just as Rashul dreamed himself to be, even if they would disagree about how to use that charisma.

The day wore on as other princes spoke. Arbul, another friend of Jasfer's father. Vedu, an older prince who had worked with Apijet on some project years ago. Girmeet who praised Apijet's guidance and mentoring when he was younger. Lokanik, who looked to be the oldest prince there and spoke of the days before Apijet came, of the bitter feuds and rivalries that dominated until Apijet helped diffuse them.

Pavresh returned periodically to the refreshment table for snacks and sweetened water to refresh Jasfer's tisane. At midday, they ate a larger meal, but he still had no time to talk with the prince to compare their thoughts on the morning. The sun rose above the mountains and, after only a couple of short speeches, set once again.

The discussion changed to what to do about the assassination. The princes discussed increasing guards and the safety of the streets. They wondered who might have committed the crime, but no fingers were pointed.

Until one young prince stood up. He hadn't spoken in eulogy of Apijet, so Pavresh glanced at Yatim. "Samatrit," he said, and added, "Prince Jasfer's cousin."

He seemed a rough one, with a note of anger just beneath the surface. "Prince Apijet was a friend of my family, yet we do nothing to avenge him?" Grief that seemed genuine nearly overcame the prince. "Surely something must be done. I can't sit here and let his killers go free. I know, we can't be sure yet who they were. But I hear rumors. There are those within our city who wish to see an end of all of us princes. Those who promote immoral behavior, against the very gods. Those who wish to end our very society. They claim the desire to abolish castes, but what they truly want is to destroy all who belong to a different caste or jati from their own. They'd set themselves up as the new princes of our valley."

He took a deep breath as if to control his emotion, and Pavresh realized he was holding his breath and staring intently at the prince. It took great effort to force himself into a servant's pose again.

"I've volunteered to lead our forces... Sorry." He bowed toward Prince Baram, though the high prince had made no move to silence him. "I will not speak of that today. But this would be a perfect training for our troops, to seek out these malcontents and destroy them wherever they might be found here in Romnai. And it would avenge the death of a great prince."

The room erupted in voices, cheering and countering and

shouting. Samatrit had sat back down, his face in his hands. Prince Dartak was on his feet applauding loudly.

Something seemed odd about Dartak this time as Pavresh's eyes passed over him. He looked more closely. Even now he felt the overwhelming sense of the rightness of this man, the sense that he was a wise and capable leader. Too overwhelming in fact. Pavresh stumbled backward. It was magic. Dartak was using arcist magic, and quite powerfully, but without any subtlety or finesse.

As he regained his composure, he thought more carefully. He didn't know that for sure. *Someone* was using arcist magic on Dartak, that much was clear. Perhaps the same person had used it on Samatrit, to make his grief resonate. Pavresh looked at the servants gathered around the prince. He was one of those who'd brought a large retinue, so it could be any of them.

Whatever the truth, it was something he'd have to tell Prince Jasfer.

But now, what to do about Samatrit's awful suggestion?

Already Jasfer was dealing with that.

"I did not know Prince Apijet was so close to you or your family, unless you include your wider family, cousin. No one would question the connection he had with my family. Like you, I wish to see justice done, and I urge everyone here to do their part to lead us to the truth. But I don't see the connection you're drawing to this rabble. Are we to assume this connection, or will you show us?"

Samatrit sneered at his cousin. "The proof is in their words. They seek to destroy us and all that our culture stands for. What other proof do you need? Assassins or not, they are a threat to us."

"A threat? The ones who rant on street corners about some made-up past? From what I've seen, these are a few mad street teachers with no true following."

Jasfer wondered if he truly believed that or if his sister told him the truth of what happened at Chaitan's house.

Before the cousins could argue more, Prince Baram broke in, his hand raised as it had been when Dartak spoke of the abandoned city. "It is true we have no proof of their involvement, and it's also true that such people merit careful watching."

He looked around the room then gestured at a prince Pavresh didn't know yet. "Shardash. I want you to look into this group. Send some of your servants to keep an eye on them, learn what they're planning. Report to me all that you learn."

"Yes, *tisrah.*"

"Now, enough of the fears and blame and plans. If anyone else wishes to speak of our brother, Apijet, do so. Let's remember his life before his body is committed to the flame."

Pavresh's religion taught that fire was too sacred to defile with a corpse. He forced his thoughts away from such desecration. He had to concentrate on the people around him, trying to understand what was going on and where he might learn more.

* * *

"I shouldn't have spoken. Damn." Prince Jasfer pounded his fist into a pillow in the drawing room of his house. Pavresh watched the various servants of the household move about, ignoring their master while he fumed.

"Prince Baram wouldn't have listened to Samatrit anyway. Now I made it look like a petty family squabble."

Pavresh shifted uncomfortably while the prince moved over to the fireplace.

"Or worse. They'll suspect my contact with Jaritta and expose my sympathies for an untouchable. Damn, damn, damn."

When he'd berated himself for twenty minutes, he turned to

Pavresh and asked what he'd learned or observed. Pavresh told of Prince Dartak's arcist magic.

"What would it take to know who was actually doing it?"

"Chaitan could probably figure it out, but I couldn't. Maybe…I'll ask Chaitan tonight if it's something that can be taught."

The prince nodded. "Good. Good. And I want to know if anyone else there was using magic." He paused and took a sip of brandy. "Do you think anyone would have noticed that you were using magic?"

Pavresh didn't answer immediately. It hadn't occurred to him to wonder. Clearly, if anyone could see it, that would immediately blow his cover. Might as well go walking through there with a sign saying he was a spy.

"I don't think so, *tisrah*, but I can't be sure. Chaitan can sense the subtlest working of magic, but I don't think most arcists can. The magic on Dartak was far from subtle."

"And your own? How subtle were you?"

Pavresh chewed the inside of his cheek. "Quite. I could probably be subtler next time."

"Do so." Jasfer sat down on a chair formed of three pillows and laid his head back. "It'll be a few days before the princes meet again. The high prince will choose a replacement for Apijet, probably one of the nephews to keep the seat in the same family. You've seen some of how the power flows among the princes. I'd like you to explore a bit more. Learn what you can from their servants and their houses and their behavior."

"Yes, *tisrah*. I will do that." He shifted on his feet, wanting to pose a question but not sure when to.

"But be careful. I can't have anyone know who you are or how you're connected to me."

"Of course, *tisrah*."

The prince was quiet then, sipping his brandy with eyes closed. Pavresh waited, uncertain what was expected of him.

Finally, he said softly, *"Tisrah?"*

"You may call me Jasfer in private, Pavresh. I am not so stuck on my caste's privileges as some."

"Yes...Jasfer."

"Did you have a question?" Jasfer opened his eyes and turned his face toward Pavresh.

"Yes, I... What about Prince Shardash? Do you think he will agree with your cousin about hunting down the...the malcontents?"

The prince released his breath loudly. "I wouldn't put him in the camp with Samatrit and Dartak. And Tarak, who seems to be a part of their group. I was studying the lines of power today, like Prince Apijet taught me." Pavresh wasn't sure what he meant, but he didn't interrupt. "Shardash wasn't a friend of Apijet or my father or that group of princes. But he didn't appear to have any connections with the other princes either."

He pushed himself to his feet and placed his glass on the mantel. "I guess if anyone's neutral, it's him. You'll have to tell Jaritta I can't visit her. And you'll need to be careful yourself. If..." Jasfer looked Pavresh in the eye now. "If they're planning anything dramatic, I ask you to keep your distance from it."

"Yes, *tisrah*. Jasfer."

"I think they'll be fine, but...you may warn them what you've heard. Tell them to beware."

Pavresh realized that this was a difficult concession. The prince expected him to keep most of what happened silent, silent even about his own involvement. The fewer people who knew of his contact with Jasfer the better.

"Thank you. I will come up with a reasonable explanation for the knowledge."

Jasfer nodded and dismissed him. Pavresh's thoughts flew wildly as he walked back toward Chaitan's house.

Chapter 8

"What happened to you?"

At first Marankiya didn't bother to see who was talking or to whom. The cold air was enough to tell him someone had come in the door. He only wanted to focus on this book Iksheen had brought the other day.

The poet and Rashul wanted to use the heretical poetry for their revolution, to inspire people to join them. Marankiya didn't like the idea. You don't use poetry, even heretical poetry. Not true poetry, and by true, he meant well written and powerful, not necessarily theologically accurate. True poetry uses you. It changes readers, forces them into new paths and toward new enlightenment.

Not that the people rewarded true enlightenment. Even the gods didn't seem to reward it. But enlightenment wasn't about getting rewarded, he supposed.

"Where have you been? We haven't seen you in days." The voices came again from the doorway, but Marankiya didn't turn to look.

He settled more comfortably into the pillows and read the words again. He'd been reading the greatest poetry of both Eghsal and the Forgotten South since he was young, and this wasn't as powerful. It didn't reach that level of mastery. The words didn't sing consistently. The images were perhaps overly obsessed with fire. But there were lines that filled him with wonder, turns of phrases that pushed the poetry close to the highest level. And when placed beside the more mystical verses accepted by the priests, this hardly seemed heretical.

They were still fussing around about whoever had entered, but the silence of the person eventually drew Marankiya's curiosity. He turned on his floor pillow to see the small crowd at the door.

The man who stood there without talking was Ekana, the dancer, but Marankiya hardly recognized him. His smooth face was broken, his clothes torn to rags, his body visibly bruised. Jaritta and some of the others were ushering him over to a seat near the fire. Curious, Marankiya stood and grabbed his mug of fire liquor. He hurried over and offered it to the dancer.

Ekana took the mug and poured it into his mouth, and the shock of it seemed to wake him from his stupor. He coughed and squeezed his eyes shut and handed the mug back.

Everyone sat quietly, and finally he opened his eyes and looked around. "We were caught."

Marankiya heard several drawn-in breaths, but no one spoke. No one needed to ask what he meant.

Jaritta broke the silence, saying in a quiet voice, "Tell us what happened."

"We were… They broke in." Ekana moved his head as if looking at the people around him, but he didn't seem to see them. "The men from her jati. They chased me. And caught me by the river. Two days ago."

He hung his head and wouldn't say any more. As the silence dragged on, one of them asked quietly as if not sure whether to mention it, "What about Indima?"

He only shook his head. Marankiya drifted back to his own pillows and looked again at the book while the others in the room fussed over the beaten dancer. He would only be in the way. What could one old man do anyway, among all these young and passionate revolutionaries? The words, though, demanded to be read. That was something an old man could do. Even if it was lesser poetry, it brought him back to those early days when he was young and brilliant, when everyone told him what wonders he would create.

When the gods hadn't yet abandoned him.

He wrote his first poetry as a teenager, laboring over the perfect words, resisting the temptation to write too much like any of his religious heroes. He thrilled to see the papers go out to the religious thinkers and prominent men of the day. And the streets buzzed with anticipation for the first words of wisdom from the boy wonder.

Until people read the poems. He'd tried too soon, they said. The lines were technically proficient, but spiritually weak. He had time. Everyone assured him that he'd simply published before he was ready. His next writing would meet all expectations. The religious world would be knocked to its core, blown back by the freshness of his vision.

Marankiya had waited then, writing often but hiding his words away. Finally, he published a poetic essay, a meditation examining the basis of their faith in fire and the ways the gods used it. It failed even worse than the poems, and his failures continued until no one wanted anything to do with him. The priests remembered his low-caste origins. The dock laborers of his own jati looked askance at his religiosity and his scholar's build. And everyone saw only his failure.

It took many years and many attempts before he finally gave up.

Maybe there was something true to this poetry from Iksheen's book after all, if it could bring him back to those early days. "The flames form shapes, / a gourd vine to bind my heart to earth." He tasted the words as they left his tongue, saw the image in his head of fire and plant superimposed, and with them rose thoughts of his youth. He lived always in the memories of disappointment, always aware of the failures of his youth, but those early years of such promise seldom surfaced in his memories.

"This is what the revolution is about!"

Marankiya looked up to see Rashul standing beside Ekana, shaking a fist. His face was pinched with anger.

"When we succeed, this won't happen. It shouldn't happen now. We need to let them know that we won't stand for this violence and injustice!"

Ekana didn't look up, but Rashul didn't seem to care whether the dancer agreed with him or not.

"We'll go into the streets. We'll gather all the untouchables and all the downtrodden, all those who feel trapped by their jati and caste."

Everyone in the room was listening closely. Marankiya wasn't sure they were all enraptured by his plan, but they were inspired to listen. He knew the young revolutionary well enough to believe he would soon have them all tearing through the streets, pulling down the mansions of the *kortru*, invading the halls of the princes, if that was what he wanted.

"And we'll let them know that we are here. Let them know that we want justice to rule in Romnai, not the corrupt castes!"

Soon they'd be ready to charge from the room and riot. Might as well, if words no longer held power, if gods ignored their poets, then maybe action and violence would mean something. Marankiya felt only the vaguest stirrings of passion from Rashul's words, but his own thoughts moved him to join those standing nearest Rashul. He didn't even need his fire liquor to keep him on his feet. Rashul talked on, stirring up the people until another voice broke in.

"Wait! We have to be careful. This is not a good time to draw the attention of the princes."

It was a young man that Marankiya thought looked vaguely familiar. He looked more closely. The man certainly belonged there among them all. Marankiya had seen him before, but who was he? It took a moment before he realized that it was the new arcist, Pavresh. They'd spoken at various times in the past few months, but he had such a forgettable face that Marankiya often couldn't recall who he was.

Iksheen, the poet, answered him. "There's never a good time to draw their attention to us, is there? If we wait until a good time for a revolution, it'll never happen."

Those gathered murmured in agreement.

"There's more going on than just this, though. We're..." Pavresh paused as if not sure how much he ought to be saying. Marankiya wondered where he might be getting this information. "We're being watched. There was a prince assassinated recently, and they think we had something to do with it."

"And it's too bad we didn't." Iksheen was about to go on, but Rashul cut him off.

"No. We are not looking to kill princes or priests. That's revenge. We don't want revenge, only justice."

He fell silent then, and no one dared interrupt his thinking. Marankiya thought bitterly of the priests who had celebrated him as a youth who knew the sacred scriptures as well as they did, only to reject him later, turn away from him as if he were untouchable. Maybe revenge wasn't such an awful, unenlightened thing. Ekana stood up and spoke. Marankiya had to strain to hear his words. "I want revenge." Then he walked out of the room into the cold street.

Marankiya expected Rashul to call him back, to warn him not to use violence, but he stayed quiet. Iksheen jumped up in his place, his untouchable cloak flying around his fancier clothes beneath, creating an image of a wild man exhorting passersby on a street corner.

"We can't let him go alone. He needs our help now. I believe in justice as much as Rashul, but true justice begins by standing by each other no matter the circumstances. Come with me!"

Rashul still said nothing against this violence or against Iksheen, although he was clearly muttering something beneath his breath. Pavresh tried convincing Iksheen that this was wrong, but he only shook his head. The others in the room shouted too loudly for Pavresh's words to reach Marankiya.

Surely, Marankiya thought, he was using his magic, trying to make his words seem wise, but if they couldn't hear the words, maybe magic lost its power. Iksheen went to the door and threw it open then stepped out proudly. A handful of others followed him.

Marankiya pretended surprise to find himself one of that handful, the burn of what had remained of his fire liquor filling his mouth and throat. But once outside, he admitted that he'd wanted to do something like this ever since his first days coming to Chaitan's house and joining the discussions of injustice and revolution. Even lately, as he'd pulled away to merely listen, sure his words were at best tolerated by the young, he'd wanted to act in some way. It was dark outside with a light snow, winter's perpetual companion, falling onto the streets.

Marankiya joined the younger men in hurrying through the streets to catch up with the dancer. He was heading toward the richer parts of the city at a fast walk, and they had nearly reached the lava beds when they caught up with him. Marankiya breathed hard and wished they would slow even more.

Ekana turned down a narrow alley that ran between two large manors. The others gathered beside him and waited for him to explain a plan or give directions. He said nothing.

Marankiya's heart beat wildly, and not just from the exertion. This was so different from what he usually did. He was the one to stay behind and sulk and relive his humiliations, not the one to run off to right a wrong or seek revenge. Had the poetry he read been so powerful? Or was one of the gods speaking to him at long last, as he'd thought they had in his youth? No, not that. The gods had abandoned him long ago.

Snow collected on their uncovered heads, and still Ekana

said nothing. These were the *kortru* manors. The silk weavers' homes. They could equally be priest houses or the homes of princes, even if not likely the families of the Thirty, but what was the difference at this point?

The thought that priests might live here built up his anger until it burned like the fire of young Iksheen's perpetual passion. Revenge on Ekana's behalf didn't rouse him like it did the others, but revenge for his own humiliation was a powerful fire. Like long-banked coals, it came to life. They were the ones who'd turned up their noses at him and his writings. They were the ones who deserved the flames of his anger. Holy flames, of course, for their pieties. Righteous fire for their arrogance.

A figure passed by the entrance of the alley, dressed in silks. Ekana didn't move, but Marankiya couldn't stand still any longer. He threw himself from the alley, bowling into the man. It was a bulky man, but Marankiya was not small either. He kicked the man in the belly as he rolled on the ground. Then he grabbed the fine silk of the man's robe and tore it. Only then did he realize that the others had not followed him from the alleyway.

He looked up the street and realized that people were watching him. Pointing. Shouting for soldiers. Running toward him to stop him.

He froze for a moment, all fire gone. This was not what Ekana and Iksheen had had in mind. He fled, not down the alley behind him, but down the street, dodging people and turning without paying attention to where. It was some blocks later when he realized he still held a piece of the silk robe in his hands. A large piece that drifted open as he ran. Footsteps closed in behind him.

He turned again. Opening the cloth fully, he spun around and flung it at the face of his pursuer then turned down a narrow side street. He had only seen the one pursuer when he turned—a face and form briefly and then images of the pursuer battling the clinging cloth. He hoped the silk had slowed the man enough for him to escape. More streets came flashing past, quick turns among the countless unnamed streets of this poorer section of the city. He didn't dare turn to see if anyone still chased him, but he thought if anyone did, they'd surely have caught him by now.

Eventually, he collapsed on an old stone bench in a tiny square surrounded by high buildings. Surely it was a forgotten part of the city for everyone but those who lived here.

His breathing slowed, and he wondered what had come over him. This wasn't like him at all. It was as if some fire inside him he didn't even know had suddenly become a wildfire. Wildfires out in the countryside often started from lightning. What lightning had struck him today?

The gods. That's what it had to be. This fire was a message from the gods. Perhaps brought also by the poetry, even if it was heretical and not as powerful as the great works of the masters.

And then he realized it. Poetry. The gods wanted him once again to write poetry. An epic. He could see it already in his mind. An epic to aid Rashul in his rebellion against the priests who perverted the truth of the fire. That's what the gods wanted. You don't use poetry, he thought once more, but now the poetry was using him, pushing him toward words that would support Rashul's ideals. "Four fires deep below / a raging dance, subterranean, / ephemeral and yet infinite." A heretical image, yet it created something in his mind, an idea of the god of water rising up from hidden caverns to teach a man to dance. "Four fires too within my flesh / calling me to join my steps to theirs. / I fall into fire." Also from the forbidden poetry, more lyrical than the epic story he had in mind, but he could feel himself falling into the sacred epic, just as that poet had fallen into what he believed was sacred fire. Already the words and images of something new and powerful were burning into his mind.

He stood and headed for Chaitan's house, the events of the evening already forgotten as he felt the words of the gods rise up within him.

* * *

Marankiya was framing the conversation between the god Perkwom and the human hero Gauran as they made war in the Forgotten South when he entered Chaitan's house, all thoughts of Ekana and violence forgotten.

Iksheen stood there, and his expression brought it all back to him. "What the burning sulfur were you doing?"

"What? Oh, I…what happened afterward?"

Iksheen narrowed his eyes and didn't answer. Marankiya looked around for the others who'd gone with them. He didn't see Ekana, but he saw another one, Rijef, one of several young people who spent time at Chaitan's who had a small level of skill with the arcist magic and performed with the dancers and musicians.

"Rijef, what happened?"

He looked almost as angry as Iksheen had, but he answered anyway. "When you ran out and attracted everyone's attention, Ekana shouted something and ran back the other way, but not far. He jumped up and grabbed a window sill. I don't know how he managed to jump that high." Rijef looked around the room, his eyes resting on the poet, who stood with his arms folded across his chest.

"Iksheen pushed on the bottoms of his feet to help him up, then he called for us to run." He shrugged. "We did. But we were chased. They captured Purunrik and dragged him off. The rest of us barely escaped."

"What about Ekana?"

Rijef held his palms up to show he didn't know. "I imagine

he was captured, too, though perhaps he managed some mischief first."

Iksheen slammed his fist against a low table. Tisane sloshed from the gourds, and those sitting around it jumped back.

"We could have done something for real. We could have actually made a strike against the ruling caste, inspired those around us to rise up. Something dramatic, a fire, a speech, anything to undermine the ruling caste." He stepped closer to Marankiya. "Instead, we were a little group of hooligans, enough to inspire extra guards in the *kortru* districts, but little more."

He stopped directly in Marankiya's face. "How you even dare come back here I don't know. Maybe you're just too old to understand the struggle. What possible excuse could you have?"

Iksheen held up the book of poems as if to strike Marankiya across the face with it. Then he threw it down at his feet and walked away.

Marankiya bent down to grab the book and watched him disappear into the back rooms. It didn't matter. The young poet could fume and be self-righteous all he wanted. The gods had spoken to Marankiya. The fire had filled him with words, and the epic that was forming in his mind would do more for the revolution than Iksheen's petty violence and angry words ever could.

The door opened, and the house fell silent. Marankiya turned and saw a high-born woman in silks standing there with two of her personal servants. Even the servants were dressed finer than most of those in Chaitan's house, and their faces made it clear that none of them wanted to be there. The *kortru* woman looked at them as if she were seeing a dead mouse drowned in her private bath.

The three stepped in, and one servant reluctantly closed the door. The other announced, "My lady, the *tisrah*, has a message she's been asked to relay."

It wasn't as if there'd been any need for an announcement. There was no noise to drown out, no whispers to speak over. Marankiya looked around and saw the same nervousness on many faces. The arcist had spoken of them being spied on. Had they sent this woman so soon to do something? No, that didn't make sense. They'd send soldiers if they meant to arrest anyone.

Marankiya realized his right hand was clenching and unclenching nervously on empty air, but he didn't try to stop it.

The woman in silks stepped forward. "I've been sent by one I love, a friend since birth. But even my love won't let me say everything she wanted me to say." She wrinkled her nose at this, as if the words themselves smelled.

"Indima asks me to send her...greetings. And her regrets that she can't come here anymore."

When they heard that it was a message from Indima, many of those there let out relieved breaths. She must have set out before hearing of any attack, or else have no idea of any connection. Still, no one spoke, eager to hear news of their friend.

The silk weaver was looking around the room, as if wondering who of them this Ekana was, who'd lured her friend away from what was right. She wouldn't know that Ekana wasn't here anymore either. And possibly wouldn't be back.

"She will be leaving the city, going to the Silk City now. Please..." She paused, and Marankiya had the feeling that these were her own words now, and no message from the dancer. "Please forget her."

"How soon?" Jaritta stood near the strangers, the beautiful side of her face turned toward them. "When will she be leaving?"

The woman hesitated before answering. "A month or more,

probably. Maybe even longer, I suppose. When the worst of winter is passed." Then she narrowed her eyes. "But make no attempt to contact her. For her sake and yours, you must forget that she ever came…here." She said this last word with a sneer, as if surprised any friend of hers would even want to be in this place.

Without another word, she turned and signaled for one of her servants to open the door. They left, and conversations slowly coalesced out of the silence.

Marankiya felt a hand on his shoulder. Even after seeing him earlier in the evening, it took him a moment to place the arcist's face. Pavresh had a concerned look to him, and Marankiya wondered if that was somehow a part of his magic or if it was genuine. That was the thing with arcists, once you knew who they were. You could never really know who was the real person beneath their magic.

"Iksheen's angry. But I think you're still safer staying here. In fact, I wouldn't go out in the streets at all. We're being watched, and they'll definitely keep an eye out for you now."

A part of him thought he should be worried by this. He didn't want to be captured by the priests, who'd already humiliated him enough. They wouldn't hesitate to use his arrest as some kind of warning to the lower castes. But the thrill of his epic was too strong.

He brushed off the arcist's hand casually and answered, "It won't matter. I'll stay here. Tell Rashul to write his manifesto and prepare to post it all over the city. I have a holy epic to write."

With a quick nod to the young man, he hurried to Kapita, who wasn't attending Chaitan at the moment, and asked for ink, a pen and some paper, and a new mug of fire liquor. Then he went into a corner and prepared to write.

Chapter 9

Pavresh walked along the Avenue of Geysers early in the morning, when the late sunrise was still long off. The sprawling manors of the princely families stood out against the glow of the lava field beyond. The manor of Prince Dartak stood over the lava beds, suspended by thick pillars of metal and ground rock. One entire wing of the building had been abandoned as unsafe, the floors collapsing into bubbling, sulfurous water, but Pavresh found the rest of the building to be plenty big.

When he returned in the late-morning darkness with a swirl of true-winter air, he carried a tall load of laundered clothes that obscured his face. He was directed where to bring them and then slipped off to explore the rest of the house. He was torn about how to proceed. He felt a strong desire to hide, to slink from shadow to shadow, to peek into darkened rooms and discover what was going on. But if he was found skulking like that, he'd have a hard time explaining himself.

Jaritta had chosen him because he could blend in so well. Dressed as a cheetah jati servant, anyone would assume that's what he truly was. He'd spoken with Jasfer in depth that morning before coming here. The prince had assured Pavresh that Dartak wouldn't recognize most of his own servants, so there was no danger of being discovered by him.

"But surely the servants know each other. Won't they realize that I don't belong there?"

Jasfer had paused as if he'd never considered this. Finally, he nodded. "I suppose they might." He turned to Yatim. "Do you know all the servants here?"

"By name, no, *tisrah*. But by face, yes. I made it my business once I began protecting you."

"Do all my servants know each other?"

"Many don't, I'm sure. And most won't at Dartak's manor, especially since it's a bigger household. More servants. The kitchen help won't know those who care for the clothes and dress their lords. The hallway cleaners won't know the footmen. You'll just have to avoid anyone in my position there."

"And I imagine that as long as I avoid the prince himself, I should be able to do that."

Yatim had nodded, but hesitantly.

That nod didn't reassure him now. Pavresh clenched his eyes briefly, stood straight, and walked down the hallway as if he had every right to be there. He did what he could with his magic, but he didn't want it laid on so thickly that Dartak's arcist might notice it. Or Dartak himself, if that was who had been playing the magic in the High Assembly of the Princes.

Several servants passed him, talking to each other and not paying any attention to him. He walked more confidently after that, looking for anything that might be worth investigating.

Doing his own spying, Pavresh couldn't help but wonder about Shardash and whoever was spying on Chaitan's house. Someone, maybe even someone he thought he knew, must be watching them, listening, reporting back to the princes. All this while Rashul made plans for something grand. Pavresh didn't know yet what it would be because while Rashul spoke freely about his frustrations and dreams, he kept the specifics to himself. Which would be good for keeping it a surprise to the princes, of course. But to Pavresh, the gatherings at Chaitan's house had come to feel dangerous, as if each time Rashul spoke and each time Iksheen urged action, they were inviting a dozen knife-wielding toughs into the room. Who knew when they might decide to stab?

Fine carvings and ancient, ceremonial gourds decorated the hallways of Dartak's manor. Everywhere were signs of the fishing he patronized—stylized helms, a false fishing net woven of silk, trophy fish as long as Pavresh was tall. Pavresh had never felt any strong connection to the sea. It was a part of his father's past, no more. But the sight of those objects stabbed some part of his heart with longing for the sea, the desire to do what his father and ancestors had done, captaining fishing vessels and trading fish up the valley.

None of the objects had any bearing on the plans for the abandoned city. He walked calmly into rooms, looking for maps or papers, but he didn't dare enter any rooms where the prince might be. In one room, he ran into a young woman in silk who must have been the prince's daughter. She glanced at him and turned her face away. Pavresh muttered, *"Tisrah,"* as he bowed his way out of the room.

A stairway led to the second floor where the sleeping rooms would be. He was about to climb up when he heard a voice say, "Stop."

Pavresh barely resisted the impulse to run. He turned calmly and faced another servant, a broad-shouldered man with only a strip of hair around back from ear to ear. If anyone was head of the servants, Pavresh thought, this man looked it.

He took a big breath and waited for the man to speak.

"You're the new footman? I'm Abhish. I'm the head footman."

Pavresh bobbed his head as if to both nod his agreement and offer the man a slight bow.

"Come with me out to the carriage. We've got to get it ready for tonight."

Pavresh stood frozen for a moment, but when no way to avoid the command occurred to him, he followed the head footman down a side hallway into the attached carriage house, lit by several bright oil lamps. Three carriages stood within, an ancient one that must have been for show, a two-horse carriage built for speed, and a stately four-horse coach. Abhish led him directly to the two-horser. Another servant was already arranging the traces.

Abhish tossed him a rag. "Polish the silver all around the carriage. The prince likes it to shine."

Pavresh thought it already shone, but he didn't say so. He went to work polishing the fittings and flourishes. The silver was especially impressive against the black fabric of the carriage.

When Abhish left for a side room on the carriage house, the other servant leaned over.

"Just be glad we're not taking out that beast." He hooked a thumb toward the four-horse coach. "We'd be getting ready all day long."

Pavresh leaned away from his work and smiled at the man, pulling a glimmer of magic over himself, *Simple worker, honest worker, friendly fellow*.

"Does the prince take it out often?"

"No, not these days. But the *tisrah* sure takes this one often enough, visiting other princes constantly."

Pavresh kept his face neutral at this, but his mind started spinning. Who did he visit so much? And why? "I guess we're kept busy then."

"That's why they needed a new footman. There's too much work for us all." The servant got the traces set and moved around to the side to inspect the large wooden wheels, painted black to match the fabric.

The two worked in silence for a while. The silver gleamed in the light from the oil lamps.

"It's even worse when he wants that old she-bear." The servant pointed at the antique carriage. "We need several days to oil the axles and air out the fabrics and repaint the wheels. I hate it."

Pavresh glanced at the carriage and shrugged. "Let's hope the *tisrah* doesn't want it anytime soon."

"No, he won't. Once Teert's gone, he won't have anyone telling him he ought to impress people with it."

Pavresh didn't answer this right away, and after a moment, the servant added, "Oh, you don't know Teert. He's the meanest slave driver in the house. He should be a galley captain or a mine overseer. He's still around for a couple twelve-days, but I don't think we'll see much of him."

"Where's he going?"

"Oh, he's been running all around the valley recently, which has been awfully nice for us. I think now he's heading to the Silk City, once the weather clears enough to travel."

Pavresh finished his polishing and stood away from the carriage. He held out his hand to the other servant. "My name's Parsh, by the way," he said, using the name he and Jasfer had decided on.

"Vipak," the footman answered, shaking his hand. "Who'd you work for before this?"

Pavresh hesitated to make sure the story he'd invented still made sense. "Well, I've moved around a bit, working for some of the priests. There's even a chance I won't be staying here. My last master said something about wanting me back, but I'm not sure if that'll happen. He'll probably take me with him out to Jarnur if he does."

"Jarnur? I'd hate to be there. I hear stories of the sea, and it scares me, so flat even when it's wavy. Give me my mountains and beds of lava."

Pavresh laughed with Vipak. "I've never seen it myself. My father was there when he was younger, and he loved it."

"No, not for me. I'll eat my fish salted and far from the sea. I hear they eat them raw, straight from the salt water." Vipak winked as he said this. The stories of the sea that came inland were always wild, but no one actually believed most of them.

"Those they don't feed to their pet jellyfish, of course," Pavresh answered with a smile.

"Or their seal wives."

They both laughed loudly, Pavresh's laugh containing a sigh of relief that he'd turned the questions away from himself. They kept up the playful talking as they cleaned.

Eventually, they stopped their work and stepped back to see the carriage.

"It looks good," Pavresh said. "So, what about you? You been working here long?"

Vipak shook his head. "Not long. A few months. I was with some of the other princes before. Not one of the Thirty, though, so this is a step up."

"So what do we do now the carriage is ready?"

"Me? I have to check on the horses and make sure they're ready. You? If I were you, I'd go hide until Abhish found me and gave me something else."

Pavresh wanted to talk to him more, to ask him about Teert and the people Prince Dartak visited and the non-ruling family he'd worked for before, but he was afraid he'd give himself away if he asked too many questions.

"Sounds good to me. Thanks for telling me what to do and who to avoid. I'll see you later, unless I get sent to the ocean."

Vipak laughed. "Say hello to the fishies for me if you do." Then he headed for the door, and Pavresh turned toward the hallway where he'd come in.

At the doorway, he turned. "Wait. How do I avoid this terrible Teert if he does show up here?"

Vipak stopped halfway out the wide carriage doorway. "I don't think you'll have to worry about it. He's on the outskirts of the city right now. Meeting with some people for several days. Or twelve-days maybe. I think the *tisrah* will name Abhish the new head of the household very soon so Teert doesn't have to worry about us here."

"Well, I hope the *tisrah* names you head footman then."

Vipak's laugh came back through the closing door. "Not likely."

Pavresh wandered through the house for a while longer, but soon he slipped out, not wanting to be corralled into any other work. He hoped his story of going to Jarnur would satisfy the mystery of where he'd gone when Vipak or Abhish looked for him. Or when the actual new footman showed up. It would remain a mystery, but hopefully one the servants would keep to themselves and not mention to the prince.

Outside he walked only a short way down the street then reached into his servant robe. The cloth he pulled out was coarsely woven and dirty. He threw it around himself and pulled the finer cloth off enough to hide it when he sat down beside the stone railing over the lava bed. The warmth at his back was a welcome contrast to the snow falling on his head. Then he waited, hands out as if to beg. The sun eased above the line of mountains, lazy and longing for its bed.

He was surprised that even though he didn't wait long, he received a few coins in his lap. Quite soon, the carriage pulled out from Prince Dartak's. Pavresh got to his feet and hurried down a side street.

He balled up his untouchable cloak and ran, not caring about the startled looks of the people he passed. He was bare-chested despite the cold, but the exertion of running kept him warm. At every few cross streets, he darted back to the Avenue of Geysers to make sure he could still see the carriage rolling along. Fortunately, the prince's driver was not pushing the horses fast, so Pavresh stayed near them.

They crossed Tanan Square, leaving behind the *kortru* neighborhood of princes. Here the street changed names to the Avenue of Falling Steam and entered a *brenil* area of merchants and soldiers. Street-lamps were more spaced apart, some unlit, and he doubted they were simply extinguished to save oil during the brief day. No single street ran a convenient short block away from the broad avenue, so Pavresh ran a twisting path of side streets before he made it back. The carriage was gone. He stopped and stared both directions. It certainly wasn't on the avenue. Had it pulled into one of these houses? Or had it gone down a side street and somehow slipped away from him? He stood a moment, uncertain what to do.

Flipping a coin in his head, he ran up the Avenue of Falling Steam, looking at each house he passed and preparing to race down a side street if he caught sight of the carriage. The public steam baths lined the southern side of the road, blanketed in wet snow that constantly plopped down to the street and melted.

A carriage door was closing as he passed one house. It was a large manor for that part of town, and men stood on balconies and at the main door. Armed men, he realized. Soldiers of the wolf jati, the fierce soldiers whose job was to patrol the mountains and keep a watch on the mumblers.

Several of them were already looking his way. He cursed himself. He'd drawn their attention easily, a half-clad man running by, stopping and staring into the house of the soldiers.

He faked a scared look behind him, as if looking for an angry husband or brother, and continued running, now stumbling as if exceedingly tired. As soon as he could, he slipped down a side street and ran faster, dropping the balled-up untouchable garment. He'd hoped to return to the street outside the prince's house and spy some more, but he could easily get another coarse robe.

He turned a corner and saw his feigning had done no good. Three soldiers were already coming his way. They must have come out the back of the manor and moved to cut him off. He looked behind and saw four more. He wondered what they would do if they caught him. Would they just kill him in the street? Would they execute him publicly? Would they question him and torture him until he told them everything about Jasfer and Rashul and Chaitan?

Stopping in the street, he took a deep breath and used his magic to make him seem weak and harmless. Then he loosened the ceremonial knots on the kusti he'd worn even over the servant robes.

He stood no chance. Three true soldiers would have been too much. Seven was impossible. His only hope was in somehow catching them by surprise and running away. But how could he keep them from simply following and attacking him when he stopped? And that was assuming he could get past them.

He looked behind him at the four soldiers. They'd surely expect him to attack the three if he attacked anyone, so he ran back toward the four, straight for the soldier on the left.

Their swords were out, and one of the four had the wolf-head cloak of a commander. When he was almost to them, he flicked his kusti at the leader, who stood in the middle. The soldier ducked, and Pavresh twisted the cord toward the weapon of the man to the right. It wrapped around the man's arm, and he pulled.

The soldiers stumbled over each other, and Pavresh jumped to the right, dashing between the tripped-up soldier and the wall. As he passed them, he flipped the cord back so the metal spikes on the end sang toward a standing soldier. He'd meant to hit the man's face, but the soldier threw up an arm, and the spikes tore into his flesh.

Then he was past them and running hard. He turned at the first street, but before he'd reached any place else to disappear, they were in view behind him. All seven, trained to be able to chase and fight mumblers in the mountains. And he'd been running for a quarter hour to keep up with the carriage. Despair nearly overwhelmed him.

He turned again and again, but he couldn't lose the soldiers.

Suddenly, he rounded a corner and saw the stone railing and wide street that marked the edge of the lava beds. No manor houses stood here, only a few smaller homes and the public baths.

Pavresh glanced back at the dusk-darkened street and saw the soldiers gaining rapidly. Slush splashed from their pounding boots. He ran for one of the bath houses, sprinting inside. A crowd was there already, men shuffling into one side and women into the other. He pushed through the line of men and into the interior where the steam was thick.

It wouldn't be enough to hide him. Even if they hadn't had a good look at him, enough people were here who could tell the soldiers that he was the one who'd come running in.

He stopped and walked calmly toward the deeper pools. Steam plastered his hair to his head. Removing his robe, he balled it up in one hand and gathered his kusti in the other. Then he jumped into the hot water.

It was far too hot after so much running. He wanted cool water, but he didn't have the luxury of choosing. He ducked under and swam to the bottom. It was stone, cut and placed there, he imagined, by the city's founders long ago. He came back up and moved to another part of the pool to dive down again.

After repeating this several times, he saw the soldiers enter. People pointed his direction.

Pavresh walked to the far corner. The water seemed warmer here, tendrils of heat rising up to the surface. Taking a big breath, he dived, and this time he found it, a small passage where the hot water flowed in. He couldn't see anything through there.

He came back up for one more breath and heard the soldiers shouting, then he went down and swam as fast as he could into the tunnel. The water got hotter. It was burning him. He imagined his skin turning red, scalding, blistering, and he wanted to scream at the pain. But he pushed on into the hot water. Only darkness lay ahead of him. He imagined the rock walls closing tighter. He pictured a wall of stone pierced with holes too small for him. His lungs demanded air. A patch of gray appeared, and he swam harder. Finally, his head came into steamy air on the back side of the bath house. Ahead of him, boiling water bubbled to the surface, a portion of that diverted into the bath house while the rest was left to mingle with a cooler stream that ran below.

He scrambled, half swimming, into that cooler water. The stream had cut a channel through the hardened lava and had only a hint of the sulfur that overpowered so much of the steam baths. Pavresh hurried as well as he could through the stream, which angled away from Romnai. He'd have to leave it soon and venture across the steam beds themselves. But he had to get farther from the bathhouse first. The soldiers would surely come outside and wait for him along the street. The afternoon darkness, at least, was in his favor.

Pavresh stayed in the cooler water as long as he could, but eventually, he noticed how far he'd gone from the edge of the city. A few lights were visible above the edge of the stream, and standing only revealed roofs, not entire buildings. Dripping, he stood on the black rocks and tried to plan a path to the city. The fumarole field was not a welcoming place, not a land he wanted to spend time in. He was soon cold, despite the heat rising from the rocks all around. He pulled his wet robe on, but it did little to warm him.

He stumbled through the volcanic rock for what seemed a couple of hours and at last reached the edge of the city. No soldiers waited in the dark. He pulled himself up to the road, glanced each direction, then walked calmly as if he had every right to be there.

Pavresh didn't relax until he stood in Chaitan's house, a dry robe wrapped around him and a gourd of hot tisane in his hand. As soon as he'd warmed up and his breath came calmly, he turned around and visited the manor of Jasfer to tell him all he'd noticed and to plan what to do next.

✳ ✳ ✳

The next day Pavresh spied again on Prince Dartak's house. This time he dressed as a walla, one of the countless who flooded the streets of Romnai all day long. He didn't dare linger long or pass often, but he watched as much as he could. The prince didn't leave his house that morning. Instead, he had visitors. Many over the few hours Pavresh was there watching.

The first arrived almost immediately after Pavresh got there with his selection of spiced squash cakes that Jasfer's servants had provided for his disguise. He made little attempt to sell the cakes and simply watched the proceedings. The carriage was not as fine as the three in the prince's carriage house, but it looked well-built. Sturdy without being fancy. He couldn't see who was riding inside, but the carriage was accompanied by a handful of wolf jati soldiers.

While the visitor got out, the soldiers examined the street, as if to find the spy from the day before, paying special attention to the few untouchable beggars nearby.

Pavresh hurried past and didn't come near the house for some time.

When he returned, he was still dressed as a walla, this time with an armload of boxes. The soldiers were gone—or no longer visible—and another carriage stood outside the carriage house. This was fancier, like the prince's own carriages, and men in the clothes of the cheetah jati stood beside it.

He didn't recognize the servants, but clearly, it was another prince coming to pay Dartak a visit. He lingered as long as he dared but found no clue who it was.

Throughout the morning, carriages came and went. At

times two or three carriages stood outside the manor, servants of Dartak and the visitors swarming around them. Some were princes, at least one was a priest, and Pavresh was pretty sure one had been a silk weaver. If all of them—soldiers, princes, priests, and weavers—were involved in whatever Dartak had planned, then this was far bigger than Prince Jasfer realized. And who knew what cheetah jati servants and even *nefli* laborers they might employ as well to further their schemes?

That question got him thinking of Rashul and the people sent to keep their eyes on his associates. Jasfer's cousin, who seemed involved in whatever Dartak was up to, had wanted to wipe them out. Was that also connected with these schemes? And would they let the fact that Shardash was watching stop them from attacking if it would benefit them? For all he knew, they also had their own spy among those in Chaitan's house.

Looking around at the people nearby, those who walked along the promenade or sat beside the stone railing, Pavresh felt himself growing nervous, even afraid. Who of these innocents was a part of the conspiracy?

Whenever he felt he'd spent too much time near the house, he disappeared into the side streets and talked to people he met. The city did not stop because of short days and darkness, so he had his choice of those to ask. The spying for Jasfer seemed to be taking up his time for hearing stories and learning from Chaitan, and it made him feel guilty.

He listened to stories of a *brenil* housewife whose husband traveled the valley to sell goods. Of a school boy struggling to learn both the sacred scriptures and the science behind the amazing things that could be done with iron. Of an old walla who labored to deliver lunches to others at their jobs. Even the story of a man who had worked for years in the hellish foundries where iron was forged into the powerful steam engines that moved the new trains.

The voice that asked him if they spoke the truth, if they

were there to spy on him, follow him, arrest him, tried to overpower their stories, but Pavresh forced it to silence and listened intently, learning from the words and facial expressions and hand motions.

In between stories, as he walked and watched Prince Dartak's house for any clue, he tried to place the stories into a system, a map of human experience.

In the afternoon, he left the *kortru* part of town and returned to Chaitan's house so he could discuss it all with the old arcist.

His observations had yielded little that Jasfer would find interesting, and they'd already agreed to meet tomorrow unless there was anything urgent. Chaitan, though, would be interested in every nuance he reported, in every person he saw and spoke with all day. And there was still so much he didn't understand, things for his mentor to explain, directions to guide him. Even as he walked into the comforting room, he could hear the little voice in his ear wondering who within these familiar walls might be a part of the strange schemes of princes and priests and who-knew-what others.

Chapter 10

Maybe the old guy wasn't so worthless to the cause. Iksheen sat back and paged through the sheets of paper Marankiya had just brought. "Fire, master burner / sovereign of ash and shadow," it began in an invocation little different from those in any other holy epic. The lines twined about the page in a set pattern and rhythm. Iksheen would have said he didn't like the form. No one used it anymore. It was stilted and artificial, stuck in the beliefs of the Forgotten South.

Worse yet, the epic form was completely a part of the caste system. The lines themselves ruled over or bowed to each other. Each stanza was identified as *kortru*, *brenil*, or *nefli*, depending on which consonants dominated, and they worked with the lines around them accordingly. Lesser vowels for the lower castes, fewer syllables. The high-caste lines told the principal story while the others were left to elaborate, to follow meekly behind. He would have said an epic could have no part in their revolution. It was another thing for them to overthrow.

There was something majestic when an accomplished poet crafted one well. Done right, it could still have beauty and power. "Kwomnep, lord of water, the many-waved one / rode the summer current high to the land of battle / where Gauran waited with his brothers, dawn-chosen soldiers." Iksheen skimmed the first pages, enjoying the sounds. Then he stopped and reread it more carefully.

Marankiya's epic did not feel stilted or artificial or obsolete. The lines followed the correct pattern, but twisted it. *Kortru* stanzas bowed with short lines as often as they commanded.

Nefli stanzas took charge of the narrative, enjambment driving them into neighboring lines. And there was a fourth kind of stanza weaving among the others, an untouchable stanza that touched and was touched by all the others. Iksheen had to set the papers down.

He looked around to talk to someone about them, but immediately picked them up again and continued reading.

> The sunlight spoke of enemy shields, glinting among
>   the banyans.
> Dawn's soldiers stirred, awaited their absent leader;
> Gauran knelt at the water shrine of his ancestors.
>
> A shape rose, slippery from the deep waters—
> a naga, Gauran wondered, come to impart lost
>   wisdom,
> to share the secrets of military might that guarantee
>   victory?
>
> No naga but the lord of nagas, many-waved
>   Kwomnep,
> lifted Gauran to his feet with a sweet-water touch,
> spoke wisdom, liquid words no human had ever
>   heard.

It appeared to be very traditional. A god—in this case Kwomnep, the god of rivers and lakes, springs and floods—carried on a conversation with a human as they prepared for battle against superior forces. Gauran, the human in this epic, seemed a typical wolf jati soldier, though that part was strange for an epic. Usually epics involved princes.

This soldier was a powerful soldier, of course, a leader within the army. Iksheen could see something of Chaitan in the way he led his troops into battle. Yet something seemed slightly off, a tiny shift from the standard epic story to make it unsettling.

Iksheen kept reading, following the exploits of the warrior as he fought off an unnamed army, all the time carrying on this conversation with the god of water. "'What is the best way to strike in the spring?'" he would ask, and the god would answer with riddles and mysteries. "'How does a river find its current to the sea? Where does the river-dolphin go to speak with the sun? What caste is the sun, what jati the dolphin?'" Of course, it made no sense literally. A battle was no place for such dialogue. But that wasn't the purpose of an epic. The key was to understand what the god wanted of the human, of all humans.

Other gods and goddesses came and went, especially Kwona, the mare goddess and sometimes lover of Kwomnep. Or sister. Or both. The stories said any and all of those things. She rode her wild horses across the sea to watch the battle. She had been a sea goddess in the Forgotten South, though here in the north, she was confined to the valley like themselves, trapped by Brilith, the goddess of the northern sea. In the epic there was no hint of the northern goddess. Kwona teased the human from her place in the sea, tempted him toward her, drove him away, all in the midst of battle.

This story didn't end in victory. Not for the soldiers. It ended in defeat and exile. It ended in the entire wolf jati sailing away, carried by Kwomnep to a distant land.

The remnant, the dusk forgotten soldiers
stumbled into the surf, arms around shoulders for
none could walk alone, none save Gauran.

And Gauran's wounds bled, turned the water its
    sunset shade,
but he held his face straight, held his arms out
to give himself to the sea, to drown his dreams in
    salt-water.

The many-waved one came, swept to shore by his
    weeping sister.
They cradled the dying man, nursed him with holy
    fire, placed him
in a boat made of flames, made of water, for they are
    the same.

The sun, remembering its chosen soldiers, shone on
    weary heads,
and ships appeared around them also, boats no sea
    could sink.
Thus they journeyed by the god's hands into lands of
    summer sun.

The final lines were such a mix of castes that Iksheen couldn't identify a single one with any level of the system. They were all the same caste, all the same jati.

He threw it down in his excitement and looked at Marankiya. "You've given Rashul his legend!"

The older man only nodded, and something about it seemed wary, but Iksheen ignored that.

"This is exactly what we need to convince our people that the caste system is wrong, an invention forced on us by the princes. We can use this for the cause!"

Marankiya winced and shook his head. "You don't use poetry. Poetry uses you."

Iksheen waved this away and looked around the room for

Rashul.

"He went in back when I showed this to him. I think he's planning something."

Iksheen didn't wait to thank Marankiya. He hurried from the main room of Chaitan's house, through the doorways, into the back half of the building. He could hardly breathe as he pictured how they might use this epic, stirring up the people, reminding them of the legendary wise man Marankiya had once been.

Rashul was in the third room he checked, some sort of storeroom, he thought, glancing around at the barrels and boxes. The revolutionary leader was hunched over a piece of paper, pen held tightly in one hand.

"Are you writing your own epic, then?"

Rashul startled at the words, looking up and pulling the paper away as if to hide it. Then he seemed to recognize the poet and relaxed.

"Of sorts, I guess. Not a sacred epic exactly."

Iksheen stepped around the wooden boxes to stand by him, but still Rashul kept the paper hidden.

Even huddled back here in the dark, there was something glamorous about Rashul. The way he held his head, the shape of his face, even the fall of his loose clothing. All they needed was Marankiya's epic and Rashul's presence in the streets explaining what it meant. There was no way it could fail. If the princes sent soldiers, the soldiers would fall under his spell. If the princes came themselves, even they would be enchanted. Priests and untouchable, silk weavers and dock workers, they'd all follow him simply for the power of his charisma.

"You've seen it," Iksheen said. "Marankiya's epic. It's just what we need. How will we use it now?"

"Shhh. Let me work on this. You'll see."

"What is it?"

Rashul only shook his head and bent over the paper again,

shielding its contents with an arm.

Iksheen didn't want to wait and see. He considered himself second in the movement, behind only Rashul…and even that, only slightly. He shouldn't have to find out when everyone else did. But Rashul showed no signs of relenting, so eventually Iksheen left. He shut the door behind him quietly, even though he wanted to slam it. Then he walked heavily to the main room of the house, grabbing a cup of something on the way.

He threw it back and gasped. It was Marankiya's fire liquor, a strong, bitter drink with an aftertaste even worse than its first flavor. Soldiers loved it, but few others. He set the empty cup down and walked to the nearest cushions to sit, his eyes watering.

It took a moment before he realized that Chaitan was beside the stage.

He almost never performed anymore. Iksheen wondered what could have inspired their patriarch to do so tonight. He sat in his customary cushioned chair with Tanjali and Kapita on either side of him, but they had pulled it over to the stage so he could face those sitting near the main fireplace.

Namrani played softly behind him, and a single dancer Iksheen didn't know stood poised on stage, preparing to begin.

When everyone in the room was silent, the dancer began his movements. Immediately, Iksheen felt a subtle snake of arcist magic. He wouldn't have known it if he hadn't spent so much time here and hadn't been ready for it, but even with that knowledge, he couldn't tell exactly what Chaitan did with it. The dancer's movements seemed to speak of distant mountain peaks and wild animals, of riding the rapids of Eghsal River's upper reaches, of standing among the geysers of the lava fields.

The magic didn't always match these images. Sometimes it ran completely counter to the dancing, calling up feelings of home or the city. And yet it all worked together in odd, unpredictable ways. The tensions added to the overall feeling of the performance.

When they finished, no one made a noise. Namrani let one last note ring, and the dancer held his final pose while Chaitan settled back into his chair, looking exhausted. The silence stretched until someone began to clap. Then the room broke into loud cheers. Someone approached Chaitan in his chair. Pavresh, he realized after a moment. Something about him was forgettable. Iksheen supposed that the old master's performance had been for Pavresh's benefit, a part of his training.

The two arcists whispered animatedly, and Iksheen wandered off. At first, he dismissed the performance as nothing more than the arcists' work together and turned his mind to guessing what Rashul had in mind. He was planning something. That was clear. He just couldn't figure out what it was. The performance kept sneaking its way back into his thoughts. There was something there, more than its surface. It was in the way it used several approaches, not merely dance, not only magic or music.

The revolution, also, he decided as the images of the performance mixed with vague guesses of what Rashul hoped to try next, would run at different levels, a variety of approaches that might not always seem matched…but eventually, they'd strengthen each other.

Soon Rashul burst from the doorway, waving a paper above his head. "The time has come! We will now show the rulers of our valley that we want things to change, that we mean it and won't back down!"

This speech was less eloquent than Rashul usually gave, but those in the room cheered anyway, Iksheen loudest of all.

"This is our manifesto. It proclaims our rights, the rights of all members of our society. The first thing we need is to copy it many times and post it all over the city."

Iksheen quickly picked up a pen, paper, and ink and rushed

to Rashul to begin copying. He and several others set to work while Rashul spoke more to individuals around the room, explaining the manifesto and his plans. Iksheen didn't need anything explained yet. All that mattered was that something was actually happening for the cause. That, at last, he was doing something more than waiting.

* * *

By the Sacred Fire that gives birth to everything, we bring new words for all people of Eghsal.

We, the people of Eghsal, have been fooled. It is now six hundred and thirty-two years after we fled the Forgotten South, and yet we live a lie created by those first settlers. They tell us we are born in certain castes and certain jatis. They tell us some are better and more deserving of riches. They tell us some are worse and may be freely abused by those above them.

These are lies.

The truth is that we are all one caste. We are all one jati. We were a warrior caste in the Forgotten South. Now, it makes no sense for a society to have only soldiers, so it is good that we follow many trades, but do not forget your warrior past. Rise up now and fight if necessary. Fight for the justice that fire has promised us all. Fight for your place in society. Fight so your children can be of any jati in a society without castes.

These are the true words of the Fire to us. The priests tell us that the universe was created by Fire, that in the early days all the cosmos was smoke. As it aged, the cosmos became mud, as it is today. The cosmos is now turning to wood, the mud distilling into its final form when it will once again be worthy of the Fire. Our nation will not be worthy of Fire as long as it holds onto the smoke and illusions of the caste system.

Today is the day to advance, to heed the words of Fire and throw off the illusions of the past, to create a society worthy of the vision of the cosmos revealed to us. No more castes. No more injustice by birth. No more bonds to shackle us as a people.

And in the new, free Eghsal we shall all be tisrae. We shall rise to new heights, we shall overcome mountains, we shall control seas, and the Sacred Fire will bless us beyond measure.

* * *

Iksheen tacked the manifesto to the door of a small temple in a *nefli* neighborhood. His hammer strikes echoed, but only a weak pinging that didn't seem worthy of the document itself. No one came rushing to celebrate or arrest him. People walked by unaware of the great change that would shortly be happening in the city.

Iksheen wanted to yell at them, tell them to wake up to the new reality. Romnai was made different simply by the appearance of that paper. They just didn't know it yet.

He took one more swing of the hammer, an unnecessary one. This time he simply struck the wood of the door itself, hoping that it would resonate impressively, but the temple swallowed the sound, so Iksheen moved off.

It was the fifth copy of the manifesto he'd posted so far. He glanced down at the papers in his hand. Only two more. It was time to be bold.

He hurried away from the rundown houses where he'd posted the others. The buildings became finer, the streets smoother. Iksheen arrived at the edge of the public baths. A half-dozen separate buildings clustered here, with other bathhouses scattered along the rest of the lava beds. He looked down at the two remaining papers.

Where would they cause the biggest uproar? And he realized, not there. He would post one here, among the bathers, but they'd probably ignore it, intent on their baths beforehand

and too contented afterward to bother. The last one he'd save for the main temple itself.

Darting over to one of the bathhouse doors, he posted the manifesto with a single blow of his hammer. Then he was off, hurrying back through neighborhoods of simpler houses toward the river.

The main temple stood directly on the river. It was an impressive building, towering above older houses, some dating back nearly to the founding of the city. Its foundation, as well as one wall visible beneath later flourishes, were said to have been the first things built here when the original city of Eghsal had grown too big.

He hesitated while catching his breath. He had thought to pound this into the door itself, but that wall… If he could find a way to post the manifesto there, it would really jump out at people, give it an immediate sense of importance.

With a quick look for any priests, he approached the ancient wall. Holes pocked it, patched by mortar that was itself crumbling. Lichen patches spread where the priests had not yet scraped it off. Yet there was a surprisingly permanent feel to that part of the building, as if not even time could ever fully conquer it.

In the same way, nothing would conquer the cause.

Iksheen wasn't sure how he was going to post the letter on the wall. He didn't dare pound a nail into the ancient structure or any of the mortar holding it together. Setting the paper down and weighting it with the hammer, he stepped off to the side and looked at the river. A sort of beach, narrow and infested with river weeds ran beneath the temple. Iksheen jumped down and felt the soil squish beneath his feet.

Ice rimmed the river bank, but digging down through the cold mud he found some that was still liquid. The dirt was dark and fine. No pebbles to mess up his plan. He scooped it up and hurried back to the wall.

The mud echoed as he slapped it against the wall, a far more satisfying sound than the hammer had made. He returned for a second handful. When it was evenly spread over the space he'd chosen, Iksheen picked up the paper and pressed it against the mud. Already the cold stone had begun to freeze the water in the mud. The dirt helped the paper stick while the ice set, but he held it in place to be sure.

People had come to see what he was doing. A handful stood behind him, peering over his shoulder. Their murmurs rose and fell as they wondered what he did to the sacred wall.

He held it by only two fingers in the center to let the mud that had been under his hands freeze. Finally satisfied, he stepped away. People crowded up behind him, trying for the first look at this strange paper.

Now was his moment. He should be giving a stirring speech to inflame them to great deeds for the cause. He opened his mouth, but no one was looking at him. Where was Rashul when he needed him? His charisma would have pulled their attention easily.

A pair of priests ran toward him, and behind them were wolf jati soldiers, not following yet, but clearly prepared to come if necessary.

Words flowed toward him from the people reading the manifesto. "Lies." "One caste." "Soldier jati." Did they believe it? Did the words fill them with fire? He needed to do something to ensure that they did. But no words came. He was a poet, used to pondering his words carefully as he wrote them down, used to reading them and changing them many times before showing them to anyone. Now the words froze in his mouth.

Footsteps sounded. Cursing beneath his breath, Iksheen turned and ran. The priests called out to him, but he didn't look back, and soon the houses of wealthy merchants that surrounded the temple became older buildings more in keeping with the neighborhood.

The whole way back to Chaitan's house, he couldn't help feeling that he'd failed. He'd missed an opportunity to further the cause. His own mouth and lungs and words had betrayed him. It wasn't something he could forgive.

* * *

Iksheen slouched in a pile of pillows at Chaitan's house, far from the fire. He didn't deserve to sit by the fire. Every time someone looked his way, he expected to see their disappointment in him. A rational part of his mind told him that he didn't see any such disappointment anywhere. But he was a poet. Rational thoughts were easy to dismiss.

In truth, no one paid much attention to him at all. Their main focus was on Ekana, who'd arrived while Iksheen was out. He said little, explaining nothing of how he'd escaped, unless he'd already explained earlier before Iksheen returned. His face was bruised, and his eyes looked haunted.

When Rashul threw open the doors from the inner rooms and stepped through, Iksheen's self-recriminations ended abruptly. There was something pure and elemental about their leader that pushed everything else out of the room, as if a fire burned in Rashul's chest, and they were all mesmerized by the flames.

Rashul went directly to Iksheen. "I have an idea, something we'll do within the twelve-day. Some people will think I'm rushing, that I didn't take the time to plan this carefully enough."

He paused and waited as if he expected Iksheen to answer.

Iksheen shook his head. "Plans never end. There's too much talk as it is. If you have an idea, then by the sulfur, let's act."

Rashul gripped his shoulder. "I knew you'd say that. That's what I rely on you for. We're going to act. We'll let the city know that we're serious."

"This is more than posting manifestos then?"

Others gathered around, and Rashul waved his arm as if the manifesto was already forgotten.

"Yes. So much more." He pulled on Iksheen's shoulder, so the poet rose to his feet. "I can't stand still right now, and it's so crowded right here. Let's walk outside."

Iksheen rushed behind Rashul as they headed out the door, hastily wrapping his thin cloak around himself. Some of the others tagged along, but most stayed in the warmth of the house.

Snow lay along the streets, though none came down at the moment. The sky overhead was a pale blue, as the days crept slowly toward spring. He'd expected Rashul to begin talking immediately, but instead, he walked in silence, jumping piles of garbage and forcing the others to hurry to match his pace.

Chaitan's house was surrounded by a small enclave of decent houses. Modestly successful merchants lived there, and retired soldiers who'd served their time without ever distinguishing themselves. But these houses soon gave way to the surrounding neighborhood of struggling *nefli*. Iksheen felt his desire for the cause swell, a strange lust that had nothing to do with any individual.

These were the people he fought for, the people he longed to free. No one could truly study and love poetry without feeling a desire to fight for them.

Rashul waited until they'd crossed much of the city to speak. "I've known of this place for some time now," he said over his shoulder to those following. "But I wasn't sure what to do about it."

Iksheen hadn't expected to go so far. After all his wanderings earlier in the day to hang up the manifesto, his legs burned to walk such a distance. The deep winter air reached through his clothing. They came to the western edge where the buildings simply faded out. No river or field of geysers cut off the city here. The roads ended in the rocky fields of this part of the valley, where much of the food for the city was grown, the rows of head squash and fields of sulfur-devouring hard grain curving around immovable boulders.

Iksheen wasn't sure if they should be asking him questions or if Rashul wanted some more dramatic revelation. He decided to wait.

At the near edge of the fields was a large storehouse. Rashul stopped before they reached it. They were at the edge of the last buildings, protected from the wind, but he still had to speak loudly for them to hear.

"This will be our first step." He pointed grandly at the storehouse, though Iksheen couldn't figure out why. To him it looked rather plain, a laborer's building. And *nefli* laborers were who they fought for, in part, but it seemed a disappointingly quiet start to their grand revolt.

He looked at the others for any clue of what was planned. The arcist Pavresh was there, but his face gave nothing away. Ekana also—he kept a length of his newly-borrowed cloak wrapped tightly around his head so no one would recognize him, but it didn't hide the tortured look on his face.

Rijef, who'd joined in the attempted attack on the silk weavers, Tanmai and Upeng, brothers who'd followed Rashul since before Iksheen met him, and the few others who'd come seemed to have no idea either. They were looking at *him* as if he might know. He shook his head.

"This place unites all levels of our society," Rashul said. "And not just because everyone must eat. It is owned by a prince, one of the Thirty, and every spring he has priests come and bless it. Merchants collect the goods here and send them on to other parts of the valley or simply to markets within the city. Of course, the laborers bring in the food." His arms swung out as if to encompass the fields all around.

"That gives us every caste, and then there are the

untouchables. This storehouse has a broken window on one side where untouchables come to steal food."

Iksheen peered as if he might see the broken window, but of course, it wouldn't be obvious from the road. He wondered how Rashul could have learned of this.

"So, what will we do?" Pavresh asked. "Burn it down? That doesn't seem kind to the lower castes."

Iksheen imagined the building burning, flames rising as high as the grandest geysers. No. If they were going to burn something, this wasn't it. But he could think of buildings nearer the lava beds that he'd love to set on fire.

Rashul answered while the poet was thinking, cutting through the images of princely buildings burning.

"No. You're thinking too narrow." Something in the way he said it reminded Iksheen of his own reactions to Chaitan's performance, the many levels. "We'll take it over. Protect it with a few armed men. Otherwise continue its usual operations, except it will belong to the people of all castes who use it, not just a distant prince. And no one will be treated differently according to caste."

Someone was approaching the building, and he turned for a moment toward where they stood.

Rashul continued, unaware of the figure at the door looking their way. "I figure it will take most of a day at a minimum before the prince even hears of something strange. And it won't be high on his priority to send soldiers to deal with. Once they come, we can clear out. Our statement will have been made. Our movement begun."

It seemed a disappointingly small first step in their revolution, yet seeing Rashul as he spoke the words filled Iksheen with a surprising confidence. He longed for it, wanted it to happen now, but it was a more peaceful longing than any he'd known, anticipation framed by certainty.

Rashul held his face up, as if looking at some vision in the sky. "Word of our deed will spread along with the words of the manifesto and of Marankiya's epic. Change is coming to Romnai, will soon be here."

They walked away, Iksheen glancing over his shoulder as if the figure at the door would follow them or send someone after them. He saw no one, and he finally relaxed and let images of the new Eghsal roll through his mind, seduce him away from the reality of the day with promises of tomorrow.

The images mixed with those of Marankiya's epic, of gods and battle in the Forgotten South, and it evoked Chaitan's performance as well—the epic and the manifesto and the warehouse each performing their part, in unison at times and at odds others, but always with the promise of tying together in surprising ways.

Chapter 11

Bhadrik strode around a curve on the slope and saw the valley before him, filling up so much of his vision. Its nearness revolted him. To have come down so far from the heights… The high country behind had required much from him, as he kept constantly alert for mumblers or the wild cats that haunted the rocks. When the winter became too much for his solitary survival in a sheltering cave, he'd wandered for more than a month with his sling always ready, a handful of bullets in the other hand. He never took the most direct route, prolonging as long as he could his isolation rather than face others as an untouchable.

Coming into the soft valley was no relief for him. He enjoyed that tension of the high country, liked the sense of danger and alertness. What was there for him in the valley?

Too soon he was there, although he couldn't have said exactly when he'd passed from mountain to valley. It was a gradual change, but finally he turned and looked back at the rocks rising behind him, and it was clear that this was valley. A stretch of level land, broken by no treacherous rocks, but only his own snow-shoe trail lay between him and the true mountains.

Bhadrik took his sling and flung a single bullet at a nearby tree. *Such a big tree. The valley is easy even on the trees.* The bullet buried itself deep within the wood.

* * *

It took some days before he saw the river and the strange ruins beyond it. From a distance, it looked like no more than he'd expect of ruins—ancient walls and piles of rubble. Nearer it seemed to change, a bulge here or a collection of material there giving the shapes of the ruins a different feel. There was something familiar about some of what he saw. He couldn't quite identify what, but it made him want to draw his missing sword.

He reached the scar of the railroad tracks and crossed, remembering journeys by train to the mountains beyond the eastern edge of the valley. *That* had been a land where a man could prove himself the fire's rival. Beyond the Silk City, beyond the cataracts where the Eghsal River forced its way out of the mountains lay a hard land, a soldier's kind of land where every rock was a chance to prove himself. If only he were there on patrol, instead of this soft valley that had no need of soldiers like Bhadrik. What was there to prove himself against here? Merely human-made train tracks, a river too wide to be anything but tame, rising clouds of steam.

At the edge of the river, Bhadrik looked again at the ruins. Still something reached out from their shapes to put him on alert, but he couldn't identify it. The water was wide here. Fire could create its own path, perhaps, by turning the water to steam, but he didn't aim to *be* fire, only match it in wildness and strength.

So much water would drown the fire anyway. The more he looked, the more he realized just how wide the river was here. It flowed too fast to freeze, though there was deep snow along its banks because of the fumarole field on the opposite bank. The air felt warmer than anything he'd known since he left the camp. Even he, strong as he was, wouldn't be able to swim it.

A few boats moved lazily near the far shore or were anchored in place while their handlers fished. Bhadrik waved his arm for someone to come get him, but if anyone saw him, they ignored the signal.

After waiting some time for a reaction, he turned and walked upriver. The bank rose and fell slightly, but always seemed roughly his own height above the water. Trees bent over the edge, forcing him away when he couldn't plow between them. Already the day was ending, so short the sun's journey during the winter. And his walking upriver carried him farther from the warmth of the steam beds rather than closer.

Bhadrik tightened his jaw. Those were valley-dweller worries. He was stronger than the cold.

Around a thick stand of trees, the bank dropped down to nothing, simply a muddy bit of ground at the side of the river. There was a hint of a road running north from there, though its snow was unbroken, and Bhadrik realized the river looked wider as well. Could it be a ford?

He walked to the edge, took off his snowshoes to stand in the shallow mud. Not frozen, that was good. Rocks rose from the river, even in the center. And a path of sorts seemed to come out from the opposite side. It still looked deep in spots. The deepest channel cut near him, where the rocks were few. Even if he had to swim that, he thought he could make it. It would be cold, but he'd have the promise of lava-heated rocks on the other side. Beyond that channel, gravel showed beneath shallow water. A brief swim and then simply wading.

Even prepared as he thought he'd been, the water made him gasp. It sent icicles through his blood. Forcing his legs to move, as if against a heavy weight, he moved toward the deeper water. The bottom sank gradually, and his hopes rose that he might be able to keep his feet, but when the water had reached his chest, the bottom disappeared beneath him.

He threw his arms forward, rotated his body so he could swim. As part of their mystery religion, the wolf jati would prove their worth swimming in cold mountain ponds or hot volcanic pools. This was as cold as the coldest of those, and the current pushed him surprisingly quickly downriver. He kicked his legs and pulled himself with his arms, aiming for the shallow water. But the current pulled him below the ford before he'd crossed half of the deep channel.

Bhadrik angled himself, fighting the current to return to the ford as he crossed. His arms tired. His breath came hard. Water splashed across his face as he breathed, making him cough.

The passage from heavy current to light was sudden, and Bhadrik instinctively tried to touch down to rest. But even the lesser current could carry him, and he was well below the shallows of the ford. Water splashed over him, frightening even if not dangerous in itself.

He resumed swimming, still trying to pull himself not only across the river but upstream. The far shore still looked too far away to swim to, but he tired himself fighting the current. The cold reached in, more powerful than his exertion. His arms lost feeling, dropped into the water.

No! He wasn't soft. This river was a valley thing, nothing to stand against him. He pulled his arms back out but found the river had turned him so he faced mostly downstream. He decided not to fight it and angled for the downriver shore. The ruins of the city came again into view, looking from the water like nothing of this world.

The boats were pulling in as he came to them. Still no one offered to help him aboard, but he grabbed the stern of one and coasted in to shore where he collapsed, shivering, on the bank.

Some time passed before Bhadrik realized that something was strange. No one had come to offer him help. And neither had anyone come to check his prone form for something to steal. He pushed himself up, his muscles complaining, and saw people moving, but they avoided each other most of the time. The boatman hadn't complained about his stealing a ride, but had completely ignored him.

It almost seemed as if the people were deliberately sending him the message that here was a city where everyone allowed anyone to do as they wished…as long as it didn't interfere with others. No censure and no assistance. At the same time, the movements of the people didn't have the appearance of people making a show of something for the benefit of the new arrival. The distance between people was extreme to the point of being comical, and yet seemed perfectly serious and normal to them.

Bhadrik brushed mud from his clothes as he stood, though he realized in the middle that there was no reason to, no person to impress in this strange place. And he set off to find a fire, borrow a blanket, and explore the twisted ruins.

They had seemed oddly familiar from a distance, but now he was here, he didn't sense that. What had it been? Something about the way the buildings were laid out. But the nearest buildings were simply collections of whatever the people had been able to find, each as isolated from the others as the people themselves. Parts of the city were surprisingly intact, although even there the people didn't seem to trust the buildings as they were but added to them with driftwood lean-tos and walls built of gathered rubble. Other buildings were visibly sinking into growing pools of hot water, stooping like a soldier too old for battle, too old to challenge the fire. He didn't want to live to be that old.

Steam vents opened where there were no pools of sulfurous water. Since no one seemed likely to share their fire with him, he paused as close as he dared beside a vent until its warmth dried him. The residents moved as if unaware of them, but gracefully avoiding even the smallest. Bhadrik found himself staring at their footwork, thinking of them as soldiers and not common people—valley dwellers and untouchables no less!—moving about their homes. Yet they had the same unconscious easiness that an experienced soldier maintained in battle, bodies moving precisely without conscious thought.

It angered him that he had to pay attention to his own feet, and he moved away from that part of the ruins into others. The houses were not always the same from one area to another. Different building materials and approaches set them apart, and occasionally he caught a glimpse of whatever it was that had bothered him before. But he could never identify it. Many of the people were already inside their houses, so he saw fewer and fewer people as he went.

Then he came to another part of the city and was punched by the earlier feeling. These houses were clustered in a way that felt ominous. He approached, walking on the balls of his feet. He was already reaching for his knife when someone stepped from one of the houses and crossed toward another. Instinct threw him to the ground before his mind could figure out what he'd seen. But then he realized. A mumbler.

He looked again. The person had disappeared into another house, but now he saw how these houses looked like the mumbler villages he'd scouted in the mountains, places he'd raided even. Not just these, but other houses among the ruins. Bhadrik saw again buildings he'd passed that seemed mumbler-constructed. They'd been scattered throughout the city!

He slid the knife loosely into its sheath and unwrapped his sling. Would they attack him? How many could he take before their numbers got him? He was an initiate in the mysteries—what did that demand of him here?

No one came out to charge him. He looked into the shadows at either side, but there was no glint of metal, no scuffle of feet. He chided himself and squirmed away. He'd known there were mumblers among the ruins. It was known for that as much as a place for untouchables and outlaws. But somehow, he'd always pictured that they'd be in their own part of the ruins, far from the dwellings of real people. They were hardly more than animals, though fierce fighters at times. He hadn't imagined that they'd be so close to the other inhabited parts of the ruins.

And stranger still, but the houses he'd passed earlier made it seem they were not only nearby, but mixed among the valley-dwellers.

He stood and walked away, eventually finding a sheltering wall of some sort—the darkness kept him from knowing any details—and lay down to sleep. It was a fitful sleep, with his sling kept fastened to his hand, and his knife in the other, a sleep constantly interrupted by thoughts. The only comfort was the warmth of the wall that made a blanket unnecessary. A city of mumblers and mumbler-lovers. He couldn't stay.

He rolled over on the hard floor and thought of wandering across the valley. Winter was here, and he didn't want to be away from the springs, not without the gear he would have carried as a soldier. Even a rival of the fire had to know when to take what protection he could. When spring came, then. He'd walk away as soon as it was possible. Or he'd find a way to get one of the boats and sail downriver for the remainder of his exile. Anything to get him away from the mumblers.

Chapter 12

The sun would not be up for hours yet, and steam from the lava beds merged with the low clouds to cover the stars and what moon there might have been. Pavresh could hardly believe that he was joining in on this folly. The building beside him was damp, the air heavy with sulfur. Yet here he was, filling the others of Rashul's band with the belief in their actions, with a sense of outraged justice. He resisted the temptation to crane his head around the corner and peek at the warehouse.

Time itself felt heavy, as if the sun struggled to push the night sky away.

He heard shouts and the pounding of footsteps. He began counting. The shouts grew louder and then cut off as he reached a hundred. Someone was quietly counting aloud, but Pavresh couldn't tell who.

At three hundred, he looked up at the dozen or so figures around him, dark shapes only. Several nodded their heads. It was their time. They turned the corner and sprinted for the warehouse.

Rashul's first group already stood inside the doorway, the two guards bound and leaning against the outer wall. Pavresh couldn't tell if they were conscious, knocked out, or dead. They pushed past the dock workers who held the door and entered.

Someone found a lamp and lit it—Iksheen, his face eerie in the unsteady light. They quickly found other lamps and moved together into the warehouse. Sacks of grain were piled high in the center with narrow aisles between them. Pairs split off to explore each aisle, returning once they were sure no one was hiding there. Some rows were much lower, a sign of winter's demands on warehouses like this. Pavresh stayed along the edge of the labyrinth, trying to look beyond the grain at the rest of the warehouse.

There was a walkway of some sort up high, and along the walls were crates of other types of food. He stepped away to check their contents. Squash. The insides would be scraped out as food and the husk left to harden for brewing tisane. He opened the next. More gourds with what looked like salad greens packed around the sides. Several more crates simply revealed other varieties of produce.

The silence of the warehouse, broken by muffled footsteps but no voices, was affecting Pavresh. With each crate he opened, he grew more nervous, as if someone would jump out from the piles of tubers to attack him.

He laughed silently. Someone might be hiding. It was why they were checking every corner. But they wouldn't be lying in wait. They'd be hiding in fear and only a danger if they caught the revolutionaries by surprise later in the day.

The crates ended, replaced by piles of sacks, like the grain sacks in the middle of the building but smaller. Pavresh stepped close and smelled the pungent herbs that were used to brew tisane. He walked to the end of the short row, glanced at the wall, and turned to come back. A noise made him look up in time to see one of the sacks of herbs falling down on top of him. It struck his face and chest, knocked him back with the surprising weight.

Lamplight and hurrying footsteps. A whispered, "What happened?"

Pavresh looked up to see Iksheen leaning over him. He shook his head to clear it, then whispered back, "Just a sack of food. It must have been stacked wrong."

Voices reached them from the doorway. One was Rashul's as he entered with another band of revolutionaries. For all the time he spent among his more intellectual supporters, he somehow managed to find others who agreed with him and had the muscle to support their beliefs. And even more striking, he seemed as comfortable among them as he did among the group from Chaitan's house. What kind of background let someone be so naturally a part of any group? It was like what Jaritta saw in Pavresh, but made real—he could seem to belong anywhere, but Rashul really did.

Pavresh returned to the main aisle with Iksheen, his eyes scanning the strange sight of those sacks of grain. In the lamplight, there was something oddly permanent about them, so perfectly arranged as if to form true walls, not temporary storage. It was a veritable labyrinth they searched.

In the old stories, nagas always hid within labyrinths, mysterious snake people that were sometimes helpful and sometimes cruel. He hoped no naga hid there.

Pavresh stopped. He looked again at the perfectly stacked sacks of grain and turned back toward the herbs.

"Come back here, Iksheen."

"What is it?"

Pavresh only gestured for him to follow. When they reached the fallen sack, he stopped and held his lamp close. It looked normal, no different from those piled beside him.

"What are you looking for?" Iksheen whispered.

Pavresh shook his head and handed Iksheen his lamp. The poet was holding two now, and Pavresh gestured for him to hold them up high. Then he stepped on the fallen sack of herbs and jumped up along the wall. His fingers closed on a ledge, and he pulled up, kicking one foot into the sturdy pile of sacks beside him.

The light below did little to illuminate that space above the ledge, but he could tell that it went back into the wall here. A crawl space of some sort. He was about to tell this to Iksheen when the lamp light flashed off something within that darkness.

He let go. A knife passed where his face had just been. When he landed, he was already untying the kusti belt at his waist.

"There's someone up there." He didn't turn to see Iksheen's response, but he heard him pass the information back to others. Instead, he focused on the darkness above him and the kusti in his hands. It had served him well twice recently. He only hoped it could do so again. Maybe he could wrap an end around the lurker's arm and pull him down.

This time the belt did him no good. Before he had it ready, a figure leaped from the darkness straight for him. Pavresh twisted, already balanced as if for the sacred moves he made for the fire. That balance probably saved his life. The knife sliced across his arm, trailing a line of fire.

Pavresh shouted as he dropped beneath the return swing. One end of his belt was caught between his body and the sacks of herbs. He yanked it futilely as his attacker stepped closer. It shouldn't have been Iksheen there near him. He wanted one of the *nefli* laborers, a strong man to knock this person senseless. Iksheen wasn't a warrior any more than Pavresh was.

Before the knife could stab him, someone jumped on the wielder. Ekana, wrestling with a fisherman's strength. Pavresh pulled himself away from the sacks and helped disarm the man and bind his hands. When the attacker was secure, Pavresh angrily retied his kusti, as if the fault had been its and not his own.

The motion brought back the pain from his arm. He made the knots sloppily and clapped his left hand over the wound. Ekana was looking at the knots of belt.

"I've seen knots like that before." He looked Pavresh directly in the eye, and Pavresh couldn't interpret the look in them. It seemed sad and curious and angry at the same time. The Enshi were fairly common in Jarnur where Ekana came from, so he wouldn't be surprised that Ekana recognized them for what they were. But he got no sense that the fisherman would reveal this to others and also no sense that Ekana shared his beliefs.

Not knowing what to say, he just shrugged, and by then others were there. They pulled his attacker away while the man shouted obscenities. Then Rashul was beside Pavresh.

"Are you hurt?"

Pavresh took his hand away from his upper arm and winced at the pain. Rashul leaned in to see it in the lamplight.

"Hmm. It could use some care, I think. Some of the women are coming by later this morning. I'll have them take a look."

He placed a hand on Pavresh's shoulder, opposite the injury. "You did well. I'm proud to have you a part of us. Not pleased at your injury, but happy that you are willing to be injured for the cause. For a new Eghsal."

Pavresh felt a flood of pride pour over him. It wasn't even arcist magic Rashul used, but he knew the words to say and when to say them. And it was something Pavresh could use in his own magic in the future. A slight variation on the sense of fighting for justice—the approval of a leader, an older sibling, a father, or a mother.

His own magic reinforcing the thrill Rashul's words had engendered, Pavresh returned to examining the warehouse with the others, searching for more hideaways. He nearly forgot the pain in his arm.

* * *

Jaritta tended the cut. The cloth around it had stuck in the dried blood, and Pavresh couldn't stop the cry of pain when she pulled it away.

"You'll need more than just water. I should take you back to Chaitan's house."

Away? His first thought was relief. He had an excuse for being away from the warehouse, away from the danger that was very real. Not a false sense of danger like riding the rail carts in the mine. His wound could give him an honorable way to get out of there. He began preparing the speech he would give Rashul as they left.

Then he stopped. No, this was part of the experience he needed. He would have to stay and use everything he observed to make his magic more intricate and believable.

"I have to stay."

Jaritta tugged on the loop of cloth that covered her burns, a gesture he'd learned to recognize as a nervous tic. "Well, if it gets worse, I'm taking you away. I don't want it infected."

Pavresh nodded and then walked with her toward where Rashul stood, talking to the captives. A bit of light came through the windows, even though the sun wouldn't rise for a while yet. The two trussed guards had been brought in from outside and propped against the wall beside Pavresh's attacker.

"You don't need to fear. We will not harm you."

Pavresh quelled the feeling that they *should* harm the one who'd cut him. He let the longing for revenge go into his arsenal of arcist magic and listened to what else Rashul had to say.

"We'll only keep you for the day. At the end of today, we will leave this building and leave you behind, untied. You are not our enemies. You are our brothers, ourselves. We fight for you, too."

Pavresh wondered how convincing this would be for someone tied up like this, but then he realized that the words were as much for Rashul's followers as for these men.

"We fight for a world where you and we and all others will be treated fairly regardless of birth or caste or jati." Rashul turned to his followers. "Now, we have to prepare for the day. All of you have your jobs, so get ready to do them. The first people should be coming soon."

Jaritta left him to prepare bags of food for any untouchables who came in the broken window, and Pavresh joined some others in getting sacks of grain ready for those merchants who would arrive to pick them up and bring them into the city.

They would run the warehouse just like the prince who owned it did, but the money would go to the revolutionaries rather than the prince, and the merchants and the laborers who arrived to transport the goods would all be treated as equals. It was a grand gesture, nothing violent, nothing to change all society immediately. But it would be a symbol, something they could point to as the revolution built up its own steam.

The bells of the city rang the morning in, and Pavresh heard a commotion outside. He rushed to the door along with the others inside and looked out on the street. It was the day supervisor, come as they'd expected. But what they hadn't expected was the group of toughs with him.

The laborers Rashul had set up around the warehouse closed on the supervisor and his men. Their shouts back and forth were muffled and indistinct. Rashul strode toward them.

His words were perfectly crisp.

"You're welcome to join us, sir. Or take the day off, if you like. We'll be doing your job for you today."

"And come join you untouchables? Never. This warehouse belongs to *tisrah* Prince Bhainu. You must allow us to enter and conduct out business."

Despite the confident words, Pavresh thought the man seemed frightened. He tried to remember if he knew anything about Prince Bhainu from his spying. Nothing came to mind.

"We'll let you enter, as I said. These others…I think they may stay out here with my friends."

The supervisor shook his head, and his men held up their weapons. Some of those inside rushed to join Rashul's laborers, but Pavresh stayed back to watch. The laborers didn't have swords, but they held heavy pins. Some of the other revolutionaries brought knives out as the supervisor's toughs advanced on them.

Pavresh unwound his belt and moved just outside the door in case there was something he could do to help. But already the space looked too crowded for him to do anything but be in the way. People cried out. Clubs thudded against knives and bodies. Cringing, Pavresh thought of the prince assigned to keep an eye on them. Surely every blow by Rashul's men, every injury of the others was a count against them. And it lowered the gesture from iconic to pettily violent.

The supervisor hadn't brought enough men to deal with Rashul's. He must have hoped they wouldn't give fight once his men brandished their weapons, but the laborers gave no ground. Pavresh watched the realization sink in that they wouldn't reach the warehouse. Their eyes stopped focusing on their opponents to glance back and plan an escape.

That led only to more blows finding their targets, and suddenly they broke.

"After them!" Rashul shouted, his voice full of a power almost like arcist magic. "We don't want anyone to escape."

The laborers chased them down the nearest streets. Shouts came back to the warehouse, soon followed by Rashul's men dragging the others back. The first captive was the supervisor himself. He struggled, kicking against his captor and the cobbled road. Pavresh rushed over to help tie him up. When he pulled the rope tight around the man's chest, the arcist grunted from pain. The wound in his arm flared like fire. This was not what he had in mind when he worshiped flames.

He stepped away and into the warehouse, clenching his mouth shut so he wouldn't cry out. He leaned against a wall and rubbed his eyes until the pain receded.

Jaritta came over to him. "It hurts again, doesn't it? You need to let me take you away to get it tended."

"Later." He brushed her hand away. "I need to be here for this."

Jaritta didn't try to argue, and he went back to helping with the preparations for the merchants. They hadn't stopped all the supervisor's men, and Rashul moved nervously around, often getting in the way of those carrying and rearranging the goods. It meant the word might reach the prince sooner than he'd hoped, and even the fact that the supervisor had come with protection might mean they were already compromised.

The first merchant came soon. Pavresh could see him through the open door, approaching nonchalantly with two *nefli* workers to carry the goods. His expression slowly changed to confusion, to worry, to fear as he noticed the unfamiliar men standing around the warehouse, metal clubs in their hands. Rashul stepped forward before he could turn and leave.

"Don't worry. We have your grain here, just like any other day."

The merchant hesitated.

"It's all here, the vegetables, the grain, the sacks of tisane herbs. And we're very willing to bargain. You'll make good money today."

This last was what appeared to convince the merchant. He jerked his head at the two *nefli* and stepped to the door of the warehouse.

"I need three sacks of grain…"

Rashul interrupted him. "And welcome to you also, sirs. *Tisrae*. The one thing we don't have today is different ways of treating people based on caste."

The two workers looked at each in surprise, and the merchant also was shocked silent.

"So start again, *tisrah*. What do you need?"

The merchant looked at those standing around, peered into the warehouse itself. His hands moved nervously over his robes. "Perhaps I shouldn't…"

"No, *tisrah*, this is for you also. Think. No bowing to princes. No need to lower your prices for the priests. Silks for your family. Come. Buy your goods."

The merchant took a deep breath and nodded, letting the air from his lungs out slowly. He repeated his list and haggled with Rashul until he had a good deal. Pavresh was amazed at how well Rashul knew the going rates for different items, both in the markets themselves and at warehouses like this one.

Pavresh helped retrieve the goods, sticking with the smaller items he could carry mostly in his left arm, using his right only for balance. The merchant's workers loaded the items onto a wide wagon that they'd been pulling, with the merchant stepping in a few times to help as if afraid the revolutionaries would be displeased at how he made them work.

Soon they left and other merchants arrived to repeat the same scene many times over the following hours.

Business slowed in late morning when most of the merchants were selling their goods in markets or directly to bakers and cheetah jati servants. Pavresh sat against a stack of grain. His arm throbbed from the lifting even though he'd done all he could to limit the strain. He looked to make sure Jaritta wasn't right there, and then closed his eyes and laid his head back.

Rashul was talking to the others. "I don't want to stay here all day. Even if that one man who got free goes directly to the princes, I can't imagine they'd send anyone this soon. They wouldn't be ready for that. But we need to be out of here in early afternoon."

Pavresh imagined the soldiers storming the warehouse. One of the local warrior jatis, maybe, or might they even send in the fierce wolf jati, hardened by their lives in the mountains? He thought of what he'd seen about the princes and their households. If a *nefli* laborer showed up, it would take a significant amount of time before he was actually brought to the prince. He'd be passed between various low-ranking servants first for a while. And then they'd have to contact the soldiers and arrange for what was needed. The soldiers would need time to decide who was going and how to best attack them. They wouldn't just march down the streets and straight toward them. Not after learning that the revolutionaries had already fought back.

Of course, Prince Shardash was watching them all this time. If he had somehow learned of their plans ahead of time, he might have prepared the soldiers already. But then they would have attacked first thing in the morning surely. It wasn't in Shardash's interests to let them come even this close to succeeding.

No, Rashul was probably right. They had plenty of time to clear out.

"That's it." Jaritta's voice woke him from a half-slumber. "You need medicine. An herbal salve at least. Some healing mud even. We're going."

"No…" he began, but Jaritta grabbed his arm right on the wound, and he cried out.

"It's hot. The skin is all red. We need to do something now, unless you want to be a one-armed arcist."

Pavresh tried to pull away. "It's only a little wound. He barely grazed me."

"Maybe, but the knife might have been dirty. We need to treat it now."

Pavresh struggled to his feet and looked for Rashul. He wasn't talking to the gathered revolutionaries anymore. Had Pavresh really fallen asleep?

"Fine, we can go. Let me just tell Rashul."

Moments later, they were walking away from the warehouse toward the river. A number of people passed them by, more merchants coming to pick up their goods. Pavresh stepped aside as one particularly burly merchant with four *nefli* workers passed by.

Jaritta pulled him farther up the road and suddenly turned

down an alley.

"Those weren't merchants," she whispered.

"What?" Pavresh hadn't really been paying attention to them as he tried to ignore the pain.

"Those merchants weren't merchant jati, and their workers definitely weren't *nefli* caste."

Pavresh stopped thinking about his wound and grabbed her arm. "What do you mean? They were soldiers?"

Jaritta only nodded.

"We have to go back. Warn them." But even as he said it, he knew they were late.

"Come with me." The words were pained, but confident. "I know where we can watch. And be close enough to help anyone who manages to escape."

She hurried down the alley with Pavresh right behind, his wound completely forgotten by both of them. After a couple of houses, a stairway climbed to a second-story door. Just before the door, Jaritta grabbed the eaves and stuck her foot into a wide crack in the wall. With a practiced motion, she pulled herself to the roof. Pavresh followed more carefully.

When he pulled up, he remembered the festering cut in his arm and cried out. Jaritta quickly grabbed him beneath his arms and helped him the rest of the way up.

"I'm so sorry. I forgot all about that. Maybe we should…"

"No," Pavresh interrupted. "We need to know what happens. I'll be fine."

"Just remember that it's hurt, agreed?" Jaritta moved back from him and rearranged her robe to cover the side of her face.

Pavresh stood to a crouch and nodded. The roof had a slight slant and was covered with clay tiles. Jaritta led him along the edge of the roof and then up the slant where it met the next building.

A maze of roofs and attics followed, twisting Pavresh about so he couldn't tell anymore where he was. Thankfully, the rest of the trip didn't involve pulling himself up with his arms. When Jaritta stopped inside a high attic, he was too winded to say anything, so he just looked at her. The light from a wide window lit the half of her face that was uncovered.

Seeing his look, she giggled and suddenly seemed much younger, more a sister than the mother she'd seemed when nursing his wound. She stopped. Against the fear of their flight and uncertainty of what was happening in the warehouse, the sound jarred. But then Pavresh felt a laugh building also, and even as it came it out, he knew it wasn't for anything funny but simply a release. The sound eased his tensions, and Jaritta joined back in, a full laugh now in place of a giggle.

When they stopped, Jaritta wiped tears from her cheeks and shrugged.

"I've been an untouchable for fifteen years. I know untouchables in every part of this city, and I was taught the streets by the best." She grew sober and lowered her eyes, and Pavresh remembered her story of the boy who'd befriended her before leaving for the abandoned city. "Even before that," she continued more thoughtfully, "Jasfer and I used to explore as much as we dared among the *kortru* manors."

In the silence that followed, their reasons for coming to this attic grew again in their minds. Pavresh looked both ways on the street below before he noticed the warehouse. It was surrounded by soldiers.

No sounds carried to them, but they watched as a figure was pulled from the building, shouting and trying to break free. It was Iksheen, and he seemed to have blood on the front of his idiosyncratic outfit. He was pulled to an area away from the warehouse. The laborers who'd been guarding the building already stood against a blank wall. One of them lay on the ground without moving.

Pavresh felt Jaritta's hand grab his, and he squeezed back without turning from the sight.

Others followed. Ekana, Rijef, Tanmai. And then came Rashul. He walked calmly, despite the sword at his back. Pavresh had a sudden sense, like an arcist image, that they would cut him down right there. He kept his head high, and Pavresh wanted to close his eyes so he wouldn't see the soldier pull his sword back and behead the revolutionary.

But the soldier held his sword steady, and soon Rashul joined the others beside the building. The soldiers, with their swords still out, surrounded their prisoners and marched off, but a dozen stayed behind and moved into the nearby alleys.

He turned toward Jaritta and realized he was squeezing her hand tightly. He relaxed and then self-consciously pulled away. "Are they…do you think they're looking for us?"

Jaritta looked down at her hand, moving the fingers as if they were sore. "Us specifically? Probably not. But I don't think it's safe to go into the streets just now."

"No. I guess we'll stay here." He paused and looked down at her hand. "Sorry, I…"

"It's all right. I'm just trying to get some feeling into it again." She smiled at him. "Don't worry."

They fell silent and sat in the dark room, lit only by the one large window. Occasional shouts rose from the streets, muffled by the heavy air. Snow fell on and off, and Pavresh tried to imagine what was happening to the other revolutionaries. Were they being tortured? Were they dead? Would the soldiers learn his description and come looking for him? He saw again and again Rashul walking proudly from the building. And Iksheen carried away with blood on his cloak.

And twisting in with these questions and images was the fact that he was sitting alone in a dark room with a woman. Was she beautiful? Not exactly, with the scar puckering the skin of her face. But that didn't really matter. Even the *kortru* beauty of the other side of her face didn't matter. The arcist in him found an image to this situation, the man and woman thrown together in a stressful predicament. It felt so ingrained in the tales and legends he'd heard since birth and the stories he'd elicited from the people of Romnai. He'd thought of her during the course of the day as mother and sister. Now his thoughts were quite different.

He kept glancing at her to see if she was thinking the same, unsure what his reaction would be if she was. The scarred side of her head was toward him, covered in cloth, so what he saw was her thin nose and the cheek beyond it. The light from the window colored them like the beautiful stained wood trim in the High Assembly.

Pavresh jerked his head away and looked out the window. No soldiers were in sight, and the snow had temporarily stopped. How long were they going to wait until it was safe?

Moving his hands nervously on his leg, he turned away from the window and looked around the room, letting his eyes pass over Jaritta as he did. What was she thinking about? Was it as awkward for her as for him? She was untouchable, but earlier they'd held hands. He felt a burning in his hand.

What was it like to be untouchable? Perhaps she longed to be touched by another person. As he thought about it, he decided that being named untouchable must be the worst punishment. To forbid someone from touching, from being touched, was to exile them from being human. It suddenly seemed crueler than blindness or deafness, and worse even than simple exile—for these exiles were forced to live so close to the life they'd had but always separated by the one word, untouchable.

In arcist terms, it was the rightful heir imprisoned. Unbridled, undeserved pain.

His thoughts still centered on Jaritta after that, but not on touching her. He imagined the pain of being untouchable, on her brother Jasfer and how he must have dealt with it, on day-to-day life in the streets. With his eyes closed to picture this, he was shocked by a touch. Jaritta had grabbed his arm and was helping him up.

"It should be safe now. Let's get back Chaitan's house. We still need to treat that wound."

He had to consciously change the image in his mind then, force his thoughts toward the mentor, the safe haven and away from Jaritta.

Again, Jaritta led him through an amazing labyrinth of rooftops and garden walls. Once they even dropped below a street and passed through a low tunnel that seemed to have been a street in an earlier age with the ruins of ancient buildings on either side. It ended shortly, on the other side of a building, and they climbed again. Watching her move in front of him, he was struck by the innate power she held, something that had been hidden to him when he'd seen her at Chaitan's place. Her brother might be a prince, but she knew this city so well it almost seemed to twist itself to serve her. Soon they were down on the streets and hurrying toward Chaitan's house.

They couldn't go as quickly as they would have liked, not wanting to draw attention to themselves. Neighborhoods passed by until they entered the square where the old arcist's house stood.

The door was open. Broken down.

A part of Pavresh knew what that meant immediately, but he refused to think it. They ran straight into the main room, not caring if there were soldiers waiting for them or not.

A musical instrument lay beside the stage, its strings broken, its body smashed. Namrani was nowhere to be seen. Chaitan's pillows lay scattered near the smoldering fire. Pavresh and Jaritta could only stare in shock.

He turned slowly to take in the rest of the room and saw Tanjali sitting on the floor against one wall, crying.

Pavresh rushed over with Jaritta close behind. "What

happened?"

Tanjali didn't answer at first, but she looked up, and her expression was angry. "Why? You couldn't just leave an old man alone? Why'd you have to do…whatever you did? You were known as his friends and guests. So they blame him, too. Didn't you think of that ahead of time?"

Chaitan was a hero of the valley. They couldn't do anything to him, could they? They might take him away to scare Rashul and everyone, but they wouldn't actually harm him. He looked again at the scattered pillows. It looked like violence to him.

"Tanjali," he said loudly, "did they hurt him? They didn't beat him, did they?"

Tanjali shook her head and turned away. Jaritta grabbed his elbow.

"We have to get out of here. The soldiers could come back any minute."

They heard noises in the street. Running feet.

"There are roofs out back. I can take us through those paths. But we have to go now."

Jaritta was already running toward the door into the rest of the house as she said this. Pavresh glanced again at Tanjali, crumpled against the wall, the image of complete loss. Then he ran.

As the door swung shut behind him, he saw soldiers pouring in, and he forced himself to run faster.

Jaritta led him up the stairs and out a window and onto the road of roofs. The untouchable city, he supposed, as they scurried from one peak to the next.

Chapter 13

"You shouldn't have come here." Jasfer let his anger overcome worry as he met his sister and Pavresh in the back room of his house. Kalvandi had let them in before telling Jasfer they had shown up at the house. She was one of his chief servants, his steward, and he knew he could trust her not to tell anyone, but he still wished she had come to him first.

Neither looked up at him. They were collapsed into the pillows on the floor, heads drooped forward in such a look of weariness or sadness or both, that he almost relented. But then he thought of the soldiers who were sure to come swarming into his house. There was no way they could have traveled across the city without attracting their attention.

He paced in silence then paused in front of Pavresh. "You knew Rashul was being watched, especially right now. Couldn't you have made them wait? Or else stayed uninvolved yourself?" The arcist and spy still gave no answer, so he rounded on his sister.

"And Jaritta, they must have known you were among them and who you are. Don't you imagine they've been keeping a watch on this very house, assuming you'd come here?"

She looked up now, and he relaxed his fists at the sorrow in her eyes. But there was defiance, as well. Whatever the sadness, she was sure of herself in a way that caught him by surprise. "We weren't seen. I know how to move so that soldiers see nothing."

Jasfer grabbed the hair at the back of his head and sat down on the room's one cushioned chair. He tried to find the words, but each time he opened his mouth, he stopped and moved his hands, to his forehead, to his chin, into each other, back to his hair.

"How can you know that?" he asked. "And anyway, even if they didn't see you, they'll likely come in here just to check."

"We...we had nowhere else to go, Jasfer," Jaritta said. "They took Chaitan."

"I know."

"I just need to catch my breath here for a moment. I can disappear among the other untouchables on the streets if you'll just let me think for a bit."

Jasfer thought he should tell her no, that she could stay and he'd think of a way to keep her safe. But, he only said, "That's probably best."

"But Pavresh can stay here." Only then did the arcist meet Jasfer's eyes. Pavresh had uncovered a good deal of intelligence for Jasfer. He wouldn't want to lose that resource...but how could he let the man stay?

Jasfer must have let his thoughts show because Jaritta pressed on before he could speak. "He's known as one of your servants already. No one will recognize him from Chaitan's house. Remember, that's why we chose him in the first place."

In his rough clothes, torn from their flight across the city, bloody even on one sleeve, the arcist looked like a ruffian, a street fighter. No one would believe he was a cheetah jati servant. But cleaned up and in fine clothes, no one would guess he was anything but. Yet, could he take that chance? What if soldiers spied on the house, interrogated his servants?

"I'll...try to figure something out. You can stay for now, but I may need to find a way for you to disappear for a little while."

He closed his eyes and debated what to do. The image of a drunken god fumbling his way through kiwan rose in his mind again. This sort of intrigue should fall to someone else, not him. If Apijet was alive, he'd try to find a job for Pavresh there.

He could try some of the other princes, the older ones who'd been friends of his father. But he wasn't sure he could pull the right strings for that to look innocent.

And besides, there was no benefit in having Pavresh there at those houses. There must be some way he could turn this to his advantage.

"Jasfer." Jaritta's voice broke through his thoughts, and he looked up. "Could we have water and bandages?"

It took him a moment to register the question. Why did she need... "Are you injured? What happened?" He was on his feet and walking toward her before he realized it.

"It's Pavresh. He was stabbed earlier this morning. Before everything happened. I just want it clean so it's not infected."

"Kalvandi!" Jasfer called through the door. She appeared immediately, water and clean cloths already in her arms.

While Kalvandi and Jaritta saw to Pavresh's wound, Jasfer stepped out to another room to figure out what to do about the arcist.

Now would have been a good time to use Pavresh as his messenger, but of course, he didn't dare take that chance. He would have liked to keep Yatim nearby for his fighting skills, but he was the only one Jasfer trusted to make the careful inquiries he would need. He didn't have the time he wanted to keep it innocuous. There was no telling when the soldiers might rush in.

While Yatim waited beside him in his study, Jasfer ran through what he knew of the happenings among the princes so he could decide where to send his servant first.

Dartak or an ally had an arcist working for him. He would love to have Pavresh keep an eye on that, but he wasn't sure how to make it work.

His cousin Samatrit was preparing to lead soldiers into the abandoned city and reclaim it. Already the wolf jati was supposed to be gathering outside the ruins, though only to observe for the moment. Pavresh might be able to pass for a soldier, but soldiers spent most of their careers among the same group. The story they'd have to invent to place him outside anywhere useful would be seen through easily.

The biggest unknown was why Dartak would send his head servant to the city of silk. And Samatrit had investments in silk, which made the question especially intriguing.

What his sister's little band of petty revolutionaries did had little bearing on the important things of the valley. But now their actions were forcing him to act when so many questions remained. Images ran through his head of soldiers entering his house, tearing apart his finery, pulling him before the priests to have him cast out.

He hit his open hand onto the desk. The picture of a perfect cheetah jati servant, Yatim didn't even react.

With a fine pen and his characteristic dark green ink, Jasfer wrote a quick message and sealed it.

"This message isn't all that important." He handed it to Yatim. "Deliver it and wait for a response, and while you wait, I want you to keep your eyes and ears open. Talk to the other servants and get me an answer."

When he left, Jasfer paced in his room, his hands fidgeting with the pen he still held.

While Jasfer waited for Yatim to return, Kalvandi knocked on the door to the room he was in and entered. He looked up, saw the concern on her face, and indicated that she should speak.

"There are men at the door, *tisrah*. Soldiers, demanding to speak directly to you before they enter."

Jasfer kept himself outwardly calm. "Thank you, Kalvandi. I will be to see them immediately. Why don't you check on our guests?"

When she had bowed her head and left, he let himself take a deep breath. They were certainly here because of Chaitan's folk. Because of his sister who wasn't allowed to be his sister in their eyes. His movements stuttered as he tried to decide how to approach the soldiers. The slightest arrogance could come across as guilt, so he decided to be as humble and accommodating as he could. This went beyond anything Apijet had trained him for. Would his former mentor even have known how to handle such a situation?

He relaxed his face into a simple smile and walked slowly to the door.

Four wolf jati soldiers waited on the street, their commander in a wolf-skin cloak, the grinning head thrown backward from his neck. He'd expected one of the other soldier jatis here in the city. There was always something wild about the wolf jati, a jarring presence among civilized people. After a brief hesitation, Jasfer inclined his head in the proper manner for a prince to acknowledge those below him. He could be humble, but he might as well remind them that he outranked them anyway. The soldiers responded in kind, with deeper bows of their heads.

"We are searching for a fugitive, *tisrah*," their commander said. "We would like to search your house."

"My house? You may come in. But I can't imagine anyone would be hiding in here."

The soldiers followed him inside and into the first room off the hallway. Jasfer pulled the door shut behind them, but one of the soldiers stepped back and opened it apologetically.

"I do not have a large house like some of the princes. So please explain yourselves before I allow you to go running through it."

The commander withdrew a roll of paper and handed it to Jasfer. Jasfer glanced at the seal and the words inside and handed it back. It was from Prince Baram himself, which meant he'd have to allow the search.

"We have been authorized to search for anyone connected

with the rebel Rashul. Please do nothing to obstruct us."

Jasfer opened his arms as if nothing was further from his thoughts. "Of course, I will help in any way I can. I will need to guide you, however. It can be a bit of a maze, I'm afraid, and I can't have you wandering lost."

He could tell that the commander didn't like this. But Jasfer kept his face as guileless and friendly as he could, and the soldier nodded.

"Thank you for your offer. If we see any different door or hallway we want to examine, you must allow us to change course."

"Assuredly." He led them back to the main hallway and then down a wood-paneled hall that led toward the steam beds.

It was a struggle to remain calm. He paid less attention to where they went than to keeping his body relaxed, as if he regularly had soldiers searching his house. He hadn't lied about the confusing layout of the building. It had been the home to many princes, switching hands when a ruling prince fell out of favor to be replaced by another, though it had been his family's home for a few generations now. As owners changed, they had extended hallways or knocked down walls or shifted how the rooms met, so he had to take the soldiers on a winding path.

One soldier remained behind in the central chamber, in view of the main entrance and the hallways down both wings. As they entered each room along the way, the commander left a soldier behind in the hallway until they came back out.

At one point in the tour, the commander broke through Jasfer's daze with a simple, "*Tisrah?*" For an instant, his precarious control wavered, but he placed a hand casually on the wall and stayed calm.

"Yes?"

"Do you have a basement? I'd like to see that sooner rather than later."

Jasfer looked around then and paused as he tried to

remember exactly where in the house they were. Stairs led up in front of them, and preserved silk hangings draped the nearest wall. "There's no basement here. We're out at the edge of the lava beds. There's a low cellar beneath the other wing. Shall we go directly there, or finish this wing first? We still have the steam bath on this level and the upstairs."

"We can save the upper rooms for later. Let's finish this floor of the wing and then go directly there."

Jasfer hoped Kalvandi hadn't directed Pavresh and Jaritta to hide in the cellar. And even worse if they remained in the room they'd been in. It was near the stairs to the cellar, and surely the soldiers would search it as they passed. The way they were looking in every room, he had no doubt they would uncover anyone hiding.

The footsteps of the soldiers echoed strangely off the walls as they walked, seemed to become the padding of wolf paws, the click of claws on the hard floors. Every few steps now he was reminding himself to stay relaxed, but his voice when he tried to chat lightly about the objects they passed sounded forced.

They reached the top of the cellar stairs, and the soldiers stopped to search the room beside it, as he'd expected. Jasfer's hand trembled as he pushed the door open.

No one sat there, and the pillows looked perfectly arranged, as if no had been on them that day. He stepped in, followed by the soldiers. No crumbs of food, no blood or scraps of bandages. It felt like the soldiers took extra long examining the corners of the room, peering beneath pillows and furniture. He wondered if they'd sensed his hesitation. But after seeing the empty room, he felt relieved, so even the longer time went by quickly.

They stepped out and toward the stairs, and Jasfer felt his fears return. Jaritta and Pavresh wouldn't have tried to hide down there, would they? They descended thick wooden steps, lighting the stores with an oil lamp. He stayed at the base of the stairs while the soldiers spread out to search the large room.

They moved efficiently, checking behind and inside barrels and sacks. Jasfer let his nervousness express itself in small movements they wouldn't be able to see across the room. He ran his hand up and down the railing of the stairs, swiveled one foot over and over, beat a rhythm with his teeth.

At last, they were coming back and seemed to have checked anywhere a person could possibly hide. He relaxed, didn't even have to force calmness on himself.

"What's this?"

All the tension returned to Jasfer's body. "What?"

The soldier pulled out a bundle of cloth, and he recognized Pavresh's clothes from earlier.

"It's torn here," the soldier said, pointing to part of the robe. "And there's blood. It's dry, but I don't think it's old."

Jasfer couldn't think what to say. His mind was completely stuck.

"I…have no idea. I suppose we can ask Kalvandi."

The soldier bundled the robe up again and nodded. They finished searching and followed Jasfer back up the stairs. The soldiers searched the rest of that wing without saying anything about the bloody clothes and without seeming to notice anything special.

Back in the central chamber, the commander spoke. "Before we search the upper stories, I want you to bring all your servants here."

Kalvandi stood along the edge of the chamber, and Jasfer nodded to her. "My steward will fetch them."

Soon all were gathered in the chamber. Only on his second time looking at the line did he realize that Pavresh was among them. He stopped himself from looking extra closely at the arcist, but he couldn't help scanning the servants one more time for his sister. She wasn't among them.

"Are all your servants here, *tisrah*?"

"All? No. I have a messenger I sent out earlier today who hasn't returned, and others may be on errands I don't know of."

"And every one of these you recognize as your own servant?"

"Yes. Some have been with me for a few months. Some for many years. I know them all, at least by appearance."

The commander nodded and sent two of the soldiers to search the upstairs rooms. Then he walked among the servants, examining them, questioning them. Jasfer had to ignore the procedure so he wouldn't accidentally reveal anything about Pavresh.

After a moment, the commander held up the bloody clothes. "I need to know whose these are."

No one said anything at first. Silence stretched out, played at his nerves. Finally, Jasfer noticed what was almost a scuffle among two of his servants. Taurav, one of his footmen, stepped forward.

"I...I apologize, sir." He bowed his head nervously toward Jasfer. "*Tisrah*." Then he turned back to the soldier and gestured behind him at the footman he'd been scuffling with. "We were play-fighting this morning. The *tisrah* had nothing for us to do for a little while, so we... We didn't want to hurt our good clothes, but we found these old rags and were pretending..." He coughed and looked down at his feet. "Pretending to be fighting mumblers. Sir."

Jasfer had to look away so he wouldn't laugh. He'd no idea that Taurav was such a good storyteller. Liar. It would be something to remember. But clearly loyal as well, if he was willing to cover for the arcist.

"We didn't want Kalvandi to discover what we were doing, so when we got a little careless, I hid the clothes."

The commander addressed Jasfer without even a hint of a bow. "How long has this servant been in your service, *tisrah*?"

"Since my father's time, I believe. I'd have to look at my records to be sure. He's always been an honest and valued servant."

"We will want that record. Thank you, *tisrah*." As Jasfer gestured for Kalvandi to retrieve the record, the soldier turned to one of his men. "Take down his name and family. And that other footman as well. The one he was fighting with."

He questioned a few others then turned back to Taurav. "Show me your shoulder."

"My...oh, yeah." Taurav hesitated, and Jasfer wondered if he'd seen which shoulder of the clothes had been bloody. As he began to pull his cloak aside, the other footman interrupted.

"It was my blood, sir. My shoulder." He bared his upper arm, which really was crossed by what might have been scratches of some sort.

The soldier held out the bloody clothes. "It doesn't match up."

The footman shrugged and pulled his cloak back up. "When you're moving around that much, with old clothes you found that don't fit well...well, I suppose it was sliding around when he cut me."

The commander studied him in silence, looked at the paper where his soldier had written the man's name and family, then moved on to the rest of his servants. He demanded no more records.

The buzz of words simply passed through Jasfer's ears, and the scene glazed over until it seemed a strange painting. He didn't think the commander had completely accepted the footmen's story, but for the moment, he was letting it slide. Maybe he didn't have the authority to push hard, or maybe he was simply toying with Jasfer, waiting to pounce. What would they do to him if they found the arcist and realized Pavresh's connection not only to Jasfer but also Rashul? If they discovered Pavresh employed the arcist as a spy?

Would they cast him out, make him untouchable like his sister? Would they simply strip him of his title, make him one of the non-ruling princely families? Either one seemed inconceivable.

A question broke through Jasfer's daze. The commander was talking to one of his servants, a younger girl who helped keep the house clean. He wasn't sure her name.

"You know this man?" He was pointing at Pavresh. "He works for your *tisrah*?"

She hunched down before the soldier and seemed ready to run from him. But, she answered, "Yes, sir. I've seen him working for the *tisrah* since a while ago."

"What about him?" he asked, pointing to someone else, and Jasfer let the room fall back out of focus.

Would they find Jaritta upstairs? He was sure they'd have other soldiers watching the house for anyone trying to sneak away. And would her presence be even more damning than the arcist's? Probably. He listened for sounds of flight or struggle upstairs but heard nothing.

Jasfer's thoughts entered an un-time that felt both eternal and the barest instant, ending when the two soldiers returned. The spoke quickly with their captain, and then he turned to Jasfer.

"Thank you for your assistance, *tisrah*. We will continue our search elsewhere. If anything else is needed, Prince Baram will contact you."

There was the hint of a threat in the way he said this, and Jasfer knew that he and his house would be watched carefully. But all he felt as the soldiers left was relief.

Kalvandi sent the servants back to their jobs, and Jasfer retired to his private study. The relief dimmed slowly, and he realized that no matter what, he would have to send the arcist away very soon. He couldn't risk Pavresh's presence much longer.

***

Yatim had returned, been sent out again for even longer, and come back a second time when Jasfer called for Pavresh. The arcist came to his study and stood before him. Jasfer did not offer to have him sit.

"First, what happened to my sister? How did she avoid the soldiers?"

Pavresh squirmed a moment, as if unsure he should tell a secret.

"I need to know, so I know how much danger I'm in from the wolf jati and the other princes."

Pavresh gave a half-shrug. "She climbed from an upstairs window onto the roof. From there, I don't know. Maybe she's still up there, waiting for darkness. But she knows how to move about the roofs of the city, so I'm sure she'll have some way to get away from here unseen."

Jasfer felt a tinge of something he didn't recognize. "How do you know my sister's ways so well? Never mind." He didn't need to protect her. He shouldn't even think of her as a sister, just to be safe. The brief memory of exploring unused passages with his sister lasted only a moment before he shuffled it away.

He looked at the arcist, dressed in typical cheetah jati clothing. He'd do for the job Jasfer had planned.

"Forget all that. This is what matters. You can't stay here. It isn't safe. And I don't just mean in my house. We need to get you out of the city for a while. I've figured out how to do it."

He stood up then and paced, wondering how the arcist would react to his plan. "I want you to go the Silk City. I have arranged for a way, if you are willing."

"Silk City?" Pavresh stepped back and closed his eyes for a moment. Then he nodded. "To follow Teert. I see."

He said nothing else for a moment, and Jasfer wondered what he was thinking. Would he go for it, or would Jasfer need to use his other option? No matter what, the arcist couldn't stay in Romnai.

"You will be a servant for a silk weaver family, so they will provide whatever you need. But I will provide you additional money for any other expenses you have."

"The soldiers noticed me. They'll remember. What story will you give?"

This was, admittedly, the tricky part. It needed to be convincing without being suspicious. But he thought he had one that worked.

"I will say that I sent you with vital messages to the mines up north. I have messages that will be going there, so they can check on that if they care to."

"The mines?" Pavresh was silent again. The arcist was from the mines. Would he rather return home, probably to stay there the rest of his life, or continue his work as a spy? Even it was a gamble. If Pavresh decided to return home, he lost a valuable tool. But he trusted that whatever had made him choose to leave the mines would still be sufficient to keep him away. Maybe even more than if the option was between the Silk City and simple exile from Romnai.

"What if I don't want to go to the Silk City?"

"Then I really do have a stack of messages for the mines. You could take them." He could hear the harder edge to his voice when he added, "Whatever you choose, you cannot stay here. I will not permit it."

A knock came at the door then, perfect in its timing to let Pavresh think of his choices. Yatim entered, which also suited Jasfer. The reminder of the force he could command if needed—not much, admittedly, but something—would discourage Pavresh from trying to just disappear in the streets of the city. He didn't want to threaten the arcist with violence outright, but if the question hung in his mind, it would be to the prince's benefit.

"Another message came from the silk weavers, *tisrah*. They leave within two days. If Pavresh would go with them," he bobbed his head briefly to the arcist, "then he must join them now to prepare their luggage."

"Thank you, Yatim. I will call you once he has given me a decision."

The warrior-servant retired from the room, and Jasfer turned toward Pavresh, his body open, inviting a response.

"How long?" Pavresh finally asked. "How long would I be there?"

"I don't know. I will call you back if it seems safe, and I'd expect you to return if you learn anything vital. We don't have time to come up with a code or way of passing written messages. If you must write me, be very careful what you put on paper."

Pavresh kneaded his face with his hands, and Jasfer remembered how long the day must have been for him, remembered the injury and his condition when he arrived at the manner.

"It is sudden, I know. All of this. But for your safety, for my safety, for the safety of Jaritta and Yatim and many others, it is necessary. And perhaps in the Silk City we can turn this situation to the benefit of us all, even Chaitan and Rashul."

Pavresh did not agree immediately, and every heartbeat that passed increased Jasfer's uneasiness. This was the best possible plan, given the way Rashul's mini-revolution had gone today. Didn't Pavresh see that? What could he do to convince him?

He was opening his mouth to add more, still unsure what words would come out when Pavresh made them unnecessary.

"I'll go. Tell me what I need to know."

Chapter 14

A train. Pavresh froze on the road as the other servants began switching the trunks and other luggage from the carriage to the train car. They were going by train. He should have realized that. He'd sworn he would never ride a train. The steam engine at the front radiated heat, bits of glowing metal visible through the protective metal around it. That red glow expanded in his sight until it seemed that the cunning invention surrounded him, as if he was the coal being burned or the water converted into steam.

He worshiped fire, but this was a hellish twist on that. This fire he wanted nothing to do with.

Was it too late to turn around, to take the messages to the mines, to simply disappear into the streets? The thought of the mines, was itself enough to discourage him from wanting to be a messenger. He'd left that world behind and had no desire to return. He didn't hate his parents or his family. He would have loved to see his younger brother again and even his older sister, to make sure his family was doing well. But he knew that going there now would only trap him. The mines were not a place to allow escape twice.

Would this steam engine allow escape even once?

"What's going on? We have to get this loaded."

Pavresh forced the image of the glowing metal away and bobbed his head to the other servant.

"Sorry, sir. I'll get it on there right away."

The servant turned away, and Pavresh took a deep breath. He could load the equipment without breaking his vow, right?

He'd only sworn to never ride on a train. He picked up a heavy trunk, and pain shot through the injury to his arm. He managed to stagger through the open door of the baggage car. Another servant was inside, directing where to put things. He paid half a mind to that while images of the broken remains of the two steam engines he'd seen months earlier pushed into his thoughts. The scattered debris of two trains. The certainty that no one survived.

Maybe once they'd finished with the loading, he could sneak off. He'd survived just fine coming through the countryside north of the river when he was heading to Romnai. And Chaitan had wandered the wilderness of the valley on his own, learning much that made him the great arcist he was. Pavresh could do the same.

It took much of the morning to unload and arrange all the goods. As the trunks piled up in the car, Pavresh realized they must be loading the possessions of several families of silk weavers, not just one. He wondered if the servants he was working with served the same family he did. Or wouldn't that even matter in the Silk City? Would all servants there serve everyone?

All the trunks and goods were loaded. Pavresh's arm ached, but he didn't think he'd torn it back open. The families soon arrived. Pavresh took one look at them and ducked back from the street, though not, as he'd planned, to dash away.

It was Indima. He should have guessed it, but with everything else going on, he'd completely forgotten. And she was still as beautiful as she'd seemed that first time he met her. After the roil of emotions he'd felt so recently in his time with Jaritta, it seemed childish to suddenly switch those nearly identical thoughts to another woman. But maybe he was still younger than he liked to think of himself, because the thoughts came. He'd been able to distract himself from with Jaritta by thinking of her role in arcist terms, of the injustice that had been done to her. But with Indima, the image that rose above injustice, above any other impression to distract him, was of the young woman in need of rescue.

There was something sad about the way she looked around at the city behind her and at the river flowing beneath the bridge. But it took away none of her beauty and did nothing to the image of her distress.

Pavresh wondered what had happened to Ekana in the raid. Dead or captured. He was certain that he and Jaritta were the only two who didn't fall into one of those two categories.

And despite everything, despite her sadness and his need to remain unnoticed, despite his worries for Chaitan and the questions raised by his spying, Pavresh felt his heart speed up. He would be serving Indima. He would see her and be there for her as a reminder of dancing and Chaitan's house. And there'd be no Ekana to stand between them, cold as it was to think of that. The fisherman had been the first to welcome him to Chaitan's and had seemed as close as anyone there to a friend. Or had been until his first capture by Indima's jati—after that he'd become colder himself, less friendly even to those who did their best to comfort him.

Anyway, it was stupid, he told himself. He couldn't risk discovery by his new masters. Surely, she still mourned Ekana. She wouldn't be looking for anyone new. A part of him insisted that maybe she would. Or maybe something would develop without her looking for it.

Running away was still the wiser course here, but he couldn't do it. Not now. He had to go along and see what happened on the trip along the valley and in the city of the silk weavers. Curiosity about the silk weavers, about Indima and about Prince Dartak's steward Teert all combined to give him little choice. He would have to board the train. He'd sworn, and such vows were held sacred by fire, but even the thought of sacred flames weren't enough to keep him from boarding.

As the train screeched and pulled away from the city of Romnai, he felt a vague sense of being a betrayer. He swore that in the future he'd keep whatever vows he made.

Betrayal did not fit how he saw himself. It was not something he wanted to become habit.

* * *

The scream of the rails did not end when they picked up speed. It came less often, but at unexpected times, it would jolt Pavresh from his thoughts or from the mesmerizing flash of scenery going past and remind him of the rails below, of the train around him, of the terrible steam engine up ahead that pulled them blindly along the river.

He fidgeted, played his arcist magic with constantly shifting themes, uncertain what he should feel, what he really felt, what he wanted others to think of him. Some of the other servants spoke with him, and he spoke back, but the conversations disappeared as soon as they'd happened.

He was on a train! The river roared by, but it might as well have been silent since the sound of the train itself easily overpowered it. The holy fire had not made people to move this fast. It struck Pavresh to worry whether he was moving so fast he'd leave some part of himself behind, his soul or spirit, the fire inside him. Even the times when the train slowed to plow away the snow from the tracks, he found no reassurance. He fingered the holy knots at his waist. They were a promise of the fire's presence everywhere, but as he fidgeted, the knots fell apart.

Late in the day, he relaxed enough to pay more attention to the others on the train. They weren't many. Most of the cars were filled with goods.

The silk weavers kept to a separate car. Or cars, really, several for sleeping in and the sitting car where all the weavers spent their days. Pavresh was required to attend them in the sitting car, carrying food and brewing tisane. There were three families. Indima traveled with both her parents and kept completely to herself. She had not yet noticed him, and her parents seemed to be keeping everyone away from her, their own jati as much as the servants.

Another family had two young children, cowed by the fierce looks of their parents and obvious terror of the train into miserable obedience. Pavresh thought of sneaking a ball to them if he could find one, or else some kind of toy to let them pass the journey.

The third family was like Indima's, two parents and an older daughter. But she didn't appear to be traveling to the silk city in disgrace. She often looked at Indima with an expression Pavresh couldn't identify, but Indima never returned the looks.

When he entered their car, Pavresh listened for anything that might relate to the ruling princes, any hint of what plans might be underway. He learned nothing.

The servants were faceless to him still. He'd learned a few names—Ravikir and Pren, Shidhi and Tejashanah—but they all jumbled quickly so he couldn't be sure which name meant which person. They were cheetah jati, just as he was supposed to be, but they'd grown up serving the silk weavers. According to the story he was prepared to tell, Pavresh had grown up serving a minor, non-ruling prince in the city of Jarnur by the sea. Society was less rigid there, and he hoped that fact would cover for any mistake he made in relating to the others. As he'd used when spying on Prince Dartak, his name would be Parsh.

Teert was among them. Pavresh watched him, but cautiously. Now especially he couldn't do anything to draw attention to himself. Teert never entered the car of the weavers. They weren't his masters. But he did assist the other servants with the tasks within their own car. He directed the cooking to keep it efficient for the servants of all three families. He organized the cleaning of the car, even doing some himself.

Pavresh found him to be a quiet and efficient servant, even humble, not the terrifying taskmaster who'd frightened the servants of Prince Dartak. But, undoubtedly, there was more to the man, and that was what he looked for, flashes of irritation or anger, moments when he didn't seem quite content among the cheetah jati servants.

The moments were rare, but Pavresh remembered each and tried to learn what he could from them. They told him that Teert had an important task, one that made him consider himself above the other servants, perhaps even above their masters. Part of the task, he was sure, was to seem a typical, minor servant, and most of the time he played that very well.

* * *

By the second day, Pavresh no longer thought of the steam engines, no longer pictured debris spreading across the river plain.

He was serving tisane to the silk weavers when someone shouted and pointed.

"Look! Across the river!" another voice added, as if it were necessary.

The river was still relatively wide here, but the far bank was clearly visible. And there, among boiling pools of mud and sulfurous water, was a city. Pavresh was drawn to the windows by the strange sight. Unbroken walls stood beside crumbled rock. The streets buckled with new hot springs. A geyser sprouted from the center of what had once been a building, its roof long gone, its walls falling as if to worship the spraying water. Growths that might have been some kind of moss or fungus and might have simply been mineral deposits coated much of the city.

All was not ruin, though. Makeshift houses stood against

the ancient rock, wooden beams and animal skins. Tumbled rocks had been rearranged to form new, circular buildings with turf roofs. It was a strange juxtaposition of ancient ruins and new life, of human-built decay and natural destruction and human hope for the future.

People walked the uneven streets freely. They were distant, far too much so to make out their expressions, but something in how they moved said they were unconcerned by either the uncertainty of the ground they stood on or the rumble of the train across the river. They did not bundle up, the fumaroles apparently keeping the ruins far warmer than this side of the river, and even from that distance, pale mumbler faces were visible as were darker tones. They—both mumblers and others—stood around large fires built directly on the streets, as if the hearths of the ancient buildings were insufficient for a new day. They grew plants where the volcanic activity had pushed aside paving slabs to reveal rich earth. They fished from dozens of boats in the river and walked unconcernedly beside the boiling pools that dotted the city.

To Pavresh, there was something both sad and hopeful in the view of the city. Squalor, destitution, the plain tragedy of being outcast. But there was excitement, as well, in the way the city overcame the failings of Eghsal's society. Rashul, he thought, would be pleased by this view of the city, though whether the truth within the city was as hopeful or not, he couldn't say.

For himself, he hadn't gone to Romnai to change society. He'd gone to meet Chaitan and learn from him, to make himself a great arcist. But now…he'd been drawn in by Rashul and Jaritta and the others at Chaitan's house. Not just by their movement, but by the individual people in it, by all their stories and where they'd come from.

Including Indima. Pavresh hadn't been thinking about her as a revolutionary. He wondered if she even knew what had happened. He would tell her. Somehow, he'd let her know that he was here, let her know what he knew and find out if she knew anything more.

It would be tricky. He couldn't risk anyone realizing what he was doing. But he owed it to her, to his own memory of Rashul's band and Chaitan's house. To Ekana, even.

The abandoned city fell behind, giving them a final look of the ruins and makeshift houses. Pavresh wondered if Jaritta's former friend—and lover, he guessed from the hints she'd given—was somewhere in that strange city.

Then the lay of the land hid the last of the buildings, and Pavresh looked for signs of the soldiers who were supposed to be watching the city. The gentle hills with only small clusters of trees didn't seem to offer much shelter for them. Most of the land was rocky with only patches of green where the toxic ground from the shifting lava beds hadn't killed the plants. The thought of setting up camp there seemed ridiculous. They should be instantly visible from any number of directions.

Yet, Pavresh didn't see any sign of soldiers anywhere. Maybe the land was deceptive, with pockets to hide the army. Or maybe they were all on the west side of the city, laughing and drinking and playing pranks on each other.

He turned from the window, working out a plan for contacting Indima.

* * *

Pavresh found a pen and paper, and that evening he sat by the window of the train and wrote, pretending even to himself that he was writing to a lover back in Jarnur.

When I think of you, I think of the first time we met, you working in the main room, your movements like a dancer's, and I performing the shifting music to go with your steps. Not real music, I know, but that's how I picture it now.

This is so far from that place of fishermen from the sea, the place that seemed so innocent. I worry that none are left there now, even the kind proprietor gone. This train is another world taking me far from that one. I wonder what stories I will learn as I go, what stories you will experience while I'm gone.

And years from now, what story will our valley tell of us? Will it speak of our jati, mine and yours? Will it remember our caste, or will such things be forgotten? Our names, perhaps, will be remembered no more.

But for now, I simply wanted to let you know that I'm here and doing well and wishing you all the best where you are, so far away from your true love.

He looked the note over carefully. If anyone found it, it should seem innocent, the letter of one cheetah jati servant to another. To Indima, if he could get it to her, it would announce his presence. She would catch the reference to Chaitan's house and Rashul's revolution and dancing and arcist magic.

He hoped. She'd always struck him as intelligent, though he knew that beauty could blind people, make them believe what they wanted about someone else. She might be incredibly stupid, and he'd assume intelligence because of his attraction. Or she might be far more intelligent than he realized, but her beauty made him not notice the fact.

Well, it didn't matter. He'd have to assume she could figure it out. The tricky thing would be to get it to her.

It was the next day when he found his first opportunity. The train had stopped, as it did periodically, to get more coal and unload goods for the scattered households away from the cities. A snow-covered track wound into the distance both to the north and south of the river, reminding Pavresh of the road that carried goods to the mines. They were farther east than that road, but otherwise, it could have been any stretch of it, twisting among what in a month or so would reveal itself to be bare, gray rocks and patches of hardy bushes and lichen. Clusters of tall, thin aspens, bare of leaves, huddled together at irregular intervals across the landscape. The southern track, he realized, must lead to the third great city of Eghsal, Pashun, too far away to be visible from the river. Even the mountains high above that city were so distant they could only be a dream.

The train laborers unloaded goods onto the flimsy-looking ferry for carrying south while the cheetah jati servants watched from the window.

Pavresh entered the silk weavers' carriage to see if they needed anything. As he walked around, pouring hot tisane and adding honey, he held the letter, folded very small, in the palm of his left hand. Like their servants, most of the weavers stared out the windows, though Indima's father and one of the other men took advantage of the still train to play a game of kiwan.

Pavresh passed quietly among them, responding to their quiet commands. The girl near Indima's age, Datri, grabbed his arm as he passed, and the paper nearly slipped from his fingers.

"Watch out." She shook her hand, and Pavresh realized some drips of tisane must have struck her. He reached out with a cloth, but she pulled back. "Never mind that. I'd like some dried fruit. Pears. Apples. Raisins. Whatever you find."

"Yes, *tisrah*." Without thinking, he played up his arcist magic as a rugged adventurer and rising star and added, "And I apologize for the tisane."

She cocked her head, and he held her eyes for a moment longer than he ought before dropping them.

"It doesn't matter. Bring my fruit now."

He caught a smile at the edge of his vision as he turned away. Why had he done that? It felt fun to flirt, but he hadn't planned it. And it seemed opposed to his purpose, drawing her attention when he should be blending in with the others. He winced briefly before schooling his face back to its cheetah jati mask. He hadn't been able to play with his magic for too long. It felt good to use it, like stretching his legs after too long sitting; he only wished he'd found a safer way to stretch. He filled a bowl with fruit and a few nuts and wondered if he could turn his spontaneous blunder to his benefit.

Handing it to her, Pavresh watched to see if she would look at him. His eyes dropped immediately when she did, but he let a smile show on his face. It might come in handy, he decided, during the trip or in the city to have someone fond of him. He'd seen enough of Datri that he didn't think she'd actually do anything against her parents' wishes. But she might like to pretend she would.

He'd have to be careful, use his arcist magic in secret now and then so it didn't slip out like it had here. And be extra careful whenever Datri might be watching him.

He approached Indima's customary corner and cursed silently as he realized his situation. This was the worst time draw attention to himself! What a fool he'd been! Datri's attention would only make it more difficult to pass messages to Indima.

"Servant," a voice called from the kiwan board. Pavresh turned away from Indima's corner, snapping around so quickly he worried it might look guilty. No one said anything as he approached.

He couldn't resist a quick glance at the board, enough to see that Indima's father was vastly outclassed by his opponent.

"He doesn't stand a chance, does he?"

Pavresh glanced up at the man. Not Datri's father, the father of the young children. Ambal, a thin man with delicate fingers.

"*Tisrah?*"

"I saw you look at the table. You're familiar with the game, I can tell."

Ambal spoke to Indima's father then. "See? A man of our caste may play against his servant, if he has no other competition." He turned to Pavresh. "That is how you learned, I assume?"

"Yes, *tisrah*," he answered, since it seemed the safest. Ambal, he imagined, wouldn't believe that the other castes played the game as well, though it was true their children often couldn't devote as much time to mastering it.

"Then I will call on you to play with me sometime."

"I would be honored, *tisrah*."

Ambal had already turned away to finish his game with Indima's father, whatever he'd called Pavresh over for apparently forgotten. Pavresh rushed from the car, cursing himself trebly. He'd failed to deliver the message, and the one thing he'd wanted to avoid was attention. Now he'd earned the notice of a teenage girl and an adult weaver and master kiwan player.

The note was slightly damp against his palm.

* * *

Later that day, Pavresh was again in the weaver's car, serving their dinner. The kiwan board was abandoned in mid-play, and several of the adults sat at a small table in the center of the car. The children and other adults each sat alone, eating in silence.

Pavresh circled the car, planning to end at the central table. Another servant, Vinyala, poured the drinks, and Pavresh noticed how naturally she moved with her eyes down. There was no way she would have let herself fall into the gaffs he'd made earlier in the day.

As he handed Indima her hot food, he let the note fall from his sleeve. It tumbled down her robe and disappeared beneath. She took the food listlessly, giving no indication she'd noticed the paper. It must not have landed against her skin, as he'd feared when it fell, and he wasted no more time beside her.

He saw no indication that others had noticed the drop as he continued around the car.

As he turned to leave, Ambal called to him. He was one of those at the central table, but he pushed himself away and staggered over to the kiwan board.

"Come. Jinshu has left his side in complete disarray. Again." He swept his hand over the table as if in disgust. "Rather than start over, I'd like to see what you can do with it."

Pavresh stepped over to the table and looked down. The green markers were ridiculously vulnerable. A competent blue player could eat through them within a few turns. He glanced at the remaining pieces and saw nothing special among them.

"I'm afraid such a challenge is beyond me, *tisrah*." He kept his eyes down. "I will play if you choose, but I fear it will be over soon."

"Too true. Jinshu has left you few options." He picked up one of the blue pieces, however, as if preparing to play it. "But, I'll give you two turns now before we resume to move or add the pieces you want. And then it will be your turn to begin as well. Can you right the loom in three turns, servant?"

He looked at the pieces more closely. There were a few obvious moves that would cover the most glaring weaknesses of the arrangement but wouldn't set him up to do much more than prolong the game. He looked deeper, trying to imagine a way to go on the offensive. An open space near the center would be a good beachhead, if he could get a piece there. He'd have to roll the piece in.

The weak side he'd just have to abandon. Pull a couple of pieces away before it was overwhelmed, if he could.

Pavresh picked up a heavy piece and said, "I'll do it."

Ambal gave him the ritual nod, and Pavresh placed the piece against the ramp. The movement of the train made any attempt ridiculous, but he didn't seem to have an option. He needed the right angle so it would curve into place. The piece curved and bounced toward the opening in the center, but it hit one of the other pieces and ended up too far to the side. Not a terrible place, but not enough to go on the offensive.

It meant one fewer piece to pull back from the weak side. He winced as he picked a different piece, one that was heavier on one side than the other. A glance at the weaver showed him the man was watching carefully, making note both the play itself and his body language. Pavresh debated using his magic to cover his plans, but he decided not to. He doubted anyone would notice, but he'd already used the magic once today and was still wishing he hadn't.

This piece went to the square he'd hoped, and he used his final move to retreat a piece from the right side of the board so it could add to his attack on the left.

"Fascinating. It isn't what I expected you to do."

Pavresh didn't answer and concentrated on keeping his face expressionless as Ambal slid a piece over toward his weak flank. He responded by pulling one more piece away from there, and the game continued in earnest.

The weaver still had the better position, and Pavresh knew it'd take luck to actually win. A botched move or bad roll by the weaver. One or two minor slip-ups, and if he could avoid any stupid mistakes himself, he might be able to win.

Ambal made no attempt to engage him in conversation as they played. The train stopped at a station that was no more than a lantern in the dark, but they played on.

And finally, Pavresh lost.

"A fine match, servant. You lasted longer than most would have from that mess." He gestured for Pavresh to gather the colored pieces into their bags. "One of these days, I'll play you in a full game. Be interesting to see your opening moves."

His ritual nod then was to dismiss Pavresh. The arcist finished putting the pieces away and left the car.

* * *

The next day Pavresh wrote a second message for Indima. He struggled over the safest words as the tree-lined river roared past. The other servants said they would soon leave the train, switching to a caravan of wagons as they left the river behind. A part of him still tensed when he thought about the train they rode in, especially when he first woke in the morning. The creaks and roar of the rails brought it all back to him, and he thought of his vow and the terrible destruction he'd seen months earlier.

Had it only been months? It seemed as though he'd been gone from the mines and his family for years at least…though at the same time, it felt that he'd laughed at his brother's jokes and antics the day before yesterday. A twelve-day or two before Pavresh had left, his brother had bought a hat from some peddler, a low-caste or even untouchable man that their parents didn't want coming near the mines. It was a ridiculous hat that couldn't cover the ears and would do little to keep anyone warm. But his brother wore it all around the mines, twisting it occasionally, as if he could never tell which was supposed to be front. And to the women among the laborers who cared for their house and garden, he would remove his hat and give a half bow, like the men in stories from the Forgotten South.

Thinking of his brother made Pavresh smile, and he forgot about the paper in his hands for a moment.

Until Teert snatched it away.

"Looks like a delicious love letter. Shall we read it?"

Some of the other servants laughed, but none seemed terribly interested. Pavresh wanted to snatch it away, but he thought trying to fight back would only make the teasing worse…if teasing was all it was. Otherwise, it might just raise the suspicions of Prince Dartak's steward.

"Ah, leave him be," Ravikir said. He was a large man, with a commanding voice, but he made no move to push his body up from his pillows or follow through in any way.

"It's mine," Pavresh said quietly, adding a touch of magic in the form of a love-sick young man.

"'The train is a loud contraption,' it says. What a profound statement to his lover."

When Pavresh didn't reply, Teert continued reading. "'It feels like a trap, a cage on rails. The screech of its motion a terrible form of torture. Perhaps I will be free of this trap soon, and you of yours. Does your life feel like a trap, too? Sometimes it seems the train is taking me to a new world, and I wonder what valley I'll step into, what strange society might be waiting for me, what castes and jatis will exist there…'"

He threw the paper down onto Pavresh's lap.

"That's all?" Teert laughed. "I hope you already have the lady well wooed. You won't win her with letters like that."

Pavresh's fingers crushed the edges of the paper, and Teert turned away. The confrontation had all the feel of a juvenile prank, a minor attempt for Teert to show some sort of superiority. But…Pavresh doubted it. Somehow the man must have been suspicious.

He smoothed out the letter to reread it. It *was* worthless. He wasn't actually trying to woo Indima. Or anyway, he wouldn't admit that he was. Even so, she wouldn't be interested in a letter like that.

He crumpled the paper and stuffed it into his bag.

Chapter 15

Indima kept her eyes on the servants who moved in and out of the silk weavers' car. She couldn't figure out when the note had been slipped to her. Was it here, in the sitting car, or had it been already in the morning, in the sleeping car? There was a hidden message within the simple note, one she didn't feel she'd fully understood yet. Her time back at Chaitan's house seemed so distant she'd forgotten many things.

She hadn't forgotten Ekana. The note alluded to him, but who sent it? It wasn't Ekana himself. She'd notice him immediately if he were on the train. She read the words again.

The references to dancing and music, to Chaitan and Ekana, to Rashul's plans... Had something happened to Chaitan? Something about the revolution? It must have been the fifth time reading through the note that she remembered the arcist. What was his name?

Pavresh. She tried to picture his face but couldn't.

Of course it was him, though. Indima looked more closely at the servants, trying to remember, to pick him out from those faceless people who'd been catering to her throughout the train ride. It was so easy to let her eyes slide past as she'd always done. They were hands and arms for serving tisane, feet for retrieving a pillow from the other side of the car.

When she focused on their faces, it made her mind wake up, made her aware of other things as well. Of the train itself and her reason for being there. Of Ekana and the people and places she'd never see again. Even of Rashul's naïve dreams.

But this note meant there was one person from Romnai she

could see again, if she could only recognize him. As she stared at the faces and failed to remember, her longing grew. She needed that connection to her past. She needed to talk about Chaitan's house and Rashul's revolution and the music and dancing of those beautiful days.

As she searched for Pavresh, Indima found that she spent less time isolated in her corner. She spoke a few words to Datri, she joined her parents to eat, although she wouldn't speak to them, and she even played a brief game of kiwan with one of the young children. He was only about five years old, but he almost beat her because she couldn't concentrate on the game.

A servant came with small cakes for them. Was this Pavresh? No. His head was too big, his skin not quite the same. Not darker or lighter so much as a slightly different tint. Pavresh's face had had a hint of red, she remembered, like the dried bark of the cinnamon trees that were cultivated at the edge of the steaming lava beds.

Would he be disguised some way? She looked at the women, but she doubted he could pull off such a disguise. All looked convincingly female.

There was another servant keeping to the servant car, sent by one of the princes for some reason no one had told her. That would be a convincing cover for Pavresh, but then how could he have left the note for her? No, he must be one of the other two male servants. Eventually, they both entered the weavers' car at the same time to serve a midday lunch.

A glance was all it took to tell which was Pavresh, even if she never would have noticed if she hadn't been looking. He saw her gaze and gave a discreet nod, and she felt a brief flash of his magic, the sense of a good friend who would be there when she needed him. That was all, but it was enough. He moved about the car, serving the other weavers, flirting innocently with Datri, and as he left, he glanced one last time at Indima.

She had to force herself not to smile like a little girl. Smile. She hadn't done that since she'd been caught with Ekana. But it was so good to have that connection to her past, to the beautiful times in Chaitan's house.

Indima didn't smile—it would be obvious to her parents that something strange was happening—but for the first time since that night, The Night, she felt something inside relax. Maybe her life was not over.

* * *

In the little time that remained aboard the train, her correspondence with Pavresh consisted of quick glances and innocent smiles. He gave her no more notes, and she never wrote him. But she joined the other weavers more often and found the time passing much more rapidly.

Soon came the time to disembark. The train stopped at a desolate station, but a well-maintained road led off to the east, plunging through low rocky hills, as the river—and the rails—curved away south. A line of covered sleighs awaited them, carriages really, sturdy and large. All that separated them from the carriages of the streets of Romnai were the blades that replaced the wheels. Indima played a mindless game of cards with Datri as the servants unloaded some of their luggage and piled it into the sleighs—the rest of the luggage would stay on the train until a station farther along with a cargo-only rail-line.

It would be a three-day journey, and Indima was surprised to feel excitement and nervousness dancing inside her when she thought of that trip. No, not the trip itself, when she thought of the Silk City at the end of it. She'd never been there but had heard stories of the legendary city all her life.

"You cheated!"

Indima looked down at the table, saw the round cards

without understanding what Datri meant. "That's a fair play."

"On this round it is," Datri said, a hint of annoyance entering her voice. "But you should have played that card a couple hands ago. Look."

She started digging through the pile of played cards.

"Never mind." Indima reached out and grabbed the younger girl's wrist. "Don't worry about it. My mind isn't on the game anyway." Even with the game interrupted, Datri still had the intense look of someone debating how to play a card or how to roll a kiwan stone.

Indima turned away and looked out the windows. The mountains were distant here. Because of how the river angled away from them, this was farther from the mountains than they'd been the entire trip, as far as Romnai itself was from the mountains that formed the northern edge of the valley.

The servants moved as if they'd been born to loading and unloading, and maybe they had. Maybe there was more to the castes than Rashul believed, an inborn sense of labor for the lowest castes, of ruling for the *kortru*. But then Pavresh hadn't been born to it, yet he moved no different from the others, marching back and forth with boxes and chests and bales of cloth.

It was a role for him. Maybe it was a role for everyone. Every society had its castes and jatis—its roles—and people would fill them, whether society forced it with iron castes or not. And what role would she play, if she weren't forced into this one? Who would come to fill her own role if she had the option of running off to escape?

"Oh, come on." Datri snapped her from her thoughts. "There's nothing else to do anyway. Or do you have your eyes on those servants for some reason?"

There was a gentle mockery to the girl's words, even though her eyes still seemed intent on the moves of a game of strategy, and Indima forced a laugh. The sound of her own laughter sent a brief stab through her as she pictured Ekana and all that she'd lost.

"Them? No. Sometimes I wonder if you do."

Datri's lips thinned then opened into a smile. "No. They're like children, you know. It's fun to flirt with them, but it means nothing in the end."

A part of Indima cringed at the easy dismissal of the other castes. What would Ekana have thought to hear that? Yet, it was the way she'd been raised, to see the lower castes as simply separate, like children. Or even animals. So instead of answering, she picked the cards up and shuffled them.

"What will you do in the Silk City?"

Datri picked up the cards Indima dealt as she answered, "Mostly just see the place for the summer. We're planning to go back to Romnai before winter."

"All of you, or just your parents?" Indima teased.

Datri laid her first card and giggled. The sound made her seem much younger than Indima. "All of us, I think. Unless…" She shrugged and giggled again. The innocence in the laugh made Indima relax. Given time, this might be someone she could actually confide in. "Really, I think my parents have their eyes on another jati, looking to match me with a priest or prince."

After a few more cards, Datri added, "How long…oh, that's right. Do you think you'll really be forced to stay out here? Forever?"

Indima looked away from the cards, saw her parents sitting across from them, talking quietly. "I don't know. They'll try, for a while. If they can marry me off, then I guess it depends on my…husband."

They focused on the card game then, speaking occasionally but never of anything important. Some of the women servants came in to serve them lunch as the morning shifted to afternoon.

* * *

It was strange to ride in a horse-drawn sleigh after so long on the jerking, screeching train. These were not much quieter, as the body of the vehicle creaked about over its blades, but there was a grace to their movement that lulled Indima despite the discomfort of where she sat. It was a rough bench across from her parents, the other weaver families in separate sleighs. A small table stood between them, and one of the servants was wiping it clean after their dinner.

Shidhi, that was the woman's name. Indima felt a bit guilty that she never really noticed the servants. Shidhi had been with her family for years, cleaning and cooking—not as a personal attendant, but even so, the name should have been there immediately, not waiting for her to unbury it.

Indima glanced across the table. Her mother looked at her with the same disappointment she'd had ever since she'd been discovered with Ekana. They'd barely spoken beyond a few words about the food or weather during the entire trip. Indima shook her head and looked away. She wasn't ready to try to talk about anything either. Let her mother while away her own anger in silence, as far as Indima cared. Shidhi finished with the table and moved away to the bench at the back of the sleigh for servants.

Most of their servants had remained in Romnai, watching the house her parents would return to without her or serving another *kortru* family in the interim. Her family would be assigned other cheetah jati servants in the Silk City. Only Shidhi had offered to accompany them, and so they'd retained a second servant. Pavresh. He sat now on the servant bench with his head down, his dark hair falling forward around his face, though too short to completely obscure it. If he was using his magic, she couldn't sense it.

Her father broke the silence.

"There's little to do on these rides, it seems."

Neither Indima nor her mother answered him.

"Three days of this? Three days without talking. Fine." He snapped his fingers. "Boy. Servant. What was your name?"

Pavresh looked up in surprise then quickly got to his feet, the motion of the sleigh making him awkward. "My name is Parsh, *tisrah*. How can I serve you?"

"I wish to play kiwan, Parsh."

"Kiwan?" Pavresh asked. Indima saw a confused smile pass briefly over his face. "Will that work in the sleigh?" He swung his head back and forth, as if looking for a kiwan table.

Her father laughed, and Indima felt an uncertain nervousness for Pavresh arise.

"Not table kiwan," Jinshu said. "Card kiwan. Surely you know the game?"

Pavresh shuffled his feet, and for an instant he didn't look at all like a cheetah jati servant. "No, *tisrah*. I don't believe I'm familiar with that one."

"Huh. I thought all cheetah jati servants were addicted to the game."

Indima's nervousness grew. Would her father uncover Pavresh's deception? For some reason, she felt his discovery would be seen as reflecting on her, also. As far as her family and her jati knew, she'd simply been having an affair out of caste. They knew nothing of what actually went on at Chaitan's house or what kind of people she'd been involved with.

Whatever Pavresh was here for, she didn't want him exposed, but she also wanted her own past protected.

"I think you'll find many little differences," Pavresh said, "between the cheetah jati of the capital and those of us from the sea. And even among the cheetah jati in Jarnur…well, my master often kept us pretty isolated."

It seemed a reasonable explanation. Indima looked at her father. For all his superficial gregariousness, he wasn't stupid.

He studied Pavresh more closely. She watched his eyes move slowly and then his face suddenly return to its superficial charm.

"That's great! Then I can teach you and hopefully win a few games along the way."

Pavresh smiled in return. "I would be honored, *tisrah*."

Jinshu gestured for Indima to slide over and Pavresh to sit. Her mother frowned briefly as Pavresh sat beside Indima, but she said nothing.

Jinshu quickly absorbed himself in teaching the game, a game similar in strategy to the movement of pieces on the kiwan board but with other twists. Pavresh asked the right questions, quickly mastering the basics of the strategy, and the two fell into the game.

The game had special cards, not the round traditional cards she'd been playing with Datri. These were smaller and square and had different designs painted on them. She wondered if there was a jati somewhere with the sole job of creating such works. Did some people spend their entire lives crafting the cards and painting the pictures? Like anything, it probably became tedious, but at the moment, the idea of joining in such work appealed to her. There was a simple beauty in the miniature paintings.

Indima watched them play and thought about how she could warn Pavresh to be careful. Her father would be watching him with a seed of suspicion tucked into every glance, hiding behind every word.

* * *

Late in the evening, the drivers pulled the sleighs to the side of the road in a small clearing, and everyone simply found places to sleep inside. There were no inns here, so far from the steam beds, but a high wall had been built along the edge of the clearing, which cut off the fierce wind. Still, away from the steam heat, these lands were bitterly cold, even as the sun showed itself longer each day. Spring had come while they were on the train, but the cold didn't feel much lessened. Their driver came inside with them and slept beside the large brazier that heated the sleigh, tending it throughout the night.

The air became warmer as they continued the next day, though the sleighs still had no trouble gliding. Most of the time, Indima simply stared out the sleigh's windows at the piles of snow and stunted pines. She sat at the right-hand side of the sleigh, so the nearest mountains were opposite her, but at times, she could glimpse the peaks of the southern edge of the valley. Unless those were merely mountain-shaped clouds. The valley should be narrowing here, bringing both lines of mountains together, but she wasn't sure exactly how narrow it was. In Romnai, it was the southern mountains that were visible, just beyond the bed of hot springs, but those had fallen away quickly to the south as they'd traveled along the river.

Tall deer watched them pass, unafraid of the line of sleighs. Their antlers seemed like crowns, and Indima thought that if the animals had castes like her people did, then surely these deer were the princes. Once she saw a strange dog-like creature. A large and very long-legged fox, perhaps, or a slightly built wolf. It had a mane around its head and like a fox, a sort of feline grace as it paced among the trees. Was the wolf jati named for such as these? She doubted it. The name likely went back to the Forgotten South, just as the cheetah jati did. No cheetahs ever lived up here, but stories remained of the hunting companions of their ancestors, the great cats who ran down game. The foxlike animal bounded through the snow, into the trees and out of sight.

Other mighty animals were said to live out here away from cities. Lynx with their thick fur and deceptively friendly faces. Wild goats the size of deer, with small horns and nimble feet.

Hump-backed wisents as big as two horses side-by-side, with fearsome horns and thunderous hooves. She saw no such monstrosities as they rode toward the city, and no wandering pale-faced mumblers either, for which she was grateful.

After the midday meal, Pavresh played card kiwan again with her father and then offered to play a game against her.

Indima looked at her mother, but she said nothing.

"Yes, servant. I would enjoy the distraction."

Pavresh bowed his head gracefully. "I fear the *tisrah* will quickly defeat me, but I will do my best to keep the game from ending too soon."

Indima looked at her cards and at the playing surface. Like table kiwan, the goal was to move the pieces—cards in this case—over toward the opponent's side, capturing ground as she went and protecting her own cards. There was also the added need for building patterns as she moved, patterns made of the different numbers and suits on the cards, in addition to the need capture her opponent's cards.

But it wasn't the normal strategy of the game that filled her mind now. The cards struck her as words in a strange, constructed script, and she wondered how she could play them out to talk to Pavresh, to ask him about Chaitan and Rashul. About Ekana.

His letter had hinted that something went wrong back in Romnai, but she couldn't figure out what. Each time she imagined the cards stringing together to form a message, she lost it. The pattern fell apart, and the meaning was lost.

"I believe you go first, *tisrah*."

Indima looked at Pavresh's face, wondering if he would have any idea if she did play a message with the cards. He looked perfectly innocent, the model of a cheetah jati servant. She decided to try to communicate.

"Yes, it is my turn." She laid a card with an older man on it, letting her finger linger over the picture for a moment.

Pavresh's card with a cat on it bore no relation to it, not as the meaning she'd given it in her mind, so before she laid another card, she turned to her father.

"Father, what stories do you remember of the last time our soldiers fought the mumblers?" As she asked it, she kept her finger on the old man, whispering over and over in her head, *Chaitan*, as if Pavresh would be able to hear her.

Jinshu looked up from a sheaf of paper he'd been reading, a bit bewildered. "The war, Indima? What makes you ask that?"

Indima kept her face relaxed, though it was a struggle, and shrugged. "These woods, I guess. I haven't seen any mumblers, but it makes me think of them."

The land was rough here, exposed rock showing through the snow on the sides of hills. Trees struggled in the cracks of the rocks.

When she looked back from the windows, her father was shaking his head. "I don't think you have to worry about them here, dear. Besides, we have soldiers riding with us."

He went back to his reading, and Indima was relieved. She hadn't wanted him to actually talk about the war, but she hoped the exchange was enough to get Pavresh thinking. She looked directly into his eyes until he nodded. It was the ritual nod of table kiwan, but she thought she saw more than that in it as well.

With a slight smile, she played a musician to make sure he understand, resting her hand so it touched both pictures. Then she nodded to him.

He played a soldier.

She couldn't stop the gasp that came then, and her mother immediately looked her way. "Sorry. I just thought of something." The words came out quickly and didn't sound quite natural to herself, but her mother shrugged and looked away.

Play continued, and they weren't limited to the new cards

but could point at the earlier ones as well, and the game approached a true conversation. Pavresh pointed to the soldier card over and over and a card that was supposed to show night, but she decided he meant it as the darkness of a cell.

Neither paid any attention to the actual strategy of the game, and if anyone had looked at the board, that would have been obvious. Finally, they seemed to have reached the limits of the cards, and Pavresh gathered them up.

Indima sat back to try to understand what he'd told her. She wasn't sure how much she could trust the conversation, not that Pavresh would have lied to her, but that the cards were so open to multiple meanings. But as far as she could guess between their strange conversation and the cryptic note earlier, Rashul had staged some kind of demonstration and been arrested along with many of the others and even Chaitan himself.

That made her angry, a stronger emotion than any she'd felt in many twelve-days. She'd been curious and somewhat excited at learning of Pavresh's presence among them. The thought of being in the fabled Silk City gave her an odd twinge of something that wasn't quite excitement but near enough. She'd felt sad, of course. And angry at herself and her family and jati. But all those emotions had been subdued compared to this. Chaitan didn't deserve any ill treatment. He was a hero of the land, someone who strove to make it better. He was a great man who should have been given his own place among the council of princes to help guide the valley toward greatness.

Pavresh had somehow escaped—if he told her how in the game, she hadn't understood. And Jaritta was safe on the streets. Namrani, the musician, he wasn't sure. Ekana, Iksheen, Marankiya all captured as far as he knew. The city of Romnai wasn't safe for him or anyone known to be connected to Chaitan, and strange things were happening among the princes, though that part was especially unclear. Intentionally so, she guessed. Pavresh was caught up in this somehow. He was doing more than simply fleeing the dangerous capital. But what that was she couldn't divine.

Thoughts of Chaitan's house filled her then, images of dancing and music and arcist magic, of hot tisane and impassioned speeches. Tears rose to the corners of her eyes and threatened to fall, but she couldn't let them. Not with her parents sitting right there. She tried to lose her thoughts in the view of the passing land, but the images of Romnai were too strong.

The afternoon passed, both slow and fast it seemed later, the strange timeless hours spinning around in her head.

* * *

That night they pulled in again beside a high windbreak, but this evening was milder, and they came out from their sleighs to gather around a large fire. There were more soldiers traveling with them than Indima had realized. They joined the servants and the weavers, and for a few moments, it seemed there were no castes there, no jatis, only a group of equal travelers.

It didn't last long. One of the young weaver children began complaining of the cold, and Kisar, their mother, sent a servant for a cloak and a blanket. Then another for the other child and their father Ambal demanded a gourd of freshly brewed tisane.

And like that, all the pieces of Eghsal society fell back into their places. The soldiers drifted to one side of the fire, keeping an eye on the darkness beyond their circle. The servants enjoyed the fire in their own clump when they weren't fetching things for the weavers. The sleigh drivers, whom Indima guessed to be lower caste *nefli*, stayed farther from the fire as if they didn't enjoy its heat. And the weavers reclined on wooden benches, covered in warm cushions that the servants brought.

They acknowledged the others only to demand things.

Rashul, she was sure, would have felt sickened by the behavior. Indima watched Pavresh for a while, but he blended in well with the other servants, and she soon found herself staring into the high flames.

Fire. Her people worshiped it as the source of all gods. She tried to imagine Tiespetre stepping from that fire. What would he look like? In the sacred paintings, he was always tall with a handsome *kortru* face and a strong body. His skin danced with flames, and his dark hair trailed into smoke. He was what young girls learned to desire for husbands. Or at least lovers.

As she pictured his descent from fire to earth, it wasn't the sacred images she saw. She saw a shorter man with a lighter, *nefli* face and fisherman's hands. And more disturbing, she saw her mental picture of Ekana transform to a thin man with cinnamon skin and a shifting face that matched the faces all around.

She glanced at Pavresh among the servants then forced Ekana's image back into her mind.

Just then a voice spoke in her ear.

"Ekana sends his love."

Indima startled and turned toward the voice. She didn't recognize the servant standing in the dark. There was something malicious in his voice.

The other weavers were clumped a bit away from her, engrossed in some discussion, so none noticed the man beside her. She didn't like the way he'd spoken or the fact that he approached her like this, but if he knew something about Ekana…

"What? What do you know about him?"

"I know much about him, *tisrah*."

"What news…" she began, but he continued without waiting for her.

"I know about his…" he paused, and in the dark, she

couldn't see his eyes, but his head clearly moved up and down as if seeing her body beneath her robe, "indiscretions. I know about his capture."

Indima's heart pounded, and she noticed her fists were clenched.

"And escape."

She drew in a sharp breath. Had he broken free? Escaped to the sea and his old life?

"And recapture."

Indima's shoulders dropped, and she bowed her head.

"But I know more than that, as well. I know of his activities. With rebels and revolutionaries."

He leaned close to her then, and his smile was a cruel thing in the firelight. "And he was not alone among those people. I know that, too. Indima."

She drew back from him, feeling her name as if it were a slap. He knew too much, things her family and jati didn't—and couldn't—know.

"Why are you telling me this? What do you want?"

He pulled away from her and stood in the perfect cheetah jati pose. Except for his smile. "Nothing now, *tisrah*. I merely want you to know and beware. Sometime in the coming months I may have need of your assistance. I want you to be perfectly ready to give it."

With that he left her and rejoined the other servants. Indima shifted closer to the fire, but the chills she felt couldn't be warmed by any fire, no matter how sacred. She whispered a prayer but didn't know which god to send it to. Perhaps Paxu, out here in the wild, but he was unpredictable and often drunk, so the priests said.

After offering the prayer to him, she said a quick word to Kwona, the mare goddess who herself had been in trouble for an affair from time to time. If anyone would understand and sympathize, it would be her.

* * *

The first Indima knew of their approach to the Silk City, late in the third day, was the cry of the drivers up ahead, passed down the line sleigh to sleigh. She was playing a form of solitaire, not with the kiwan cards but the circular playing cards. She threw them down on the table and leaped to her feet, hurrying to a window at the front.

The driver's legs dangled in front of her, and through them were the heads of the horse team, another sleigh beyond them. But farther up, between the lead sleigh and the columns of steam from the lava bed that warmed the region, was the city. There was something powerful in the sight of those gray walls, crafted to be as fine as any silk cloak yet strong enough to withstand the mumblers. The lava field itself helped the walls with that purpose, curling around the city to form an odd sort of peninsula. The twists of steam gave the city an otherworldly look, as if they were about to ride into one of those stories of the Forgotten South.

A rail spur from the south met their road up ahead. A train that looked significantly different from the one they had ridden was pulling away, car after car that must have carried grains and other goods to the city. None of the cars would have been fit for travelers, even of the lower castes.

On the northern side of the road, running right up to the steam beds were fields of cotton. She recognized them from stories of the city. Each narrow strip would contain a slightly different variety of cotton as her people experimented to create new forms of cloth for the day when even their skill and magic could no longer preserve the silks of the Forgotten South. Farther along the steam beds themselves, sunlight glanced off glass roofs where other experiments grew.

There was a feel to the place of antiquity, as if it was far older than Romnai. It wasn't, though the weavers had first established themselves out here centuries ago, not long after the founding of the capital city. But Romnai felt more modern, with its ever-shifting buildings, its constantly improved streets, its yearly expansions. Perhaps it was the lack of walls in the capital city that made the difference. The mumblers were a much lesser threat that far downriver.

The sleighs stopped outside the city a fair ways, and Indima looked around in confusion. They were at the top of a rise with a gentle slope that could lead them right to the front gate of the city. Why should they stop here?

She didn't wonder for long. The driver jumped from his perch and came inside while Pavresh and Shidhi joined the other servants gathering beside the sleighs.

"The snow's too wet up ahead, *tisrae*, and doesn't even cover the road as we get closer to the city. So we'll have to get out here."

The snow looked plenty deep that Indima didn't exactly relish the thought of walking through it. She hadn't brought the boots or furs for such things, but she supposed she could if she must.

Deciding to be sure, she asked, "Must we walk through that snow then?"

"For you, *tisrah*? No. I will carry you on my back, a trunk of luggage in each hand."

She looked at the little man and laughed. "I think not, driver. I would rather walk."

Her mother muttered something to her father. She couldn't hear what, but it seemed the driver might have overheard.

"Forgive me, *tisrae*," he said. "I do not mean to forget my place. I am simply pleased to be back here for a time, with no need to drive again to the tracks for a twelve-day or more." Even trying to sound chastised, he couldn't keep the excitement from his voice.

"And how will we honestly reach the city, driver?" her

mother asked. The melting snow outside had entered her voice.

"Wagons will soon arrive for your goods and luggage, *tisrah*, and carriages for you. Wheeled instead of blades." He stuck his head out the door and looked toward the city. "Your servants are already deciding who will stay to serve you and help the city's servants load the wagons and who will go on ahead on foot to make sure all is prepared for your stay in the city."

The servants were splitting into two groups, and Indima looked beyond them at the city again. The snow did not look so deep over the road.

"I will go to the city now, then."

"You will wait, Indima." Her father moved to block the door.

"No. I will take Shidhi with me and see to our accommodations." Neither of her parents looked as if they were going to allow it. "Listen. We're this close, and I've never been to the Silk City before. It's been a part of so many of the stories you told me, so many tales from everyone else in the jati. I don't want to stay cooped in this sleigh waiting when the city's this close."

She glanced at the driver as she said this and noticed a smile play at the edges of his mouth. But he'd already pushed the limits of what her parents would allow and wouldn't be likely to say anything in her defense.

Neither said anything for a moment, but her father nodded. "You may then. I suppose it is a safe city. Be mindful nonetheless, and keep the servant with you. Take the other one also…Parsh. It will look better to arrive with a pair of servants rather than just one."

"Yes, father," she said, and quickly stepped out into the wet snow.

She hurried over to the servants and told Shidhi and Pavresh to attend her. Pavresh, she understood, had been assigned to stay behind and assist with the unloading, but with her instructions, the other servants had no choice but to rearrange their groups. With her two servants breaking the trail, she headed down the slope toward the city. Her own city in some ways, more than Romnai ever should have been.

At the head of the peninsula, they crossed a bridge over a dry moat. Indima looked to the side and saw a strange device beside a pool of boiling mud and wondered if they had some way to divert the mud into the moat. The ground beyond was broken by further defenses that she didn't bother trying to understand. Her focus was on the wall ahead.

Its height compared to the size of the city lent to the silk-like image, and it wasn't smooth but billowed vertically like cloth draped over a fine piece of furniture. The southern sun cast shadows along the ripples, making them seem to move as she approached looking up. She had to bring her gaze down to stop her dizziness.

The gate was equally difficult to focus on, an intricate weaving of stone and iron. It had less the look of a silkworm's silk and more of a spider's web, fine but, she guessed, deceptively strong. Not so delicate as it seemed.

It was open for them, and they walked through into the city itself.

"Where are we supposed to go?" Indima asked the servants.

Shidhi stopped walking to address her with proper respect. "We have directions, *tisrah*. Ahead and down some side streets."

"You don't have to stop to talk to me, Shidhi." She laughed as Shidhi continued leading her up the street.

"Yes, *tisrah*."

Both servants looked around and stared as much as she wanted to, but she kept her looks to glances, trying her best to appear confident, familiar with the sights. To her parents it was vitally important how she carried herself here and what kind of impression she gave to anyone who saw her, especially any unmarried men. When they were several blocks past the entrance, Indima turned and looked again at the gate. From the inside it was less impressive, but the view beyond was a fascinating one, of rolling steam and melting snow and the plots of land fenced off for cotton.

A figure walked through behind them, then dashed off to one side. She looked more closely as he disappeared down the side street. It was the servant who'd approached her at their camp the other night.

"I wonder what he's doing there."

She hadn't meant to say it out loud, but Pavresh turned immediately and asked, "Who?" He added a hasty, "*tisrah,*" before she could answer.

"That other servant, the one who didn't serve us during the trip. I'm sure it's nothing."

"Where did he go?"

Indima looked at Pavresh and realized that whatever reason the arcist had for coming to the Silk City, it must have something to do with that other servant.

She explained where, specifically but breezily for Shidhi's benefit, as if it were nothing, and they continued on their way. But the Silk City suddenly felt a lot less welcoming, as if a threat had come with them, a danger from the capital city.

The sounds of the city were lost in the echoes of the man's voice, cruel and threatening, and she feared what further humiliations might yet befall her.

Chapter 16

Even when Ekana could smell the salt and decaying fish of the ocean, he hardly dared walk openly. Salt replaced sulfur in the air here in Jarnur where warm ocean currents took the place of steaming volcanic pools to heat the city. Ekana looked up and down the road that ran beside the tracks and stepped out from the winter-bare brush. He wasn't sad to leave the game trails and unmarked paths behind for the road. A twelve-day and a half it had taken him to come from Romnai, what he could have traveled on foot in eight or nine days if he'd dared walk openly on the road.

Maybe it hadn't been such a good idea. By now, word would have reached the coastal city of the failed revolution, and anyone looking for him would have arrived. Would anyone be looking for him? He wasn't even sure who to avoid. The government leaders wouldn't be pleased that he'd left, wouldn't be pleased that anyone involved in the attempt had escaped. So, the princes and their soldiers could be after him.

Ekana resisted the urge to swing his head constantly. The street was straight, with a number of people in sight, both mounted and afoot. Looking suspicious would only attract their attention.

The silk weavers, meanwhile, still bore a grudge. That thought didn't make him scared so much as angry. If he found a silk weaver here, he'd probably pick up a rock from the side of the road and use it as a weapon. He wondered where Indima was. In the Silk City already? Still in the train on the way? But that image of the train wasn't one he wanted to dwell on.

And either way, she was a captive of her family and jati. Ekana wanted to picture her in her ancestral home on the east end of the valley, to see in his mind how she passed her days, how the silk weavers welcomed her, but he had no idea what to imagine.

Out here beside the sea, there would likely be a few weavers, but not many. So that should be a lesser worry. Still, he watched those on the street leading into the city, looking for the telltale silks. Everyone was so bundled against the cold that it made careful study difficult.

People nodded to him as they passed, and Ekana made himself nod back. Jarnur was not a small city by any means, but it still felt much smaller than Romnai, and the people, mostly *nefli* fishers, extended their greetings without judgment. Here was a place that at least approached Rashul's ideals, where caste was less rigid and society more free.

But he didn't want to think of Rashul either. Rashul whose fancy words had done nothing to change society or protect him and Indima. He saw again the soldiers storming the warehouse, saw Iksheen fighting back with a knife, saw Rashul being led away. It made him wonder if he was in more danger from them than the princes and soldiers and silk weavers combined. It wouldn't look right that he had escaped while they were all imprisoned. If Rashul had supporters out here, would he be branded a coward? A turncoat? Betrayer?

As the road passed into the outer edge of houses, Ekana couldn't help relaxing somewhat. These were streets he knew, houses he'd grown up playing around. He walked more quickly, heading straight for the riverbank. The road came in on the southern side of the river, where the city was only a narrow strip. But it was in this strip that he'd grown up.

Ekana reached the river, wide and fast here at the mouth. Trying to make his ragged cloak as presentable as possible, he turned from the main road and the ferry at the end into the unpaved streets that straggled among fish-wife houses. The men wouldn't be here at this time of day, but out in their boats, which were their own houses in many ways. He made for his mother's house.

Women looked from their windows and doorways, gazing suspiciously at his ragged clothes, far too light for Jarnur, even as spring warmed the city. He nodded back to each, doing his best to imagine he'd never left the sea. The children running about the streets appeared to ignore him, but their play always took them conveniently away from him. When they had to come down the same road, they dashed around along the far walls or chased each other into the gaps between houses until he passed.

The walls of his mother's house showed their age. This bank of the river had been settled a century earlier as the northern bank became crowded, and most of the houses were still the original buildings. Moss climbed up the sides, shifting to ivy higher up, the roots slowly eating into the clay and rock.

His mother stood outside the door.

She froze when she looked at his face, her eyebrows up, her mouth open slightly. Ekana stopped also, taking in her appearance. She looked no older or younger than he remembered. Just the same woman who'd always cared for him until he was old enough to join the boats out in the bay.

She was first to speak. "I'd thought you drowned."

"I went to Romnai, not to sea, Ma."

She shrugged and narrowed her eyes. "A man can drown on land, too. I've learned that much. A man can drown anywhere."

For some reason, her words brought to mind Indima's face. Maybe he *had* nearly drowned. He saw her boarding a train, looking only down at her feet but still graceful, still a dancer, still his Indima. The image shattered when his mother stepped forward and gave him a brief embrace.

As she pulled him back into the house, she added, "Well, at

the least it's clear you've been shipwrecked. Come inside and we'll take care of that."

The inside of the house looked as he remembered, and for a moment, he felt like an adolescent again, awkward and uncertain of his place. But then he remembered making love to Indima and he remembered fighting for Rashul, and the moment passed. He was not a youth. He walked easily to a rough chair and sat.

His mother asked him nothing and said little as she moved about the small space. But soon he had a gourd of hot tisane, slightly salty as the people of Jarnur preferred it, and a plate of steamed shrimp.

"Eat," she said simply. "Recover. Tell what you want later, tomorrow when you're out in the boat with your father."

Ekana cringed at first at the thought of going fishing so soon, but it passed quickly as he realized he looked forward to it. There was a comforting familiarity to the boats of the sea, just as there was to his hard-edged mother and her little house where he'd grown up.

He drank another sip of the tisane then turned his attention to the shrimp. Only this existed, the plate of food, the familiar house, the taste of the sea in the air. For a time, all other thoughts and memories could disappear.

* * *

When the memories overcame his sense of ease in that house, it was one in particular that performed itself over and over in his mind, like a dance at Chaitan's house with no end, the musician and arcist cruelly repeating a theme, forcing the dancers to keep moving in the same exact motions. Memories allowed for no improvisation.

He'd tried to forget the image as he'd journeyed, and at one level, he had. But he could never completely banish it.

After he'd escaped the soldiers, Ekana hadn't immediately fled the city. It was dangerous, he knew. Foolish. But he found places to hide near the river docks, beside the bridge that crossed the river to the train rails. He hadn't stayed long, maybe two days, although he couldn't be sure anymore. But in those few days, he saw something that branded his mind.

What wind there was blew the steam of the volcanic fields away from the river, but the cold air lifted mist from the water below so it reached up to touch the bridge above. A line of carriages crossed together, and Ekana watched them as he had every carriage since he started hiding there. The carriages stopped beside the train tracks. The servants had already been there most of the morning, loading the luggage onto a waiting car. Now their masters arrived, ready to depart.

Ekana ignored the servants, trying to see inside the carriages. Was that her, seated in the shadows of that carriage in the center? He longed to run across the bridge to her.

Soon the servants had the last of the luggage arranged and came over to help the passengers into another car. Indima stepped out, head bowed and covered with cloth. But he knew it was her. He knew those shoulders, knew the way she walked, her poise that of a dancer even then. She looked weary and sad, or was that merely his wishes? The river was too wide here for a perfect view.

She climbed the train and disappeared, and some part of him was sure he'd never see her again. Not dancing on a stage, not lying in his arms, not even peeking from a window for a last glimpse of her former home.

He nearly turned away, but something caught his attention. A servant, but he looked somehow familiar. Ekana studied the servant until he entered the train and stood there watching as the engine pulled the cars away with an awful shriek. The train disappeared beyond the curve of river, a puff of smoke marking its path.

Ekana's mind flipped back and forth between his final image of Indima and the familiar figure that would be journeying with her as he walked away, down the river. Who was he? It was only when he stopped seeing the final image of Indima and imagined her dancing that he realized how he knew that face. The arcist! Pavresh. Why was he going to the Silk City with her? What did it mean?

That same day, with thoughts spinning in his head, bubbling like the thick mud in the volcanic fields, he fled the city for the sea.

And now in Jarnur, he wondered again. What was Pavresh doing there? Clearly there was something more to the arcist than he'd known back in Romnai. Had he somehow betrayed Indima and Ekana? Had his words brought an end to their relationship? And what would he do now, with Ekana out of the way? There had been nothing suspect in the arcist, nothing in his words or magic that should have warned him. Pavresh might have looked admiringly at Indima when they met, but most men did, and that had always pleased Ekana. Except not now. Conversations took on new meanings, the magic Pavresh had used as she danced, their body language that he didn't remember but now invented to match his suspicions. As much as he tried to deny it, he couldn't help but see Indima with her arms around the arcist, leading him into a secret room in that distant city or stepping with him into the shadows of an empty hallway.

Ekana forced his fists to relax, although they resisted it. Maybe some time fishing with the other men of his jati was exactly what he needed.

* * *

The waves hit the sides of the boat, sending up spray that froze on the edges of Ekana's thick coat. The ocean currents kept Jarnur warmer than it might otherwise be this time of year, but that didn't mean it actually kept it *warm*. Ekana thought of the steaming baths of Romnai and shivered.

They were net fishing that day, dragging specially-constructed nets through the sluggish saltwater, nets that wouldn't snap in the cold, even as they rose out of the water and became lined with ice. The fish they drew up protested weakly, themselves slowed by the cold water. Ekana pulled them aboard and quickly helped the other men empty the fish into the bins that filled most of the center of their ship.

This time of year, the catch was all these over-sized, dark fish, called *rebes*. They were not the best-tasting fish, but their meat was easily preserved with sea salt and shipped upriver to the capital and the rest of the valley. Would Indima eat these very fish he pulled up, months from now after their long journey? Would Pavresh?

No, he couldn't think of trains, wouldn't think of Indima and Pavresh. He grimaced and forced the thoughts down. Let his mind be like the cold water of the bay. Let those thoughts drown. Here, in this boat. Now. That's what he needed to think about. Nothing else.

Ekana had avoided eating *rebe* as much as possible in Romnai, though he would be willing to eat some freshly cooked tonight when they returned. Even uncured, they had an overwhelmingly salty flavor.

His body still remembered this kind of work, and he fell into it easily without losing any of the grace of dancing he'd developed in Romnai. The boat moved in the waves, and he moved with it, sliding up and down the deck, wondering and then forcing himself not to wonder what kind of theme an arcist like Pavresh might put to this dance.

As they moved to another place to drop their nets, Ekana looked west and south to the horizon. The waves became wilder farther out, seas too much for their small boat. The

214

success of the train inland meant that some were experimenting with putting a steam engine in a ship and taking it beyond the limit of the fishing boats, and who knew what they might find? Six centuries ago, their ancestors had somehow traveled through those impossible waters, coming up the coast from the Forgotten South, which was anything but forgotten by the people of Eghsal. Since then, none had ever arrived to tell them how things fared there. And none had survived the attempts to return, not by hugging the coast, not by sailing farther out in the sea, and certainly not by attempting the mountains that bordered their land.

Maybe that would be a better fate for him. Better than brooding on Indima's absence. Better than thinking about the arcist who could see her while Ekana was so far away. Better than remembering the failure of Rashul's movement. No, there was little good in his memories of Romnai except a few brief moments with Indima. Rashul couldn't protect that relationship, and Chaitan couldn't protect them, and nothing anyone did could make them acceptable.

"Watch out!"

Ekana jerked from his thoughts and ducked, but it was a person walking he needed to avoid, and ducking did nothing for that. The man knocked into Ekana, and both fell to the deck.

The man pushed himself back up and glared at Ekana. The captain, Ekana realized with a wry shake of his head. The one *brenil* on the ship, and not ashamed to remind the *nefli* workers.

"I apologize, sir."

"Get to the stern and help pull the net into place. And stay out of my way." He hurried to the bow and directed the men in arranging the net just right. Ekana brushed off his thick clothing and hurried over to work the net.

Yet one more reminder of the impossibility of Rashul's naïve dreams of a new society.

* * *

The streets on the north side of the river mouth were finer, wide, and evenly paved with smooth stones. After wandering various neighborhoods nostalgically, Ekana returned to the river-side avenue and strode up the wharf. The current of the river met the waves of the ocean here, freshwater and salt mixing with the tides. He'd forgotten how much he loved it, the sights, the sounds, the ocean scents. Arctic birds circled and dived for food.

He walked past many side streets and many docked fishing boats before he reached what he'd come to see. The steamer. It was an awkward-looking ship, not at all like the graceful boats he was used to. Huge metal smokestacks up top, a wooden hull, a bow that looked as if they'd tried to make it resemble a train rather than a boat. No, he wasn't going to think about trains.

Ekana approached it more closely. A section of the side was gone to show passersby the interior of the ship where the monstrous furnace burned. He joined the crowd that was gathered, staring into the newest technology. Some whispered, as if the engine were a holy thing. Others shouted and pointed. Ekana said nothing but peered inside. The metal of the engine glowed red.

Glancing up and down the length of the ship, he noticed something else. At the river docks in Romnai a few people had been experimenting with steamboats, but those were propelled by giant paddle wheels that dipped in and out of the water. This had no such thing. As far as he could tell, whatever moved the ship was entirely underwater.

He walked away from the showcase of the engine to see the rest of the hull, imagining as he did what it would be like to sail such a ship deep into the sea. And what would they find if they reached the Forgotten South so many years after leaving? All they had of the south were half-formed tales of silk and demanding kings and religious stories that spoke of battles but really told more of what the gods wanted than of any actual history.

Perhaps somewhere in the south they'd already achieved the ideal society Rashul only dreamed of, a land without castes where anyone could live where they wished and marry whom they wanted to. A society without betrayals. And even if there wasn't such a place, Ekana could easily forget Rashul's empty promises in exchange for the excitement and adventure of discovery. Was that willingness itself a betrayal? No matter anymore.

Ekana returned to the space before the engine and noticed one small knot of gawkers. They whispered, as some of the others had, but as Ekana approached he realized that for them there was something religious about the engine. Or nearly so.

"The divine changes as our world does," one man said. "It reminds us explicitly that it is the source of all we have, even this mighty power to sail the seas."

Ekana's eyes fell to the belts around their waists, the roped kustis. Many men of their society wore kustis to gather their robes, but these were slightly different. They appeared to be made of a stronger material, and the knots that held them in place were distinctively ritualistic. These were Enshi. Only in Jarnur were they allowed to practice their religion openly. The arcist Pavresh had worn such a kusti. Ekana hadn't put that together at first, but in the midst of the attempted revolution, it had occurred to him. What was the connection? Was it something religious that sent Pavresh to the Silk City with Ekana's beloved? And why must his thoughts keep returning to that man here in his own home, a place the arcist claimed he'd never been?

"So you say," another answered. "But perhaps it's simply another example of humans trying to harness the divine, yoke it to their own purpose. Surely there's a danger in it, for the power of divinity is greater than our control."

Ekana turned away, no longer interested in the steamer or the crowd around it. Whatever reason Pavresh had for tagging along with Indima while Ekana was trapped out here beside the sea; whatever divine power he thought was leading him there, Ekana hoped it would break from his control. Push him down. And maybe sling Indima away, straight back to his own arms.

Chapter 17

Pavresh wiped cooled steam from his face to better see the volcanic fields that surrounded the city. From his vantage at the edge of the narrow wall, the Silk City looked to be in perpetual danger. It seemed that any day would bring a shift of the molten rock below and melt the city and all its silks. But whereas that exact thing had forced the ancestors of the people of Eghsal to abandon their original city, the Silk City had stood for centuries, protected by the dangerous land surrounding it.

Something about those fields felt different from the much larger ones south of Romnai. Maybe it was nothing more than the fact that here he could see all the way across them. The mountains on the other side were perfectly distinct, the gray rocks cut by streaks of yellow, the bushes beginning to turn green, an impressive waterfall where a small stream of snow melt fell down from higher than the height of the wall to wander off, away from the steam bed. This time of year, the water cascaded wildly to the valley floor.

Despite the majestic and terrifying surroundings, the Silk City itself had a way of taking urgency and turning it inside out. The need for information had seemed so important when he arrived. He had followed Teert whenever he could in those first days, sneaking through the streets and casually walking past windows. Nothing seemed to happen. Teert visited people, but Pavresh couldn't find out anything about those people, and often Teert simply disappeared.

So the days passed, and Pavresh paid less attention to Prince Dartak's servant. He worked for Indima's family and occasionally played card kiwan with her. In the evenings, Ambal often summoned him to his house to play real kiwan, so he came to know those servants as well as the servants assigned to Indima's family. But none of it led to any new information that would help Jasfer.

He resigned himself to the fact that he'd been sent here simply to keep him away from the trouble facing Chaitan and Rashul rather than for any useful purpose.

Atop the wall several twelve-days after arriving, Pavresh felt the first hint of urgency return.

Beside the waterfall a track descended into the valley, and figures stepped out onto it from the deep fissures of the mountainside. They came down quickly, as if sure of themselves despite the steep path. At first Pavresh thought he should run and warn someone. Surely these were mumblers, descending from their mountain homes into the valley that had once been their ancestors'. But he stood and watched, and the precision of the line of people struck him. This was not how the stories told of the mumblers, not this marching in perfect precision.

They swung around the western edge of the steam beds, between the geysers and the stream, which meandered off to the west and presumably to the distant river itself. Then the figures came clear, their dark faces visible beneath modern helmets. They were soldiers. Wolf jati, undoubtedly. The helmet of one was covered with something that might have been a wolf pelt, falling down his back to create a cloak. So why come down from the mountains?

Pavresh thought of the abandoned city he'd seen from the train, and all the complexities of his mission, of Jasfer's mysteries, came back to him.

The troop of soldiers, several dozen in all, continued around toward the road that led from the city to the train tracks. Soldiers from the city, not wolf jati but from a small jati unique to the place, rode out to meet them. Pavresh watched them and wondered where the soldiers would be going. Already months ago, Jasfer's cousin Prince Samatrit had been ordered to post soldiers around the abandoned city for surveillance. These couldn't be going there, unless he'd decided to rotate units. But with everything they carried, it was clear they were leaving for an extended time. This was no quick foray to catch a wandering band of mumblers.

So how would he manage to learn about their mission? He began plotting where he could loiter, what tavern they might visit, where they might choose to talk, and how he could place himself nearby to learn what he could.

The two groups of soldiers met on the road, a friendly meeting it appeared. Pavresh supposed that the city's soldiers felt they had more in common with the wolf jati than with the weavers and servants who surrounded them. It was probably a welcome change to talk with other soldiers.

Before he could leave to get himself settled anywhere strategic, the wolf jati troop swung away from the city and headed along the road. In too great a hurry to even spend the night in comfort. Pavresh leaned against a crenelation and tried to imagine where they might be going and why such a hurry.

It had to have something to do with Jasfer and Dartak and the intrigue of princes. No other arcist theme fit.

The Silk City soldiers returned to the walls, and Pavresh wandered back toward the house of Indima's family, his mind racing over ways to learn anything from those soldiers who'd gone out to meet the others.

* * *

Now Pavresh walked the streets with different eyes, not looking for Teert or wondering where he might go, but paying attention to the soldiers. They moved throughout the city as a police force, stopped often at certain taverns, patrolled the high walls, and slept in a converted house near the gate.

In the house directly beside these barracks, the other family from the train was staying. Datri. She'd shown him some measure of fondness on the train. Probably forgotten him already by now, but it might be enough to simply get to her house and speak with the servants.

Later that day, he was back serving Indima's family. When he went up to her room to deliver a load of wood for the small fireplace, he struggled to find some way to convince her to take or send him to Datri's house. Shidhi was there as Indima's personal servant, so he didn't dare speak openly, but, he pulled the arcist magic around him like a thick coat, adding layer on layer so that she might notice.

"Forgive me, *tisrah*." The magic named him an innocent helper, the ideal servant, or as close as arcist magic came to the concept of a servant. "You seem to be stuck here in your room often. Perhaps you should visit the other *tisrah* from the train sometimes and play cards with her." As he said this, he sent a sharp dart of arcist magic that changed his image into that of a spy sneaking through dark alleys. It was as brief as he could make it and returned immediately to the innocence of the earlier image. His hope was that Shidhi would notice nothing or quickly dismiss anything she did happen to pick up. But Indima, knowing his past and guessing some of why he'd come out here would pick it up.

Her eyes widened as he did it, and he knew she must have noticed.

"Perhaps, servant. Thank you for your concern. I will consider it."

As careful as he'd tried to be, Shidhi watched him suspiciously as he left the room. He bent all his efforts, magical and otherwise, on seeming—on *being*—the perfect servant.

An hour or so later, he was summoned to attend Indima as she and Shidhi walked through the streets to Datri's house. She could have ridden a carriage, but then she would have had little excuse for bringing Pavresh along.

At the house, he accompanied her inside and smiled briefly at Datri. Her responding expression was far less coy than he would have expected, which worried him. As soon as he could, he left to join the house's servants in their own room downstairs.

That first time he did nothing more than meet them. He'd learned by now how the cheetah jati servants interacted, though he still had to draw on his supposed isolation with a reclusive master in Jarnur to explain the jokes he didn't get and the cues he missed. Fortunately, he'd yet to meet any servants who'd ever served in Jarnur.

As they returned to Indima's house, she said casually, "That was good, actually, to get out for a bit. But I'm not sure if I would keep finding it good many times or if it was just a nice break that would soon grow as dull as everything else in this city."

The way she said it was clearly directed at Pavresh. He tried to think of a way to let her know that he'd like to return often in the next few days.

Shidhi answered, apparently unaware of the hidden meaning. "Whatever seems suitable to you, *tisrah*. I can attend you as easily there as at your house."

"And I," Pavresh quickly answered. "However often you wish to go, I can accompany you."

Indima nodded, and Pavresh hoped it would be enough. The following days proved that it was as Indima spent most of each afternoon with the younger girl. Each time they entered, he offered Datri a proper bow, and each time her responding smile became more knowing. It cast an odd cloud over his mind as he descended to spend time with the servants.

After a few days, he decided to simply ask directly about the soldiers next door. Pavresh relaxed next to Phangun, a slightly built man approaching middle-age who had spoken with him the other times he'd been there.

"What about these soldiers next door? Out west there was nothing like them, just the larger soldier jatis."

Phangun shrugged. "They're good people, I guess. Keep to themselves a lot, but maybe not as much as soldiers where you come from. We're pretty isolated out here, so they'll mix with us sometimes. Go out drinking."

Afraid that the servant might get curious for his reasons for asking, he pulled a bit of arcist magic around himself, giving the sense of an eager lover. Then he asked, "And their women? You get to…mix with them too?"

"Not usually." Phangun shook his head. "They marry with the other soldier jatis is all. Not us."

Pavresh let disappointment show on his face. After a brief silence he added, "Oh, that's right. I remember seeing some soldiers pass by the other day. Wolf jati, I'd guess. They didn't seem to be picking up brides at the time."

Phangun laughed. "No. And they've been streaming by since last fall. I sometimes wonder if there are any soldiers left up in the mountains."

Pavresh moved the conversation to other topics and later spoke with some of the other servants, but his thoughts kept coming back to that final statement. So many soldiers were leaving the mountains. At whose bidding? And where were they going? He hadn't seen the numbers he'd expect around the ancient capital. Perhaps they were gathered on the south side, away from the river and railroad tracks, but was that enough to explain it?

When Pavresh was summoned to attend Indima on her way back through the streets, his mind raced through all the questions and possible answers. He forgot, for a moment, to keep his eyes downward as a servant ought to. Only when he looked directly into Datri's wide eyes did he think to lower them.

As he hurried out with Indima, he wondered what the other girl had seen in his eyes.

* * *

More twelve-days passed, and Pavresh learned little else, either about the wolf jati or about Teert. He continued spending time with the servants at Datri's house and other servants also, learning the ways of the City of Silk. It felt so different from Romnai, though mostly in ways he couldn't quite identify. The manner in which the people spoke to each other. The way they walked up and down the streets. Even the baths laid out along the edge of the steam beds. All subtly different. Each spoke of the people's isolation together, the way the people were so far from other places and therefore forced to come together often, even across caste and jati lines.

In Romnai, it seemed to him now, it had been the opposite. The people were crammed all together, but being directly on the connecting river and railroad, they were tied to all places, anywhere within the valley. Somehow that very closeness drove them each apart. So in the capital, they were more isolated as a result. A paradox, and one he wasn't quite sure he could grasp yet.

It seemed an important understanding, one that would improve his ability with his magic and maybe even help with his task out here. So, he wandered the streets whenever he wasn't needed by Indima's family. Watching, listening, thinking. He remembered Prince Jasfer talking about being able to see the lines of power and influence in a gathering of princes and wondered if perhaps he was learning to see the same things in a more general way, the interactions of people and their surroundings. It was almost like the city itself was made of words he could read. Each building a sentence, the movements of each person a paragraph to be read and translated into a more human language.

He was so focused on the way the streets and buildings pulled people in specific ways, the way certain doorways exerted pressure on those people—words—passing by, that he didn't at first register the voice coming from one of those open doorways.

It was a distinctive entrance, wide with intricate carvings in the wooden jambs. The way it opened onto the street with a small halo of light drew gazes from passersby. Including Pavresh. He was staring directly at the entrance when a familiar figure stepped out, still talking to someone inside. Teert looked straight back at Pavresh and started on noticing his stare.

Pavresh tore his gaze away, trying desperately to figure out what words they'd been saying. They'd been talking loudly, so it probably wasn't anything secretive, but even so, it might be a clue. The words were too jumbled in his memory. He'd been paying attention to other things, another language that wasn't made of speech.

As he hurried around a nearby corner, it occurred to him how suspicious his actions must have looked. He'd forgotten so much since his brief time spying for Jasfer. He should have walked confidently by, perhaps nodding his head to the servant. They knew each other from the train, after all, even if only superficially. But now if Teert had recognized him, then he'd made himself suspect.

Tired of the city streets, Pavresh went to the servant quarters in Indima's house. The room was dark when he entered, the other servants likely waiting on the family. He stepped to his bed and sat down.

Then a voice spoke. "A kiss and I may tell you a secret."

Pavresh bounced quickly to his feet and turned to the voice. The darkness was too much to reveal the figure there, but he knew that the voice was Datri's.

"What are you doing here?"

"I already said. Offering you a secret, one that might help you on your mysterious wanderings."

Pavresh backed away, though she'd made no move to approach him. What did she know? And how? He thought again of Teert seeing him in the street and brought one hand up to his face nervously. He was clearly not the spy Jasfer had hoped him to be.

"I don't understand. What do you mean, *tisrah?*"

Datri laughed, a young laugh, but not purely innocent. Pavresh tried to understand her through his magic. A seductress? That didn't seem quite right. There was something else, as if whatever lust she might have wasn't for seducing him but for something else, or something beyond that.

"You are not as good at playing innocent as I am, servant." She took a few steps closer. "I've seen you talking to the other servants. I've seen you walking the streets. I even remember the way you acted on the train. You are not who you claim to be."

When he said nothing, she added, "And I know something about the one you've been following."

"What do you want?" This was all too strange for Pavresh to understand. What exactly was going on here?

"I already told you. A kiss."

Pavresh stepped back and felt a bed against his legs. He moved to the left as she approached. "Why?"

Either a hint of light was now entering the room or his eyes had learned the dark and adjusted because he could see her shoulders rise in an exaggerated shrug.

"I seem to remember some smiles from you. Can't I just long for a kiss?" She stopped a couple steps away from him. "A girl from your caste…no, I guess I don't know that, do I? A cheetah jati girl, let's say, might be married by my age. A *nefli* laborer might have been married five years ago and already have three children. A kiss is a small thing."

She wasn't speaking the truth. Pavresh could sense it. The seductress theme still didn't quite fit her. For a true seductress, the thrill was in the seduction, nothing more. He wasn't even sure she wanted to seduce him. She was simply playing with the idea of it for some other purpose. For power, he thought, though he couldn't quite tell where that would fall in his magic.

As she took another step, Ekana's face came to his mind, bruised and bloody from the men of her jati. He moved to a side but could see no easy way out. "Maybe, but I know what your jati does to those who kiss their girls."

Datri seemed to know exactly where his thoughts had gone. "My friend Indima, of course, has tasted more than just a kiss. I wonder if she's taken a lover here, also. I wouldn't want anyone to make such an assumption."

Pavresh froze. It was a strong threat, one he didn't like. But equally strong was the thought of Indima as his lover. He could picture it if he wanted to, but now was not the time to imagine that.

"You seem to have me trapped, *tisrah*. What is the secret you would share?"

"A kiss first, servant." She moved to him, but didn't embrace him or anything else he might have imagined. Instead, she held out her hand toward his mouth.

It was another power move, and he thought he began to see something of who she was and what she wanted. He took her hand and dipped his head to kiss it.

"And now your secret, servant. The man you follow has been talking to many in the city, men who owe a part of their silk trade to some of the Thirty."

Pavresh nodded. It was a small bit of information, but even so, it was enough to connect Prince Dartak and Prince

Samatrit since Samatrit was the prince involved in the silk trade. Unless some other prince was as well and he didn't know it.

"He's calling in debts," Datri continued. "Even asking for additional loans against future trade. Unbelievable amounts of money. What he wishes with this, I don't know. That will be your job to find out, I suppose."

As she turned away from him, she patted his cheek, as if he were some exotic pet of hers. At the door, she said, "And I made sure my own personal servant knew I came here. She could easily betray our tryst if it was necessary." She let the word tryst roll off her tongue like some rare delicacy. "I may call on your assistance in the future so that it doesn't become necessary."

Light flooded the room briefly as the door opened and closed. In the renewed darkness, Pavresh sank to the nearest bed and leaned his head into a hand. It was good knowledge to have and an intriguing lead to follow. But what had been the cost? That, he wasn't sure of yet, and it frightened him. He didn't want to think what would happen if Datri called in his debt to her. He'd moved into a new level of political manipulations, one that didn't suit him at all.

Chapter 18

The streets were not the same as they had been, as Jasfer had known them to be since his childhood. No one did anything openly against him or the other princes. He rode in his carriage now to and from the gatherings of the princes, and from the windows, he saw nothing that should have frightened him. People walked as they always had, wallas delivering all variety of goods or messages and others going about their business. Untouchables sat along the streets begging like any other time in the history of Romnai. At least as far as Jasfer knew.

That was the thing, though. Many of those walking didn't believe it had always been so.

The carriage came around the corner onto the Avenue of Geysers and toward his house. Jasfer watched the usual beggars, wondering if any of them would jump up and attack his carriage as some sort of preemptive strike. Yet it wasn't violence that hung in the streets. It was something else, something strange and indefinable as if the fire that gave birth to reality was now tilted differently. Or, he thought, that was how the priests might describe it, and for once in his life, the priests seemed worth listening to. If anyone understood what was happening, they should. Their stories of the Forgotten South, of gods and heroes and the fire that created both must make sense even of these times.

Little had happened in the High Assembly, simply more talk of the abandoned city and the jailed revolutionaries. One surprise for Jasfer had been that Prince Dartak argued passionately for the release of Chaitan while Samatrit glowered as if he wanted to run the old hero through along with everyone else who even whispered their sympathy for the rebels.

High Prince Baram decided to grant the release. No doubt the old man would be watched carefully in the days to come.

The carriage pulled into his carriage house, and Jasfer stepped out. Kalvandi awaited him at the doorway into the main house, which surprised him.

"You have an urgent invitation, *tisrah*."

"Urgent?" Jasfer frowned. Who would wish to see him?

"Prince Shardash, *tisrah*." That made Jasfer pause. The man who'd been assigned to spy on Rashul and that group before the tiny rebellion. The group that included his sister and his spy. "He simply said he wished to speak with you in private and asked that you join him for lunch, *tisrah*."

Lunch. That meant right away. He couldn't even use eating a light meal as an excuse to delay and to think about what it meant. "Thank you, Kalvandi." He dismissed her with a bob of his head and went to his room. A servant helped him into a change of clothes, and within a brief time, he was back in the carriage.

Even more than the houses of most of the princes, Shardash's manor stood out over the edge of the volcanic field. Swirls of steam accompanied Jasfer to the main doorway, and for a moment, Jasfer fancied that the swirls were spirit helpers of the prince, like in the folk tales of the Forgotten South. Spirit messengers, perhaps on a level with the cheetah jati. If so, they did not bother to call him *tisrah* as the door opened to admit him.

Jasfer wanted to plan, to be prepared for whatever this invitation meant, but his thoughts couldn't settle long enough for him to think it through. Had Shardash connected Jasfer to Rashul through Jaritta? Through Pavresh? Was this some kind of warning? Only the high prince could remove him from his position, but Baram could be pressured if the priests believed he deserved to be cast out.

The thought of being made untouchable was what kept him from thinking of anything else. He didn't know how Jaritta had handled it, but he knew he wouldn't do as well as she did. She had some kind of strength that he didn't see anywhere in himself.

Servants led Jasfer to a sitting room sparsely decorated with fine trinkets where Shardash already waited. A variety of foods lay on the table, and Shardash gestured for him to take some.

"Thank you for coming so quickly, Prince Jasfer."

Jasfer selected some fruits and a bit of creamed head squash while Shardash spoke.

"It was short notice, and I apologize. I felt we needed to meet immediately."

As he sat on one of the cushions to eat his food, Jasfer studied the other prince. He was older than Jasfer, but certainly not old, the lines in his face still shallow. A thin layer of fat covered his features without obscuring the strength there. Apijet had trained Jasfer meticulously in reading a group of people, seeing the ways conversations shifted in power, and it was something he'd grown increasingly comfortable with in the months since his mentor's assassination. But reading a single person was different. He couldn't see anything in Shardash's face or movement to give him any clue, except that he had no doubt that all the power in their conversation would come from the other prince, not Jasfer.

Shardash allowed him to eat in silence for a few minutes, though he himself ate little from his own plate. Finally, he explained why he'd invited Jasfer over.

"You know something of these malcontents."

Shardash took a sip from his gourd of tisane, as if to let the words themselves lower slowly like a weight on Jasfer's shoulders. A threat, even if the prince's next words seemed to disarm it.

"I'm not saying this as any kind of warning. I simply wish to understand them better. In private seemed easiest."

Even that was its own threat, dragging along the question of when it might turn public. Jasfer wondered how to answer. "I know little. I believe my former sister spends time with them, or did once anyway. But I know little else."

"What do you know of this Rashul, their leader? There are those who clamor for his release."

Very little. He tried to think if Jaritta had ever said much of him. "He's charismatic. And idealistic, of course. But I don't know much else."

"Is he violent?"

"I don't think so." Jasfer didn't think Jaritta would be intentionally involved in any violence. "But what do your spies say?"

Shardash shrugged the question away, and it seemed intended to mean that they said nothing useful. But to Jasfer, it felt more like he didn't wish to share his information. Despite his apparent friendliness, the other prince was not being completely open, and he would do best to keep that in mind.

"The people seem to love him, anyway. There was some violence at the warehouse, right? But did he begin it?" Realizing how that might sound, he quickly added, "Or one of his followers?"

"The soldiers won't say. They've been given some special leeway in this that I don't like." Shardash stopped abruptly as if he'd said something he hadn't meant to.

"You could set him free and watch him closely, I guess."

Shardash looked at him intently, and Jasfer could see all the power in the room gather around him again. "I have wondered. It doesn't seem safe to keep him imprisoned, not unless we want to face down a full rebellion in the city. But to set him free..."

"So why call me here? I don't see how I have any insight that you don't have."

Shardash reached for his plate and picked up a spoonful of squash. "This is a strange fruit. It's from the Forgotten South. Did you know that? Yet it thrives here beside the steaming pools of our valley."

Jasfer was silent as he ate the bite.

"Some things can exist in two worlds, it seems. Like your sister." His face turned hard beneath its fat, like the parts of a steam engine after it has cooled. "I want you to speak with your sister about this. Ask what the untouchables want. And others, if she knows. What would they do if we executed him? If we exiled him to Jarnur or Pashun? If we set him free?"

"I have not spoken with my sister in some time." Shardash's eyes were as hard as his face as he looked straight at Jasfer. "But I will do as you ask. She may come to me soon, and if not, I will seek her out."

Shardash's smile didn't look genuine, but he thanked Jasfer and urged him to finish his food. Jasfer took a few more bites to be polite, then rose to excuse himself.

As he stepped out of the room, he decided to pull a portion of power back to himself. "If she doesn't wish to be found, she won't, Shardash. Keep that in mind."

* * *

Jasfer was about to set the red cloth out the upstairs window when he stopped. For years he'd used this as a way to get Jaritta's attention if he needed it, but now he wasn't sure he dared. Would Shardash be watching him now as well, looking to see what he might do to find her? He didn't want that secret way of communicating to be known.

He stashed the cloth again on the shelf beside the window and stalked away. Jaritta might stop by the house—she occasionally did—but did he really want that either? Equally then she'd be observed, and even though Shardash had asked him to speak with her, the fact that they met could be seen as wrong, subversive. She was still an untouchable, no matter what.

The hallways turned around him in their maze-like way without drawing his attention on any detail. He wished Apijet were still alive. His old mentor could have advised him, could even have provided a safe place to meet perhaps. What of the other princes? Perhaps he could trust some of his father's old friends. Maybe Arbul.

Jasfer hardly noticed that he was putting on his cloak and heading for the door. With his hand beginning to push it open, he stopped. He had been about to wander the poorer parts of the city in hopes of running into her. That was probably the worst choice of all. If he did find her, it would look highly questionable and may even place her in danger. And if he didn't, it would still look bad for him and possibly attract attention he didn't want.

Now he was at the door, he couldn't stand the idea of going back inside. He needed to move. His house had access to its own private bath and even a small, private chapel—as Jaritta had cause to regret—so that eliminated some of the reasons he might have for leaving the house. But he thought he might go to a public chapel anyway. The dark interior with sacred flames all around would be a relief, a place where it seemed unlikely anyone could be watching him.

One glance at his clothing told him that, while he wouldn't be mistaken for one of the wallas or a *nefli* laborer, his appearance wouldn't scream *prince* to everyone, so he walked.

Walking felt good. He swung his legs briskly and headed along the edge of the hot springs for a local chapel. No snow came down. It was stunning how every spring that was a strange and surprising change. Snow seemed almost permanent, like the constant stage scenery of fire in a sacred play. Even after the air warmed and the sun became visible for increasing periods, the steam only rose so far before hitting a colder place and falling back down as snow. But today: nothing, holding out the promise of that brief summer when twelve-days would go by with the sun scarcely setting and nothing to interrupt it but the rare rain.

Jasfer looked at the passersby. Many clutched sheaves of paper as if afraid to lose them. It seemed odd behavior, so he let his eyes follow the trail of papers until suddenly someone shoved a stack in his hands.

The first page, he wasn't surprised to see, was the same manifesto that had been circulating ever since the brief insurrection. The following pages were unfamiliar. Jasfer stopped beside the road to look through them. It was poetry. Some epic he'd never studied. He almost threw it down, then tucked it under his arm and continued walking.

The chapel was quiet, the darkness a relief. Jasfer knelt in the center of the room, farthest from any light, and stared at the sacred fire up front. He'd never been a religious man, but he'd grown up visiting the family's private chapel and the large temple beside the river, so there was something comforting about being there. He could almost imagine that the fire and the gods that descended from it really did have something to do with the world around him, that there really was a purpose to all the craziness of the city, more than just a drunk god playing kiwan.

He lost track of how long he remained in the darkness. People came and worshiped and left. Priests tended the various fires set around the room. Eventually, he rose and approached the central blaze. Here the people gave their offerings to the gods, not riches or goods, but simply little things that would burn and remind the gods of the people stuck here in the world.

Jasfer reached for something to offer, and the only thing he found was the sheaf of papers. He took the first page, the manifesto, folded it in a pattern he remembered from childhood, and threw it into the fire. The paper unfolded in the heat and curled up again as it ignited. It struck Jasfer as sad, the way the paper resigned itself so easily to its fate. He almost threw the rest in as well, but he feared it would draw attention to himself as it flared.

After a brief look at the mural on the far side of the fire, a painting of Tiespetre and the other gods, Jasfer stepped away and left.

On his way to the exit, his attention was caught by a dark doorway, and it reminded him of his childhood, of the explorations he and his sister would make before she was cast out. Without taking time to think, he turned down the side hallway. Light shone up ahead, but he crossed another dark door first and entered there. Rooms led to rooms in a strange maze that might have dated back hundreds of years. Some were dust-covered, others clearly in frequent use. Whenever he thought he might run into someone, Jasfer turned down a new hallway. Students of religion had once studied in these rooms, he guessed, slept in them even, and priests had stored the props they used to teach the populace about the gods.

The thrill of exploration came back to him, the hint of danger, the promise of finding something new. When a passageway led him out to a side alley along the chapel, he noticed a doorway on the opposite side and ran in. This was an old part of the city, not renovated in a generation or more. Abandoned wings of the larger manors ran into each other with fallen debris in the hallways and unintentional windows above, open to the elements. Maybe this was what had always attracted him and his sister, the sense of ancient disorder that simply did not exist in their own home. The city of Romnai filled the land between the steam beds and the river, but it didn't fill it tightly, so abandoned ruins like these weren't uncommon. Untouchables might move in to some, and soldiers might sweep through to clear them out once every few years, but there was no urgency to rebuilding them.

He came out again, this time beside the volcanic fields, and there he remembered something Jaritta had shown him. Not when she was his sister, but after she'd been cast out. There was another part of the city much like this that she'd discovered. A group of manors that had been built over the volcanic fields themselves then abandoned when they became dangerous.

She went there often, she'd told him, she and another untouchable who'd become her friend. He hadn't seen that boy in a while. But Jaritta still visited the area, or at least he thought he remembered her mentioning it more recently. He couldn't go openly looking for her, but he could leave her a message.

Jasfer headed back into the main flow of pedestrians, flinching as the sudden change of surroundings brought back all the worries and pressures he'd tried to leave behind in the chapel. At his manor, he grabbed the red cloth that was the signal and stuffed it under his robe. Then he stopped. How to explain going out this time?

Whose houses were they? Some were princely families that weren't among the Thirty, none of them closely related to Jasfer. But Arbul lived near there, and he'd been wondering about visiting the old prince anyway. They'd scarcely talked since Apijet's assassination.

After one more glance at the red cloth hidden within his clothes, he nodded. Arbul it would be, and he hoped he could figure something out to keep it looking as innocent as possible.

* * *

"It is always good to see my old friend's favorite son."

Jasfer laughed and answered, "As it is to see my father's

good friend. I only apologize I have not visited sooner."

Arbul waved the thought away. "It is a crazy time we live in. All is understood, all forgiven."

Forgiven? He hadn't quite considered it a fault in need of forgiveness. But he ignored that, and they spoke lightly of many things, Jasfer always speaking with careful respect. Finally, he got to the reason he'd invented for his visit.

"I've been trying to keep my mind off all the unrest and was looking into my mine holdings." At first he'd thought about making the pretext something to do with arrangements to find a wife, but business seemed safer, more impersonal.

"Oh yes, your father always kept his fingers in all sorts of such things. Coal mines. Iron mines. I never knew what else. If tisane could be mined, he'd have found a way to be involved."

Jasfer smiled, though it didn't fit the image he had of his father. "There's a cluster of mines to the north, and it occurred to me that they must waste an excessive amount of time transporting their goods back to the river."

"The north? Oh yes, you sent a servant there recently, didn't you? Or a messenger or something?"

"Yes. I might have." Why would Arbul know such a thing? The messenger he'd sent had been Pavresh, who of course, hadn't gone there at all. He didn't worry about Arbul suspecting anything. He always seemed quite traditional and might disapprove of Jasfer's contact with Jaritta, but nothing else would likely bother him. But the fact that others were aware of such an action disturbed Jasfer. "Often my servants deal with the smaller matters such as messages."

Arbul only nodded, his eyes innocent.

"So as I wondered, I thought of your involvement with the railroads. And I'm curious what it would take to send a spur out there."

"The railroads?" Arbul wiped a hand across his mouth then reached for a chilled fruit. "It's worth exploring," he said around the berry. "You and the mine operators and transporters or whoever's involved in that side of it would have to pay for most of the construction."

Jasfer allowed himself to look hurt by the idea. "I was hoping a shared profit deal could pay for the construction."

Arbul sat back and looked straight at him. "Perhaps in part."

They spent the next hour discussing and debating. A servant opened a window, letting in a cool breeze that soon became cold. Jasfer sipped a hot tisane to keep himself warm, but Arbul didn't seem bothered at all, still eating chilled fruits and other snacks.

Over the course of that hour, they agreed to some basic plans and promised to continue exploring the idea, and Jasfer bid farewell.

The manors here ran together, so at the entrance Jasfer slipped to one side and into a neighboring walkway, covered by the upper story rooms where the two manors met. After a short ways, the walkway opened up in a small garden. Voices came from the open windows, but he could see no one among the hardy plants. He passed through quickly and turned down another covered walkway, which brought him into a narrow alley. Across the alley were the abandoned wings that he'd been looking for.

No one walked in this alleyway, but Jasfer paused. For a moment, he thought he'd seen movement among the abandoned windows. He stared at each, shifting his gaze suddenly as if to catch the shadow by surprise, but he saw nothing new.

It could be an untouchable, finding shelter here, though he'd expect them to be out begging by day. Were there even untouchables that weren't beggars? He'd never really thought of that. Well, the death workers, but they wouldn't be hiding now either. It'd be nice to have Yatim with him. In his mind, he saw Apijet lying on the pavement, killed by an untouchable.

Well, killed by a sort of malfunctioning railroad steam engine, but it'd been placed there by the untouchable. And who put it in the hands of the untouchable? That was a mystery no one had solved.

He glanced at the passersby at the end of the alleyway, torn by wanting to avoid their notice but wanting them close enough to somehow protect him. But why would strangers protect anyone? Not in today's Romnai. Steeling himself, he crossed the alley and entered the abandoned wing through a broken door. Dust filled the most recent footprints, which was some relief, though he guessed there would be many possible entrances to those rooms.

He'd only come here a few times with Jaritta, and the twists of the hallways spun him quickly around. More than once he had to backtrack from a room with no exits, and always in his mind was the thought that these rooms hadn't been abandoned randomly but because of the molten rock beneath them, melting away the foundations. He pictured cracks appearing behind him, red rock flowing upward and cutting off his escape.

Jasfer found the overgrown garden in the center of those rooms. A hoary pear tree dominated the space, crowding out most of the original plants, although the descendants of some had spread across what had once been pathways and benches. The steam seemed especially thick, as if it sank into the garden overnight and became trapped. The air was heavy with sulfur.

Jasfer crossed to the branches of the tree, ignoring the plants underfoot, and tied the red cloth around one prominent limb.

He turned and someone stood directly behind him, face obscured by a loop of cloth. He stumbled backward, then was brought up short by his sister's voice.

"You wished to see me?"

He would have laughed if his heart wasn't going so fast.

"How did you know I'd be here?"

Jaritta shrugged. "I've been staying here."

"Here?" Jasfer looked around the overgrown garden, imagined the lava underneath the stone, ready to destroy it. "No, there must be a better place. What about the room I've rented for you?"

"Not safe." There was no irony in her voice, though Jasfer imagined he could feel the floor shake its reminder of danger. "We've been careful, but if someone wants to, they can trace it to you."

"But we…" He didn't finish. He'd been as careful as he could, but if there was any possibility, any hint of what would be seen as inappropriate behavior…now was not the time to take such a chance. "Still, there must be somewhere else."

"I'm looking. And moving often. But this is a good place in between." She walked over to the pear tree and looked up into its untended branches. Last year's fruit lay decomposing beneath her feet.

"What about the steam beds under us?"

"Never mind that. What did you want?"

Jasfer briefly explained his visit with Shardash that morning.

"Set Rashul free? I wouldn't have thought anyone would support that." There seemed an angry undertone to her voice that surprised Jasfer.

"What, are we princes not capable of good deeds? You were once one of us. Do you truly think all our jati cold and ruthless?"

Jaritta shook her head slowly, almost sadly it seemed. "Only focused, I supposed. Blinded by what's in their own interest."

Perhaps there was a truth to that, and perhaps that wasn't an awful thing. "Might not someone's interest include setting the revolutionary free?"

Jaritta froze at that, slowly turning her eyes—one half-shadowed—directly toward his own. "That perhaps is most frightening of all."

Jasfer broke away first and placed his hand on the nearest tree branch. There seemed to be a strange power in his sister that he hadn't ever seen before, a confidence coupled with bitterness. Maybe it had always been there, but he was sure recent events had hardened it, brought it to the surface. "Will you visit Prince Shardash?"

"No. I don't trust meeting anyone but you right now. But you can let him know my opinions."

He had to agree that it was smarter that way. "Well, what do you think? What would his followers do?"

"Execute him and you're asking for trouble." She took a dead twig from the tree and snapped it in two. "Everyone will rise up. The untouchables, the *nefli*, and most of the *brenil*, even. And I'll be right with them. You've seen the epic?"

"The what?"

"The poem."

Jasfer remembered the papers he'd been given earlier that day and pulled them out as Jaritta continued.

"It was written for Rashul by the wise man Marankiya. A poem to put the gods on his side. Those are the papers, yes. They've been spreading throughout the city for a few months now, ever since the attempt at the warehouse."

Jasfer turned the pages, scanning the lines, but he'd never paid much attention to the holy epics the priests liked to recite. "This would seem to make him even more dangerous then, Jaritta."

She shrugged. "And probably he is. But killing him certainly won't get you out of that danger."

"Exile?"

"Probably not much better. Some of the more violent members will probably take charge, maybe even claim that the exile is false, that it was invented to cover his execution."

This became more complicated as they went. What could they possibly do to appease the people without completely destroying their society? And he had no doubt that their society was threatened. Rashul's words sounded good. And Jasfer could even accept that he genuinely believed his ideals, not like some populist speakers of the past who said whatever words would bring attention and popularity. But the caste system was vital to their society, vital to stability and progress. It could be made more just, certainly—girls who stumbled while carrying fire should not be cast out—but to tear it down was to descend into the chaos of mumbler villages deep in the mountains.

"So something public. A house arrest, perhaps, though he doesn't seem to have his own house to be confined to. Thank you. I will suggest such to Shardash."

"Jasfer." Jaritta reached out and touched his cloak-covered arm. Even with it being his sister, the idea of an untouchable touching him was enough to make him step back, but she went on as if he hadn't. "You may need to use the same caution with the poet. Marankiya. He was a prodigy as a child, many years ago. But people have remembered his name."

"Thank you, sister. I'll do what I can. Be safe, too, and be wary of visiting me." He fumbled in his robes for a moment and drew out a small bag of coins. "It's all I'll be able to get to you for a while. I fear I may be watched as well these days."

Jaritta smiled, or at least seemed to. Ever since she'd covered half her face, he found it hard to read her expressions, as if the hidden part would reveal more depth and nuance to each smile or frown. "I'm sure you are, brother. I've found my own way that should keep me from trouble, I promise. Be more careful yourself."

Jaritta ran to one of the walls and scrambled up onto the neighboring roof. She didn't seem as nimble as she once had, but she'd learned how to move on those roofs so well that she no longer needed to be, he supposed. He imagined her old and gray, limping along the streets with a cane but still able to climb and dance from rooftop to rooftop.

With that image bringing a smile to his face, Jasfer left the garden through the abandoned wings and returned to his house. Marankiya's revolutionary epic was still curled in his hand.

Chapter 19

Pavresh followed Indima's father Jinshu silently through early morning streets. The sun had been bouncing along the horizon almost since the night before, so Pavresh wasn't even sure the time. Few people were out yet, and Jinshu set a fast pace toward the center of town. Pavresh was struck, as he never had been before, by the bright colors of flowers in the upper windows, a shocking contrast against the monochromatic stone of the buildings. He wondered if they were a new thing, maybe even a part of the upcoming festival to honor the goddess Kwona. Or no more than a part of the season, bursting to life to take advantage of the long days of sunlight, thriving on the steam-heavy air. The steam felt different to him here, not so thick as in Romnai, though still enough to keep that corner of the valley warm.

Jinshu met with another silk weaver after a few streets, and Pavresh bowed. The man ignored him. Others, some accompanied by silent servants and some alone, joined them as they neared a series of large buildings that didn't look like houses. In their time in the Silk City so far, Indima's family hadn't yet asked him to go there. He'd simply remained in the residential parts of town, serving in their own house and the houses of others. But Jinshu and his wife would put in their hours of some kind of leisurely work in one of these central buildings.

They entered one that was as close to sprawling as anything in that cramped city could get. In Romnai, it would have been the type of restricted place where only a select few could enter, but the Silk City as a whole was that way, so there was no need of guards at the entrance. Instead of any kind of reception area, the door brought them directly from the street into a large gallery of people at work. It felt too abrupt, as if a piece of the building were missing.

An impressive-looking weaver met them in that first gallery, her silk clothes finer than any Pavresh had ever seen, with intricate thread-work and several hues of cloth. She welcomed them and began their tour.

Only then did Pavresh realize that it *was* a tour. Jinshu had simply called for a servant as he prepared to leave, and Pavresh had been the first available. He hadn't told Pavresh anything of where they went or why. These weavers, Pavresh realized, must all be from the other cities come to see the latest advances in research. He wondered if any had come from Jarnur and would question his story.

A servant stationed in the gallery gestured for Pavresh and the other servants to assist him with serving, so Pavresh missed most of the guide's presentation. That room had many people leaning over bits of cloth, pulling at them, dripping various liquids onto them, writing down whatever it was they observed.

"Most of the cloths don't make it past this stage," the guide was saying as Pavresh returned with hot tisane. "A few go on to make the lesser silks available to the merchants and other lower jatis."

The visiting weavers nodded and murmured, and then they moved on into other galleries. Pavresh constantly moved between the group and the various locations for refreshments, but he saw the rooms and tried to understand their purpose without the guide's explanations.

One room was filled with spiders. Pillars designed to resemble trees lined the room, branching out into ever smaller twigs of masonry. Among those limbs were countless spider webs, and Pavresh imagined he could hear the sound of millions of legs carrying the spiders up and down the trees to their webs. One corner of the room was completely bare, as if the weavers had recently harvested the spider silk.

They passed through that room quickly, though Pavresh wanted to stay and wander among the fake trees.

For once, he heard the explanation of their guide. There was much shuddering among the weavers as they stood in the next gallery to hear her. "All of you have probably seen this room in the past. But there's little new to report on them. We keep trying different varieties of spider and different manners of using the silk they spin, but the result is just as it's always been."

Other galleries followed, most filled with rows of people working, bent over strange instruments or stirring unknown solutions. As he passed among these people, Pavresh noticed a different air to them, something that set them apart from the weavers touring the place and from any weaver he'd ever met away from the city of silk. They were intense and focused, though he supposed that the other weavers might be the same when working. But there was more that he tried to understand as they continued.

Further galleries brought them to stores of cotton, from the plots and glass-roofed buildings Pavresh remembered passing on the way to the city, but also some "specially cultivated out over the steam beds on movable platforms of earth," as the guide explained, and others "from a hybrid variety that grows on terraces in the mountains just east of the volcanic area." Pavresh tried to picture what that would look like, either the movable beds or the terraces, but it seemed so unlike anything he'd ever seen that he could hardly imagine it.

Huge looms dominated another room. A few were strikingly new and powered by steam. Older looms occupied most of the people in that gallery as they wove a variety of cloths.

These people seemed more like the weavers on the tour, and Pavresh realized that what really set the others apart was the sense of discovery. It was an arcist theme, the inventor, that settled on many of those working here. Most of the weavers were antiquarians, preserving the lost past in ancient silks. They concerned themselves with the theft of time, grasping to hold what they could against loss. Not so those he'd seen in many of the galleries here. They saw the past and the future differently. The past was something to learn from, but little more. The future was something to welcome, a promise of new things that didn't mean all that was good was gone.

Not that each person was either purely an inventor or purely an antiquarian. If arcist magic taught him anything about people, it was that things were never so simple. But realizing the difference helped him understand the weavers better.

In another room, he saw a familiar face. He couldn't tell what it was they were doing there—something with pulling and crumpling endless swatches of cloth—but among the workers was Datri. Pavresh saw little of the inventor in her demeanor and nothing of the antiquarian. This to her, he imagined, was knowledge, nothing more or less. She must have taken work in the research galleries simply to learn what she could and store that knowledge away for later use. The princely jati didn't exist within arcist magic, but she was the arcist embodiment of what most people assumed the princes to be. Calculating and manipulative despite her innocent exterior. More like the spiders in the other room than any of the silk weavers around her.

Their group passed directly beside Datri, and she looked at them, studying the weavers as they passed. Her eyes seemed to pass right over the servants, and Pavresh breathed easier that she hadn't looked directly at him.

The final gallery contained a wide pool of water. It did not steam. After a moment of staring at it, he realized the only other time he'd ever seen such an expanse of water that wasn't heated was the river. It gave him a chill feeling, the sense of it being something unnatural. He'd helped refill the weavers' gourds with hot water before entering, and he noticed that many gripped their beverages tightly, as if they also felt the unnaturalness of that dark water.

Here was no table of refreshments for him to hurry off to, so Pavresh stayed to hear what the guide said.

"This will be new for all of you. A very recent discovery." She gestured to one of the nearby workers, and he began pulling on a rope that led into the water. "These are fish found at the mouth of the Eghsal River, living in the mud."

The rope pulled up a mesh cage, and inside were a number of wriggling fish. Pavresh leaned closer to see.

"When frightened—and I imagine they will be frightened right now—they secrete a slime that covers their bodies, often allowing them to escape predators."

A number of the fish displayed this very thing as they slipped away from the cage and back into the water.

"It usually sticks nicely to them until they tie themselves in a knot and slide the slime right off their bodies."

Pavresh realized then the eel-like nature of the fish's bodies. They looked to be about the length of his arm from fingertips to elbow. No variation marked where its head merged into its thin body. Their mouths were framed by tiny whiskers. Ugly was not an arcist theme, but if it was, he thought sure this would be it.

"That's when we harvest the slime. It's not a pretty thing, nothing like spider silk, nothing like the thread of silk worms in our ancient stories. But we've found that it works very similarly if we treat it right."

The worker tipped the cage until only one remained and

then reached inside with his gloved hand. It had already been slimy. Pavresh could tell by the way the light of the room hit its head. But as the thick fingers closed around its body, he *saw* more slime appear. The fish's eel-like body seemed to grow, but it couldn't escape the worker's grasp.

He carried it to a small tank of clear water that was raised up beside the pool and let it slip from his glove into the water. There it did just as the guide has said, looping its head back and then through the loop and sliding the knot quickly back along its flexible body. The worker used a net to scoop out the slime that came off.

There was some talking after that, but less than Pavresh would have expected. A number of the weavers seemed vaguely sickened by the fish.

As they left, Jinshu turned to another weaver and said, "Those fish…they aren't nagas. Are they?"

The man only shook his head and shrugged. Pavresh's mind raced. Nagas. There were stories, of course. Tales of the wise and mysterious and tricky nagas who lived in the Forgotten South, but no one believed them anymore. Or did the silk weaver jati?

He couldn't imagine that it would have anything to do with Prince Jasfer and the other princes, but it seemed a fascinating thing that could influence arcist magic. He decided that as long as he remained in the Silk City, he'd try to uncover what he could about the nagas and their connection with the weavers.

* * *

Pavresh dangled a pen over a blank piece of paper. He wanted to get the information on Teert and the wolf jati soldiers to Prince Jasfer, but how could he keep it safe? Ever since he'd learned of it from Datri some twelve-days earlier, he'd been trying to find a way, but each time he brought the pen down to the pot of ink, he stopped, stood up, walked around, and came back. Then repeated the process. A few times he got as far as dipping the pen in the ink and holding it long enough over the white paper to leave drips of black across its surface.

Then he thought of kiwan and the information he and Indima had managed to convey to each other. How might he use that with Jasfer? A letter with nothing more than the description of a game would surely raise suspicions. He'd have to bury it in other text. But that gave him a place to start.

Mind racing with how exactly to word the letter, he managed to bring the pen to the paper. He addressed it to Jasfer's servant Yatim.

> *Greetings, cousin. I hope that all is well in the capital. Do you miss the sea as much as I do? Some say the mountains out here are their own sort of sea, unimaginably vast. People can enter them briefly, like the fishermen in the bay, but they daren't go far or stay long. And like the sea, they cut our valley off from the rest of the world. Maybe, but to me there's nothing like the smell of salt and the cries of gulls.*

Even so, life is good here…

He went on in that vein for the rest of that page, trying to evoke the sense of the exile, the wanderer longing for home. Finally, he came to the important part.

> *I played a game of kiwan the other day, and I wanted to share it with you, see if you have any ideas how I might have played it better. It was a perplexing game, so I apologize if I go into too much detail, but I want you to understand how things stood.*

Then he told of an imaginary game of kiwan, of the arrangement of the pieces in surprising places, "like wolves on the prowl," and of the way his opponent moved her pieces, "striking sharply across the board, as ruthlessly as a lender calling in loans." And with further oblique references, he kept pointing to the same things, the soldiers coming down from the mountains and Teert gathering all the money he could for no reason Pavresh had determined.

At last, he sat back, three sheets of paper filled with text, though most of it was filler that hid the account of the game. He read it again, then sealed it.

Tomorrow he could deliver it to the departing supply men.

* * *

The preparations for the Kwona festival increased as early summer passed, but Indima and her family seemed prepared to do nothing for it, not even to go out for any of the many celebrations taking place around the city. Pavresh suspected it might have to do with Indima's dalliance with Ekana. Kwona would be the last goddess they'd want her to venerate after that, at least as far as he understood the pantheonic religion.

So Pavresh prepared to spend the evening in his masters' home as well, seeing to their needs and hearing the celebrations all around. It would be its own minor exile for any who longed for those celebrations, but it wouldn't bother him in the least.

Then Raksh, the head servant who'd been assigned to the household, surprised him. "You've been asked to attend another *tisrah* this evening."

Pavresh set down the boiling water he was pouring and cocked his head at Raksh.

"Another *tisrah*? Why is that?" More than a twelve-day had passed since he sent the letter to Prince Jasfer, and the thought flashed across his mind that someone had intercepted the letter and tracked it to him. But that didn't seem to fit with him serving a different master for the night.

Raksh shrugged with his hands. "For the festival, I imagine. Other than that, it doesn't matter. You were requested. Here's the address." He handed Pavresh a paper with a rough map sketched in. He didn't recognize the place.

"Do you know which silk weaver it is?"

"No. And it's not for us to worry about such things. They'll have a celebration there, and you will attend and serve in whatever capacity is needed."

"Yes, sir." Pavresh gave a quick bow of his head, wondering if his questions had marked him as not truly cheetah jati. "I will serve."

He hurried out into the streets to the nearby address. The house blazed with light, and many people moved across the windows. Pavresh approached the front entrance where more silk weavers were arriving. A few looked at him askance. The entryway was crowded with the weavers, and Pavresh saw he would have to wait. That was when he remembered his place among these people. He was a servant surrounded by *kortru* peers. A high-ranking servant, perhaps, but servant no less. He turned away and walked along the outside of the building until he found a side door. Inside scurried the other servants.

Pavresh fell into the work of delivering and arranging. Yet it struck him how effortless these servants who'd been born to their roles made it seem. He watched one servant, while balancing a tray of cheese and bread in one hand, pick up an empty gourd that had been set down, cut across the crowded floor offering cheese to the revelers as she passed, gather another discarded cup of something, and weave toward the kitchen, all without once seeming off balance. These servants never appeared to be rushing, but the tasks got accomplished with amazing speed. He tried to glide as they did, tried to be everywhere without breaking a sweat, but it was a strain.

The evening progressed without any clue why Pavresh's presence had been requested, unless it was simply that the weavers hosting the party had requested any servant and Raksh had chosen him. But that hadn't been the sense he'd had from the head servant. On top of her fabled romances, Kwona was goddess of horses and the sea, so the festivities included intricate fountains of lukewarm tisane cascading over beautiful horse sculptures. Across the largest of these fountains once Pavresh noticed Ambal and wondered if the man had requested him with the thought of playing a game of kiwan. If so, the game never happened. His wife Kisar also attended the party, looking young and beautiful away from her tiring children.

Musicians played in one corner, the sanctioned music of the priests to which temple-trained dancers moved. Some of the songs also allowed the guests to dance slowly with each other. Pavresh thought of Namrani's music, of the blending of music and dance and magic in Chaitan's house. That had been living music; this was mere motions.

Late in the evening the festivities ended with a light-hearted invocation to Kwona's sister, Gouwind, the cow goddess who was the opposite of her sister. As far as the prayer went, Pavresh guessed that they considered her a simple goddess, full of laughter and free of the conflicting shadows and uncertainties of the mare goddess.

With that laughter still on their lips, the guests trickled away, and the work for the servants eased up. They still had much to clean up in the dance rooms and beside the tables of food, but the urgency was gone, the tension of serving perfectly and fluidly evaporated. The servants showed their weariness at last as they rearranged large tables and heavy chairs, but a few weavers still remained in some of the rooms.

As Pavresh passed one empty room, an arm snaked around his arm and pulled him inside. He was within before he realized that he might have resisted the light hold. Light from the hallway was just enough to reveal Datri's face to him before she pulled him farther into the dark.

She wasted no time with vague threats. "Who sent you? Tell me why you follow the servant Teert."

Pavresh sucked in his breath and tried to see her expression in the dark. "I can't do that."

"You know what I can do to you, yes? Whether it's for pulling me into this darkened room and assaulting me or for impersonating a cheetah jati servant."

Pavresh had to close his eyes, but it didn't stop the images of soldiers coming to him, pulling him away, casting him out as untouchable. It was a feeling he'd learned for his magic, but never one he'd experienced, not the longing for home of the exile, but the terror of being driven off. What would he do as an untouchable?

"I know, *tisrah*. Yet, I can't tell you. Ask something else, and perhaps. But that…"

Datri moved around him then, trailing her fingers across his back, down his arm. "Someone powerful then." He jerked his arm up and stepped back as her hand came down his arm and brushed his waist. "Or someone you care about."

Cared about? Not as such, he thought. He cared for Jaritta in her way, he supposed. But Jasfer was simply an offer of employment. No, there must be more than that. As far as princes went, he seemed a decent man. If he'd come in among the princes without knowing any, he would have rather sided with Jasfer over Samatrit. But really, cold as it sounded, what he cared about more than anything was the magic itself.

"A beautiful princess, maybe?" Datri's voice went silken. "Their jati is less vigilant than ours about liaisons with their lessers, I hear."

When he said nothing, letting her imagine what she would, Datri continued. "I'd first thought you were here for some merchant wanting in on the silk trade. Or maybe another prince wanting his piece of it. But it isn't that, is it?" Her voice had lost the seductive edge and seemed simply curious, although he guessed it was more than that. "You were sent by a prince. Can you at least confirm that?"

Pavresh didn't want to, but then he thought of her threats and decided it was safe enough to play along. "Yes. I was."

"Good. We're figuring out how this works, you and I. Now, what can you tell me of Teert? What is his true purpose here?"

"I don't know, *tisrah*. That's why I'm here. He serves one prince but seems to be here for another. That's the mystery, and it's all I've put together." He didn't think telling her the names of the princes involved would be wise, since it might not be difficult to narrow in on his own connection with Prince Jasfer.

"Fair enough," Datri said, and Pavresh was surprised by how easy her voice had become. "For now. I think you have work to do yet, servant."

As he turned to leave, she ran a proprietary hand once more along his back. Pavresh shivered and stepped out into the light of the hallway.

* * *

The next time Indima invited Pavresh to play kiwan with her, he decided to broach the subject of the nagas. He waited while Shidhi was in the room, bringing the *tisrah* her food. Pavresh played quietly and without any refreshment. He tried a few times to replicate the spinning move he'd seen Chaitan use once, but it never managed to land where he wanted. When Shidhi left for a moment, he spoke.

"Your people seem to honor the nagas from the old stories. Why is that?"

Indima took her hand from the piece she'd been about to play and looked at him.

"Yes...I suppose we do." She picked up another piece and moved it about in her hand. Then as if she were her own echo, she repeated, "We do. I don't think I can really explain it. Not without taking so long it'd be suspicious. But I'll have you accompany me tomorrow, and you'll see."

She said nothing else about it, and Shidhi soon returned, so they played in silence.

The day after, she summoned him to attend her and Shidhi through the streets. They entered a part of the city near the front gate, as far from the volcanic bed as any part of the city wall. The streets were narrow here, claustrophobic. It almost seemed an older part within the rest of the city. Hadn't he been taught that the entire city was equally old? Maybe it was simply that the narrower roads gave an antique air so it fit some preconceived idea of what an old city should feel like. Moss grew in the cracks of the street where the sun seldom reached the surface.

Among those buildings they came to a slight hill. The streets curved around, and buildings cut off most of the view of the rise. Between houses he saw the ground go up to what looked like a small garden.

Indima turned down an alley Pavresh would have completely missed. It didn't head straight for the garden, but twisted around. No debris cluttered the alley, but even so, there were points where they had to go in single file. Indima led without bothering to look at the buildings beside them.

The house on their right ended, replaced by a tall fence. Pavresh looked through at the bright green of the garden. Branches spread from the trees as if stretching after a long time confined. His own limbs longed to do the same. How much longer would he have to stay here in the Silk City?

Another curve of the alley brought them to an opening in the ground. Not quite a cave, but a sunken end to the street. At the far rock wall was a shrine.

Indima approached the shrine and knelt, Shidhi beside her. Pavresh stayed standing behind them, his head slightly bowed. The faithful servant, he tried to convey with his magic. Respectful but still alert, though he knew they faced little danger within the Silk City.

While standing thus, he surreptitiously examined the walls of the shrine. Like the nearby streets, they gave the impression of great age. The carvings in the rock were worn around the edges, but still quite clear. Words ran among the images, an ancient script that he would need to study in greater detail if he were to read. Fortunately, the images themselves told the story well.

Along one wall were the fabled nagas, eel heads with stylized horns or some other protrusions on their heads and long, sinuous bodies with arms that seemed too small. Some held weapons, some treasures from deep underground, some the wreckage of ships lost beneath the sea. Over and over among the figures was repeated the image of a small pool of water.

On the other wall were carvings of silk weavers. The fabled worms spun their silk in the trees of the Forgotten South, and weavers gathered it together to create their cloth. He'd never given any thought to what must have been involved in weaving silk, but even a short look at those carvings showed the process to be far more intricate and detailed than he ever would have guessed, from harvesting the cocoons to doing something with water to release the threads to then carefully wrapping threads together and dyeing and weaving. It fit well with the magical folk tales that were all that remained of the Forgotten South. Surely there was some kind of magic involved in such a process.

The figures on the two walls faced all directions at first, but farther in, they tended more and more toward the back, and in the middle, directly before the shrine, the nagas and the weavers met. The nagas gave the humans some gift there, and behind them were ships waiting to carry them away. To the north, of course. This was their myth, the story they told of how they'd learned to preserve silks where no silkworms lived.

The magic or science of it had been a gift from the nagas.

It didn't fit well with Rashul's claim that all the people of Eghsal had once been of a soldier jati. But then, the point of such a myth, whether this one or the one Rashul told, wasn't its truth but how it influenced people. Like arcist magic.

Indima finished her obeisance and stood, glancing at Pavresh. He gave a slight nod to say he'd learned enough, and she led the way out of the garden and back through that close-looming part of the city.

As they walked, Pavresh tried to work through this new myth and place it among all the stories he'd been learning. The ancient gift from wise ones. Yes, it also belonged, a powerful part of arcist magic. It would be a good one to remember for when he did return to Romnai.

* * *

It was morning, and Pavresh closed himself in the little room he'd found. He didn't dare light a proper fire, but he had a lamp, and he imagined it blazing high. With his kusti in his hands, he moved through the motions of honoring the fire. It felt as if he hadn't performed the rituals for months. His first movements were off-balance, but then he felt his mind enter the fire, become the fire, and his limbs found their grace.

Time disappeared as he moved through the motions over and over. His mind ran through the maxims of his faith. The fire is endless. It exists at all times, as do the embers, the ashes, the smoke, coexisting in eternity, creating in their dance the cosmos. An illusion, but real at the same time. He didn't try to understand, didn't try to penetrate the mysteries or solve the paradoxes. He simply entered the fire and let himself be, nothing more. Nothing less.

The oil in the lamp was nearly gone when Pavresh came out from his trance to the sound of knocks on the door. It was an empty room, scarcely more than a closet, one he'd never seen used in his time in the Silk City. Why would anyone be coming here now?

He cautiously moved the heavy box he'd carried there to block the door and opened it. Indima slipped in and shut the door behind her.

"Pavresh, you have to go."

At first he thought she meant she wanted him to leave the room, but then he noticed the way she'd said it. If she were an arcist, it would have had the theme of the rightful heir sneaking out of the castle before the usurper could catch him.

"What is it?"

"Datri betrayed you. That man you've been following..." She paused, and he thought he saw her shiver. "He's a dangerous man, and he's looking for you."

"How do you..." he began, but she hadn't stopped talking.

"I can't help you. He knows about my connections with Rashul and will use that to force me to help him. You need to leave before he does."

Pavresh said nothing as he searched her face. She was frightened, and a part of him wanted to stay and comfort her. Another part of him wanted that very much, to let her lead him to her room, or anywhere. But the fear was enough to cut through such thoughts. She was afraid for him and for herself, but also afraid of what she would be forced to do if he stayed. Still, he let himself marvel at the beauty of her face longer than he needed to before he broke away and nodded.

"Yes. I...I will leave. I think the time's come to see what's happening to Chaitan and the others anyway."

They both stood there for a moment as the lamp flickered. Pavresh tried to imagine something to say, slowly lifted his hand as if to take hers and kiss it. Then the light died, and Indima stepped forward to embrace him. He could hardly believe it, scarcely knew what to do in response. The feel of her body against his sent shocks up his scalp and down the backs of his legs. He held her tightly against himself.

"I'm glad you were here, Pavresh." Indima's voice sounded strained. "You were my connection to Chaitan and…the others. Now…"

That's all it was? He'd been her reminder of Ekana? He pulled himself from her arms, but as he did, she kissed him on the cheek, an affectionate kiss that seemed to mean more than her words had implied.

With his thoughts still stuttering in confusion, he stepped to the door and pushed it open a crack.

"Here." Indima held out a bag of coins. "There are horses at the gate that you can take to the train track. Leave the horse there and catch a train or whatever you need to do."

"Thank you, *tisrah*. Indima." He put the coins into his cloak. "I'm pleased that I could serve you and your family." As the light coming through the opening fell on her, Pavresh was struck with a powerful image of how she fit in the arcist magic. It cut even through his roiling emotions. She was the quintessential exile, three times over. All those of the valley were in exile from the Forgotten South, and their society never let them forget it. Second, she'd been born a weaver but away from her jati's home. But the truly poignant one, what made her the image of all exiles was her complete absence from those things that mattered most to her, a former lover, dance performances, plans and heated debates of revolution. She was fully cut off from that with no real hope of it ever being restored to her.

If Rashul's revolution succeeded, that might free her to return, but even that he doubted. The silk weavers would hold on to their old ways out here as long as they could. This would be the image he would take of her, even after all the mysteries and intrigues resolved into whatever form they took, he would still picture her here an exile. It seemed so final, a door closing on her story simply because that was how society worked.

"Be...be well, Indima. Do as you must for your family. Do all you can for yourself."

She answered nothing as he left the room and headed out to the streets. His thoughts were still too confused to make any sense of his own feelings about leaving, but he managed to realize that he needed to maintain his image as a cheetah jati servant. He headed for the gate with the confidence of those servants who knew themselves so well, knew their place in the valley, knew that all they did was sanctioned. He wasn't sure he'd ever know his own place so well, not now that Chaitan was imprisoned and his guests as well or scattered. But he could pretend. Their certainty bordered on arrogance, and he tried to emulate that also, but it was an arrogant humility, if that was possible, an arrogance that never threatened the superiority of the caste above them.

Trying for this exact balance, he strode through the gate and paid most of the coins Indima had given him in exchange for a horse. The man, one of the few servants in the city who was not of the cheetah jati, promised that he would receive most of the money back when he gave the horse to the stable master at the railroad tracks.

As he rode away, Pavresh resisted the urge to turn around and look at the city walls and the volcanic beds. Cotton wisps floated around him, and he pushed the horse as fast as he dared toward the distant railroad track.

Chapter 20

Jaritta stood to one side while Tanjali opened the oven. She couldn't keep herself still, wondering what the things would look like. But at the same time, she couldn't get herself to be the one to pull them out. She closed her eyes.

"They look like piles of dung."

Jaritta felt something inside her drop as her eyes jumped open. She looked at the figure. Dung. Tanjali was right.

"The glaze works anyway. See how smooth it seems to flow?"

Jaritta couldn't help the bitter laugh that came. "Perfect. *Smooth* shit. Who wouldn't want to buy that?" She almost reached out to knock the pile of clay to the floor before remembering how hot it must be. She walked over to the far wall. They were in an abandoned *brenil* building near the river. It was a rare find, and Jaritta expected any day to find the owners returning. It had likely been a merchant's house, and the merchant was called away suddenly, taking his family with him. Or perhaps a tradesman of some sort who jumped on an opportunity to work his goods in another city for better pay. Whichever the case was, she'd found a rear window loose and let herself in.

Now she and Tanjali made use of the generous oven inside and the piles of coal.

"Not all of them are so bad." Tanjali still stood beside the hot oven, taking out the things one by one.

Jaritta walked back and looked at the other pieces she'd made. Maybe so. Some might work for what she wanted. The glaze pleased her, giving the clay's surface the natural coloration of wet stone. That had been the first thing she worked on when she decided the usual life of the untouchable had become too dangerous. For several days, she'd hidden herself above the window of a potter to watch him work, and then stolen in to see what exactly he used. The result was good—surprisingly so, given how awful most of the clay figures looked.

Jaritta wrapped her hand in a bundle of rags to pick up one of the figures. She'd tried to recreate the image of the weird rock formations in the lava beds, where minerals coated the stone in wild layers. The clay she'd been most faithful in shaping were the ones that collapsed into ugly piles. In others, she'd added a bit of fancy, swirling the clay into more bizarre configurations. These were the ones that had survived. She held one close to inspect it. Swirls in the glaze spilled around the edges, giving the whole thing a sense of motion.

She set it down and looked at the others. No more than five of the dozens she'd crafted would be worth trying to sell. The rest could go in the house's courtyard. Or in the river. She stepped away and looked at Tanjali. The girl was also untouchable, and Chaitan's release hadn't meant she could get her job back as his attendant. Now she was looking back at Jaritta and obviously struggling not to laugh.

Jaritta shook her head and gave a wry smile, which was enough for Tanjali to let out her laugh, a full-throat, young-girlish laugh that didn't seem to belong to an untouchable. She supposed maybe there was something funny about the ridiculous things they'd tried to bake. She'd wanted something they could try instead of begging, which was becoming increasingly difficult in the capital. Soldiers regularly assaulted beggars, accusing them of plotting against the princes. So far women had been safe, but Jaritta wasn't going to assume that would continue.

Meanwhile, the lower caste jatis, and even some *brenil*, were becoming more sympathetic to the untouchables as Rashul's manifesto and Marankiya's epic spread among the people. Well, not all the lower castes felt that way. Many were as contemptuous of the untouchables as the priests and soldiers had always been. Some more so. But it was the growing sympathy in certain quarters that made Jaritta think of her current scheme. These were not the usual people to offer anything to beggars, but they might be willing to buy a trinket from an untouchable where the higher castes wouldn't.

Tanjali interrupted her thoughts, still half laughing as she spoke. "Well, what did we expect, I guess? Digging up our own clay outside the city and using stolen ingredients for the glaze. Not even knowing how hot to bake them."

"I suppose so. But…" Jaritta gestured at the worthless lumps of failed clay, ending with her hands in the air. "I guess I didn't expect this."

They separated the good pieces from the trash, piling the worthless ones in the corner of the room. Jaritta looked down at the few that remained.

"We might as well wait until we have more before we try to sell them. Back to the clay beside the river, I guess."

Tanjali stopped her with a hand on her arm. It was strange how such a touch shocked her again, as if everything that had happened to Chaitan and Rashul and the others had made her once again truly untouchable by anyone. "You try to sell these. I'll get us some more clay for the next batch."

Jaritta hesitated, and Tanjali added, "It can't hurt to get a sense of where we might want to bring more to sell."

"Fine. We can do that." She began gathering the figures she would try selling, then stopped as she thought of the slight Tanjali wandering to the river alone. She'd been born untouchable, true, but not like the street-dwelling beggars. Her family were death workers, a jati, even if excluded from the castes. She hadn't been forced to survive the streets on her own.

Setting down the wooden tray of figures, Jaritta picked up another pail and shovel. "Maybe I should come with you."

Tanjali smiled as if she knew what Jaritta was thinking and stepped to the wall. Neatly folded on the floor was her roughly made black cloak. "I will be fine with this." She swung it around her shoulders, and Jaritta realized what people would see. A death worker, carrying a shovel even. Only the lowest of corpses—criminals and heretics—would be thrown into the ground rather than burned. No one would disturb her, superstitious of the bad luck even looking directly at her might incur.

Jaritta nodded and resumed loading the tray as Tanjali slipped out the side door. She followed soon after with her tray of whimsical figures.

Everywhere in Romnai the streets felt different, as if the moment was poised on the edge of a tremendous fall and no one knew where it would land. She moved about the not-quite-familiar streets, offering her clay figures to passersby. No one could mistake her for anything but an untouchable. Most ignored her with the same intentional, half-guilty way they ignored beggars, their faces turned slightly away, their pace increasing, their movements becoming stiff.

Jaritta pursued them with all the shameless persistence of the beggars, but with little success. She sold one to a *brenil* merchant who clearly bought it simply so she'd leave him alone. As she hid the coins within her coarse, untouchable clothing, she looked up and realized she stood near Chaitan's house.

Without any conscious decision, she wandered closer, her mind replaying all the times she'd come here in recent years to sit inside, to talk with others, to rail against the bonds of the caste society. She entered the square outside his house and stopped. A guard stood before his door, another visible inside at a window on the second floor.

Jaritta scurried into the shadow of the nearby buildings. If she blocked out the guards, it looked so familiar. She could hear Rashul's voice, strident but inspiring. Namrani's music, ranging from quiet to overpowering, like a foundation that everyone else built on. Other voices rising and fading. Iksheen, passionate and impatient. Marankiya, sullen, withdrawn.

For the first time in days, she thought of the arcist Pavresh. Jasfer wouldn't tell her where he'd disappeared to, though she suspected he'd gone to Jarnur beside the sea. And what of the rest? Many imprisoned. No more laughing together or dreaming of a better city, a better world. Those were the old concerns. Now was a time of survival and nothing more. Those who made it through these times of beatings and imprisonment could dream again. Jaritta had to put any hopes away—save them for later, she told herself, but what it really felt like was killing them. What else could an untouchable do at a time like this? Hope wasn't safe.

Even so, Jaritta found a shadowed roof where she could see Chaitan's house, and she sat there until late in the afternoon. People visited Chaitan's house, but they weren't familiar people. The strains of some song reached her, but it wasn't the songs of their performances, only the sanctioned music of the temples coming over the roofs from a hidden musician.

Finally, she left, hardly looking where she went.

* * *

Their next batch of figures, each whimsically designed to match the best of the first batch, failed utterly. Jaritta again left it to Tanjali to open the oven and look first. As soon as she opened the oven door, she began coughing. The smell of smoke made Jaritta open her eyes and look. The figures were charred and broken. The lead that seemed to be in her stomach told her even before she'd examined each one that none was worth salvaging.

"What went wrong?"

Jaritta reached out without touching the blackened figures. "Did we leave them in too long?"

"No." Tanjali sounded surprisingly confident of the fact. "It was the same amount of time as the others."

Jaritta thought of the work they'd done piling the fuel around the brick oven throughout the day before to get it to the right temperature. All the careful laying of the coal such that it would stay constant overnight while they slept. The times she'd roused in the middle of the night to check on the fire and add more. "I guess we must have left it too hot." The lump of lead grew even heavier. "Next time we'll have to…"

Did she even want there to be a next time? Such a pointless exercise while people suffered, while Rashul and so many others were imprisoned and the entire city cringing in fear. She wanted to shape events, not clay.

Tanjali said nothing as Jaritta moved away from the oven to the corner where the shards of their earlier failures lay. She picked one up and threw it into the floor, scattering a dust of hardened clay. As she picked up another, she paused.

"Pull them out and let them cool, Tanjali. Then I know what to do with them."

Her hand wrapped in cloth, Tanjali pulled out all the charred figures and laid them on the floor beside the oven.

"Shall we let the heat out or keep the fire going?"

Jaritta stepped over to the table where more figures were already formed and drying. "Keep it going. We have enough figures here to make another batch tonight."

While they waited for the latest rejects to cool, Jaritta set to work on the drying figures, checking their wild shapes and curves to make sure they were ready for the swirls of different glazes. Her fingers moved quickly, as if she'd been painting clay since she was young.

When she finished the figures and left them to dry, she returned to the corner full of shards. "Help me gather these up," she said to Tanjali, who'd been preparing some food. Jaritta didn't feel hungry and had no wish to wait until after they'd eaten.

Fortunately, Tanjali said nothing, simply moving the food to another part of the iron stove. Without a word, she came over and helped Jaritta gather the pieces, first from the corner and then from the newly cooled figures. When every sliver was gathered up, they left the house through the side door and marched through the early-evening streets toward the steam baths.

They talked of nothing as they went. When they reached the steam baths, Jaritta led straight to a gap between two of them. Steam-slick steps led down to a slab of rock running out into the volcanic bed.

Jaritta slowed to descend, but even so, her feet slipped on the rocks. A handful of shards spilled from her robe as she reached out to steady herself.

"You all right?" Tanjali came down and grabbed her elbow.

"Thanks." She smiled at Tanjali, realizing then how she hadn't smiled without a bitter hitch to the expression in so long. "Let's go."

Helping each other down the last steps, the two passed beyond the bath buildings. Sulfurous water pooled beside them, its heat quickly warming them uncomfortably. Gray mud bubbled ahead, belching and spitting in a shallow depression. Jaritta spilled the hardened clay onto the rock at her feet and picked one up. Tanjali mimicked her.

Then as hard as she could, Jaritta threw the piece into the mud. The next one went into the boiling water, and the rest followed. Some she simply threw as hard and far as she could,

Tanjali trying to beat her for distance.

Each throw pulled something from her as it left her hand. The splashes as they hit water or mud and the shattering as they struck rock sent something back, a sense of some emotion growing inside of her. Not quite happiness, but satisfaction. As she threw the final slivers into the water, it seemed to her that satisfaction was a deeper and truer and more desirable emotion than happiness or any other emotion.

Tanjali shook the clay dust from her robes. "That felt good. I almost hope for some more broken and worthless figures so we can do it again." She laughed, and it was a surprisingly young and innocent laugh. A part of Jaritta was surprised that any untouchable could ever sound so young, but the thought felt too cynical for her current state of mind.

The feeling of satisfaction lasted as they returned to the house, but shifted. It wasn't a feeling that everything was perfect, not a feeling that she could stay in that moment forever and be pleased. It was a satisfaction that demanded change, that longed for something more. Yes, she seemed to be saying and, but not yet. Even that was naïvely optimistic. It was an emotion full of nuance and complexity that seemed to lie just on the edge of all the familiar words, a slight angle away from any word she knew. She could be satisfied shaping only clay for now, and her hopes didn't have to die while she did so.

At the house, they added fuel to the oven, bringing its heat up a little but not as hot as before, giving the glaze extra time to dry sufficiently. It was late, the summer sun already set for its brief night when they placed the figures into the oven and retired to sleep.

In her dreams, the strange emotions took bodies, first as frightening mumblers, then as majestic maned wolves, then as the sly and wise nagas of myth, and finally as bizarre flying creatures she could never quite focus on. Each of these groups paraded before her as if to ask if it was the right representation, as if to ask her to name them. And each time she found herself answering yes and no, not quite, and the names she gave them were in no language she knew and had escaped from her by the time she woke.

* * *

They tried again to sell the figures a few days later when they had a fair number that seemed good enough. Both Jaritta and Tanjali wandered the streets of the lower castes, sometimes together, sometimes in adjacent blocks. They chose the neighborhood north of where Jaritta had gone earlier, an area that was less rundown with wider streets and its own small market, but still filled with the laborers and craftsmen and lesser merchants that were their targets.

Jaritta was elated with her first sale, a sympathy sale, no doubt, from a passing tradesman. She nearly ran from there as she sought out another customer. It took time, but eventually she sold another, and a third came soon after. But the euphoria lasted shorter each time, and she found herself growing angry with each person who turned her down. Now that she knew she could sell the figures, knew that some people appreciated them, it seemed insulting that anyone wouldn't agree and buy one themselves.

She turned a corner after one such rejection, her thoughts still on the encounter. Had she approached the couple wrong? Could she have done something differently to convince them?

When she looked up, she saw three men approaching her, spread out in a sort of net. Jaritta stopped. They were from a *nefli* jati. Laborers of some sort, she guessed. They didn't appear to have their minds on laboring. Jaritta had been on the streets for years and usually knew how to avoid any danger like this, but a glance at the narrow street showed her she hadn't put herself in the best position this time. It was more of an alley than a street, and no other people were in sight. She could try to climb—leaving her figures behind—but she'd have to get past them to reach the nearest way up to the roofs.

She took a step back. "Would…would you like to buy a figure?" How far to the street behind her? She glanced back as she stepped away again, but the three men were uncomfortably close now.

"Maybe. If you show us your figure."

"I'm untouchable." Often that fact was enough to keep most people away, though she wasn't sure with these men. "You wouldn't want to make yourself unclean."

"Way I see it," said the same man who'd spoken earlier, slighter in the shoulders than the others, but still muscular from whatever work he did, "if you're untouchable, then no matter what I do to you, I haven't really touched you." He moved to the side as he spoke, and she saw that soon they'd have her completely cut off. The way he said the words made her decide she couldn't wait any longer.

With a wordless cry, she threw her tray of whimsical figures into his face. Clay shattered as it rained down around him, and Jaritta ran. She made it past him, but before she could get away, a hand grabbed her arm, and then a hand on her other arm helped push her against the wall.

The two holding her still said nothing, though they were laughing as the leader recovered from the things she'd thrown at him.

"Bad move, woman. We'll see now just what you have worth touching." He came toward her, but stopped without warning several steps away. "What…?"

He turned around and then backed toward Jaritta so she couldn't see what had frightened him. When he bumped against her, he made no attempt to do anything, but only slid to the side. A figure in a black shawl glided straight toward him, her arm out, finger slightly bent as if with age.

Of course, Jaritta knew it was Tanjali, and she told herself there was no need to be frightened. But even so, she felt a bit of what the men must be feeling, the ingrained fear of the death workers, dressed as if in the ashes of a fire long gone cold. She felt that cold, and it felt like the fire that gave birth to the cosmos withdrew from the alley for a moment. It had the touch of arcist magic, like when Pavresh or Chaitan or one of the others had joined their magic with music and dance.

The men ran.

Tanjali pulled the black cloth from her shoulders, and Jaritta glanced up as if to catch sight of a dark cloud pulling away from the sun. But the sun didn't reach into that alley, and she knew it had been no cloud. She said nothing until they had reached a wider street where she could soak in the sunlight.

"Thanks. I…" Another shiver made her leave the statement unfinished, not even sure what she'd been intending to say.

"So which of us should be careful wandering the streets alone?" Tanjali asked with a smile that was maybe not quite as naïve as Jaritta had thought earlier.

"That's some magic you have there, Tanjali. You ever discuss it with Chaitan?"

Tanjali grabbed her elbow and guided her to a place to sit, the sill of a long-closed window. "I don't think it's magic. Not like Chaitan has. But sure, we talked about it."

Jaritta said nothing as Tanjali settled herself on the sill beside her.

"I guess it might tap into his arcist tricks, but then everyone does in some way, right? The difference is that the arcists do it intentionally."

"I suppose so."

They sat in silence for some time, and then Tanjali walked across the intersection to retrieve her tray and remaining figures. Jaritta debated returning to the alley to see if any of her figures were worth retrieving, but she knew they weren't. The two women set off through the city, away from the river, to see what they could sell, but Jaritta's heart was only half in it.

After a few more turns and a few more rejections, they paused along one wide street, curious about a commotion coming their way. At first, it was nothing more than an unfamiliar sound, but then they noticed people moving to the side of the street, people pointing and watching. They moved to another spot but could see nothing more besides the crowds gradually growing larger.

Finally, soldiers parted the crowds, marching around something still hidden. They neared where the two women waited, a dozen or more soldiers forming a circle around a man with his hands bound. The prisoner walked with his head high, moving in step with the soldiers as if they were his honor guard.

It took Jaritta a moment before she recognized him, as gaunt and disheveled as he'd become, but his bearing overpowered that, his charisma clear even with the chains. Rashul.

Other soldiers followed, discouraging the crowd from chasing after the captive, though not forcefully, as if they wanted some, at least, to bear witness to what was done to the revolutionary. Without needing to discuss anything, Jaritta and Tanjali both joined the small group of followers through the maze of streets.

The soldiers really did seem to be treating the neighborhood as a sort of maze, weaving up and down streets and even one of the smaller markets in that part of the city in what was surely not the quickest way to their destination. They wanted the people to see him, Jaritta realized. The house they stopped at stood alone, though surrounded by streets of row houses. Guards already waited nearby.

Jaritta led Tanjali to a low wall that brought them to one roof and another until they could look down on the house. The soldiers brought Rashul inside. She looked for some way to get to the roof of that house, but she saw nothing. It had been chosen well to keep Rashul visible but isolated.

Just as she'd suggested to her brother, it was almost as if she'd shaped the actions of the princes like so much clay.

The soldiers made a great show of checking around the house and talking with the soldiers inside, not because they really feared the house wasn't suitable, Jaritta guessed, but to give extra time for everyone to see Rashul standing there before the door. The windows on the lower level had iron bars over them, and some on the upper level as well. Others appeared to be completely sealed shut. One soldier even stood on an upper-floor balcony, giving him a view of part of the roof and some of the surrounding buildings as well. He wouldn't be there long, but it was an effective part of the pageant.

Already her mind was inventing and discarding plans to contact Rashul when they brought him inside. Plans to further shape the city of Romnai.

Tanjali had to pull her away. They returned to the house where the oven was still warm and ready to be heated again for another batch. But Jaritta had already forgotten the earlier events of the day and had no wish to work on more.

"Maybe tomorrow, Tanjali. I can't focus on clay right now. I need…" Her eyes fell on a kiwan board in one corner of the room. "Let's play kiwan."

Tanjali narrowed her eyes and raised one eyebrow.

"And while we play, we need to think of a way to talk to both Chaitan and Rashul."

The city lay before her mind like a lump of clay, and she only hoped that her attempts to shape it didn't end as formless as her first attempts at the figures. There could be no trial run or botched attempts in a craft that involved more than a million people.

Chapter 21

As the Silk City fell away behind him, Pavresh gradually increased the speed of his mount. The road had been transformed since he arrived, hard-packed dirt replacing grooved snow. He wondered how long before the snow returned out here, though it wouldn't affect him. He hoped to reach the tracks within two days.

Soon he found he couldn't focus on the trip ahead. He was constantly looking behind him, wondering when the pursuit would come and what he'd do. He tried to imagine what he would have thought a year earlier as he left the mines to go to Romnai about his new journey, his return to the capital. In so many ways that seemed like a different person, ignorant and arrogant. He was still ignorant, no doubt, of much that went on in the valley, only now he knew it. If he could approach Chaitan's house now, it would be as a much humbler person, not as the cocksure prodigy, not as the rugged loner, but as the earnest seeker of wisdom.

If anyone chased him, they hadn't caught up by the late summer nightfall. He made his camp off from the road, tying his horse behind a line of trees. There he imagined a fire among the rocks since he didn't dare light a real one, a fire of pine needles and slivers of stone. He performed his movements with his kusti, but the forms never came fluidly, as if a part of him was too aware of the road on the other side of the trees. His sleep also seemed merely an imitation of true sleep, and he woke early before the sun had risen above the nearby mountains.

As he saw to the feed and care of the horse, Pavresh heard sounds from the road. He had chosen the spot to be completely hidden, which also meant he could see nothing of those passing by. He was torn between sneaking into the trees to spy on the road and staying beside the horse to keep it quiet. The travelers themselves made little noise.

His indecision made his choice for him as he stayed beside the horse. Pavresh tried to count those on the road, but he didn't have the experience to be confident in his guess. He had tried to choose a rocky stretch when he left the road, and he hoped he hadn't left any tracks. He untied his kusti, wondering how such a little thing would help him if soldiers came around the trees to find him.

No one came. The noises moved on down the road, and Pavresh stayed beside the horse until well after he could hear nothing. When at last, he decided it was safe to move, he returned to the road.

He didn't move as quickly that day for fear of catching the riders ahead of him, but all day he saw no one in any direction. He and the horse grew too tired to continue before the sun set, and Pavresh again found rocky ground and a sheltered spot.

The next morning he'd only ridden a little ways when he decided he'd come far enough. His trip out had been so long ago and under such different conditions that he had no real idea how close he was to the railroad tracks and the river, but he didn't dare take the chance of getting close. If those other travelers had been soldiers, they might have simply been instructed to wait for him at the station. He would have to leave the road and swing around to the north, meeting the tracks farther downriver.

Pavresh dismounted and looked at the land to his right. Rugged land, full of rocks and pines and low shrubs. He thought of Indima back in the Silk City. They knew that her money had secured the horse. How much trouble would she be in if he took it with him? Another study of the land ahead decided him. It wasn't land for a horse. He'd probably end up leading the horse more than riding, so it'd be only good to carry supplies. His journey from the mines to Romnai had taught him how to live on what supplies he could carry.

What would be useful to have? A hunting sling and some bullets, though he wasn't adept at their use. A skin of water. Thick blankets for sleeping. And all the trail food he could manage. After grabbing those items and securing them, Pavresh gave the horse a slap and sent it along the road. It took off fast at first, but soon slowed to a walk. With the fire's luck, it would take its time reaching the station, and they'd be too late to search for him.

But who knew if the station might be just around the next bend? Pavresh left the road and made his way among the jumbles of rock. He tried to guide his steps to leave few prints, but didn't want to sacrifice much speed to accomplish that.

Late that afternoon, he heard a train whistle. He looked west. Far across the rough land, a line of smoke moved. It was farther than he'd hoped. So far to walk, and already weariness bogged down his pace. The distance made any pursuit less likely, anyway. Nothing for it but to keep moving. As he crossed the terrain toward the tracks, he forced himself to consider how exactly he planned to continue once he reached the river.

The easiest would be to find a boat and simply sail down the river, but he knew nothing of boats. Or rivers. Instead, he hoped to find one of those small stations where their train had stopped on the way out and sneak onto an empty car.

Apart from the surprising variety of animals Pavresh frightened as he walked—including the long-legged wolves and huge wisents, which seemed terrifying and graceful and cumbersome all at once—there was little to interest him until he reached the tracks the next day. He set off downriver in search of a station.

As the evening wore on, he grew frustrated. The station stops had seemed so frequent on the train ride out, as if they were constantly stopping to unload or collect goods. But now he couldn't find a single station. No trains passed by either, which might be good or bad. It would be awful if a train came and went just before he reached its stop, but he entertained the image of leaping onto a passing train, grabbing the rear railing, and hiding in one of the last cars. It seemed worth an attempt.

He hadn't found a station yet when it came time to stop for the night, but as he prepared his sheltered camp in a hollow in a rock, he heard a train approaching from downriver. He had no reason to watch it pass, but he crawled out nonetheless and crouched beside the tracks. It was on the farther of the two sets, the upriver tracks.

The train didn't whistle—it had no need to out here—but the noise of the steam engine and the cars on the tracks astounded him. He'd known it was loud when he rode upriver, but not this loud. As it passed, he realized that even if it were going his direction, he'd have no hope of jumping aboard. Unless the train slowed down, there was no way he could grab a railing and hang on long enough to get his feet planted.

Before the train had passed, he left, returning to his hollowed rock. But as he turned, he thought he saw movement on the rear cars, as if people were gathered on the platform at the end. He froze and looked again, but the light was dim. Pavresh waited until the train had disappeared before he moved again.

* * *

Finally, late the next afternoon Pavresh saw a collection of low buildings and a road leading away from the river. There had been no trains since the night before. When he reached the buildings, he saw a bridge as well and a road heading south. The bridge seemed a good place to wait, so he settled in at the edge of the river to watch the water flow past.

A train pulled in during the darkness of the short night. Pavresh woke and pulled himself from under the bridge. The engine was just past the road, not where he wanted to hide on the train, so he made his way along the top of the river bank toward the rear of the train. He caught glimpses of movement as people unloaded or collected something—in the dark he couldn't quite tell. They were all on the other side of the train from him, so he moved more confidently.

Little grew between tracks and bank, and the rocks were easily avoided, so he soon reached the last cars. He studied them, trying to decide where he could hide. A railing ran around a walkway on several of the cars. Or maybe it was a porch on the back of the cars. It seemed the ideal way to get aboard. With a final glance toward the front of the train where the people were loading, he ran for the second car from the last.

As he was about to reach up and grab the railing, he was struck with a powerful arcist theme. That of the rash youth hurrying into danger. Without thought, he pulled his hand down and veered to the side. His body crashed into the side of the car, fortunately without sound. As he'd twisted, he'd seen a figure on the porch, and he wondered if some part of him had noticed that and sent the message to his body faster than his mind could make a decision.

A voice sounded almost right beside him. "I thought I saw something out there."

"A person?" a second voice answered from inside the car. "Be alert if he tries to board."

"I think he might…bring a light, would you?"

Pavresh ran, and shouts came from all along the rear cars of the train, followed quickly by the light of a dozen gas lamps.

"There!"

Pavresh dodged in case they had slings or bows. He ran toward the front of the train, wondering if maybe he should have gone the other way and disappeared back into the wild land around. But he'd run without thinking, and now he feared there must be soldiers at the front of the train as well.

He'd heard no swish of arrows yet, but still he dodged as well as he could in the dark. Gas lamps approached from behind, and shouts passed the alert to those ahead. Just before the front of the train, Pavresh reached the bridge and sprinted with everything he had left over the river.

He'd known the river was wide but never realized how wide until then. It was no mystery where he'd gone, so Pavresh expected to hear the sound of footsteps behind him, but no one came. He was more than halfway across when he heard a whinny, followed by the unmistakable sound of horseshoes on wood.

He tried to run faster but stumbled, scraping his hands against the wooden bridge as he caught himself. More horses followed the first onto the bridge. The other side of the river still seemed too distant. An ache spread in his side, and his palms stung from his fall.

A glance behind told him that the horsemen carried no lamps or torches, which would be good if he managed to find a hiding place, but for now, it meant he had no idea how close they were. The echoes of their hooves seemed impossibly loud.

A low wall ran along the bridge. Pavresh angled toward it, placed his hands on top, and vaulted over. As he fell, he heard hoofbeats directly behind him. He pulled himself into a ball for protection from whatever lay below. He steeled himself for cold water.

Instead, he hit shrubs and wet ground that felt impossibly hard. At first the pain was distant, the ache of something missing, vague and unformed. Then it struck him in perfect focus. Not a pain from any particular part of his body, but pain with no source that simply descended on him, smothering his breath. He tried to lift himself into a crawl, but he couldn't even do that. The smallest movement brought more fire.

People were shouting. The sounds of the horses came from across the bridge where their riders searched by the light of the stars. It might take them time to descend to this place, but he knew they'd find him if he simply stayed there.

He pulled himself forward, crawling like a snake. Like a naga, perhaps. The images he'd seen with Indima in the Silk City threatened to overwhelm him. He thought he saw a naga rise from the marshy ground, but then the vision disappeared.

The ground, he realized now, was very soft, despite how it had felt when he landed. Pools of water alternated with bits of land, clumped by the roots of the shrubs. He slithered from clump to clump.

Someone shouted from the other side of the bridge, indistinct but the answer from the nearby horsemen was clear. "Bring some lamps. He must be hiding along here somewhere."

Again, there was a question, and the soldier answered, "I don't think he jumped. We would have heard a splash." After a pause he continued. "It's possible, I suppose. We'll check down there."

He couldn't have much time. Pavresh forced himself through the muck. With light, they would surely see the path he made. He angled into deeper puddles where the water chilled him.

Further images swayed above the water, flashed, and disappeared. Pavresh crawled toward them without thought, moving downriver among the reeds and brush and wet mud. The rich scent filled his nostrils, a heavy, rotting smell mingled with hints of a thousand other odors. After a pain-wracked time that felt eternal, Pavresh approached a low bank. Long grasses overhung the sides, and for an instant, nagas seemed to dance before it and on the lip of the bank. The images disappeared, but Pavresh went straight to the grasses and pushed them aside.

He thought he should be surprised to find a dirt cave hidden behind them, but he wasn't, as if he'd been expecting just such a place all along. It was not a large cave—not much more than a hollowed-out bit of ground—but he found enough room to lie down, curled against the cold dirt at the back of the cave. The sounds of the search continued outside.

Between his fear of discovery and the unending ache of his body, Pavresh thought he'd never sleep. Shouts continued to punctuate the night, and in his mind, he saw the lamps swinging about, moving along the bank and down beside the river. He imagined them finding the path where he'd dragged his body and following it straight to his cave. Slowly the cave teased out his tiredness, and despite the occasional shiver that passed up his spine, he grew sleepy.

He awoke to light coming through the grass, unsure what had woken him, though he knew instantly where he was. He could hear a low hum of something over the sounds of the river, and then he heard it again: a train whistle. The train was pulling away from the station. Were the merchants involved frustrated at waiting so long for nothing? Were the soldiers embarrassed at not finding him? Or did they remain behind, waiting for him to show himself?

He stayed in his cave, not daring to look out yet. There was no other sound from outside except for the noise of the river. Pavresh lay there long after he'd fully awoken, listening for any hint of soldiers. He pushed the grasses away. There were no signs of people at the station or on the bridge. He studied the scene for a long time before crawling out. Keeping low, he turned and peered over the edge of the bank. No sign of soldiers there either. Pavresh made his way downriver from wet-soil shrub to a stand of reeds, splashing across deeper water when he had to, stopping and hiding periodically to look for any sign that someone observed him.

Only when a broad curve in the river hid the bridge and station completely did Pavresh climb onto the bank. He moved more quickly on firm ground. Late in the day, he found a track leading straight west, away from the northwest flow of the river and decided to follow it. If he was picturing his location correctly, the river made a large loop here, heading west for a ways then curving back most of that distance to the east before it righted itself to head for the sea. He hoped that the track would cut out that extra distance.

He kept a wary eye behind as he went, but the long evening passed uneventfully.

* * *

Pavresh had underestimated distances in the interior of the valley. Even as his aches faded and he could walk faster, he seemed to get nowhere as the days went on. Three days from the river, he came across a wide north-south road. The people of Eghsal didn't travel often, not for the sake of travel. But merchants would surely frequent this road, and there was always the possibility of a *kortru* prince or priest needing to visit another city to plan some aspect of governance. So, a steady trickle of carriages passed through the day, and Pavresh waited among a pile of boulders until night. Then he crossed and continued on his rough track. That had to have been the road between the river and Pashun, which had seemed to be near the end of the train ride out. If he kept this up, how long would he be walking before he reached Romnai? Months?

On the fourth day after crossing that road, Pavresh looked out on the combined fumarole field and city ruins that were the former city of Eghsal. It took him another day to descend to the edge of the unsettled ground and then among the dangerous pools to reach the city itself. Throughout his approach, he kept a careful eye out for any sign of the wolf jati encamped around the city.

He saw nothing.

No one accosted him as he entered the broken streets. He studied the strange buildings, remembering the way his mind had read the lay of houses in the Silk City. They spoke mainly of chaos. In places, the original houses were whole, but more often makeshift houses had been made of ancient walls and more recent, rougher construction. Mortar-less stone walls, long sticks lined with wisent skins, mud bricks, planks of wood scraps pressed together all combined haphazardly within any given dwelling.

Pale-faced mumblers watched him, and Pavresh stared back. These were the original inhabitants of the valley before his people, but their language, unintelligible to his ancestors, had earned them their name. Now he stood among them and couldn't look away.

He half-expected one to attack him, and his hand went to the sacred knots on his mud-caked kusti. But no one attacked. The looks he got ranged from curious to indifferent to vaguely hostile, but never outright violent. The most hostile, he realized as he tried to put an arcist theme on it, were simply protecting their homes, wary of a stranger and what his arrival might mean. He nodded to them and moved along the street.

That first neighborhood of mumblers was the exception. Throughout the other streets, Pavresh encountered untouchables and others who had fled society living alongside the mumblers as if there had never been a war between their peoples. No one seemed terribly concerned by his presence, but neither did anyone invite him to join them or inquire about his reason for being there.

It was late already, so Pavresh found a recess in the only remaining wall of a building, a small alcove raised knee height above the ground that provided a bit of shelter. He lay down to sleep.

Dawn light crept over the ruins of the wall opposite him when he woke to someone trying to sleep beside him on the bench. A large person, and seemingly unaware of Pavresh. He smelled something potent in the person's breath, like the fire liquor Marankiya used to drink at Chaitan's house but rougher. Pavresh pushed back. The stranger was a man, he realized as he saw the unshaven face, and despite his size, the man resisted and sank down to the floor beside the alcove.

Pavresh debated finding a new place to get a few more hours of sleep, but he couldn't imagine the drunk would possibly wake before Pavresh planned to leave. So after lying awake while the early morning sun rose, he rolled over and slept again.

When he woke once more, he stepped over the prone form beside the bench, but the man stirred at the movement, fumbling for something among his clothes as he sat up. He gave up and squinted at Pavresh. His face was darkened by several bruises.

"What do you want then?"

Pavresh shrugged, not knowing what to say to the man.

"Another mumbler-lover, are you? Don't worry. I'm leaving this town." He struggled to push himself to his feet but only fell back onto his face. "Just give me a minute," he said, his voice muffled by the ground.

Pavresh left him there to wander the city. He knew he ought to press on and get to Romnai as quickly as he could—he guessed now that it would take him at least a twelve-day to walk the rest of the way. Maybe more, depending on the terrain and how easily he could forage as he went. But the city piqued his curiosity. He wanted to see more of it and hear the stories of the people who lived there.

He walked down streets that were half gone, one side completely dissolved into a pool of sulfurous water. He saw walls visibly crumbling, trails of dust streaming to the ground. One small segment of an ancient building—little more than a brick or two—fell into the street just after he'd passed by. Pavresh stepped away quickly then turned to look at the wall. A steam spring bubbled just beyond it, and what was left of the wall looked ready to collapse at any moment.

Yet the people here seemed to live without worry. Not carelessly exactly, but as if the encroaching danger of the lava beds was simply a normal part of life. Nothing worth dwelling on. Nothing worth moving for. He spoke with some. Most were reluctant to talk, and if they spoke at all shared little of their pasts. From some he learned what brought them there and heard their stories of living in that place. Most were untouchables. Some had been laborers who fled their caste and jati. He met no one who'd been born *brenil* or *kortru*, though several people had stories of some high-caste person who'd just left or was out hunting or had died a month before.

With one older woman—he guessed she wasn't as old as she looked, the rough life aging her faster—he asked about the mumblers.

"What about them?" Her voice became sharp, almost shrill. "They're here like anyone else. Go beyond the steam field to hunt when they need to. Or across the river."

"And that…" Pavresh paused as he wondered about this reference to crossing the river. He couldn't remember seeing any sort of wharf for boats, but now he thought of it, an image appeared as he'd seen the city from the train, and that image included boats. That wasn't what he'd meant to ask her about. "Are there fights? Between mumblers and…regular people?"

The woman peered at him for a moment before answering. "Sure. And among mumblers. And among the rest of us. But those who think like that," she paused, and Pavresh felt like she was including more than just those people of Eghsal and mumblers who fought often, but other divisions as well, "don't end up staying here long."

She picked up the basket that she'd set down when he started talking to her and looked at him as if daring him to ask anything further.

Pavresh shook his head and said, "Thank you for your time," and she left.

Next Pavresh wandered near one of the mumbler houses, a frame of sticks and skins on two sides, an original wall on a third, and a jumble of rocks on the fourth. He stopped, trying to be as inconspicuous as he could, and wondered if he dared approach them to hear their stories. A long splinter of wood lay under a pile of stone near them, so Pavresh acted as if he was trying to free it for firewood and listened to them talk.

They mumbled. He'd half expected that these mumblers would have learned the language of his people, but they spoke the same senseless sounds as their people in the mountains. His attention wandered away from the wood as he listened, trying to imagine what words might lie hidden in such sounds. The mumblers noticed him then, and one called out, some shouted words that Pavresh couldn't understand, but the motion of his arm was plain enough. Pavresh walked away, leaving the length of wood beneath the rock.

As he went, the shouted words seemed to resolve into words he *could* understand. Had he simply not understood a strange accent, or was his mind trying to force the meaning of the motion into the mumbles as well? Had the mumblers learned to speak the language of Eghsal, the words of the Forgotten South, in their time here? And if they had, then their sobriquet no longer fit, and the image he'd grown up with, that the mumblers were too primitive to speak real words, was false. In fact, it spoke to intelligence greater perhaps than his own people's, since in six centuries none had learned the mumbling language.

Throughout the day as he spoke to people, he'd been offered

bits of food, but he felt hungry again, and he realized that he'd passed the entire afternoon wandering. He decided to return to where he'd slept the night before. If the drunk was still there, he could find a new place.

He tried to place the mumblers within the arcist magic as he went. In one sense, they were an obvious part of it, or at least the way his own people saw them fit the magic well. They were the others, the not-my-people. As soon as he thought of it, he realized the power of that image. It must have been a large part of what Chaitan had used years ago to influence the soldiers in their war with the mumblers. But now Pavresh wondered if there was something wrong with that approach. Or if not wrong, then over-simplified.

The mumblers fit the magic in other ways. They were the more primitive folk, free from the corruption of civilization. That, also, was a powerful arcist theme. And the stories of them cast them as warriors, no less than the wolf jati itself.

Back at Chaitan's house, Rashul and his circle had been fascinated by the fact that the castes didn't exist in arcist magic. It was proof to them that the castes were unnecessary, an evil that had been created by their society. And Pavresh had come to see arcist magic as revealing the world as it ought to be, cutting through the lies of reality to allow people like him to examine the truth, as he might part the smoke of a wet-wood fire to see the flames. But now… He looked at the mumblers as he passed and realized there was more to arcist magic than he'd thought, and not all good. When it came to the mumblers, arcist themes had the power, not of revealing the truth beneath the lies, but of hiding it, of allowing him to continue to see the mumblers as the stories of his people had always portrayed them.

He bent down and picked up a stone, balancing it in his hand. He'd forgotten some of the central ideas of his own religion, that the world itself was illusion, smoke from the holy fire, but worthwhile nonetheless. The rock in his hand, no matter how worthwhile or worthless it may be, was also false, forcing his mind to accept a certain way of seeing the world. Arcist magic might have the power at times to peel back a part of the illusion, but it could form the illusion itself at other times.

He was still trying to think through these things, twisting the stone in his fingers, when he reached the alcove. The drunken man was there, but appeared to be sober. He moved through a series of forms, similar to the religious forms Pavresh used.

Before Pavresh had come near, the man called out, "Don't come live here. It's not a good place."

"I'm sorry. I just needed a place to sleep last night. I'll find another place."

He relaxed his stance and faced Pavresh. "No. I don't just mean here. I mean this city. It's completely wrong. So, run back to whatever..." he looked up and down at Pavresh as if to guess his caste, then continued, "trade or delivery job you had."

"I'm only passing through on my way to Romnai. I hadn't intended to stay."

"Oh." He was breathing heavily from his exertion, but on hearing this, he came toward Pavresh. "I'm leaving tomorrow. How will you travel?"

Pavresh shrugged and tossed the stone at his own feet. "I've been walking."

The man said nothing for a moment, but stood there studying Pavresh. The arcist shifted on his feet. "I guess I'll find a different place to sleep then."

"Come by boat," the man said, as if Pavresh hadn't said anything. "I'll have a boat tomorrow, but it's really a two-person boat. I'm Bhadrik."

It seemed a ridiculous suggestion. This was not a man who inspired confidence, not a man Pavresh wanted to travel with.

But the mention of a boat made him pause. How much sooner could he reach Romnai by river? The water was wide and fast here, and as far as he could picture from maps went almost straight between these ruins and the capital.

While he was thinking, Bhadrik bowed to him, his movements almost a stutter. He seemed to pause at the level of someone greeting an equal and then went lower. He stopped in the middle of it and looked at Pavresh as if to guess his caste.

"I'm Parsh," Pavresh said. "You may stand up."

"You're untouchable, too?"

Pavresh shook his head. "Only a traveler. I was curious about this city."

Bhadrik looked at him skeptically. "I'm only untouchable for a few more months. Then it's back to fighting."

He left the word hanging as an invitation for Pavresh to tell his jati, but, Pavresh wanted to hear about the boat.

"How long do you think it will take by boat?"

"I don't know. I'm not an expert."

"How'd you get a boat then?" This wasn't looking so good to Pavresh. He was returning to his earlier thought to turn down the offer and walk.

"I've been doing some hunting for the man that owned it almost since I got here."

Pavresh was already shaking his head to turn down the offer when Bhadrik's earlier statement struck him. "You said back to fighting?"

"What?" Bhadrik cocked his head.

"Earlier. You said you were cast out for a while. And then back to fighting. What'd you mean?"

"I'm a soldier. Wolf jati. Is that what you're asking? I figured that should be obvious."

Pavresh thought of the soldiers that should be camped all around the city and the empty, open plains he'd seen as he entered. "Yes. I'll join you in your boat."

Bhadrik shook his head. "You do jump the conversation around." He shrugged. "We leave early, when the sun's still low. You'll be ready?"

"Anytime."

Both stood awkwardly for a moment, then Pavresh stepped past him to the alcove where he'd slept the night before. He thought Bhadrik was about to say something to him, but he stayed silent and gathered some dirty blankets together at the base of the crumbling wall.

Pavresh's last thought as he fell asleep was of the mumblers, not as something distant or unknown, but as people he could join, sitting at the fire before their front door, sharing their food, learning their stories.

Chapter 22

Bhadrik was not sorry to leave the ruined city behind. The boat floated high in the water and handled well as it carried them to the fast current near the far bank of the river. The others in their fishing boats, mumbler-lovers every one, wouldn't look their way as they left. The buildings became less distinct, a thing of the past. He was tempted to take out his sling and fire one bullet back at those walls, but he forced himself to keep paddling. The fastest current wandered back and forth between the banks as the river curved, but usually, they stayed near the center, and the river ran quite straight.

From the front of the boat, his companion did his share of the paddling as well, such that Bhadrik couldn't complain. Parsh didn't have the glorious body of a wolf jati soldier, but he seemed to be doing what he could with inferior strength. There was something about the man he hadn't told Bhadrik, some mystery to his wandering. He claimed to be merely walking back to Romnai, but if he had legitimate business, why wouldn't he take the train?

Not that Bhadrik was worried, as long as Parsh did his share of paddling. The man was unassuming and slight, obviously a valley-dweller who posed no threat to a soldier like himself. No peril for a member of the mystery religion, for a rival of the fire. It did make him curious.

As the city and its huts disappeared behind a curve of the river, followed soon by the western edge of the steam beds, Parsh seemed to be looking for something on that side of the river. He twisted backward, paddling without watching.

"Where are the soldiers? Shouldn't your wolf jati be camped here?"

Bhadrik pulled his paddle from the water and looked at the shore. "Here?"

Without his paddling, the boat spun away from that bank. Bhadrik corrected with a deep stroke, but his paddling was half-hearted as he studied the area.

"How long have you been cast out?"

"About nine months. What's going on?"

"And you never saw camps of soldiers around the city in your time there?"

Bhadrik's grip on his paddle tightened. The way this questions were heading...did others outside his jati—valley-dwellers!—know more about the soldiers than he did? He let his anger come through in his answer. "No. And they wouldn't be able to hide from me either. They are camped nowhere near those old ruins."

But it wasn't only the fact that this lowlander knew something he didn't. He pulled hard on the paddle but without skill. Parsh's questions implied that his brothers were doing something unexpected. Bhadrik thought of those visitors to his camp and the fact that he'd been told not to seek them in the mountains when his time as an outcast ended. What were they doing?

Parsh still said nothing, and Bhadrik tried not to let his anxiety show in his words. "My unit came down from the mountains just after I left, but why would you expect them here?"

His companion was quiet for a moment, then answered, "The council of princes instructed them to keep an eye on the city. The priests want to reclaim the city as someplace holy to the gods."

Bhadrik laughed. "Reclaim the ruins? That's worthless."

"There are rumors of an uprising against the princes

starting from there."

Parsh studied him, as if to see if there was any truth to it. There wasn't. The idea of those mumblers and mumbler-lovers mounting any kind of attack or plotting any sort of threat was ludicrous.

"The priests have been drinking too much, my friend. And a thousand wolf jati soldiers will die if they try to drive people out. They're not much as soldiers, the people there, but they'll defend their homes, drive the attackers into boiling pools and under crashing walls."

"And those in charge must know this." It didn't seem that Parsh was talking to him so much anymore, but simply musing aloud. "So, the question is, where are the soldiers, if not here?"

* * *

Until Bhadrik saw the first train going by, he thought they were moving pretty fast. The current seemed to race in places where the terrain became rockier, and even in gentle stretches, the riverside trees flashed past. But the thunder of the train told him how deceptive that was. The river's fastest was no match for steam-powered speed.

After the train had passed deeper into the valley, they sat in silence until Parsh began asking him about his time as a soldier. The man had an easy way with questions, and Bhadrik found himself telling more than he would have expected. He spoke of easy times within the camp buildings, of struggles deep in the mountains, told anecdotes about his fellow soldiers and his commanders. He said nothing about the mystery religion of the wolf jati or about any secrets known only to soldiers, but otherwise, his answers ranged all over his life.

At one point Parsh asked, "How far have you gone into the mountains?"

"As far as anybody. Until they become too high and too

snowy to pass."

"But do you think someone could? I mean, if they had the supplies and the climbing ropes and toothed shoes? Wouldn't they eventually come through somewhere?"

Bhadrik thought of the deepest he'd been in the mountains, where even the paths of the mumblers ended. Sheer cliffs and treacherous ice with little shelter and nothing to hunt. "No. Not in the north anyway. It only gets snowier and colder."

"The south." It was a whisper, not a question, but Bhadrik heard the longing in it, the same way all the valley people spoke of the Forgotten South. The passing rocks and scraggly trees seemed to pale, as if even they were only memories of better landscapes in the south. He'd never felt drawn to the south as others were, but for once, he understood that longing and felt it himself.

"It's been tried," Bhadrik said at last. "Wolf jati and others, and no one can get through."

"Did you think of trying it yourself? When you..." Parsh paused as if unsure how to say it delicately, "...were cast out?"

"No. I honestly didn't. It's never interested me enough." Though now that Parsh suggested it, what could be a better way to rival fire than to conquer the mountains and return to the lost homeland in the south?

Parsh's next question shook this from his thoughts, though it stayed at the edge of his mind, teasing him. "When you were cast out, was it fair?" Gone was the hesitation he'd shown a moment earlier, replaced by a sense that being made untouchable was a completely normal and natural part of most people's lives. "Did you deserve it?"

"No," Bhadrik answered immediately, then paused as an image of a broken body in the snow came before his eyes. He remembered the blood against snow, remembered carrying the other man, the injured one, at a run to the camp, remembered the sling bullets he'd sent flying through the air. His tone softened when he said, "No, I deserved to be punished, but…it should have stayed within the jati. Not something dictated by the visiting priests."

"Priests in the mountains? Why were they there?"

"I wonder that, too. They were telling our unit to move somewhere else. I don't know where."

"The priests told you to move? Since when did the priests direct the army?"

Such a simple question, yet it dredged up anger that surprised Bhadrik by its force. He dug his paddle deep into the water. Not anger at the man's question, but at the priests, at the way outsiders were using his jati. Outsiders! The very idea burned. People who were inferior to them, even if society set them up as a higher caste, those who worshiped fire instead of competing against it. He didn't consider himself an emotional person, yet somehow Parsh's questions seemed to bounce his emotions all around. It was far more unsettling than the physical jolts of the occasional rough water they passed through.

Finally, he managed to speak. "Never. That's the problem. The priests are not our masters."

Parsh nodded without turning. "They seem to be growing in influence, back in the capital. The priests and a few princes who've joined with them."

He said nothing else after that, and there was nothing in the statement to make it seem especially important, but it played through Bhadrik's thoughts the rest of the day as they paddled downriver and that evening, too, as they camped and he hunted. The hunting was easy here, and he returned soon to where Parsh waited beside a small fire. But he didn't revel in the hunt like he had other times. He kept thinking of priests, imagining himself striding into a temple and putting them in their places. Let them worship him, let them serve him, the equal in every way of their sacred fire.

* * *

The first two nights they didn't bother setting a watch. Few people lived away from the cities since it would mean being away from the warmth of the steam beds. This land would seem to be fertile, but even the farmers kept to the volcanic soil nearer the cities. And see how weak such softness made them. Most travelers would be on the trains, which meant that any outlaw bands would be on the north side of the river as well. So as long as they camped on the south side, they had little to fear from bandits.

As they approached Romnai they took turns at watch and often alternated staying alert in the boat as well to catch a few more hours of sleep.

One night Bhadrik woke, unsure why, and saw a figure approaching, lit by the lingering late-summer dusk. He reached for his knife, then paused at a gesture from Parsh, hidden opposite a small tree from the figure. Bhadrik relaxed his posture as well as he could, though he kept his hand on the hilt of his knife.

The figure—a man, Bhadrik guessed by how he moved—had paused when Bhadrik stirred, but now he resumed his approach. He had no weapon out but was crouched as if to pounce on anything, either dangerous or valuable. Bhadrik wondered why Parsh didn't simply show himself and scare the fellow away. He doubted the man would advance if he realized he was being observed. Parsh had something in his hands that Bhadrik couldn't identify.

When the man reached the edge of their camp, lit red by the embers of their fire, Parsh stepped from hiding. He moved gracefully, some kind of rope in his hands, and Bhadrik felt a thrill of excitement. Those moves—they were similar to those of the mystery religion but far more fluid, as if it wasn't that his companion moved his limbs to match some ideal but that his body truly was each of those stances, flowing as easily as the river did over its bed.

The rope flicked out, Parsh danced around to one side, and the intruder was bound even before he could give a cry.

Bhadrik sat up as Parsh prodded the man toward the fire. Bhadrik added more wood, then sat back to see what his companion wanted with the man. He said nothing at first, only untied and retied the captive's arms so he was bound to a small tree. His hands moved so fast the man had no time to attempt an escape, and Bhadrik couldn't tell what kind of knots Parsh had used, though he could see how well they held.

Then Parsh squatted beside the man and spoke in a calm voice, little different from the way he'd spoken in their boat, asking questions of Bhadrik.

"We don't intend to hurt you. I'd just like to hear some gossip, if you'd care to share it. How near are we to Romnai?"

The man said nothing, though he was visibly shivering at being tied up and interrogated.

Parsh eventually spoke again. "I should say that *I* don't intend to harm you." He gestured toward Bhadrik, who rose from his blankets. "My traveling partner may have something else in mind. See, he's a soldier—wolf jati. Or was one. They cast him out for killing a man."

Had anyone else shared his background this way, Bhadrik would have been angry. But coming from Parsh in the middle of this bizarre situation, he had to struggle not to laugh.

"Did you answer my question yet?"

The man had sat up straighter as Parsh spoke and answered as if the words were in a race to leave his mouth. "A day by cart. Loaded cart with vegetables, and an old pair of horses." His eyes shifted between them, darted around what was visible of the campsite. "Probably a little shorter for the two of you to walk."

"Less than a day. Good." Parsh said nothing about the boat.

He picked up a stick and drew in the dirt at his feet, then asked a new question. "And what's going on in the capital these days? I've been away for some time."

"We don't really…" The man swallowed when he looked at Bhadrik. He started again. "I guess we do hear *some* stories. People don't like it. Some group tried to kill a bunch of priests or something, which made everyone angry."

"Killing priests could do that." Something in Parsh's voice made Bhadrik think he doubted the story. It was probably the story as twisted by the priests.

"I don't think they actually succeeded. The princes even set some of the leaders free, from what we heard. Or sort of free but with soldiers stationed in their own homes."

"Do you bring your vegetables to the city often?"

"What makes you think I'm a farmer?"

Parsh didn't answer, and again the captive looked over at Bhadrik's size and gulped.

"No, not often."

Parsh moved from his crouch into a seated position, as if he intended to stay there talking for a long time. "Tell me about your last time there."

As the farmer and would-be thief talked, Bhadrik found himself nodding off. He hadn't slept as long as he'd hoped, and his body remembered that. Parsh and the captive spoke of so many details about the city, about people who lived there, even about some poetry. Poetry! How was a man supposed to stay awake in a discussion like that? He returned to his blankets and lay down.

The man was still bound when he woke, though asleep against his tree. Parsh nodded to him silently as soon as he noticed that Bhadrik was awake. Making as little noise as they could, they gathered their few things and loaded them into the boat. Last, Parsh untied the rope that bound the captive and looped it around his waist. Only then did Bhadrik realize it was no more than a belt, a kusti like many men of the city wore, a bit rougher at a glance than those worn by the *kortru* caste, but a closer look showed it to be especially thin and strong, more than the rope it appeared.

The man did not wake even with his hands free, and they got into their boat and pushed off. The morning was cold, but less so than on recent mornings, and the air carried a hint of sulfur. Buildings appeared along the river. Still not many—even here few people lived outside the prescribed limits of the city. Most appeared to be warehouses or clusters of buildings for farm-workers and their families.

Parsh slept briefly as the current carried them, but Bhadrik woke him when he saw the first buildings of the city proper. A few stood on the northern bank, but they were mostly tied to the railroad and older buildings from the days when the river itself was where trade and transport took place. The river passed close to the steam beds here, so the stretch of city between the water and the rising clouds of steam was narrow, but ahead the river took a sharp turn to the north, such that the bulk of the city lay directly before them. Even with how fast the river carried them, it would probably take a wolf hour to reach the northern edge of the city, up near where the river curved again toward the west. Where in all that stretch should he leave the river?

As if reading his thoughts, Parsh asked, "Where will you go now?"

"I…" He was supposed to report to the commanders in the city once his exile was over, but that was still some months away. He realized that he'd simply been imagining showing up in the neighborhood, not far from where they floated now, where the rest of the wolf jati had houses, as if they'd welcome him and give him a place to stay until he could rejoin his unit. But then, what would be the point of exile? "I'm not sure, I guess."

Parsh was silent for a moment, then said, "I might be able to find a place for you. Not that I know where I'll stay either. But I might."

"I would be grateful."

They came to the wharf, which had a few larger ships arriving from or preparing to leave for Jarnur at the river mouth but otherwise was primarily a place for the boats of river fishermen. A few odd boats moved noisily about that stretch of river, moving by the fire's power, as Bhadrik understood it. Let them move by his power, and they would do better. When they pulled up to a dock, Parsh jumped out and secured the boat with knots like those Bhadrik had seen the night before on their captive.

"Stay here and try to sell the boat. I need to check on a place for us to stay, but I'll meet you back here as soon as I can."

Without offering any idea how soon exactly that would be or what to do if he didn't return, Parsh nearly ran as he left the docks.

Night came surprisingly soon, a clear sign that summer was ending. And with it, Bhadrik's time as an outcast. He sat against an abandoned warehouse with a few coins in a pouch he'd secured within his robes and waited for Parsh to return. He'd received a respectable amount for the little boat, and all he wanted was to go to one of the riverside taverns and spend them, but he told himself he could wait a little longer and see if his former companion returned. The longer he waited, the less highly he thought of the man. Parsh had kept his own origins and purposes mysterious, had done his share to get them downriver but little more. Sure, he'd made a show of offering to help find him a place to stay, but that hadn't happened after all. And why make the offer in the first place? What did he want of Bhadrik?

He stood up and headed along the docks, telling himself at first that he was only going to look at the taverns to decide which one would be best if it came to that. But, he gave up the pretense and headed for the entrance of one. Even from outside he could see that people crowded the room, which would seem to promise good drinks and good fun, although there was a slightly muted tone to their celebrations, as if fear was heavy in the city. But what else should he expect from valley people?

As he was about to enter, he felt a hand on his elbow.

"I've found a place," Parsh said and walked away. At the corner of a nearby street that led away from the river into the city, he stopped and looked back.

Bhadrik still hadn't moved. Tavern patrons pushed past him to enter or exit, but intimidated by his size, they did no more than mutter. The smells of the kitchen, of barrels of beer, of freshly brewed tisane came to him, and he reached his hand into his money pouch. But where would he stay if not with the little man? His money might get him someplace to lie down for a twelve-day, but then what would he do? Some kind of meat was roasting in the kitchen, and he caught the scent of fresh squash.

Parsh returned to his side. "Follow me. I've found more than just a place to sleep."

Bhadrik swung his gaze from the door to Parsh, and the images seemed to bleed from one to the next. *I'm tired*, a voice inside said, but another part of him thought it was hunger, no more or less. He still didn't leave his position at the doorway.

Parsh whispered, "You wish to avenge yourself against the priests, yes? To restore your honor and the honor of your jati?"

Bhadrik shifted his feet, took a small step toward him. How much had he told him in their time together on the river? He'd alluded to that surely, but had he stated this so plainly?

"I know a way to do that, a way that shows the priests that they don't rule over you. I can feel that need, like a fire inside you."

A fire inside him? No. The merest suggestion broke the spell Parsh had seemed to place on him, and he took a step back toward the doorway.

"No, it's not a fire," Parsh rushed to continue. "I was wrong. It's as powerful as fire. It's…it's the equal of fire. And I know a way for you to prove it."

Parsh stood before him, his stance open and challenging at the same time, the image of a friend who believes in him, who dares him and encourages him to try something bold simply because he believes it's possible. Because he trusts his friend.

Finally, Bhadrik nodded. "Let's go there then. Is there food? I'm tired and hungry."

Chapter 23

"I did not give you leave to return." Jasfer studied Pavresh for any clue about what he might have learned. He looked composed, his straight posture framed by the doorway. Jasfer had received the letter Pavresh sent and managed to decipher something from it, though it was mostly guesses. The papers in his hands demanding his attention, notes from relatives who were working on arranging a marriage for him, did much less to keep his interest. He was curious what Pavresh would say, but that didn't lessen the danger his presence posed.

"I apologize, *tisrah*."

Jasfer's ears invented the sounds of soldiers marching up to his door, the ominous crunch of boots on the aging flagstone.

"I couldn't stay in the Silk City," Pavresh went on, "without putting you in deeper danger. They would surely have connected me to both you and Rashul's crowd given more time."

"Who would? Tell me about this."

Pavresh proceeded to tell him about the actions of Prince Dartak's servant, about calling in loans, about soldiers coming down from the mountains but not gathering around the abandoned city. For a moment, he forgot about the danger Pavresh posed as his mind leaped through the information, trying to understand how it all fit together. If the soldiers weren't around the abandoned city, then where were they? And what was all the money for? A bribe of sorts for the soldiers? Paying for their supplies wherever they were and paying off those who stumbled across them?

It took him a moment to remember the spy standing before him. His curiosity retreated as he imagined someone having seen Pavresh come to his house. "You didn't answer why you had to leave."

Pavresh shuffled his feet on the stone floor. "There was a silk weaver who knew of my association with Rashul. And Teert knew of her participation with that group as well and was beginning to ask questions about me."

"You were careless." Jasfer ran his thumb along his clenched fist. Carelessness could easily ruin him. "Do you think he could connect you to me?"

"No. I think he suspected I was sent by a prince. He wouldn't have any idea who, though."

"You sent a letter to me." Jasfer's hand felt around on his desk for the cryptic letter he'd received a month or two earlier.

"I sent a letter to a cousin of mine living in Romnai."

"A supposed cousin who happens to work for me. You don't think they'd look into that? A suspected spy sends a letter. Doesn't matter who it's to, they'll assume it contains coded information of some sort."

He'd had the letter for a while now with no hint of anything changing in how the other princes treated him, and certainly no accusations. Still, he didn't like the possibility. His hands moved among the other papers before him, shuffling them as if in a blind attempt to choose a wife.

"I don't think I was under suspicion then, *tisrah*. It was only at the end that anyone took any interest in me."

Jasfer said nothing and stared at his spy. He didn't think the words sounded quite as confident as Pavresh pretended. But Pavresh endured his stare without flinching, and Jasfer broke the silence.

"Coming here was still a dangerous thing."

"Your sister knows how to move unseen. She brought me here."

"I don't have a sister." Jasfer pounded the desk once with his fist. "It's essential that you remember that, and that she remembers that, and that I remember it, too. In the eyes of the city, I have no sister." He picked up a quill as if to examine it, but he didn't really see it. "Even in the privacy of this office, we must remember that."

Pavresh lowered his head. "I apologize, *tisrah*. Jaritta, an…untouchable I know, has found me a place to stay and knows how to guide me where no one will notice."

Jasfer said nothing at first until he put the quill back down. "Beware with this woman. Don't let her presence get you in trouble. Or me." He looked at Pavresh's face until he saw that Pavresh had understood the unspoken caution that he not bring trouble to her either.

Pavresh nodded. "Yes, *tisrah*. I will take care."

Jasfer waved him out and turned away. As the arcist made for the door, Jasfer's fingers reached for something to fiddle with. They found a paperweight made of what appeared to be highly polished coal, or perhaps a briquette of coal with some kind of varnish over it. It had come from the mines, the same ones where the arcist had grown up.

He spoke before Pavresh could leave the room, though he didn't take his eyes from the hints of color that hid deep within the black of that coal. "Your…cousin will be on an errand every morning at this time. Pass him by, and if I need your services, he will let you know."

"Yes, *tisrah*."

Jasfer heard him leave but didn't look up. He was a useful man and had uncovered some important information, so Jasfer didn't want to lose him. He posed some danger, but already that fear was fading as he wondered how to fit the new information together. There were lines of influence all over the place, but still too many uncertainties for the prince to grasp exactly where they led.

* * *

Jasfer rode in his carriage to Chaitan's house. The few times he'd spoken with Jaritta recently (*not* his sister, he had to remind himself), she insisted that the streets were perfectly safe for her. It was only the *kortru* caste that had to worry. He hoped that was true—he didn't want to imagine her assaulted by angry low-castes, even if she wasn't his sister.

Some of the other princes were already there when he arrived. Shardash, who'd been charged with watching the malcontents. Bhainu, whose warehouse they had commandeered. And Samatrit, Jasfer's cousin. He wondered how many princes had been summoned. Jasfer joined them inside as a few more arrived. They spoke lightly while Samatrit kept silent to one side.

Chaitan himself sat at the rear of the room with one attendant. He did not rise to greet the princes, but then Jasfer didn't think he looked healthy enough for even that.

Dartak arrived, an easy smile on his face. Jasfer glanced at the two retainers with him, wondering if one was the arcist whom Pavresh had noticed. None of these princes were those he felt most comfortable with, and he wondered why he'd been invited. Had someone connected him to Chaitan? Pavresh had been back in Romnai for a twelve-day or so. If someone were to make that connection, he would have expected it sooner. Jasfer looked at the faces around him, listened to their words for any hidden threat, but he sensed nothing. Last to arrive was the newest prince, Karket, whose grandfather Lokanrik had given up his post among the Thirty.

Shardash took charge and led the princes as a group to Chaitan. The princes formed a line with Jasfer to one side and squeezed back half behind those near him.

"The city greets you, Chaitan," Shardash said as he came to a stop. "We've come to check how our storied hero of the past is doing."

There was no way Chaitan would believe such a false speech. Jasfer wanted to jump in front and get directly to the point of their being there. Except he wasn't really sure what that point was, only that it had nothing to do with pretending to be friends with the man.

Chaitan simply spread his arms as if to take in the room, the house, the soldiers all around. "Here I am."

Shardash coughed and looked unsure how to respond. Finally, he said, "We'd like to know of any visitors you've had."

An interrogation? Is that all they were here for, to intimidate an old man with a show of the power of the princes? Jasfer doubted that was all, but it seemed to be a part of it.

Chaitan shrugged and turned to his attendant. "Visitors? Have I had any, Kapita?" She shook her head, and he turned back to Shardash. "Your soldiers would surely tell you if I've forgotten anything. My memory is not what it once was."

"What of Rashul, your protégé? He must have contacted you somehow."

"He was simply one of many who came to gather here. I served our people well, and when my illness became too much, I retired here and surrounded myself with lively people. And for this you punish me."

Jasfer noticed Samatrit, opposite him in the line, shifting as if he wanted to take charge. The lines of influence, as well as he could read them, were all confused. Shardash continued his interrogation and seemed convinced that all the power was gathered in his person, like a net that he was throwing out to trap Chaitan. But instead, the princes themselves sent their lines in different directions, and what net Shardash had left simply slid off the old hero.

Chaitan talked about music, or maybe about his magic as if it were music. Jasfer focused on the faces and stances of those around him rather than paying attention to the words. Most of those gathered seemed to be enthralled with the exchange, though he caught hints of other games going on in the way Dartak stood and the seemingly random places where his gaze wandered.

"You have arrested the best of our city," Chaitan said, and the power of the conversation jumped to him, "the poets and artists and musicians. Did Rashul break a law? Perhaps. But you have no right to take all of these people away. Bring me again my musician Namrani, who had nothing to do with these things you accuse Rashul of. And then maybe we can speak again."

A coughing fit took Chaitan, though Jasfer suspected it was a sham, at least in part, a piece of the performance to drive them out in shame. And Jasfer did feel shame. He couldn't deny that. Here was an old wise man, a hero no longer revered by those he'd saved. He knew it was the arcist magic playing on his emotions, but that made them no less real.

Chaitan managed to stop coughing and said with a slight bow, "You are dismissed now." Then he turned and shuffled away, leaning on his attendant's shoulder. Dismiss a prince? That took arrogance, but all of them—Jasfer included—were too stunned to react.

Jasfer looked at Shardash. The man seemed shattered, as if any power he'd had was gone, and whatever other purpose he'd planned for demanding the presence of the others had failed. Unless it hadn't been his idea… Jasfer glanced around until his eyes focused on Dartak. Could he have planned this, perhaps even knowing that Shardash would fail? What deeper purpose might it serve? At the least, it undermined Shardash's power among the princes. Perhaps he had stumbled on some information, and Dartak wished to discredit him before he could use it. Or maybe the trust Baram put in him was something that displeased Samatrit, scared him even that Shardash might rise to greater power among the assembly. If they found any reason to suspect Jasfer's attempts to uncover their intrigue, they would certainly move more quickly to quiet him. It was a reminder, whether they'd intended it as such or not.

A soldier broke in on Jasfer's thoughts. *"Tisrae,"* he said, bowing to the now-ragged line of princes, "there's trouble outside."

Karket broke from the group and rushed to the window. Jasfer almost joined him, but even from where he stood, he could see that these windows were not glass but thick oiled paper that only let in the light. They wouldn't see anything from there.

No one spoke as they waited for the soldier to explain, and that was when Jasfer heard the noise outside. People shouting, chanting something that the walls muffled into meaninglessness.

"What is it?" one of the princes finally asked.

"A mob." The soldier looked over his shoulder through the barely opened door and forgot the honorific. "You should wait here until we get them cleared away."

"They sound well organized," Jasfer said, and thought without saying it, *and surprisingly calm, also.* "What do they want?"

The soldier glanced back at him and bobbed his head. "They keep asking you to release *him.*" He gestured toward the door where Chaitan had gone. "Don't worry. We just have to clear a way to the carriages, and we'll be fine."

Without saying a word to the man, Dartak pushed past the soldiers to reach the door. Jasfer joined several other princes in following Dartak into the street. A crowd waited for them in the square, their shouts growing much louder when the princes appeared. When he was able to see the full street, Jasfer was surprised by how many people were there. They hadn't sounded like this many from inside, and even now with their voices raised, there was something lacking compared to his expectations, a sense of volume that bordered on violence. They shouted for Chaitan's release—and for Rashul and other names Jasfer didn't know—but they weren't shouting for blood.

Jasfer was reminded of the epic he'd been given in the streets some twelve-days ago. He'd paged through it, though his patience for poetry was quite low. It had called for change, but not for violence, and that was what the noise of the crowd reminded him of.

Dartak must have sensed the same. He gestured to the nearest soldiers. "Lead us to the carriages. They'll make way for us."

The soldiers hesitated. "*Tisrah?*"

"Go on. It will be safe."

They bowed and formed a small spearhead to part the crowd. The princes followed, flanked by their own servants and a few other soldiers. There was something majestic in the way Dartak moved forward, a fearlessness that Jasfer thought would survive this day in the memory of those watching, both princes and lower castes. Even though he sensed the peacefulness of the mob, fear ran at Jasfer, making feints as if to see if he would flinch. He was glad to have Yatim walking beside him, even if the soldiers ultimately offered far more protection.

The row of houses fronted a square of sorts, large for this part of the city, but not overly big. There must have been several hundred people there, crowded into that space, some standing on the old, dry fountain in the center.

The shouts grew louder, and now they held a hint of something stronger, baser, and more dangerous. The spearhead of soldiers picked up their pace. The carriages weren't far, just around the side of the line of buildings that included Chaitan's. The faces of those nearest them were angry, but a strange sort of anger. It wasn't anger that was ready to turn into blind rage, despite the growing volume. Jasfer couldn't look at their faces for long. He tried to study the way the people had gathered for any clue to who was guiding or organizing the group, but his usual tricks of seeing the lines of influence among princes failed him. There were far too many people to see any overarching pattern.

Their progress was slow. The line of houses seemed much longer than it had when Jasfer arrived. People made way for the soldiers grudgingly and pressed against the thin line of princes from both sides. At one point, they even pressed close enough that someone touched Jasfer, reaching past the soldier on his right. Jasfer shuddered and wondered if it had been an untouchable. He would have to go to the chapel in his home when he returned and perform the cleansing rituals.

The tone of the crowd shifted with surprising quickness. Jasfer froze where he stood when he noticed it, a new undercurrent, a different kind of anger. He looked at the mob for some source, straining his neck to see farther back, but the shift rippled across them with no clear direction. Had a new contingent entered the square? Had a prince done something to anger them? He couldn't tell for sure. Even Dartak seemed taken by surprise as he halted in the lead of the line. Some of the cheetah jati servants tried to knock the crowd back with clubs, and someone lay on the ground, but that could have been a result of the growing tension, not its cause. The entire line of princes was stuck, the soldiers unable to guide them forward.

Shouts echoed off the high walls that ringed the square, twisting into more ominous sounds.

Yatim grabbed Jasfer and pulled him toward the near buildings. The crowd between them and the walls was only a few people deep, and they gave way to Yatim's pushes. No soldiers followed them.

"We're going back inside," Yatim yelled at his ear.

Bodies pressed all around him. "What about the soldiers?"

Yatim shouted something back, but even from that close, he couldn't understand it. They moved farther from the soldiers and other princes. Something sailed through the air. It passed over the heads of the other princes and struck one of the rioters near Jasfer with a sickening sound of something splattering. Other things flew, fruit and squash and small stones. Jasfer moved ahead in a crouch against the wall, with Yatim pulling him along toward Chaitan's house. He couldn't remember how many houses they'd already passed before they stopped.

Jasfer had never in his life been this close to so many people, and people of lower castes, every one. He had to remind himself that he had no time to worry about touching them as he pressed close behind the temporary path Yatim created. More objects flew through the air, and the shouts became screams—of anger? of fear? of pain? Jasfer wasn't sure. He kept his head down.

At times, their path kept them directly beside the buildings; other times, it twisted, leading them deeper into the crowd. Someone punched him in the side, directly beneath his ribs. Jasfer staggered at the pain. It hadn't seemed such a strong blow, but he couldn't believe how much it hurt anyway. He grabbed Yatim's shoulder and pulled himself along, not looking back to see who'd hit him.

Other elbows and knees struck him as they moved, but none seemed as obviously intentionally as that first one. They passed a door and came to another. Jasfer wanted to see if it would open, even if it wasn't Chaitan's house, but Yatim kept pulling him ahead.

Jasfer spared one glance behind him where the other princes had gathered in a clump, surrounded by the few soldiers. All he saw before focusing again on his own progress was the soldiers pushing back at the crowd.

Yatim used his hands as a wedge to force people apart, and Jasfer added his weight, pushing against Yatim's back, until Yatim suddenly turned around and grabbed Jasfer, pulling him down to a crouch. People nearby screamed as something fell in their vicinity, something hot and sharp, perhaps shards of heated clay. In the chaos, they advanced almost to Chaitan's door, but then the people noticed them.

They'd been mostly lucky so far, with everyone focusing on the cluster of soldiers and princes. Some few had realized that Jasfer was a prince, but most had seemed to accept them as merely members of the mob trying to get to a new location. Now that changed. A wall two to three people deep stood between them and Chaitan's door and wouldn't move.

Yatim grappled with one, first pushing him straight, then pulling him back and to the side. They moved a few steps before the others closed in. Jasfer knew nothing of fighting. He was fit for a prince and enjoyed various *kortru* sports that required some athleticism. But this was something vastly different, and the men standing in front of them were hardened by work he could scarcely imagine.

Hands reached for him, no longer simply incidental touching. They pulled at his shoulders, his arms. Yatim managed to push another person from their way, but as Jasfer made to follow, he was held back, and the crowd closed between him and his servant. With a shout, Jasfer lowered his head and charged at the gap between two men. He crashed through and into Yatim's back, who stumbled into the men he was grappling with.

Jasfer's head rang, and only part of him was aware of what he was doing. The mob's cries seemed to echo down a metal tube before reaching him. More people tried to pull him back, but he clung to Yatim, swinging elbows at the arms that reached for him.

A roar came from behind where the soldiers fought on to

protect the princes. It distracted the crowd enough that Jasfer and Yatim broke through and fell into the doorway. The prince Bhainu had stayed behind. His servants rushed over to help. Jasfer let the servants lead him to a pillow, and he sat with his eyes closed.

It wasn't long before the crowd got briefly louder and then grew nearly silent. Footsteps distilled out of the greater mass of sound, then hoofbeats, followed by the door flying open. Jasfer opened his eyes. Bhainu stood at the doorway, welcoming a bedraggled group of princes inside. Jasfer stood and went to the door.

Soldiers filled the square outside, most of them mounted as they rounded up those bystanders who hadn't fled yet. At first Jasfer was ready to relax in relief, go home and forget about the day. Then he noticed another group of servants and soldiers approaching. They carried someone in their arms, someone whose silk robes were covered in blood.

"Who is it?" he asked as they came closer. He glanced around at the princes beside him, but his mind wasn't working enough for him to figure it out on his own.

No one answered, and Jasfer was able to identify the face, broken and bloody, of Karket. The beating had aged his face so he resembled his grandfather more than Jasfer had realized before.

"Bring pillows, *tisrae*," a servant commanded, and the princes obeyed, jumping to gather the pillows about the body. No one bothered to worry about caste when they saw how ashen Karket's face was.

"Has a doctor been summoned?" Shardash asked.

"Yes," the same servant answered. "Though I don't know it'll do much good."

Jasfer stumbled away, leaning on Yatim when his servant came alongside him. It could have been him. It could have been any of them, all of them. And would Jaritta have been there among them? Would Pavresh and all their circle of friends from before? It felt like someone was hitting him again in the side, over and over. He needed to get away.

He glanced a final time at young Karket lying on the floor surrounded by pillows. Let that body be his own naïveté, he thought as he passed by. Let this day's events be what woke him up to the reality of life in Romnai—and Eghsal itself—not the perfect place it had seemed so long ago before his sister was cast out, and not the perfectible place Rashul and his ilk believed it to be, but something more dangerous, dark, and broken than even the priests wanted to admit. If it was true that the world came from fire, it was a fire that did not illuminate everything, and it rose amid plumes of choking smoke and dirty ash.

* * *

Jasfer spent the rest of the day and the next closeted within his house, feverishly working on his piles of paperwork, and applying himself more seriously to arrangements for a wife. The idea of marriage felt removed from everything going on, and that was exactly what he needed. From what his servants learned in the few essential errands that brought them in contact with other servants, all the princes stayed in their own homes, just as he did. Soldiers marched the streets, more than he would have expected they could spare from guarding the railroad and temple and other duties. No untouchables begged in the nearby streets, and few wallas delivered their goods.

Late in the morning Jasfer received a visitor, a servant of the High Prince Baram. With him were two of the high prince's own soldiers, the mysterious jati of women soldiers. The servant held out a pile of identical papers to Jasfer.

"The law requires the signatures of all the princes, *tisrah*. A formality, but he asks that you sign your agreement."

"One signature for the whole thing, all its different parts?"

The servant leaned over and pointed at the space on the bottom that already had a number of other signatures. "Yes, *tisrah*. Right here."

As if his question had been where to sign. Jasfer shook his head and read the proposal again. "Executions. Who would that be?"

"Those captured yesterday, I imagine. Those considered the leaders of that murderous mob."

Jasfer said nothing, and the servant continued. "Not Chaitan, of course. And not even Rashul. Not yet. His isolation remains complete, so blame cannot fall on him. Others though, those deemed most dangerous."

Jasfer pictured his sister among the condemned, led up to the gallows with the burnt side of her face exposed for all to see.

"And the rest of this?"

"Temporary, *tisrah*. The soldiers will simply be enforcing the princes' wishes throughout the city until everything calms down."

Jasfer felt himself again among the chaos of that mob, pictured the face of the young prince, now dead, heard the terrible shouts and screams. Perhaps such force was needed. He didn't like the thought of giving the wolf jati extra powers, not when his cousin had been placed in charge of a large part of the army, but he had little choice. The agitators had forced him into this, had forced the city away from what peace they had enjoyed into a violence that would seem even more unfair to the lower castes.

His own hand signed the papers—he watched the ink spread into the thick paper as his fingers moved—but it had been those low caste malcontents who forced his hand to do so. He handed the quill and paper back to the servant and saw him out into the ominously quiet streets.

Chapter 24

Jaritta walked in a crouch among the wounded. The ceiling of dirt and tiny, long-dead roots brushed at the loop of cloth over her head. She bent down to offer water to a man sitting against the ancient wall. His eyes showed that he recognized her as untouchable, but he took the water and swallowed, closing his eyes in pleasure.

When he gave the cup back, Jaritta moved on along the corridor, smiling at those she passed even as inside she was seething. If the demonstration had been her own idea, she would still be angry, sickened by the actions the soldiers had taken to beat these people away. And she would feel incredibly guilty for the deaths and injuries it had caused. That it hadn't been her doing, even in part, took away any need for guilt, but filled her instead with this anger that someone else was shaping events, molding them into things she hadn't planned.

She paused to offer water to others of the wounded. When she looked into their eyes, her anger shifted to all the princes and soldiers and whoever else may have been involved in this senseless attack on the lower castes. Something had to be done, something to make Rashul's dreams come true.

Jaritta still hadn't managed to find a way into his guarded house. Chaitan had been easy to visit. She could slip in from the roof, dropping to a high window, or enter a neighboring house and climb through the shared attics. She half suspected that she could have even walked right in as if she had a reason to be there—perhaps going so far as to dress as something above an untouchable, though even that might not have been necessary—and the guards would have done no more than pass on the presence of a visitor to their superiors that night. But as soon as she'd visited him once, she knew why they had no need to be more careful. Chaitan had always been a welcoming presence, an inspiration for the time he'd passed among other people of every caste and the things he'd learned. But he himself was no revolutionary. He'd been happy to see her, happy to learn that Tanjali was surviving. He promised to take her back in as soon as he dared and even offered to work out some way to drop off food for Jaritta and other untouchables. There was nothing else he could do, no power he had to shape the events of the city.

Jaritta leaned against one of the ancient walls and closed her eyes. Dirt trickled down the wall onto the hand she'd placed there.

"What is this place?"

At first when she opened her eyes, she thought Pavresh had asked the question, but the voice didn't match. Then she realized the voice had been that of the giant of a man now standing just behind the arcist, ducking to keep his head out of the threads of roots that hung from the low ceiling.

Jaritta pushed herself from the wall to greet them both. She'd been finding the two of them places to stay every night for a while, not letting them sleep in the same location more than two nights in a row. Bhadrik, the giant, was untouchable, like herself, except that it was only temporary. That fact seemed to cheapen her own exile. What did being untouchable mean if it wasn't permanent? Nothing. He was no more like her than a priest was. Or a mumbler.

Still, that didn't mean she couldn't answer him, she supposed. And Pavresh looked equally curious, though she'd shown him another one once.

"An old street, it must have been." She began walking, and the two fell in beside her. "The city's what, four hundred years old? But none of the buildings are that old, or not most of them. They must have sometimes knocked the old buildings down and built on top of them, creating these little tunnels of trapped air."

Pavresh ran his fingers through the roots overhead, bringing down a rain of dirt. He closed his eyes. "Hard to imagine four hundred years is even enough for that. I wonder if there was some kind of city here earlier." He didn't seem to expect an answer and continued with only the briefest pause. "Do many people know of these?"

"Most untouchables know that they exist. Not many know exactly where."

"I would guess the soldiers are aware of them," Bhadrik said. "Except…well, I'd never heard of them. But it seems…strategic knowledge that the leaders might know."

Jaritta shrugged. "I've lived on the streets for over fifteen years and have yet to see any sign they know these tunnels any more than they know the roofs. If you hadn't been blindfolded on the way in, you'd probably realize how little strategic value they could have."

She caught Pavresh's eye as she said this, and he nodded to let her know that they had been blindfolded. That challenge of not revealing secrets to Bhadrik that he might take to the soldiers in a few months grated on her. She'd have just let him find his own way in the streets, except Pavresh insisted he might be valuable to them. Well, maybe she wouldn't try to force him out now anyway, not after the riot. The streets had quickly become unbelievably dangerous, haunted even. She wasn't sure she could force anyone to make their own way now.

As Jaritta bent down to offer another wounded man water, she wondered if maybe there would be some strategy that *could* use the scattered and short tunnels. There really weren't many of the tunnels, not that she'd ever seen. Six or seven total with a couple more that were too small an area to be considered anything but a tiny cave. And even of those, only two extended for more than a block of houses.

At the far end of this tunnel, she stopped. A rock-strewn passage extended to one side, unlit by the gas lamps that drove off the darkness in the main tunnel.

"Pavresh." She stumbled momentarily over his name, remembering how Bhadrik had arrived calling him Parsh, but after a few days of trying to get Tanjali and Jaritta and the few others from Chaitan's place to call him that, he'd given up and told Bhadrik his real name. "I'd like to show you something. If," she turned to Bhadrik, "you don't mind staying down here for a bit and helping out with the wounded?"

The soldier looked up at the low ceiling as if it was consciously conspiring to coat his hair in dirt and cramp his back and neck, but he really had little choice and must have known it. "I'll stay."

At the surface, Jaritta passed her hands over her clothes to brush off some dirt, but she didn't worry much about it. She was untouchable, so no one would expect her to be clean. Pavresh also looked the part of an untouchable. She led him from the eerily quiet streets onto the nearest useful roofs and across the city. Only rarely did they have to descend to cross one of the wider streets, but each time they did, she had them wait and watch for a long time to make sure they weren't seen.

They reached the edge of the square overlooking Rashul's isolated house. Pavresh breathed hard, unfamiliar with the most efficient ways of moving along the roof-line. While he caught his breath, Jaritta explained why they'd come. "They're keeping Rashul in that house. I want to see him, to speak with him, but nothing I come up with gets me inside."

Pavresh looked up, though he stayed bent over with his hands on his thighs. "No roofs go near it, I see. I don't suppose one of your tunnels goes underneath?"

"No. None that I've ever seen."

"And the guards are pretty observant?"

"Very. They won't let a beggar walk through the square. Even the wallas that come must stop outside and leave their deliveries there."

"No easy way to sneak through side doors or open windows, I suppose." Pavresh straightened and studied the house again. "Why show it to me?"

He asked as if he already knew her answer, so she gave it without preamble. "Because I'd like you to get inside."

Pavresh shifted to face her, as his gaze flicked back and forth between her and the house. "Your brother would hate you for suggesting that."

Jaritta pictured Jasfer in his house, receiving news that Pavresh had been caught trying to contact Rashul. He would be angry, no doubt. Furious and frightened. But hate her? He'd never be able to do that. All she said was, "So be it. I don't think you'll get caught."

Pavresh brushed at the dirt on his clothing and didn't answer.

"I was thinking you could go in as a soldier. Get Bhadrik to tell you how to act and what to expect."

"No. I'll go as a priest. If I go. Bhadrik can be my personal guard."

The thought of that temporary untouchable meeting Rashul when she couldn't…Jaritta ran a hand over the rough scar on her face. "I don't trust him."

Pavresh looked straight at her, and she snatched her hand from her scar, tugging the cloth back over it. "It's not about trust. I'm not sure how much I trust him either. But he could be valuable, and he's…he has his reasons to join us. Given time, he'd be as revolutionary as Iksheen."

Jaritta tried to picture the soldier dressed in Iksheen's haphazard clothing and laughed. Even imagining Bhadrik *reading* poetry was enough to make the comparison silly. But she stopped almost as soon she'd started. "That's the problem. He doesn't have the time. In a month, he'll be a soldier again, and a loyal soldier I don't doubt. No matter what feelings of camaraderie he has now, they'll fade once he's back among his jati."

"Then maybe whatever we're going to do needs to happen within the next month."

Jaritta stared back at him, and he didn't blink. "You'll do this, then? You'll go speak with Rashul?"

Pavresh nodded. "I want to speak with Chaitan first, and then I'll go to Rashul."

She almost explained to him that Chaitan would be no help, then she remembered about the magic. Of course he'd want to speak with his mentor. "Excellent. I'll help you get in to Chaitan's house if I can. If everything has died down there from the riot."

Events were again shaping themselves under her hands. Without another look at the isolated house below, they left along the road of roofs.

* * *

No need to bother with blindfolds this time on the way in to the tunnel. Once inside they were greeted by Tanjali. The tunnel's dirt had added a layer to her face, like the makeup Jaritta had once worn as daughter to a prince, and the dirt was lined by tears. Not streaks, like she'd been crying uncontrollably, but a thin track beneath each eye, so matched and distinct Jaritta might have thought it was artifice, except Tanjali wouldn't do that.

"What is it?"

"A rumor, but a reliable one." There was strength in her voice but sadness, as well.

Jaritta looked at the others in the tunnel. There were fewer now. Some who'd remained looked shocked and saddened; others had faces like the ancient walls beside them that had remained straight for centuries, knowing the tragedies of the ages but able to survive in their way. Still others looked no different than they had when she and Pavresh left, the pain more distant, covered by anger. "What rumor? What do you mean?"

"They've announced executions. Including some of the old group from Chaitan's."

Executions? Jaritta's mind spun. She pictured Rashul, killed by a barrage of sling bullets or led to the edge over one of the boiling pools in Tanan Square amid the cries of the crowd. Would they surge forward, overwhelm the guards and set him free? Or would they decide it was in their interest to pretend to hate him, to be seen jeering him as he died?

"Who? When?" Pavresh asked.

"Each story is different about who, but all mention people we knew. And all say that it's happening now."

They hurried from the tunnel. Somehow Bhadrik had joined them without Jaritta noticing, and she didn't think they'd bothered to blindfold him, but she couldn't stop to worry about that. Crowds already flowed through the streets toward Tanan Square, and they simply joined the current. Moments ago, she'd hardly dared step into the streets, but now it didn't matter. The soldiers had their victims for the moment. Tomorrow they might want more, but their blood lust would be sated, however briefly.

Coming around a curve, they came to the square, a central point on the steam beds where the city's major streets met: Prince Akas Turali Boulevard coming from the main bridge over the river, the Avenue of Falling Steam to one side with its lines of public baths, and the Avenue of Geysers to the other where the princes lived. At the front of the square were those very princes, seated on raised chairs with a line of soldiers standing guard. Jasfer sat among them, his face as implacable as the rest, proclaiming a hard justice on the people of the city. In the center was the high prince himself, flanked by a ring of his personal soldiers, the women looking as fierce as any Jaritta had ever seen. She made a quick count. They were missing one prince, so the stories of one of them dying in the riot might have been true. Soldiers formed a deep wall between the crowds and the princes, and others surrounded the open square, keeping an eye out for anyone brandishing bow or sling. A quick glance up showed that they'd even found their way onto the roofs.

Notices were posted along the entrance into the square, a number of them on each side so that any who wished could read them. Someone had come and torn one in half as a petty show of contempt, but the others were easily legible even behind the rows of others reading them. In the high-flown language of the princes, it detailed the crimes of the accused, without saying who those accused were. It also set forth the strict measures the soldiers would be taking to force peace on the city. No untouchable would be allowed to sleep in the streets. Begging was allowed, but two beggars couldn't be near each other, couldn't even exchange words except in passing. Jatis would be charged with keeping a careful account of their members. Punishments would be severe.

At the bottom of the notice were the signatures of each of the princes, her brother's neat handwriting jumping out in her vision among all the jumbles of half-formed letters.

Into the square they went until the stage at the front was clear. No one stood there yet, but they waited. All Romnai waited for someone to speak. Jaritta thought it strange that here all castes and jatis were equal, all stuck in the same uncertain expectation. Even the princes, who must have known more, seemed anxious beneath their stony-faced facades. The early autumn breeze, coldly reminding them of the winter ahead, blew on each of them equally.

A voice interrupted Jaritta, drew her gaze from the princes to the person beside them. "Familiar faces!" He spoke as excitedly as the hushed circumstances allowed. "I've been looking for some of you."

Jaritta had to study the man for a moment before she recognized Ekana. She took a step back, and then came forward to give him a brief hug while Pavresh said something to welcome him.

"How did you… I thought you'd been captured back at the warehouse."

They all looked up at the stage, where some who'd been captured at that time would likely stand soon to receive their judgment.

"I made it out. Fled to Jarnur for a while, and just came back in time for this madness."

Jaritta wanted to know how he'd made it out and why he'd come back, but the presence of the crowd discouraged her from talking. "You've heard about the riot at least? You know what started this?"

Ekana gave her a look she couldn't identify. "That's the madness I meant." He lowered his voice to say, "I'd just come back and found myself outside Chaitan's."

They said nothing else while waiting for something to happen. There was a coolness to Ekana that she didn't remember from before, especially toward Pavresh. Not on the surface—he did a convincing job of seeming excited to see them—but underneath he seemed more distant than he had so long ago as a dancer at Chaitan's. But then she supposed with everything that had happened to him once he and Indima were discovered together, she shouldn't be surprised.

Finally, a priest came onto the stage, and Jaritta noticed that Bhadrik tensed at the sight. He spoke, but the words were lost in the crowd, reaching Jaritta as only a whisper of sound. When he gestured behind him, a line of prisoners approached, a wolf jati soldier beside each one.

Pavresh nudged her arm and pointed to the third in line, but he didn't need to. She'd already noticed Iksheen, looking gaunt and odd in plain, rough clothing. Others she knew also, though none as well as Iksheen, people who'd sat around on pillows beside the fireplace in Chaitan's house as they dreamed of a better world. Many more of the prisoners she didn't recognize at all, and she wondered what they had done to earn this execution. Had they been caught up by the riot and too slow to leave? Did they simply resemble people a soldier thought he'd seen outside Chaitan's house? Or had they angered a priest or a prince or a soldier for something small and found sudden revenge turned on them?

Her heart broke for those she knew, a surprisingly real pain unlike anything she'd felt since her first days as an untouchable. For those she didn't know, the feeling was no less, but it was different, a sort of pity that ached in a different part of her.

The priest spoke more words, but now the cries of the crowd covered even the hint of what he said. Then the soldiers marched their prisoners through the gap in the buildings, toward the volcanic fields. The stage extended over the edge of a boiling pool of water, not just hot like the springs that fed the steam baths. The smell of sulfur was strong in the air. Jaritta had peeked down into that pool years ago, she and a group of prince-jati friends daring each other until they all crawled out to the edge and looked down.

The first scream silenced the crowd. Only one prisoner had been pushed in, but the cries continued. Even the soldiers standing beside the prisoners shifted uneasily as the screams dragged on. The slow death made them all feel like they had a part in it, as if they'd all pushed him in, as if they all were feeling the scalding water on their skin.

The priest gave the sign for the second prisoner when the cries ceased. The princes moved in their chairs, as if to block out the sound, but Jaritta doubted that anything could stop those cries, not stone, not even distance. They must surely echo everywhere within Romnai.

Words competed with the screaming. Someone was quoting something, but Jaritta couldn't quite pick it up. Then the words were passed back among the people, row by row. It was the epic, Marankiya's revolutionary poem. It had started with Iksheen, she realized. He stood, his hands up as if to bless the people gathered there, and Jaritta joined in. She hadn't memorized every word, but that hardly mattered. The crowd carried her along past the words she'd forgotten, telling the story of the god Kwomnep and the human Gauran, of a people born of one jati, of a heritage that celebrated all its people and the god of water who blessed them.

As the words thundered through the square, a soldier pushed Iksheen into water that was not a blessing. Unless somehow it was. Jaritta felt water on her own cheeks and spoke the words of the epic as a prayer to the god of water that he would accept these prisoners, welcome them into his kingdom, and punish those who had sent them there untimely.

With the screams no longer audible among the crowd, the priest had the soldiers speed up the execution. By the time they had killed three more, Jaritta was silent as was much of the crowd. But some knew even the later parts of the epic and shouted them out, pulling the crowd through the poetic words.

One jati, sun-chosen, they raised their swords,
they charged, god-blessed, into the enemies of water
and Gauran led them, his spear glinting with sacred
     fire.

She lost count of the executions, and only a few spectators still recited the poem while along the edges of the square people slunk away, but Jaritta felt a responsibility to stay until the end. As she turned back toward the stage from glancing at the people leaving, she noticed a blur of motion to her right. She looked and realized that Bhadrik was casually winding up his sling and returning it to some pocket in his robes.

On the stage, the priest had collapsed.

"You fool," Jaritta hissed. "That's exactly what the soldiers are watching for. They'll have you marked now, and us too most likely."

Bhadrik spoke from the side of his mouth and kept his attention on the events on the stage. "They saw nothing. You saw nothing. Don't react, and they'll have no idea where it came from."

Another of the condemned was pushed off the edge while soldiers and other priests rushed to the fallen man. Jaritta could see him moving his hand, shaking his head.

"Is that better? They'll move in like they did at Chaitan's, search for slings, drag as many of us as they can up to join *them*." She pointed at the stage with her chin.

"They don't have the numbers for that. And anyway, don't you think half the people here have slings anyway? They're not uncommon weapons." While he spoke, the priest was helped to his feet. Blood marked the upper half of his robes, but Jaritta couldn't tell where the wound was, and the man stood straight without assistance. Bhadrik swore. "I couldn't get a clean shot with how cramped we are."

Nothing happened for a few moments as the most recent screams faded and no new executions followed immediately. Those in the crowd were quiet, even those who'd been shouting the lines of the epic. Everyone was looking back and forth as if to find a clue of who could have slung a shot at the priest. Jaritta forced herself to mimic the behavior.

"They'll be on the alert now," Bhadrik said as he also glanced from side to side. "But they won't do anything. Not here. They don't have the men. If they try to take anyone now, the crowd will turn on them."

Jaritta stared at Bhadrik, wondering where this strange wisdom came from. He hardly seemed the same man she'd seen these past days. A calmness had fallen over the anger he'd often shown, not replacing it, but controlling it. And he actually seemed intelligent, a word she would never have associated with him. She supposed that like any jati, his own had taught him the intricacies of its power and purpose.

Pavresh leaned across from the other side to say, "Based on how they've been playing this, I agree. Think of the pauses, the pageantry of all this. They want everyone who came today to return to their own families and tell of the horrors they've seen, of the fierce justice of the princes."

"I wouldn't worry about it turning into another riot like outside Chaitan's," Ekana said. "That was very different and built slowly to its eruption."

They fell silent so they could pretend to be as innocent as the rest of the crowd. Jaritta wanted to hear more about Ekana's recollection of the riot, to see if she could figure out who'd been shaping events then. The way he'd spoken, the thought flashed across her mind that Ekana himself had helped shape those events. But that could wait until they were someplace safe to talk. She was sure that some of those nearby must have seen Bhadrik's actions, but none gave him away. Any who knew managed to hide their knowledge from her gaze.

The executions resumed, and Jaritta forced herself to listen to each scream, to memorize the pain she heard there so she could call on that sound when she made her plans for the city. Others would scream so because of her before the revolution would be complete, people she would mourn who didn't deserve such pain, but, the princes and priests who sent these prisoners to their deaths would also have to account for every cry.

As she thought this, she looked at her brother and wondered if he would pay a price as well. And wondered if it mattered to her.

Chapter 25

Pavresh tugged on the fake vestments as he and Bhadrik walked through the quiet streets. If Jaritta was right, Pavresh could get in to see Chaitan without any problem. No disguise or careful planning needed. But he wanted to try out the role he was planning to play to visit Rashul, so he got Jaritta to dress him as a priest and Bhadrik as a soldier, which wasn't difficult. Jaritta never explained exactly where she'd gotten the outfits, only that she'd found them. They walked openly to Chaitan's house. The market sounds from the main market two streets away sounded as muted as everything else in Romnai these days.

The soldiers looked up as they entered the house, their gazes lingering longer on Bhadrik than on him. They'd decided to dress Bhadrik as a member of one of the smaller soldier jatis that provided personal protection for priests and others. Still, the wolf jati soldiers looked at him curiously, and Pavresh had a twinge of a fear that they'd somehow recognize the jati he'd grown up in. But they said nothing and held a book out for Pavresh to sign. Columns of names filled the paper inside. Pavresh handed the pen to Bhadrik and turned away as he thought a priest might treat a servant.

Chaitan sat in a corner, as he had so often when Rashul and the others had gathered on a circle of pillows before the fire, sharing dreams and making plans. It struck him with a note of nostalgia. His eyes flicked to the stage where he'd performed his magic for the dancers. Soldiers lounged there, betting on cards to pass the time. Pavresh approached his old mentor.

"I would speak with you, old man." Kapita looked at him without recognition, and Chaitan's eyes remained closed. "Could we go to a back room to talk?"

Chaitan still said nothing, so Pavresh gathered the magic around himself without any particular image in mind, playing it simply as a musician might hit a number of notes at once without bothering with tone, aiming only for volume.

Kapita must have noticed it, though she wouldn't have any idea what it meant. "I'm sorry, *tisrah*," she said. "Chaitan is worn out today. Perhaps you can…"

Chaitan cut her off with his hand. "We can meet. Come."

Kapita hesitated before helping him to his feet, her surprise overcoming her familiarity with her role. Pavresh turned once toward Bhadrik and gestured for him to remain in the main room.

As soon as they were through the door, Pavresh took Chaitan's other arm. Kapita's eyes narrowed as she studied him from across Chaitan's sunken chest.

The room they entered had only one chair, so when Pavresh had helped Chaitan to it, he sat at his mentor's feet while Kapita positioned herself behind Chaitan's shoulder. Sitting there, he saw her eyes widen and her face relax—not quite into a smile, but close—as she realized who he was.

"What would you learn?" Chaitan's voice was rough, as if he desperately needed something to drink, but Kapita made no move to offer him anything.

He wanted to know how his mentor had been doing, what Chaitan thought of Rashul and the revolutionaries and everything going on, but with this opening, he knew he ought to start discussing magic. "Is arcist magic true, teacher? Or is it illusion?"

Chaitan waved the question aside with his hand. "Ask the priests these questions. They will say that all is illusion, the smoke of a fire we can sense but never see."

"Fine, but we'll leave those ideas to the priests. Within this illusion then, does the magic reflect the illusion truly, or only what we want to think?"

"What do you mean?"

Pavresh drummed his fingers on his leg while he tried to put the thoughts he'd been having since the abandoned city into words. "What I mean is…your discoveries in arcist magic helped inspire Rashul. You learned that the castes don't exist within the magic, and that got people like Rashul thinking about our own society. But does it mean what they take it to mean? Does it mean that the ideal for the world, whether it's illusion or not, is caste-less?"

Chaitan leaned forward in his chair and looked Pavresh directly in the eye. "Do you question Rashul? Do you question the actions of his followers?"

Pavresh didn't answer immediately. Did he? At times, yes. He still believed that they were after a good thing, something just, but he wasn't sure they'd always taken the right way. Finally, he nodded.

"Good. Those who never question become dangerous, but those who always question do as well. We are reaching a time for action, I believe."

Pavresh nodded again while the old man paused to cough, a violent fit that had Pavresh worried about him.

"Arcist themes have power," Chaitan said after he'd finished coughing. "In a sense that makes them true, whether or not they reflect some reality or illusion."

Pavresh shifted on his pillows and looked up for a moment at the beams of the ceiling. "What of the mumblers then? The magic seems to speak for a more just society for us, but it seems unjust in how it places the mumblers."

Chaitan sucked in his cheeks for a moment, making him look even older. "Do the mumblers deserve justice?"

Pavresh remembered then that Chaitan's discovery of arcist

magic had come during the last Mumbler Wars, that he'd been a soldier fighting them at the time, a soldier, perhaps, like Bhadrik. It was an odd juxtaposition, this old man, frail but wise, with Bhadrik's strength that seemed to hide little depth or wisdom. He tapped his finger to his lips while deciding what to say. "I saw them in the abandoned city of Eghsal. Living among our own outcasts. If the untouchables deserve justice, then so do they."

Chaitan didn't look convinced. He moved a thin hand up to his face and briefly closed his eyes. When he opened them, he said, "The only way for the magic to bring them justice as well is for someone to go listen to their stories. An arcist must take what they tell, take what they believe, and expand the pool of our magic to account for them as well."

As he said this, he looked directly at Pavresh, as if he was sending his apprentice out on such a task. Pavresh recoiled. Surely there was another way, a way through his contact with Prince Jasfer or the revolutionaries. When the city was settled down—for good or ill—he could prevail on Jasfer or Rashul or whoever it was to reconsider how the mumblers were treated, to seek a peaceful way to communicate with them. He'd returned to Romnai so recently, he had no wish to leave again now.

A noise from the main room caught his attention, and he realized he ought to get going. He hoped Bhadrik had found no troubles out there. "Thank you, teacher," he said as he stood, then he paused. "What do you think about Rashul and all of…us? Are we doing right to change the way things work here? Sometimes it seems we've only made the city worse, more dangerous for every caste."

Chaitan made as if to rise and return with him to the front, but Kapita held an arm on his shoulder, and he subsided. "I don't know, Pavresh. I've been forced to distance myself from all of that, and now I find it all mixed together." He looked tired, as if the thought of trying to understand the right path was too much. "I suppose no one can know beyond doubt."

Pavresh bid farewell and returned to the main room where Bhadrik had joined the soldiers with their game of cards. Bhadrik didn't jump away quite as soon as he probably should have if Pavresh had been a real priest, but then he seemed to recollect their roles and stepped away, offering Pavresh a quick bow and a *tisrah*.

Pavresh said nothing as they left.

✳ ✳ ✳

Before Pavresh had a chance to make good on his plans to visit Rashul, one other task took precedence. He received through Yatim a message from Prince Jasfer, asking him to spy on his cousin Samatrit.

"Whatever's happening," he said through the message he'd had his servant memorize, "it will happen soon. Samatrit is pushing for even harder measures, as if daring the lower castes to rebel."

"That's it?" Pavresh asked. "Just prance in and see what I can see?"

Yatim shrugged. "I suppose so." He cocked an eyebrow then and half smiled. "Though prancing may get you more attention than you want."

Pavresh laughed. "Fine. Tell Jasfer that I'll get over there today."

Yatim nodded and walked away, adding over his shoulder as he did, "You be careful. There and...wherever."

Pavresh debated going again as a priest, but he feared that would lead to too many questions and too much attention. He wanted to be invisible within the house, not welcomed and offered choice foods and beverages. So, leaving Bhadrik behind with Jaritta and the others in their most recent dwelling, he dressed himself as a walla and walked toward the manors of the princes.

The streets were heavy with soldiers and little else, but they had no reason to suspect he was anything but an ordinary walla on delivery. They looked at him, even studied him briefly as he passed, but no unrest could interrupt the vital job of the city's wallas. Pavresh carried a large sack over his arm, filled with food, as if he were delivering lunches for a number of workers. The smell of the food helped make his disguise believable. He was less sure how well it would hold up for the servants at the prince's house. It was far from the quality of food the prince and any family he might have would expect, and even the servants might be accustomed to better food—Pavresh had certainly enjoyed better in the Silk City.

When he reached Samatrit's manor, he looked at it through the eyes of the cheetah jati servants. It was much larger than any home could be within the tight walls of the Silk City. Still he was able to identify the different entrances, that for the prince and high-caste visitors, that for the cheetah jati, and a third for deliveries and other lower-caste visitors. The main entrance drew the eye, while the others seemed placed to hide themselves. Pavresh wavered between the second and third doors. The third fit his disguise, but the second seemed more likely to give him quicker access to the rest of the house. What if he entered the delivery door and found he could get no further? Still, given his disguise, he had no real choice.

People moved quickly about as if preparing for some feast. One gestured for him to set his food down in the adjoining room, and Pavresh ducked inside, away from the noise. More importantly, away from any eyes. After unloading his food, he slipped from that room and wandered the manor.

For an hour or more, he moved about, sneaking into rooms to look for paperwork, trying to eavesdrop on any conversation that might hold a clue. He found better clothing, cheetah jati clothing, in a closet, and changed into that to blend in better. Whenever someone came near him, he simply nodded and kept moving as if he belonged there. His emotions alternated between the giddy excitement that he could do this without raising suspicions and the horrifying thought that any moment he might be caught, that his luck would run out.

His luck, if that was what it was, held. Pavresh played the arcist magic subtly and explored nearly the entire house, but in all that, he found little. He lingered longer than he'd meant to stay, frustrated by his lack of success. The one room he hadn't been able to examine was the prince's study, which, of course, would be the most valuable to him. But Samatrit never left it. At last in desperation he entered with a tray and tisane with the hope of peeking at whatever the prince had out, but Samatrit waved him away without looking up from his work before Pavresh could even get near.

Eventually, he left, going through what little he would have to give to Prince Jasfer. Talk of soldiers, but no clue where they were except for a code-name of nonsense syllables. What seemed a strange obsession with railroads, as if the soldiers—or maybe even the servants—had been riding the length of the valley many times throughout the summer. Preparations for a fancy dinner that involved other *kortru* guests. And derision for the rabble of the streets, as even the servants called them, a hint that some in the house longed for violence and none were frightened by the prospect.

Not much to show for his time, but he hoped it would be sufficient to placate Jasfer until Pavresh had his chance to meet with Rashul.

* * *

Their latest place to sleep and gather was a fourth-story apartment near the river. The shadow of the Bridge of the

Forgotten South fell across the rundown buildings, and the main temple was visible over the nearby roofs. What people lived in these buildings were all *nefli* and unlikely to report anything to those of higher castes, if they even noticed that one of the empty rooms was occupied.

When Pavresh returned in the late afternoon, he saw that their group had grown. Not only Ekana, but other faces, some familiar from their times at Chaitan's house and some unknown. They were deep in a heated discussion, Bhadrik as involved as the rest.

"Your brother can help, Jaritta," Ekana said as Pavresh joined them. "Wouldn't he?"

Jaritta shook her head. "He…I don't think he dares. He has to be wary himself or the priests and other princes will cast him out among us."

Wary. Pavresh nodded. That was the exact word for Jasfer, wanting to do what was right but afraid of what it might cost him.

"Not if he was the high prince he wouldn't."

Everyone stayed silent after Ekana said these words, and Pavresh looked at Jaritta's face, wondering what her reaction would be. Her face had gone still and perhaps slightly pale.

She shook her head. "Even if he had the desire *and* the support to overthrow Baram, I'm not sure he would use his power to help us. Certainly not as quickly as we want. He might bring some reform, but…" She let a shrug finish the sentence.

"Think what we could do with an advocate as high prince. Isn't it worth suggesting it to him?"

Pavresh spoke up. "I don't think so. He's not one to take well to that. He'd probably turn us in just for suggesting it." He looked at Jaritta and added, "Even if it was his sister."

"And how do you know the prince so well?"

Pavresh froze at Ekana's question. There was something in

the question that seemed not quite innocent, and he realized that he and Jaritta had always kept his spying for Jasfer a secret. And on top of that, Ekana himself seemed more forceful than he remembered before. The memories made him think of Indima, trapped in the silk city. If he'd thought he might see Ekana again, maybe he'd have asked Indima for a message, but he knew that would have been far from his mind anyway. Nothing had happened between them, but even so, he felt jealous of the memories of her on the train and in the Silk City.

The pause as these thoughts rushed through him seemed incriminating itself, and he stuttered out, "He…I mean, his connections with the mines where I grew up." As soon as he said it, he knew it was a logical reason and wished he had thought of it immediately. "My father had many interactions with him and his men. And when I came back here with Bhadrik, I presented myself to his steward to give my father's greetings." He stopped then, afraid it would be obvious he was covering up part of the truth.

"Can't we just set ourselves up as the new princes?" Bhadrik asked. "Why must it be someone from that jati if we aim to destroy those divisions anyway?"

Pavresh tried to imagine himself as a prince, the servants bringing him sweetened tisane as he debated the city's future. Except…there wouldn't really be servants either. He couldn't see it. "The city wouldn't accept it," he said when no one else answered. "A single charismatic person maybe. Chaitan, if he were healthy. Rashul, if he wanted it, and I can ask him if I get a chance to. Maybe even Marankiya, if he still lives, with how popular his epic has become. But a strange group of unknowns? No."

Bhadrik shrugged. "We'll make ourselves known then. Become heroes in our own ways."

"I don't think it would work, even if we had twenty years to establish ourselves. You need to recognize that most of those who dislike the castes still find some comfort in them. The *kortru* caste gives people authority even if they haven't earned it. Us? Enough would say, 'What's special about them? Why shouldn't I set myself up as prince?' And we'd be stuck spending all our time stopping rebellions."

Ekana stood and paced. "So, then what? We simply let the undeserving rule because it's tradition?"

"No." Pavresh closed his eyes. "There has to be a better way. Something the city will accept, something that will bring justice without violence."

A train whistled from across the river, and Pavresh looked out the window. The sky was already darkening, the days growing shorter. If he wanted to visit Rashul today, they had to go now.

He excused himself from the discussion and gestured for Bhadrik to join him. As they left, Ekana addressed him. "It's a good dream, justice without violence. A great dream, but it won't happen. The time for dreams is over, the time for action come. And actions will always involve someone hurt."

"I hope you're wrong, Ekana."

Ekana didn't answer him, and soon Pavresh and Bhadrik were walking through darkened streets, a priest and his personal guard. Anyone watching them for a long stretch might have been confused why a priest walked as far as he did, but to those who simply saw them pass for a block or two, there was nothing strange in the sight.

Rashul's house was farther from the steam beds, north of both the princes' manors and the worst of the *nefli* neighborhoods. It took them longer to walk there than Pavresh had planned, and gas lamps lit the bigger streets by the time they reached the house.

Pavresh looked Bhadrik in the eyes. It felt like he ought to ask if the soldier felt ready, but he knew the answer. They'd prepared as much as they could, and now they'd have to see how it played out.

Rather than talking, he used the break to build up his arcist magic. On his first attempt, he started with piety, the devout worshiper, the sacred monk. As he built from there he could feel the magic crumbling. That was the wrong image for his role. There were likely plenty of such people within the pantheonic religion, priests who dutifully served, who loved the people that came to worship and did all they could for the sacred fire. But they weren't the ones likely to come to this house. Piety had little place in the role he was after.

Power was what he needed to convey, the hidden master, the secret behind the throne. He kept it subtle to not overwhelm the soldiers here and added hints of more flattering traits as he went.

At last, it seemed as ready as it could be. With a quick gesture to Bhadrik, he crossed the empty street to the darkened doorway. Bhadrik knocked for him and spoke to the soldier who answered the door.

"The *tisrah* would like to speak to the prisoner."

"By whose orders?"

"His own." Bhadrik stood back as if to afford the man a better view of Pavresh. "You see who he is."

The soldier shook his head, but it was an uncertain shake, one that showed they'd already begun to make him question himself. Even so, he said forcefully, "No, I don't know this man."

"This is Father Parshtun. You spend no time at the temple, then?"

There was something in the way Bhadrik asked this question that Pavresh couldn't quite interpret, as if the words hid another meaning only a soldier would catch. And their interrogator seemed to realize it, as well, as he took a small step backward.

"I'm a devout worshiper, sir." He turned to Pavresh. "*Tisrah.*

I apologize. Perhaps I have been more often to the smaller chapels of late, so I do not know you."

Pavresh made his voice sweet with only a hint of an edge to play on whatever fear Bhadrik had summoned. "No need, soldier. As long as you worship somewhere, the sacred fire is pleased."

"Thank you, *tisrah*." He waited as if hoping they would leave of their own accord. "Even so, *tisrah*, I cannot let you in. Our orders are very strict."

"And we are blessed to have such dedicated soldiers. You bring honor to your jati, especially now when you must all long for the mountain heights." These words brought a slight relaxation to the soldier's face. Pavresh could imagine him thinking that he must be one of the influential priests who could be trusted if he knew about their descent from their mountain homes. "But who gives you your orders if not us priests? You need fear nothing when you let one of us come inside."

Again, a flicker of fear crossed the man's eyes, and he glanced at Bhadrik. It seemed to Pavresh that there was something that these soldiers knew, some secret of their jati that they must at all costs keep hidden from the priests. Giving himself to his role, he offered a silent prayer that the fear and his own words would be enough to gain them entrance.

The soldier stepped back and allowed them to enter. Other soldiers sat about the room, looking at them curiously.

"Where is he?" Pavresh kept his head high, his gaze fixed just above their eye-level.

A different soldier from the one who'd answered the door stepped toward them. "What is your business with him?"

"Priest business and none of yours."

"We have our instructions to let no one in."

"And I'm giving you new instructions." Pavresh played up the authority of his image as he lowered his gaze enough to stare into the soldier's eyes. "Time runs out to keep our city safe from the rabble. The prisoner has information we priests need."

"Priests have questioned him already many times."

Pavresh lifted his chin and fixed his eyes above the soldier's head. "Which is why they've sent me. Send a runner to the temple if you wish. But let me in while he goes. I won't sit around waiting."

After a few more exchanges, they agreed to let both Pavresh and Bhadrik through to an upstairs room where they'd bring Rashul as well. A runner set off for the temple. Pavresh tried to figure out how long it might take to run there, find someone who could answer a question, and then return. He feared it wouldn't be long.

The wait in the upstairs room seemed far too long. And maybe that was fortunate because when the soldier brought Rashul in, Pavresh had no problem hiding his relief at seeing Rashul beneath his irritation with the soldier. He snapped at the man, who darted out, leaving them alone with Rashul.

He didn't look Pavresh in the eye, and his body slumped against the pillows where he sat. Pavresh came closer and spoke quietly. "Rashul." The prisoner looked up, and his eyes narrowed as if trying to place the face before him. "It's Pavresh. From Chaitan's. I'm an arcist."

At last Rashul recognized him, and his eyes widened. A mask fell back over them as he saw Bhadrik.

"It's all right," Pavresh said. "He's with us, though I'm guessing they have other ears trying to listen in."

Rashul still said nothing, so Pavresh asked, "How are you treated here?"

He shrugged. "Like a criminal some days. Pampered on others, but those are almost worse because they always end. How'd you get here?"

"Don't worry about how. What news do you hear? Do you

know about the others and what's been happening in the city?"

"I heard of Iksheen's execution, of people killed in the streets for gathering, of how the priests and princes will soon crush anyone who remembers me."

"I'm sure there's much you don't yet know and much that the soldiers tell you twisted." Pavresh then rushed through a summary of everything that seemed important, of the spread of Marankiya's epic, of the protest outside Chaitan's house, of Jaritta and Tanjali and Ekana and the others, of the vague feeling that something more was about to happen, though he didn't dare speak of Jasfer or exactly where he himself had been for the last months.

Then, finally, he got to the discussion of that night, of the idea of completely overthrowing the princes and setting up new leaders headed by Rashul.

"It wouldn't work," he said immediately. "I wouldn't be accepted by enough people, and certainly not by the soldiers."

"I may be able to convince enough soldiers to support us," Bhadrik said. "There are...ways to influence us. Them. Ways that go beyond priests and beyond any other force outside our jati."

"That is good to hear, but still I am not the one. I can speak for the people, and I can speak to the people for whoever would be in charge, but I couldn't be the leader. Let me think."

Pavresh said nothing and tried to guess how long they'd been there, how close the runner was to returning with a message to stop them. They had little time left.

"Jaritta." Rashul's eyes suddenly came to life as they hadn't through their entire conversation. "She was born to the princely jati and so is eligible to take the throne room for herself."

"She's untouchable."

"That won't matter. We can find some law to support her, enough to convince whatever princes she chooses to rule beside her, and we can reveal that the priest who cast her out did wrong. That she didn't deserve to be made untouchable. That will appease the people of the street."

"Will they accept a woman?" Pavresh turned to Bhadrik. "Would the soldiers accept a woman?"

Neither answered immediately then both tried to speak at once until Rashul let Bhadrik answer first. "If I frame it right, they would. Or enough would anyway."

"I think the people of the street would," Rashul said. "It's the other princes who might be more problematic. She'd have to choose thirty to be legitimate, and they'd have to be both willing to accept her as their high prince and work with her for our aims. I don't know if there are thirty who fit that. Even her brother might not."

Pavresh said nothing for a moment as he pictured them barricading themselves behind the ornate doors he'd seen in the High Assembly. Even if all went well, it wouldn't be easy.

"We have to get out of here now, before their runner returns."

"Let's take him, fight our way out." Bhadrik unwrapped his sling from his wrist. "I can take a couple before they even notice it, and you're pretty good with that belt."

Before Pavresh could either consider or argue against this, Rashul answered. "No. Don't take me with you. I'll be more distraction than inspiration out there, drawing soldiers out, taking attention away from the hardships."

He stopped and looked at the walls of the room. "I'm here. Let everyone know that I remain imprisoned. Declare it on the streets, and let them call for my release."

In the silence that followed, Pavresh heard footsteps on the street outside, coming at a run. He jumped to his feet.

"Let's hope we haven't waited too long that we're forced to fight our way out. Let's go!"

Still, they didn't dare run down the stairs. The soldiers in the main room looked at them as they descended, but made no move to attack. One rose halfway and opened his mouth, but already Bhadrik was opening the door for Pavresh. He simply nodded to the soldier and stepped out.

The runner was in the square before the house, a sword out. Pavresh ran the other way and heard a whistling sound that he guessed was Bhadrik's sling, followed by the outcast soldier's own footsteps.

There was a shout behind them, but Pavresh didn't turn to look. Was there a tunnel nearby? Or access to the strange road of roofs that Jaritta knew so well? He wished she were there. He didn't pause to look for anything. Better to chance the streets than climb to a dead-end roof and be trapped.

The streets here were more widely spaced than near the bridge, making it difficult to lose their pursuers. The echoes off the nearby buildings made the number of people following them seem high. Several streets followed in quick succession. Pavresh pulled Bhadrik down a road and then into what was too narrow to be an alley, a brick path of sorts squeezed between two buildings.

They came out on another street and turned down it, finding themselves soon in the middle of a small market. No one remained there, buying or selling, but the widened street had a double row of rough stalls down the middle and others lining the sides. Bhadrik took the lead this time, ducking among the twisted lanes that ran between stalls. Pavresh tripped over a prone body, barely keeping his balance. An untouchable most likely, who groaned and turned and fell back into drunken sleep.

Pavresh had hoped that the stalls might provide a hiding place, but the market ended too soon. It was nothing like the huge market near Chaitan's house. The sounds of pursuit grew louder as if the noise itself would grab them, hold them until the soldiers could come. At the other end, they found a road angling away from the market and toward the river. They sprinted to the wharf buildings. Pavresh glanced upriver as they crossed to the run-down warehouses and saw the temple brightly lit. But no army of priests or soldiers poured from it, and the maze of storerooms and buildings whose purpose Pavresh couldn't fathom swallowed them.

They collapsed in the shadows between two buildings and waited to recover their breath, waited until they thought it might be safe to pass the temple and join the others beside the Bridge of the Forgotten South. Pavresh removed the fine-looking, though cheaply made, outer clothing and tossed it in the river, then rubbed dirt into the rest.

Chapter 26

Bhadrik watched bemusedly as the others discussed Rashul's suggestion to set Jaritta in the place of power. Jaritta said nothing, looked shocked by the whole idea. Even Pavresh seemed a bit uncertain, but Ekana took the job of convincing the others. There was something forceful about the little man. Not in the way of soldiers, but as if he drew power from a deep source of anger, a fire of sorts. He argued that it was the only way to make Rashul's dreams reality.

It wasn't that Bhadrik didn't feel the thrill of excitement to be doing something, but it didn't seem nearly as shocking to him as they seemed to take it. He was a soldier, even if outcast, and soldiers served those in charge or served those longing to be in charge. Their jati told stories of countless attempts, both failed and successful, of a prince occupying the inner sanctum. Always there were soldiers defending it, and always there were soldiers trying to enter and throw the pretender out, not only the high prince's falcon jati, but their own as well.

Which made Bhadrik wonder—where would they get the soldiers for their attempt? He was one, of course. And they were talking about people Rashul knew from rougher parts of town—dock workers and such who had muscle but wouldn't be able to do much against true soldiers.

But if he could convince some of his fellow soldiers to support them… While the others talked, he let his mind stray. Something nagged at him, a tingling like what some of the old soldiers claimed to feel when they'd lost a leg or a hand in the Mumbler Wars. And then he realized that, in a sense, he *was* missing a limb. His sword. How had he not considered his sword earlier? That was like forgetting a sibling or a lover, like forgetting himself.

Deraj had agreed to get the sword to Romnai. Bhadrik had sworn not to retrieve it until his exile was over, had sworn on himself, the most sacred oath for a member of the wolf jati's mystery religion. And yet, what was an oath against the need to challenge the flame? This was his chance to prove himself the equal of fire. Compared to that, an oath meant nothing. He let his mind picture his body in detail, each muscle and joint, in the centering ritual of the mystery religion. In this way, he worshiped himself.

People spoke excitedly all around him, but he shut out their noise and became the only thing, not just the center but the embodiment of the cosmos. At last, he knew he was ready.

"Where are you going?" Ekana stood between him and the door, although Bhadrik hadn't noticed him move.

"To get you an army." Bhadrik glanced around at the people there and focused on Pavresh, who was moving as if to join him. "No, you can't come with me. This is something only I can do. I'll join you again…" he turned to Jaritta, "here?"

She tapped her fingers against her smooth cheek, the one she kept bare. "If we move from here, we'll leave someone behind who can bring you." She paused, dropping her hand self-consciously to her side, then added, "If no one is here, wait, and we'll find you."

Bhadrik nodded and left before anyone else could bother him with questions or challenges.

He made his way through the dark streets toward one neighborhood along the eastern edge of the city where the steam beds didn't quite meet the river. The streets were close together here, as if crowding each other to be closest to some beloved prince. Even at this hour, the sounds of children and the shouts of their mothers filled them, echoing off the high buildings.

Bhadrik found one particular building, identical in appearance to its neighbors, and walked down the stairs at one side into a basement apartment. An oil lamp lit the inside, but not enough to reveal much of the furnishings. An older man sat there, bent over piles of a variety of items as his hands darted among them, tying and twisting them together.

He glanced up, and then said as he looked back at his work, "My charms are sold in the shop across the street. I don't do custom work at this time. Go there tomorrow during the day, and you can buy them."

"I'm not here about your charms, *sitrah*." The word of address was a play on the formal address of the *kortru* caste. Knowing the man would be watching him now, Bhadrik gave a brief bow that did not abase himself. "I seek to challenge the fire."

The man said nothing at first and continued to tie his charms. Bhadrik stared at those fingers, fascinated. They were hard fingers, fingers that had gripped a sword and sling for years, that had clawed up mountains, battled against enemies, that had themselves challenged the fire. Now he sat here tying up junk late into the evening. Did he still worship his own body during the mystery rites he led, or did those mysteries change with age? Did he now worship the bodies of the young men who came to the ceremonies?

When *he* was that old, he would still worship himself. His body, if he still deserved it, but if not, then his past, the memories of all the times he had excelled, had proven himself worthy.

Finally, the old man stopped. Not just his fingers, but his entire body became perfectly still. Bhadrik tried to make his own body as still, but it seemed to obey him only on the surface. "Three wolf hours. The grotto of seven flames."

Bhadrik gave a shallow bow to indicate he accepted this,

that he'd never attempted to challenge the fire there before. "My name is Bhadrik, *sitrah*. You were given my sword for keeping. If I defeat the fire, I would like it returned to me."

The mysteriarch did not answer as Bhadrik left, but would be there with the sword, as would a number of other soldiers, some to test themselves against fire and some to observe. The grotto of seven flames was the oldest of the secret chambers, secreted within the steam beds. He'd never had to test himself there, but he doubted it would be much different from the challenges he'd endured in other grottoes within the city or high in the mountains.

While he waited, he walked briskly until he'd drawn a light sweat. Temple bells somewhere marked the valley hours even at night, but the wolf jati had devised their own way to measure time away from such things as bells. The steam made it impossible to tell the passing time by the stars as he might have in the mountains, but the wolf hour was such a part of him that he had no trouble timing his walk to bring him back to the edge of the steam beds three hours later.

Officially the city ended at the steam beds, and no one walked among them. Children were raised to believe them dangerous and shown certain safer roiling pools of stinking mud and sulfur-rich water to defuse the attraction of forbidden things. But a path started here, between some of the older houses. Several paths, really, each scarcely visible even by day, but they all came together not far into the fields of twisted rock to form a clear trail.

Boiling water spattered to one side of Bhadrik as he walked. There were no lights ahead to guide him, no other people on the path. Was he early or late? He refused to let the question worry him.

The trail wound through strange rocks that were no more than dark shapes in the night and brought him at last to a mound. The path descended into what must have once been a pool of water. The far wall, as well as he could make it out, looked fashioned by humans, as if centuries ago someone had dammed the water feeding into a pool and drained it dry. Now, at last, he saw light, squeezing out from behind some sort of a door.

He reached the door, a piece of river-smoothed wood, still slightly curved from what must have once been a gigantic tree, and pulled it open. The nearest part of the cave—benches made of sand-filled cloth clustered together as if around low tables that weren't there—was empty. Farther in, before the altar with its single torch and the painting of a man behind it, people were already gathered, kneeling silently. Deraj was not there, and none of the men he'd known up in the mountains—only then did Bhadrik realize his mind had been wondering, hoping, fearing to see them. Not many men were there at all, in fact, so Bhadrik doubted he was the last.

He wasn't, but it was only one more person. The soldier entered shortly after Bhadrik, and Bhadrik had to wonder where the man had been. It seemed he should have seen anyone that close behind him on the trail. But his wondering was cut off by the entrance of the mysteriarch.

When he reached the torch on the rough altar, the old man spoke the words of ritual. "We have come to overcome fire."

"The fire is powerful," the soldiers all answered.

"But not so powerful as you."

"The fire is quick and deadly."

"And you even more."

The exchange continued in this way for some time, and Bhadrik felt the temptation to simply settle into that comforting familiarity. But that was always the danger when one came to perform the challenge rather than simply partake of the mystery's ceremonies. Fire was not and could never be familiar or comforting, and to allow himself into that trap would disrupt his chance to prove himself. He shifted on his knees, letting the harsh stone of the floor irritate his skin through his robes. He focused on his body and let the words come out on their own.

The mysteriarch spoke the last words of the ritual. "Who would fight fire this night? Come forward and prove yourselves."

Bhadrik shrugged off his robes and stepped to the altar naked. Only two others joined him.

"You go down a path of difficulty, one you must walk alone."

"I do this willingly," Bhadrik intoned with the others. "The fire is not my master. The flame is my servant."

Then they stepped around the altar to a low door. One of the others stepped through first, and the door swung shut, so Bhadrik waited. No noise came through from the soldier himself, but Bhadrik did catch the rumbles of the mysteriarch's voice, deep and indistinct. Time passed, but it seemed to neither drag nor speed. It just was, the moving present that carried him along parallel to the others but as if untouched by them.

The first soldier came out, his jaw set, his face the stone of the cave walls. He had not lost to the fire, Bhadrik felt sure, but he had not won either. It was the look of one who met the fire, proved himself the fire's equal. Bhadrik had performed thus a handful of times and knew he wouldn't fail tonight. But he couldn't simply equal the fire. This time he had to overcome, to earn his sword back, to draw together a group of other soldiers.

Bhadrik entered next. At first, he saw nothing. Slowly his eyes made out a green hint of light within the steam that rose to either side of him. It was enough to reveal a narrow walkway before him. The heat brought sweat out on his chest and back, and his mouth felt painfully dry.

The mysteriarch spoke from somewhere, but the words were swallowed by the walls, becoming simply a deep and ominous backdrop to Bhadrik's journey. They stopped after a moment as Bhadrik felt the steam wrap itself around his body, chains to bind him into the earth. He pushed ahead, fighting the steam. The other times he'd challenged fire had been nothing like this. Each sacred grotto had its own unique method, as did each holy mountain, but what was he supposed to do here?

Then the voice of the mysteriarch returned, this time clear even as it created dark echoes. "Behold the fire!" A jet of flame appeared, a pillar it seemed, one that stretched from the floor almost to the ceiling above. Bhadrik squinted and turned his face half away. "Creator of gods. Originator of the cosmos, of all things seen and unseen, known and unknown. What is this that dares approach?"

Bhadrik took another step and no longer looked away from the light. "I do, a man."

"Only a man?" Though he knew the voice was still that of the old man, it seemed to come from the fire itself, and the flames jumped with the words.

"A man. There is no *only* in it. I am your equal. I am your master."

What happened next didn't make sense. A part of him knew there was no logical way that he could be doing what he did, wondered if the steam of these springs carried some strange drug that tricked him. But what seemed to happen was that the fire twisted and beckoned to him, a sensuous woman leaning from a doorway.

Bhadrik took a step nearer, and the jet of fire became something else, something more sinister. It reached for him to crush him, and Bhadrik reacted, wrestling against the fire, trying to throw it down.

The fire was slippery. *How could flames be slippery? How could smoke be slick?* It didn't matter that it made no sense, only what he did in response. He dug in with his fingernails and held tight as the column of fire thrashed, trying to shake him free.

If time before had seemed simply an unchanging present, now it seemed to compress an endless past and an eternal future into each breath. Every twitch of the fire reminded him of the moments of his life, the dreams and fears of what was to come. All he could do was hang on. That must surely be the key to the trial in this grotto. He tightened his arms around the slender column.

A current ran through his muscles. He'd kept himself in shape since being cast out, but he'd seldom used his muscles like this. He thrilled at the feel, at the exertion. He was doing it, overcoming the fire.

When he walked out of this chamber, he wouldn't have the hard face of the last soldier. His face, his body would be exultant. He would receive the sword and the shouts of acclaim.

Except…Bhadrik faltered for a moment and struggled to renew his grip on the fire. If that last soldier had only equaled the fire, how was that possible in this grotto? To lose his grip would be to be defeated. And now his feet slipped beneath him, the fire threatening to do just that. But then, what was the middle ground between failure and victory? It must be this stand-off that left a man the fire's equal. He needed a way to truly overcome the twisting rope of fire. Never again would he be able to test himself in this particular site, and elsewhere he would have to wait. He didn't think Jaritta and the rest would wish to wait, even if it meant attempting the inner room without the soldiers.

He tried to imagine the fire as another man that he was wrestling, tried to throw it to the ground, but that didn't work. The flames slipped from his grip, and he nearly fell away. He had to think of this differently. It was already impossible. Let his body imagine impossible ways to smother the fire.

Bhadrik began to twist himself then, as if his body shared the properties of the fire, and he felt himself rise up until his eyes looked directly at the tips of the flames. He imagined his body growing extra arms to embrace the fire. He didn't. At least, he could see no additional limbs growing from his torso, but his grip on the fire strengthened.

Then he pictured himself rising, becoming a cloud of smoke without losing any of his strength, and he pressed down into the column of fire. It shrank, but it pushed back.

The minutes or hours that followed were perhaps the strangest of the entire trial, and his memories after were fragmented images that made little sense. He seemed to fight the fire in a thousand guises, in a thousand locales from the lands of folk tales of the Forgotten South to empty spaces between the stars. The fire itself constantly transformed its shape, and he had to do the same, meeting each change with his own to bear it down to the rocky floor, which throughout the dizzying changes was always half-visible beneath them.

At times the fire seemed a mumbler, a cruel enemy to be fought. At times a lover pressed beneath him or atop him, worshiping his body. At times a member of every caste and jati, and they struggled together or against each other at some impossible task that seemed in some ways to be the creation of the world itself.

At last he was back in the cave, back in a body recognizable as his own. And with a final cry, he pulled his opponent to the floor, smothering what remained of the fire. A voice spoke somewhere, but it was meaningless, a whisper of insects compared to the voices of the world he'd been hearing, speaking, muting.

Bhadrik stood, and the cave was dark without the fire, but he could see. He retraced the path between the steam—though he didn't think even the boiling water could harm him—and pushed back the low door.

They could see his success. He knew there was no way they could miss it. He stepped to the altar and faced them, letting them look on his fire-touched body. There were no burns, but his brown skin had been changed by the fire, darkened and brightened at once, it seemed, his body become more real, more capable of extremes than it ever had.

At last he spoke. "I am fire's equal. I am the fire's master."

The mysteriarch appeared to one side as the soldiers cheered. In his hands was the sword Bhadrik knew well. He licked his dry lips and took the familiar hilt into his hand. Now was the time to gather other soldiers to him. He took a breath, tasting a lingering hint of smoke and chemical-rich steam.

"As fire's champion, I have a task, a journey, a challenge. It will be the proving of others, of the power of the wolf jati over the fire and those who prostrate themselves to it. Come with me if you wish a part in this new testing."

Both the soldier who'd already gone through the testing and the one who had been waiting to make the attempt were among those who followed Bhadrik out of the grotto. He hardly saw the steam beds as he led them into the city. The eastern sky was graying with the sky's fire, but it seemed rather his own light that brought in the day.

He didn't lead them to the hiding spot of the others, but gathered them in one of the innumerable rooms within the neighborhood of the wolf jati. Bhadrik wondered what to say, how much exactly to reveal and when so that he didn't risk betrayal. And yet…he'd seen their faces when he came out from his trial, and the power of overcoming fire still filled his body. They would trust him no matter his words. It didn't take an arcist or a charismatic speaker to move a group of soldiers to action. It took power.

And in the grotto of the mystery religion of the wolf jati, he'd shown them that power. Whatever he said now, he had them.

Chapter 27

Something wasn't right. Pavresh could feel it laid over the room where they had gathered, a strange tension on the same level as arcist magic. It should feel right. He could sense the early-morning excitement as Jaritta and Ekana made their final plans. The Just Revolution was a powerful arcist event, and it filled the actions of all the plotters, even without Pavresh needing to do anything. But to his arcist-trained mind, there was a dangerous undercurrent to those emotions.

Bhadrik had returned an hour earlier with a sword and a promise of a handful of wolf jati soldiers to fight for their cause. They'd been able to recruit a number of Rashul's contacts from the dock workers and other laborers as well. Everything seemed to be falling into place for them to make their attempt that night.

So why did he feel uneasy? He tried to tell himself that it was the magnitude of their plans, that it was nothing more than nervousness. But that didn't fit.

Jaritta spoke to Bhadrik about their plans. "There is one of those old tunnels not far from the High Assembly. If you can gather the soldiers there, we'll join them soon."

Bhadrik nodded. Something had changed about him ever since he came back with the sword, and not just the fact that Jaritta seemed to trust him more. It was that he was a soldier again. Pavresh almost said this aloud when he realized it. Not that he'd been reinstated by the jati itself, but that he no longer considered himself an outcast, an untouchable. He was a soldier because he believed it of himself.

Ekana spoke before Bhadrik could answer. "Get them there right away if you can. Even as little as they know, we don't want word of it to be guessed by those they might talk to."

"Yes, we can prepare ourselves there. I will need some sleep then, but none will leave." He paused and looked between the two, and Pavresh could see how he wasn't sure whether to treat Jaritta as the one in charge or Ekana. In the brief time since the fisherman dancer had returned from Jarnur, he had taken a leading role in their plans, propelling them toward their conflict. "We still haven't decided on the exact time to converge on the High Assembly. Will someone come to summon us, or can we decide that now?"

Ekana stepped back as if deferring to Jaritta, although something in the motion struck Pavresh as false. She accepted his deference as natural and answered, "The sixth night bell exactly. It will be dark and quiet by then. But…" she paused and looked around at the revolutionaries already gathered in the room, "we'll all meet in the tunnel and head out together."

Bhadrik frowned. "We'll be awfully conspicuous that way."

"I didn't mean we'll march through the streets together. We'll still split into smaller groups. It'll just make it easier to coordinate when we meet at the High Assembly."

"Very good. We will make our plans on how to defend the room from what stories we've heard of its interior."

Bhadrik left, and those who remained fell to discussing the details of their attempt. Not that there seemed much left to discuss. They could plan as much as they wanted, but they really had no idea how the soldiers for High Prince Baram—the mysterious women of the falcon jati—would counter, and until they knew that, planning seemed pointless.

The thought of soldiers resonated with his uneasiness, as if there was a pitch correspondence between the two. He needed to ask Bhadrik something.

"I'll be right back," he said to the others as he rushed from the room. They had no time to answer him before he was out the door and onto the street.

Their new hideout, a basement apartment in an abandoned complex, lay not far off the Prince Akas Turali Boulevard that ran from the bridge to Tanan Square. Pavresh reached it just in time to see Bhadrik head down a street on the opposite side. Pavresh dashed between carriages, ignoring the shouts of their drivers. An uneasy imitation of normal life had returned to the streets, a pretense of people acting as if they could return the city to its more peaceful past through force of will. But the quick pace and furtive looks belied that. Wallas cluttered the other side with their deliveries, but he avoided them and entered the street where the soldier had gone. He was not yet far away, and few pedestrians were here, away from the main streets.

Pavresh called to him. He paused, cocked his head at him, but waited.

"I forgot to ask," Pavresh said as he reached the soldier. Then he lowered his voice. "Did you ever ask these other soldiers what they knew about the mystery of where all the wolf jati soldiers have disappeared to?"

Bhadrik laughed, a short bark as if the question seemed unimportant to him. "No. I completely forgot about that."

"Could we ask them?"

He frowned but resumed walking. "You joining me? I don't...I suppose that's acceptable."

They weren't far from Chaitan's house, but Bhadrik took them south into a part of the city Pavresh didn't know well. Even in his story-gathering wanderings he'd mostly kept to other parts of the city. Here were many small dwellings clustered together, but not in the same way that *nefli* neighborhoods were. It was crowding that celebrated its closeness and gave no sense of deprivation. They entered one large building that clearly belonged to the soldier jati. Armed men—some of the few men Pavresh had seen in this neighborhood of the women of the wolf jati—guarded the entrance, but Bhadrik spoke some words Pavresh couldn't hear, and they were allowed inside.

Small rooms lined the hallway, about half of them empty, their doors left open. Bhadrik knocked on one that was closed, and a man opened it.

"I'll get the others," he said, stepping into the hallway. Then he stopped, his eyes on Pavresh.

"It's all right. He has just one question."

The soldier studied Pavresh briefly then shrugged as if to say he could ask, but no answer was promised. Pavresh thought of how to frame the question, of what arcist twist to add to the words. The rugged wanderer, wilderness survivor. He made his voice slightly hoarse to match the magic.

"Where are all the soldiers?"

The soldier said nothing, and his stance seemed to say he didn't intend to answer.

"So many rooms here empty," Pavresh continued, "and they've been coming down from the mountains. Only, Bhadrik here can confirm that we saw no sign of them around the abandoned city where they're supposed to be."

His body relaxed some, and Pavresh added, "It could be important for our plans."

Bhadrik nodded, and it was clearly more than just agreement with Pavresh's statement. It was an instruction for the soldier to answer him.

"Nearby. They've been stationing us in small camps scattered on the north side of the river. Upriver mostly."

"Do you know why?"

He didn't answer immediately. Was he debating whether to tell the truth or not? Or did he not like to admit ignorance?

"No," he said at last. "Only that the priests coordinate it."

"And that," Bhadrik said, "is a part of what we will remedy

tonight."

"Yes." Pavresh tried to guess the time of day by the light coming in from the windows, but he couldn't tell. It should still be morning. "I should get back to the others. Thank you." This last was to the soldier, who ignored him, and Pavresh left.

He didn't take the most direct way back as he pondered what the purpose of the nearby soldiers could be. He wandered across the Akas Turali near the steam beds and headed toward the hideout from there. He was several blocks away when he noticed Ekana walking away from him on a side street.

Pavresh stopped the shout that almost passed his lips and paused at the edge of the street. Where was Ekana going? There was an arcist swirl around him, as if his actions hadn't settled into a pattern. Pavresh decided to follow quietly.

Something about the way Ekana was walking, slightly hunched, furtive, gave the impression that he was torn by what he did, like he was two men fighting each other. As they went west into the richer neighborhoods, he straightened and picked up his pace. He still looked around often, but Pavresh kept well back and didn't think he was seen.

Ekana led him through clusters of silk weaver houses but didn't stop, and Pavresh was surprised to see that he didn't seem any more troubled by that neighborhood than any other. He tried to imagine what memories must come as the former dancer saw those silk-clad figures, but Ekana's pace didn't falter. Beyond them, he went right to the edge of the volcanic springs, the Avenue of Geysers. This time without a look back, he entered a manor familiar to Pavresh, that of Prince Dartak.

Pavresh wanted to wait, to think through and understand what might be happening. He needed time to place everything together so he didn't miss some key clue or event. This behavior was strange, so unexpected that he couldn't get his mind to fit it with everything else he knew. But it seemed more important that he get inside now and find out everything he could. Understanding could come later. Now he needed action.

He had no time for a disguise. His clothes would never pass for a cheetah jati's clothes, but he might pass for a walla or a laborer of sorts. He went to the servant entrance and let himself in. His magic was running as strongly as he could make it. If he were a horn player, his lips would grow tired within minutes, a string player and his fingertips would be ready to bleed. But he couldn't afford to stop from either pain or tiredness with his magic. "I belong here," he said over and over, both in his mind and with his magic.

Several servants moved about within sight of the entrance, but they were not high-ranking servants and ignored him. Pavresh turned down the first hallway before anyone could notice him.

He'd been in this manor once months ago, but he found little that felt familiar. He was wandering as blindly as he ever had in his work for Jasfer, as blindly as his first attempts at developing his magic.

Other servants passed him by or worked in the rooms he passed, but none said anything. He belonged. This was what Jaritta had seen in him so long ago, but so much more, too. He was the unnoticed color of the walls in a forgettable room, a part of the background in an intense painting.

Some part of him that seemed at the back of his throat, or maybe even farther back, outside his body, felt raw with the magic. He knew he wouldn't be able to hold it much longer. The pain was creeping into his vision, into his hearing, dulling both. He heard voices ahead and forced himself onward. The voices became clearer until Pavresh decided to duck into a side room.

It was more than a closet, but not much more. Cushions lined one wall as if it had been used as a retreat for reading, but the pillows were dusty. The wall between this room and the one with the people speaking was no thinner than a typical wall here, but either it was thin enough or the words echoed perfectly through the open doors.

Once inside, he hid himself behind some pillows and released his magic so he could focus on the words. As they distilled themselves into recognizable sounds, he identified Ekana's voice, though not his words. The voice that answered was familiar from his times spying, though he wasn't sure whose it was. Dartak's? Perhaps.

"And this will happen tonight?"

"Yes, *tisrah*," Ekana answered, and Pavresh was struck with a powerful arcist moment. The traitor. Not that he hadn't already begun to suspect as much of Ekana as he followed him, but this made it real.

"And the soldiers?"

A new voice answered, and Pavresh identified it as Jasfer's cousin Samatrit. "Ready to move in at my word."

He thought of what he'd learned from Bhadrik's soldier. How many thousands were nearby? Jaritta didn't stand a chance at holding the room. He ought to leave now and warn them. They had to call it off before it was too late. But he waited to find out what else they might say.

"Notify them to be ready," the voice that might be Dartak said. Pavresh imagined all those soldiers storming into the city. Would they go directly to the inner sanctum to head off the attempt, or wait, flood the High Assembly after Bhadrik and his handful of soldiers were already inside? Probably the latter so they could catch all the conspirators.

But what Dartak said next jarred Pavresh from his thoughts. "We'll give them two days of chaos. Have them enter the city in three days. Mid-afternoon for full pomp."

"I will."

Pavresh tried to puzzle this through without missing what was said next. Letting the day pass wouldn't help them. They'd be giving Jaritta the time to establish her own circle of princes.

Time for her to command the soldiers of the high prince's falcon jati, to gain the support of people in the streets. And wouldn't some of the wolf jati commanders defend the position of high prince? Maybe he shouldn't rely on that if the priests and this group of princes had as much influence as they seemed to.

"What about me, *tisrae?*" Ekana asked.

"What do you wish? It was a woman, I believe?"

"I…" Had he paused, or were the words simply not reaching Pavresh? He couldn't tell, but then Ekana continued, and the words were quite clear. "I'm not sure anymore. Sometimes I think I'd rather just leave."

This struck Pavresh as even more insulting than the simple betrayal. To betray them for Indima was hateful, and yet understandable in a way. To betray for…for nothing was beneath human.

A laugh greeted Ekana's statement, and Samatrit said, "That's easy to do."

"Peace," Dartak's voice cut him off. "Where would you go instead?"

"Raise my caste. Put me in charge of one of the new steamboats in Jarnur."

There was a brief discussion after this—it seemed to be principally between Dartak and a voice Pavresh didn't quite recognize, one familiar from the High Assembly but no one he'd been asked to focus on. An older voice, he thought, that quavered slightly as it spoke. Dartak's interests were in Jarnur, he remembered, so it would make sense for the choice to be his. Unless the steamships themselves were somehow tied with something else. The railroad, perhaps?

The discussion ended abruptly, and Dartak said, "We can do that."

There must be something he was missing here. Clearly all the mysteries he'd been following among the princes and as far as the Silk City were tied into this intrigue. He couldn't quite believe that even Rashul's revolutionary ideas had been a part of it, but at the least these princes had taken advantage of his stirrings, goading them on as a blacksmith who pumps the bellows on his fire. Advantage. That was the key. What was their advantage in this?

If Jaritta was successful, they would lose their positions as ruling princes, but that didn't seem to bother them. They spoke of a day of chaos. Did they imagine her ascension would cause so much violence in the streets? Maybe, if they created it themselves. A pattern emerged from his thoughts, an idea of what shape their intrigue would take. They would allow and foment this chaos, turn the people against Jaritta before she'd had any chance. And then the soldiers could sweep in, remove her, and install...someone new as high prince. Someone who would have acclaim from the streets and unprecedented power.

And the priests' role in this? Power as well. Whoever would take charge—and Pavresh was guessing it would be Prince Dartak, as he'd already used magic and words to establish himself as a wise and brave and charismatic leader—whoever that was would owe something to the priests. He would pay it by granting them greater power. And the soldiers also, perhaps, though he doubted the power for them would translate into Bhadrik's coveted freedom from the priests.

And the castes of Eghsal would become even more rigid as a result. That he could see quite clearly, even as the exact details remained fuzzy and uncertain.

He had to leave now and warn Jaritta. The conversation had continued as he'd thought this through, and he'd paid enough attention to know the information wasn't vital. As he prepared to step back into the hallway, he drew his magic around himself. The intense pain had faded to a distant ache, and it only needed to last long enough to get him back outside.

Before he'd taken his first step, he heard a new voice from the other room say, "Stop!"

"Who are you, to talk that way…" Samatrit's began.

Dartak asked over him, "What is it?"

Pavresh paused to discover what was happening, and the voice said, "Arcist magic. Someone is using it nearby. And very strongly."

Pavresh dropped the magic immediately, but he knew he was too late. He ran.

Shouts followed him. A servant stepped into the hallway, and Pavresh crashed past her, knocking her aside. He hardly touched the steps as he descended, slipping past more servants on the way. None tried to stop him, but he knew someone would eventually.

That someone had a familiar face. A coachman, positioning himself directly in the center of the hallway. Pavresh had cleaned the fixtures on a coach with him that day so long ago. What was his name?

"Vikpa," he called as he closed the distance. It didn't sound quite right, but it must have been close enough. The coachman hesitated, and Pavresh ducked past. His fingers, or perhaps his knuckles, brushed Pavresh's back as he stepped out of reach.

He reached the door and stepped out, but already footsteps sounded behind him. He heard Ekana's voice and didn't think he could trust his uncanny anonymity to keep the former dancer from recognizing him. That meant he had to get to Jaritta now.

Pavresh glanced back and saw a pack of soldiers following him. His time in the wilderness had strengthened him. He could keep running for a long time, but he wasn't especially fast. The soldiers gained, the distance shrank.

Pavresh looked around the nearby streets. Could he climb onto Jaritta's roof-road? Not and lose his pursuit. They'd simply follow him, and he wouldn't have her advantages of familiarity and climbing agility. On the other side was only the black rocks and columns of steam of the volcanic beds. No place to hide there.

He ran past another building, and the soldiers came even closer. Now people in the streets were paying attention, and there could easily be soldiers among them who might trap him. His only hope was the steam beds.

The space between this building and the next looked promising, but he just caught himself as he was about to run down it when he noticed a wing of the building cutting off the far end before the gap could reach the steam beds. After the next building, he found a fence and vaulted it. The rock on the other side was not soft, but he had no time for pain. An irregular-shaped pool of boiling mud bubbled to one side of him. He ran along it, finding the rock underfoot more uneven than he'd expected. The soldiers were climbing down behind him more carefully, but still they came.

Pavresh looked for something that might offer a way to hide. Columns of steam. Jumbles of rock. Everything looked so flat, even though he now knew it wasn't, and he couldn't slow down to study the land.

The ground became more uneven with wildly shaped rocks and the hint of hills and valleys. Now when he chanced to look back, he would sometimes see no soldiers. When he passed near a fumarole at the bottom of one of these slight valleys, he dashed behind its thick steam and up into a cluster of rocks. He dropped to his belly, facing the way he'd come, and slowly wiggled himself backward.

He could see the soldiers as they came over the rise, although they didn't see him yet. They paused and milled around a bit, studying the land around them. Pavresh stopped moving and kept his head as low as he could without losing sight of them. As the pounding in his ears decreased, he was surprised to hear the sounds of the city, distant but not as much as he'd have expected.

Another soldier joined the group, followed shortly after by Ekana, who scanned the area as the soldiers spoke. His dancer's grace stood out even in such a motion. None of the soldiers wore the wolf-head cloak of a commander, but that was only a small relief. The words of the last one to arrive reached Pavresh.

"Leave him. Commander says to go back and keep a watch…" The rest of his words were lost before they reached Pavresh.

"He must…nearby," another said. "Let's check…first."

"Doesn't matter. Commander says we only have to keep him out here till evening. Then it'll be too late to matter."

There was more muttering, but the soldiers left. Ekana waited until they were gone then called out, "It's only me, and I know you can hear me." He paced around the fumarole. "Come out and we can talk."

Pavresh lay as still as he could make himself. His magic would do little to make him blend in with rock, but he did what he could.

"Of course, you're a betrayer yourself. That's what started this, didn't it? Who did you tell about me and Indima? I suppose it was Jaritta's brother."

The temptation to jump up and defend himself was strong. He'd done no such thing and hated the thought of anyone, even this traitor, assuming wrong of him. He imagined himself pressed into the stone, part of the rock even, to keep himself hidden.

"Whatever it was, it worked, I guess. They got me, her stuck-up silk jati. And the soldiers and then the princes." Ekana darted up one side of the valley as if to surprise him among the rocks there, but fortunately, he'd picked the wrong side. Pavresh untied his kusti in case Ekana chose right next time. "But then, you're back now, without Indima, so it didn't work out, maybe. Or you grew bored and left her."

Pavresh ground his teeth together at the recriminations.

"And so it ends, the great dreams of Rashul. But he never could protect us anyway. Chaitan couldn't protect us, and Jaritta won't be able to either, no matter what happens. They're great dreams but nothing more, lovely stories to tell beside the fire when the reality of Eghsal becomes too much."

Back at the bottom, Ekana looked one more time around the sides of the shallow depression, stared a final time at the rocks. Then he shrugged and headed back the way the soldiers had gone. At the top, he turned back a final time and cupped his hands around his mouth.

"Don't bother trying to warn the others. There are plenty of soldiers around, I'm sure you've realized, and those guards will have our pitiable group of revolutionaries well watched. You'd never get through. Besides, by the time you reach them, no one will trust you anymore anyway. They'll know you for a traitor."

He left, and Pavresh lowered his head against the black rock.

Chapter 28

The ground snaked about, reminding Pavresh of the twisting bodies of the nagas in the carvings in the Silk City. Rocks rose into improbable shapes, undercut by tiny pools of scalding water, perfect circles, narrow channels, and shapes in between. The ground appeared to be burning, the steam rising like smoke. It was fitting. What was the world, except for smoke, illusion? Somewhere the sacred fire burned that created this smoke, but all he would ever see was illusion. Peel it back, wave away the smoke, and find only more in a never-ending circle. The fire was outside that, and therefore unknowable. If it even existed.

He didn't circle back toward the city. He'd already tried once, hoping to sneak through and warn Jaritta despite what Ekana had said. But the soldiers had guarded the Avenue of Geysers well, and not half-alert soldiers like those who'd guarded Chaitan's house. So now he wandered through a land that could as easily be another world.

He moved cautiously. The mudpots and scalding vents could surprise a wanderer. Every step was a step toward danger. It put his mind on a thin edge, ready to shift any way to maintain its balance. Any action seemed primed to cast him down, not just his mind but his body as well.

That was exactly how he had to picture it, he realized. Not just out here among the volcanic dangers, but back in the city as well. So much was happening, so many people with motives and counter motives. He wasn't even sure how much they were in control of themselves. Had Jaritta truly longed to take over ruling the city? Did Bhadrik want to overthrow the priests? Did Ekana want to betray them all? Yes to all, but he guessed that each was conflicted, each had acted out of half-understood motives and emotional reactions. Out of illusions.

A wide pool that seemed more steam than water interrupted his path. Pavresh backtracked and circled the edge as close as he dared. Maybe the steam could renew him. It fit the image of these pools, the promise of a cleansing that was deeper than any normal water could give. Even the thick mud offered a form of cleansing. But he resisted the temptation to enter the steam fully, skirting around it and heading deeper into the volcanic fields.

No people came here. Not mumblers or untouchables, not criminals, not the devious among the princes. It was empty except for him, and for that reason seemed almost an extension of himself, as if by exploring the barren land, he could better understand himself.

And what motives and counter-purposes did he find within himself?

At first it had been about the magic, nothing more or less. He'd become enamored of the strange hints of something unknowable within the magic, the intimations of power, and he'd come to Romnai to grow in that. In many ways, this remained his ultimate purpose, but his understanding of the magic had developed as well. As he learned more and fit more stories into the magic's pattern, he saw things that didn't fit the society around him. He began to long for change, to long for justice. Rashul's principles became his driving force. Now it was slightly different still. Now the magic seemed to carry its own demands, as if simply by plunging himself into the deeper parts of arcist themes he'd incurred a responsibility.

Not necessarily to Rashul's revolution, though. That was what made this so hard. To justice, certainly, but justice was no simple concept. To decide what to do now, he had to understand himself better, understand his place within the arcist magic, his place within society.

For all the stories he'd worked to form into a matrix of the magic, this was the hardest. So instead of pausing to contemplate its mysteries, he walked. Not to avoid his responsibility, even as a part of him accused himself of that, but to let his whole body work to understand, his feet as much as his mind.

A geyser shot its spray high into the air nearby, and Pavresh walked toward it, wondered what the shooting water could say about his dilemma.

The water eased off, and Pavresh stopped at the edge of where the dangerous water fell back to earth. He decided to address these thoughts to the water and to the broken, violent land all around.

"Ekana's betrayal. That's what weighs on me most right now. Why did he do it?" The words echoed strangely, as if curving around the nearby rocks to enter the ear of some listening creature. Perhaps a naga that lived in those heated pools. He made a brief bow, deciding that he would pretend that such a creature did live there. It would make it easier for him to speak.

"Though now I think of it, I remember the haunted look in his face after he returned from his first captivity. He spoke vaguely of his escape, never explaining exactly how it happened. His betrayal must have gone back that far then. Did they promise him something? Indima's return? Was he so angry with us that we hadn't been able to protect him and Indima?"

Pavresh paused to circle the dormant geyser, heading in the direction he imagined the naga to be. As he did, he remembered Ekana's return from Jarnur, and his explanation seemed evasive now. Had he tried to run away to Jarnur and been forced to return so he could betray them?

"And now…now it comes to me to betray someone. Simply allowing Jaritta to make her attempt, in a sense, was already a betrayal of Jasfer. But that never bothered me. Now that betrayal pierces deeper since it's not only Jaritta I'd be helping, but Jasfer's enemies among the princes. Even allowing it isn't really helping Jaritta, but is a betrayal itself."

The ground underfoot was broken, throwing off his balance momentarily. He climbed up to some higher rocks that were more even. The sun was heading downward now, though still hours away from setting. The days and nights were fairly balanced this time of year. He would have to choose a path soon, or simply being out here would make the decision for him to allow the attempted coup.

He addressed the imaginary naga again. "But I don't wish to help Jasfer's enemies. It won't achieve Rashul's goals except for a day or two. After that, the injustices would become even greater. So instead, I could betray Jaritta by letting the high prince know of his danger. Betray Jaritta. It seems cruel to even entertain the thought. And what will that do for Rashul's cause? Likely nothing. The princes who remain will try to strengthen their hold as well."

Pavresh's path took him toward a pile of rocks on the far side of the geyser. Trickles of hot water spilled beneath his feet, as if one large pool filled the top of that rise, emptied by many tiny rivulets. It seemed a fitting place to find a water spirit like the nagas.

"If I can't warn Jaritta to postpone her attempt, then maybe the best is to allow the coup, even if it means they will be thrown down after a day. The memory of that brief success may just be enough. Justice will be thrown back for a time, but with the right stories told, the right memories preserved, maybe someday others will rise up and be successful where Rashul wasn't. But can I be so cold, so cruel to both Jaritta and Jasfer?"

He reached the top and found a pool much as he'd imagined, but not quite as regular a shape. Rather, it was more like several interconnected pools with paths of slick rock cutting between them. He knelt at the end of this maze and said, "I just don't know. It is a betrayal whatever I do, and I don't wish to be a betrayer."

After these words, he stayed silent—not only aloud, but even in his thoughts, trying to find the peace of the sacred fire within the steam of that pool. No naga emerged, though he didn't think he would have been completely surprised if one had. Eventually he stood, removed his kusti, and performed the patterns of his worship.

* * *

When Pavresh came back to himself, he stepped out among the pools of steaming water, following the narrow strips of solid ground. Even after he reached the far side, his mind seemed to sense a path ahead, as if the maze of that hilltop extended into the field around. He was only half conscious of controlling his own body as he wove among the dangers of the fumarole field. A part of him that was either above or below his conscious self knew exactly where to step to find his way through the labyrinth.

Paths opened up. What seemed a single mudpot became two. What seemed an impassable channel of boiling water plunged briefly underground. Pavresh walked without questioning along these paths.

At last the labyrinth led him to a single arch, a natural bridge of stone that stretched over a confusion of fumaroles and pools and tiny mudpots. There whatever had been leading him stopped, abandoned him again to make his own choices.

The drop was dizzying. Pavresh lowered himself carefully onto his knees and peered over the edge. The mesmerizing landscape below called out to him, urging him to jump. Wouldn't it be strange and wonderful and, most of all, new to go flying through the air on the way down? What would it feel like as he fell?

Pavresh pushed himself to the middle of the bridge to think. Maybe the answer lay within his magic. But the image he got whenever he tried to think of a betrayal didn't seem to fit. Betrayal was so deeply opposed by arcism, the ultimate wrong. It was the brother who turned against his family, the child who led an army against her parents.

He pictured a sinister figure, a mumbler not how they really were in the abandoned city but how his people imagined them. He pictured evil deeds done in shadows, cruel laughter, a smell of trickery like some perfume not quite covering a foul odor.

Where was the space for his actions against such images?

He imagined the betrayer delighting in the act. That was the main thing. It seemed that he would be forced into betraying someone, but he wouldn't enjoy it. He hadn't joined in with Rashul and Jaritta and the others thinking from the start that he wanted to betray them. He hadn't agreed to help Jasfer in his spying while gleefully considering how he might betray that trust. It was the reluctance that was missing in all these images.

As he thought, he let his gaze wander. The bridge gave him a wide view of the fumarole fields, with a taller rock just to his north blocking out most of the city. He could see all manner of strange formations and features, the pools and vents and streams of mineral-heavy water. How did such a land fit within the magic? It was a fearful land. He could sense that much—a lack of potable water and edible vegetation coupled with the unpredictable dangers of the steam vents.

But that wasn't all there was to the land. It served a purpose beyond what images it evoked in the magic. This was a cold valley, far north of the equator lands of his people's past. The sun struggled to warm it for much of the year, yet they had good growing seasons and water that didn't have to be melted. The size of this part of the valley boggled him, the thought that he could walk all day and not reach the mountains on the southern edge. Given what the arcist image was for this place, he should be terrified, but he wasn't.

It was these very dangers that made his people able to live in the valley with the comforts they had. These immense fields and the others by Pashun and the Silk City and abandoned Eghsal made the whole valley warm. He'd traveled enough away from the cities to know that even a little distance made a difference in temperature, and in the mountains, if he could believe Bhadrik, the cold was far greater.

The terror of the arcist image of these lands was only a part of their nature, a simplification.

Simplified! It was obvious in many ways, even something he may have been aware of at times during his training, but now it struck him as something profound. Arcist magic was useful. It could peel away lies and illusion, could dig beneath the surface to help people understand things. But it would be wrong to think it matched the cosmos of the sacred fire perfectly. It was a map, a guide created to assist visitors—and all people were visitors in a way—but it simplified everything, didn't replace the world.

Even if he had to betray someone, and he still didn't see a way to avoid that, it wouldn't make him that arcist image of betrayal, the sinister figure he'd been picturing. That might be a part of him, as it might be a part of any person if they really looked at themselves honestly, but it didn't tell everything, it didn't define him.

With that thought, Pavresh pushed himself up and climbed carefully from the bridge of stone. He still wasn't sure which would be best, which betrayal would be lesser within the context of everything he knew and suspected. But he knew he would act. He would give himself permission to regret it later.

Now he had to be in Romnai when the attempted coup took place.

The strange features of the land kept getting in his way. Pavresh could see the city whenever he decided to climb a little way up the piles of stone he passed, but it always seemed that a steaming pool or a crack in the ground cut him off from it. After reaching yet another gully whose bottom he couldn't see, he decided to jump across. It was easily within range for any fit person to jump, even without a running approach, but something about that emptiness below made it frightening. Pavresh found a relatively smooth approach and carefully cleared it of any loose stones that might throw off his jump. Then he ran and leaped.

A brief blast of warmer air hit him as he crossed, but otherwise, he made it over without anything strange, landing well beyond the far edge.

After that, it was as if the hostile land released its hold on him, and he merely had to weave around what obstacles remained between him and the city. Soldiers still stood along the border between the city and the steam beds, but with darkness not far off, Pavresh was sure he could find some place to slip past them. It should give him just enough time to be within the city before the attempt began. Time to neither prevent it from starting nor assist it, but in time to be a part of it in a way.

That was what mattered.

Chapter 29

Jaritta made them wait in the rough tunnel longer than they'd planned, hoping Pavresh would return. She knew what Ekana had said, that he'd seen the arcist that afternoon, apparently trying to betray them, but she couldn't believe it. As darkness came, it became clear that it didn't matter. If he hadn't shown up, then he was too late.

And that did make him look either guilty or cowardly.

A bell sounded somewhere in the city, late for any of the usual bell ringings, and Jaritta stood up. "Let's go."

She hadn't needed to say anything. Already the others were moving out, following their careful plans. At last count, they'd had over fifty, and more of Rashul's contacts had arrived after that. Bhadrik's soldiers, the rough-edged laborers, and even some of those who'd spent time at Chaitan's, though for this night's attempt, those thinkers and dreamers were of much less importance. It seemed a staggering number, that so many would support her attempt to claim the prince-ship, and yet insufficient at the same time. Jaritta and a few more who would travel with her threw on black cloaks that in the light of dusk should make them look like death workers. Some others made attempts at disguises of one sort or another, but mostly their plan relied on them to move quickly and draw no attention to themselves.

Once out, they split into their groups and walked as fast as they dared without drawing too much attention to themselves.

Jaritta's group consisted mostly of laborers and one of Bhadrik's soldiers. She didn't know the names of any of them.

The laborers had sacks on their backs filled with a variety of items. One even carried a large piece of lumber. According to Bhadrik, they would need such things to fortify the inner room. All Jaritta carried was a single long knife.

The streets were empty, even more so than she would have expected. They saw no soldiers as they went, even as they neared the High Assembly. With how crowded with soldiers Romnai had been ever since the riot outside Chaitan's house, this made her uneasy. It had to be good, she told herself, a sign of the gods' favor, but she couldn't stop herself from wondering why it would be so.

Light from open windows across the city reflected off the low-hanging steam, so they didn't move in as much darkness as Jaritta had expected. Strange shadows shifted in that orange-tinted light. The farther they got without seeing soldiers, the more ominous those shadows seemed.

It felt like hours had passed by the time they reached the building and rejoined as a single group. Glorious arches formed the main entrance, but they kept around to the side. The High Assembly was not and had never been a fort. It had not been built to keep people out by any stretch. More than a dozen doors opened onto the square surrounding the building, though all would be locked at this time.

Bhadrik's soldiers had known something of the inside of the building, and they led the way to one particular door where the surrounding square narrowed to little more than an alley. One of Rashul's laborer contacts stepped forward with what looked liked an oddly twisted crowbar. The tool shrieked as he pulled on the door, but no heads poked from the nearby windows. At least not from those that were lit. Jaritta began seeing forms in every darkened window, a hint of a profile, a gathering of heads and shoulders, skeletal arms pointing their direction. Did the shadows whisper, or was that imagination?

The bar locking the door bent and slipped free, and this

time the noise brought attention. Voices cried out from the nearby darkness. Jaritta heard footsteps on the square, though she couldn't be sure that was in response to the conspirators.

"Hurry," she whispered. No one needed to be told. The men at the front pulled the door open, and everyone pushed to get them inside.

Jaritta was ready for a battle right there, had expected at the least a few guards bravely standing their ground. The hallway was empty. For a moment, the sense of disconnect between what she saw and what she expected was so strong that she glanced around to see if Pavresh was using his magic to manipulate her feelings. But no, the arcist was nowhere.

The soldiers led, their swords out and poised at a precise angle. They'd debated giving slings to the others coming behind, but none had enough experience with the weapon. So they carried knives and sections of pipe as clubs. They surrounded Jaritta close, as if she were a child. Ekana walked beside her.

The dark hallways felt even stranger empty than the streets had, as if someone had come through ahead of them to clear things out. She wanted to reach a hand out to the polished wood and stone of the wall for comfort, but there were people on every side of her. Too close, it seemed now.

Footsteps sounded down a side hallway, and they picked up their pace. At this point, it shouldn't matter much if news reached the high prince. He'd have the usual number of guards in place, a number established by tradition, but by now, it should be too late to mount a full defense. That was what Bhadrik told her, anyway, and he and his jati had countless tales of past attempts to draw from, passed from generation to generation.

The main room of the Assembly opened before them, the towering doors of the adjoined temple nearby, lit by the room's few lights. At first Jaritta didn't recognize the room because they entered from a servant passage, but as they rushed across to the ornate doors of the Inner Sanctum, memories slammed into her. Families weren't regularly allowed among the princes at work, but there'd been enough times when she'd come here, tagging along with her father or accompanying her mother to bring him some news or item from the house that couldn't be trusted to servants.

Even as they ran, her mind lit the room with remembered lamps, filled it with arguing princes and not-quite-invisible servants. And she felt that little girl that had been her, the young woman even, descend into her own body. What was she doing? Being surrounded by soldiers, strange but fine. The wolf jati regularly protected the princely jati. But these others… And where were her servants? The questions flooded her, but even through it, Jaritta knew who she was today, remembered herself as untouchable. It seemed that the room itself was an arcist, battering her with images she struggled to resist. She tried to picture herself as a rock in the middle of the river, the water sweeping by but not moving her.

And almost without her knowing it, they were at the door, the imagined waters receding, while wisps of her teenage self lingered at the edges of her mind.

Tradition kept this door always unlocked, and they would have to abide by that as well once they were inside, though they intended to do what they could to block them. It was not the only entrance into the room, as the high prince's falcon jati had passageways and tunnels from their quarters with direct access to the Inner Sanctum. But it was the only way a pretender could enter the room to claim it. The door pulled heavily, and guards on the other side jumped as Jaritta's soldiers revealed themselves. The guards moved as if underwater in the steam baths, reaching for weapons, calling out commands. These were the fabled women who fought for the high prince, would fight for her soon, if she succeeded. Their fighting style was unique and hypnotic, a combination of specific kicks and jabs paired with sword thrusts.

One turned to run, and Bhadrik felled her with his sling. Felled. That was exactly the right word, just as she imagined a tree would fall, gracefully in that slowed-down air.

But there was nothing graceful in the form lying on the ground. Jaritta stared at it as her soldiers and the room's guards fought. These were not wolf jati soldiers, but they were no less trained to fight. Their mesmerizing style posed a distinct challenge to her soldiers because of how different it was to their own.

Jaritta dragged her eyes away from the guard on the ground to watch the fighting directly in front of her. They were doing this for her. Not fully, and maybe not even at the deepest level, but in some sense, this was for her, and she couldn't let herself look away. Each flash of red that became a wound was a fire that threatened to burn her. Her hands wanted to pull her cloak down over her scars, but she kept them still and simply watched.

The guards were easily outnumbered, and even she could tell that they weren't necessarily fighting to drive her wolf jati soldiers back. They fought to delay them. They would give their lives simply so the rest of their jati would more likely succeed in taking the room back. They fought to wound, to make later fighting more difficult.

Jaritta could sense this honor in them and wished there was something she could do to reward it instead of killing them. But events had turned as they had, and she could only go along now. If she needed to be purified later, well, the sacred fire had already rejected her once, so she couldn't be more damned than that, according to the priests.

She wished for a sword for herself, something more than her knife, which seemed so small now. At least then the effort to stay alive would keep her from seeing the rest of the fighting.

She'd experienced her share of street fights, but she was their key to the plan—without her, they had no chance of claiming the position of high prince. And besides, she was a woman, and despite the women they were fighting against, it seemed the default to assume that fighting was for the men. Watching the fighting made her think that they had the easier role. Men chose to be the fighters not out of a desire to protect others, not to prove their worth, even if these reasons existed, but to lose themselves, to hide from the bigger picture of war. It was those forced to watch who endured the entire scope of terror and disorder.

Jaritta shivered at the cries, at the violence of every swing, but she watched each of the guards fall, saw several of her own soldiers fall as well. When poets called war madness, it wasn't a figure of speech or an exaggeration—it was truth. She could feel a part of herself going crazy as the fight progressed. The sacred fire had not created the human mind for such things.

At last they entered the room, the soldiers pulling the bodies of both friend and enemy with them so they could shut the door. Some stirred, and one of the soldiers bent down to check on them, but Bhadrik grabbed Jaritta's arm and pulled her further inside.

The Inner Sanctum was a maze rather than a single room. Each new high prince changed the layout of the space, adding different entrances that led to the rooms of the falcon jati and false doors at the end of other hallways. The passageways were long and twisted, with false ends and hallways that continued beyond those doors that proved to be true. Some ancient tradition kept the high prince's guards beyond the building itself. Bhadrik and his soldiers had figured that even if they were identified as a threat to the Inner Sanctum, as soon as they entered the High Assembly, they should have an hour before the soldiers would be ready to mount a full counterattack. A few small groups might attempt to keep them off balance, but the full force would wait until its leaders had judged how best to fight.

That gave them time to explore. They needed to get a rough map of the rooms within and an idea of which doors were true. Then they could block those doors off and set their own defense. The soldiers and laborers ran in groups of three and four throughout the labyrinth. They banged on walls for hidden doors, peered into the shadow-darkened ceilings for trap doors, listened for a hollow sound to their footprints for passageways underneath.

While they did this, Bhadrik and Ekana forced Jaritta to wait in the center, with them standing guard beside her. The walls formed a small room of sorts, carpeted like the rest of the Sanctum, and with a single cushioned chair. Jaritta refused to sit.

"This is the most important part," Bhadrik explained as if they hadn't gone over the plan in detail already, while Jaritta kept her gaze shifting erratically around what was visible of the Inner Sanctum. Ekana's head jerked about no less anxiously.

"If we can just get ourselves established, then the demand to last a full day isn't difficult. We have the numbers to hold it."

"I was expecting more of a fight to get inside in the first place," Ekana said.

"They don't care about us getting inside, only about us staying here."

"That can't be all there is," Jaritta said. "They wouldn't just sacrifice those guards at the door for no reason." As she said it, her eyes went toward the entrance, now out of sight, and in her mind, she saw the bodies propped against the door. Her stomach churned, and she reached up with a hand to cover her mouth.

Bhadrik shrugged as if the deaths meant nothing to him.

They fell into an uncomfortable silence for a moment, and Jaritta strained her ears for any hints of fighting. An hour,

Bhadrik had said in planning. If they could have an hour to search the rooms and passageways, they should be able to set their defenses and hold for a day. With the fire's luck.

Jaritta jumped at a crashing noise down one passage, and Bhadrik stiffened as well before saying, "They're setting up a block, sounds like."

The noises continued, and Jaritta realized that it was the sound of wood being laid down, wedged at angles at a narrow point in the passage. It certainly wouldn't stop anyone from coming—they would have needed much more material to do that—but the purpose was simply to slow the soldiers down. Soon similar noises came from other passages.

Bhadrik nodded at each sound as if seeing progress through the tones and vibrations. "Just a little longer," he muttered.

Jaritta tried to create a map in her mind from those sounds as well, but all she could do was imagine each passage continuing as it was when she last saw it. This only brought the hallways into intersecting each other, twisting into a snarl that made even less sense than a maze would.

Soldiers came within sight, a few coming all the way to the center room to tell Bhadrik about what they'd found or what they expected. Jaritta couldn't concentrate on their words, but she pictured them as an army of spiders scurrying about to maintain the web of their queen spider, herself. Ekana fidgeted beside her and kept looking up the different hallways and at the door. She felt bad for him—this was surely very different from fishing, very different from dancing. What would he have thought when he first came to Chaitan's house to dance if he had known he'd end up here? But then, what would any of them think?

No, not end up. This was only one step along the way, not an ending. A crash punctuated this thought, and all three jumped and turned. There was nothing for a moment, no sound, no co-conspirator in view, but then a laborer stepped around the corner and looked their way without looking at their eyes.

"Sorry, *tisrae*. Or, *tisrah* and sirs."

Jaritta tried to wave away his discomfort, but he wasn't looking high enough to see her hand. This was what the revolution had to do, destroy this sense of inferiority in people like him, allow them to look even at those in power with their heads held high.

She didn't say anything along these lines, of course, and the man continued. "It was only some lumber that we…that I knocked down."

"Fine. Get back to work." Bhadrik turned away to say something to Jaritta, but before he could get the word out, the laborer dropped. Jaritta shouted. Maybe it was a scream, though she didn't want to call it that. Blood appeared on the man's shirt.

Bhadrik swore and said something like, "too soon," as he stepped in front of Jaritta. His sword lay within reach on top of a pillowed chair, but it was his sling he had ready. In his left hand, he held bullets, their metal dull but still somehow mesmerizing.

The hallways were silent, but it was a silence on the verge of crashing into chaotic noise, a geyser at the point of going off. The tense silence stretched longer than Jaritta thought possible. It had to break now. No? Then now. But it didn't, and the body of the laborer lay unmoving as if to taunt them.

The first noise to break the dam of silence was only a trickle of sound, meaningless, unidentifiable. Jaritta strained her ears only to have them assaulted by the cacophony of noise that broke through. Shouts and cries. Sharp commands. A sound of stone moving. Jaritta wanted to move, but she didn't know which way to go. Even if she'd known where the fighting was, she wasn't sure if she wanted to rush there and join the fight or run the other way.

Even Bhadrik hesitated, though Jaritta didn't think it had anything to do with uncertainty about his prowess. He seemed to radiate his own heat, a fire that meant war. All he lacked was where to channel it. Immediately after this thought ran through her head, Bhadrik shot away from her down a side tunnel rather than the one where she could see the still form of the laborer. Beside her, Ekana clenched his teeth and shifted his stance but didn't go anywhere. He held a sword not much bigger than her knife.

The shouts and noises went on and on without any clue of what they meant, a language Jaritta couldn't understand. She wanted someone to come back and translate for her, let her know how the defense went, but, all she heard was Bhadrik's mutter repeating itself in her head. *Too soon. Too soon, too soon, too soon.*

The words grew louder, pushing against each other, echoing off the twisting walls of the maze. *Toosoon, toosoon, toosoon.*

Jaritta gripped her knife. The blade seemed especially ludicrous now as she stood in that place. A child's toy. Good for scaling fish, perhaps, but little else. The words became too powerful. *Toosoontoosoontoosoon.*

Leaving the frozen Ekana behind, she ran from the central room to the corner where the body lay. Kneeling, she peeked into the tunnel, exposing only the top of her head. Here, the sounds of fighting drowned out Bhadrik's muttered words.

Not that it was a pleasant replacement. Each scream grated. The cries were more animal-like than human, except for the brutality. Only humans were capable of that. Her eyes lagged behind her ears in taking in the battle fought in those tight tunnels. At first all she saw was fractured bits of images, a mosaic of the Forgotten South scattered into pieces. When her mind put the pieces together, she saw soldiers entering from a hidden door in the hallway. Women in the distinctive headpieces of the high prince's guard, but others also, wolf jati if she had to guess. Compared to them her own soldiers seemed ragtag, a bunch of incompetents.

They fought, though. They fought and bled and died for her. The hidden door opened a short ways behind one of the makeshift blocks so that those entering had been able to cut Bhadrik's soldiers into two groups, an isolated one trapped against the barrier, and those who came from other passageways to stop them. And the soldiers kept pouring in. This was no small group sent to slow them down until the full force was ready. How could they have prepared themselves so quickly?

Jaritta saw when the resistance from the trapped group ended. Had all been killed, or some captured? She wasn't sure. A face on the ground looked familiar, Rijef, one of the people who'd argued and dreamed with them at Chaitan's house. She thought about running down the hallway and adding her knife to the chaos, but she knew it would only get her killed. These were trained soldiers, not pickpockets and petty thieves. They would hardly be distracted by an old woman swinging a knife. And she definitely felt old. She wasn't—far from it be the standards of the caste and jati she'd be born to—but she felt the years of her life on the street pressing against her, multiplying themselves many times over.

The knife began slipping from her fingers, and she leaned into a wall. Her hands. Hands that had meant to form clay didn't know how to hold a knife. And yet...letting go of the knife was letting others shape her.

She tightened her fingers and stood straight, preparing to charge. Before she could, someone else entered the fray. Bhadrik had found another side passage that brought him into the middle of the growing body of guards and soldiers, surprising them, and he moved with a grace and breath-taking speed that stunned Jaritta. He was a primal force, fighting not only with his sword but with his feet and elbows, spinning and twisting and driving through the now-confused fighters.

The soldiers Bhadrik had recruited, those who remained, took up a strange cry as they saw him. It seemed a word, though no word Jaritta knew, and the wolf jati soldiers among their enemies paused as they heard it, some turning to Bhadrik with what looked like awe.

The high prince's falcon jati fought on, seemingly unaware of what had stunned their comrades. But no matter what they did, they couldn't get close enough to touch Bhadrik. They counterattacked, and his sword cut a swath of flame, his kicks burning those opposite the blade. They were too crowded together to take advantage of their numbers, and the growing pile of the fallen hampered them even more.

His appearance and the surge by his fellow soldiers seemed about to push the others back through their hidden doorway. They wavered and fell back or simply fell, and Jaritta allowed herself a moment of pride at their resolve. The battle seemed to pause, poised at an edge between two dizzying drops, and she expected it to fall her way, for the door to be sealed and the passageways secured. But with surprising swiftness, it rolled the other way as more soldiers came out pushing hard.

Then a bang came from behind her, the sound of debris being removed, and before her soldiers could react, other fighters came running from another passageway. Jaritta spun with her knife out in a vain hope to stop them, but after one swing that would have driven back any street thief, if not disemboweled him, she found her arm pinned and her knife on the floor.

Bhadrik fought on, but as unstoppable as he seemed, there were simply too many against him. What remained of the rest of the rebels were subdued or killed, and the soldiers pulled back from Bhadrik to give just a few the space to take him down.

A sling bullet zinged Bhadrik's arm, but there wasn't space for anyone to sling at full speed, and too many people to make it safe. So, no more came, and Bhadrik appeared unaffected. He approached the nearest soldiers, swinging and focused, but even before he could fully engage, another soldier darted in from the side. Bhadrik caught the sword and swung into a counter, but the action opened his other side, and swords came flowing. He twisted, parried, kicked, but the flood of soldiers was too much, the strange fighting style finding openings.

Jaritta watched the fight from against the wall of the passageway, a soldier holding her silently.

Bhadrik slowed, his wild fighting, perhaps, having consumed the fuel that drove him. His sword still bit, but without the quick shifts of before, and the circle of soldiers closed. A line of blood flared along his side, despite the leather armor there. Then one on his thigh. He stumbled, righted himself, struck again. One of the soldiers attacking him fell. Jaritta didn't think she'd been seriously wounded, and another stepped forward in her place.

He refused to give up even as it became clear that he was doomed. There were shouts from the other soldiers. Did they want him taken alive to be tried? Killed on the spot? She didn't think he'd give them an option unless they wounded him so badly he lost consciousness.

The swords tore into his leather, ripped it away slowly to expose his body. It seemed to dissipate like smoke in a wind. And then the blades pierced the muscles of his belly, three almost simultaneously while Bhadrik's sword swung just above their exposed edges. He crumpled still weakly swinging, his arms still trying to fight as he fell.

Jaritta hadn't loved him, had hardly liked him and only recently dared to trust him. But if she'd been a different person, she knew his death would have made her cry. Even as an untouchable who'd sworn never to cry, she felt a twitch, a ghost of a tear. Her brother would have wept. Perhaps Chaitan would have, or Tanjali. Maybe Pavresh. She turned that impulse into a jerk at her elbow, a tug and jab that briefly freed her as her captor stumbled away.

She took one step. The cloth over her head came loose, exposing the full scar, scaly skin back behind what remained of her ear, but before she could take a second step, the soldier leaped from his stumble and tackled her to the ground. She squirmed, tried to get an elbow on him again, but he was ready now and kept her down.

It was from this position, her face resting on the carpeted floor, that Jaritta saw the new arrivals. First came the high prince himself. He'd been a young prince when Jaritta last saw him, before she'd been outcast. Just one of many princes, though it wasn't long after that when the former high prince retired, and Baram managed to take his place with a lot of deals and little bloodshed. As far as she'd ever heard, this was the first time he'd had to deal with an attempted takeover. He looked surprisingly calm for that.

Jaritta was pulled up and shoved among a handful of other survivors as the high prince approached. She looked again at the arrivals as she joined the huddled group and noticed other figures behind. Servants some, and more guards, but also more familiar faces. Jasfer, her brother who wasn't a brother.

And Pavresh, the betrayer.

Without being able to use her hands, she still managed to mold her face into a perfect vessel of hatred.

Chapter 30

Pavresh ran through the words he would say until he felt ready. The trial of the princes was not a public affair in Tanan Square as the earlier trial of the rioters had been. This was held in the High Assembly and attended by princes and others of the *kortru* jatis. Pavresh expected to be compelled to tell what he knew, all that he'd seen. He entered with Prince Jasfer and a circle of his household servants. They took their places near the ornate doorway of the Inner Sanctum.

People crowded the room, far more than the times he'd been there when the princes were in session. Families with young children. Silk weavers and non-ruling princes. Priests clustered together near the door into the adjoined temple. People spoke, and the room was far from quiet, but it didn't feel loud either. Something in the air muffled every noise, reminding Pavresh of the way Namrani used to dampen the sound of her stringed instrument for certain parts of her improvised songs.

What noise there was faded to nothing when guards entered, escorting the disgraced princes. Dartak came first. Whoever his arcist had been, he wasn't there to cast a glamor over the prince, but he retained his stately appearance, his face more that of a martyr than a traitor. Samatrit followed, and two more princes. Jasfer stiffened when the last entered, an older man whose name Pavresh thought he should remember. Arbul, perhaps. A friend of Jasfer's father? The few days they'd spent in prison while waiting for Baram to convene the trial had left these last three more bedraggled than Dartak.

A handful of priests also shuffled in, and about a dozen wolf jati soldiers, bound as if even lacking weapons they posed a threat to their guards. Both groups, but especially the soldiers, were certainly simply a token number among those involved. Pavresh doubted Baram knew exactly who was most responsible, and he wouldn't want to punish every soldier who'd simply followed orders. But these would have been chosen to send a very specific message to their respective jatis.

Pavresh tried to guess what thoughts were going through the minds of the families of the wolf jati, the wives and children of the priests. Whether their husbands and sons and fathers were up there or not, they must be feeling that the ground had become uncertain, must be wondering if a geyser would explode beneath their feet.

The prisoners were made to kneel, facing the Inner Sanctum, and then the doors opened. Baram stepped out in full regalia, his ceremonial robes of ancient silk, his headpiece that was said to date back to the Forgotten South. But even those weighty clothes did not overpower the high prince himself. They seemed a mere afterthought to complement his authority, and Pavresh knew that arcist magic had to be at work in such an image. What he was less sure of was if it was a person casting that sense or simply a natural part of the role of high prince that evoked it. At his side stood a quartet of falcon jati soldiers, also dressed for ceremony with feathered spears and loose clothing that left their legs bare.

Pavresh licked his lips and thought of his words again, but Baram did not ask for witnesses. He moved first to the soldiers.

"You have betrayed your jati, your high prince, and the Valley of Eghsal. Your trial will take place tomorrow before the people of the city in Tanan Square."

His words were flat, not meant to inspire or move the gathered people. It was a death sentence, in spite of the simplicity of how it was announced.

Seemingly as an afterthought, he added, "Along with the survivors of the rebels."

Jaritta. Pavresh looked at Jasfer for a reaction, but he showed none. Pavresh tried not to picture her falling into scalding water, screaming as the rest of her skin became as scarred as her face. Not that she'd live long enough for such a burn to scar, but that was the image that wanted to take over his thoughts.

The soldiers were led out, and Baram had already moved to the priests by the time Pavresh managed to banish the images enough to pay attention. They showed no exceptional signs of fear, no change after the sentence on the soldiers.

"I name you traitors as well, traitors not only to the city but to the sacred fire." That was a strong claim, and some of the priests seemed shaken by it, their shoulders dropping, their heads falling lower. "You made claims of what the gods wanted merely to advance your own desires. Such an act is abhorrent. You are stripped of your jati, stripped of caste, and given to the final judgment of the fire as untouchables."

It sounded harsh, and no doubt some of the priests thought it so. Whispers passed through the room as those gathered discussed it. Was it just? To Pavresh, it seemed lenient. The soldiers got death, but the priests, of whom better was expected and who probably had been more instrumental in the plans and intrigue, were only cast out? Or perhaps not even that. If they stayed in Romnai, they'd likely find some members of their former jati who sympathized with them enough to offer what shelter and food they dared.

Last, he came to the four princes. Arbul—Pavresh had now heard the name and confirmed his guess—Tarak, who wasn't familiar to Pavresh, Samatrit, and Dartak. Was this really the extent of the conspiracy? Probably the core of it from what he'd seen, but other princes had likely been aware of some of the deals and manipulations.

"My cousins, whom I trusted. You deserve no less than these. Lest anyone doubts the severity of your crimes or the rumors that have reached them…" Baram gestured for one of his servants to step forward.

The woman held out a scroll and read, beginning with a list of the princes' names and titles, the names of their fathers, and some of the details of their past service to the valley. Then she retold their crimes for the people gathered there. "You perverted the cause of holy priests, bribed high-ranking soldiers. You used money gained from the silk weavers to position the wolf jati where it had no right to be, leaving the valley vulnerable to the mumblers of the mountains. You used your influence over the railroads to twist this new technology, this future of our valley, to your own uses, to the detriment of princes, priests, and silk weavers. You encouraged rebel forces to violence so that you could, in turn, defeat them and liberate the city from a threat of your own devising. You plotted not only against the high prince, but against the city itself, against the valley as a whole with attempts to turn people against people and jati against jati.

"Your crimes go beyond simple intrigue, beyond both business and government, into the realm of reprehensible betrayal."

The woman stepped back, tucking the scroll under her arm, and Baram resumed speaking. "Crimes of this nature call for punishment. For exile, perhaps, a stripping of rank, a banishment not only for yourselves but for your children."

Only banishment? After the death and pain they caused, the violence and betrayals? Banishment to the mountains at the least, something that would lead to a lingering death if possible, though the children could be left unharmed. But Baram didn't seem to agree with Pavresh on this.

"Perhaps that is excessive. You will be stripped of rank and jati, declared untouchable with no hope of restitution. Your children, however, will remain within the jati of princes, but none of them may ever succeed to the Thirty as long as you, their fathers, live."

There was some murmuring at this. Pavresh wasn't sure if it meant people were surprised by how heavy the punishment was or how light. It seemed grossly unfair to him, a spitting on all those who'd died. He wanted to jump up and give his own sentence, to slap the high prince across the face for his effrontery, and take his place. Not fully. He didn't long for the power or responsibilities of leading the council of princes. But he wanted for a brief time to control the fates of these men who'd manipulated him and others he'd come to respect, even love.

Yet he remembered that he was a betrayer, also. Like a whisper among his shouts for justice, a voice reminded him of what he'd done, and that voice kept him seated more than the impossibility of making a difference here.

"You will be untouchable, but you will not be allowed to disappear. Not in the ruins of Eghsal, and not in the streets of Romnai or the other cities. You will be imprisoned from this day forward."

Pavresh took pleasure in the way Samatrit's shoulders drooped, the fierce whispering from some of the princely jati, who might have been their relatives. They thought it too much, although Dartak's straight back seemed to imply he thought it wouldn't last, that someday he would be free again. It still seemed too easy a punishment to Pavresh, not fitting the image he had of their cruelty, their cold-hearted intrigue.

The guards marched the princes away, and Pavresh imagined tortures for them, imagined ways he could sneak into their cells and take revenge. Some part of the magic seemed to argue that revenge never fit, images of those seeking revenge ending equally unjust, equally separated from fire. But for the moment, that didn't matter.

The prisoners out of sight, the crowd became restless. High Prince Baram was saying nothing more, simply speaking with some of his servants, but he hadn't dismissed them either. The crowd trickled away on its own.

As Pavresh left with Jasfer's entourage, the high prince gestured for Jasfer to approach. They whispered briefly, and one of the guards joined in the discussion. Jasfer spent most of the conversation nodding and soon rejoined his servants, and they left.

Back at Jasfer's manor, the prince asked Pavresh to join him in one of the studies. It seemed unconscionably fine, the polished wood and worked stone, the elegant decorations. That he should be here while Bhadrik lay dead, while Jaritta and others awaited execution in prison, while Rashul and Chaitan were imprisoned in their homes—and who knew what reprisals might come against them even despite their lack of involvement? Marankiya imprisoned as well if not dead—no one seemed to know, or if they knew, willing to tell him. It was wrong at some deep level, a flaw in the cosmos.

Jasfer motioned for him to sit against a single pillow on the floor while he reclined against another pile of pillows. Pavresh sat on the bare floor, letting his back touch the pillow, but without leaning against it.

"What can you tell me about the spy who infiltrated Rashul's group? This, uh, Ekana?"

Ekana? Why did that schemer matter now? "He's a fisherman from Jarnur. One-time lover of a silk weaver who is now in the Silk City."

Jasfer cocked his head at this and peered at Pavresh's face, but Pavresh shrugged and sat quietly. "Truly. Would he seek to be reunited with her?"

"Has he escaped?" Jasfer only nodded as if Pavresh should have already known this, but it came as a surprise to him. He'd been there for part of the night. Pavresh had heard enough from others to be sure of that. Had he somehow slipped out as the loyal soldiers came? Pavresh let himself sink into the arcist magic. What would Ekana try to do? If he fit the pattern of the separated lover, he'd surely make an attempt at the Silk City. But if he considered himself the common man broken by the ways of the world, he might simply return home.

"He might. Or back to Jarnur."

What had he asked the princes for? He'd been a broken man already then, wanting to leave Eghsal entirely. He had a startling image of the slight fisherman loaded with supplies, pulling them on a sled as he climbed into the southern mountains. Simply to survive in the wilds? Pavresh doubted it. He would seek the Forgotten South.

The image was so powerful, he was sure that it was what Ekana had actually done or was preparing to do. Arcist magic didn't work that way, offered no guarantees that any one individual would follow a certain path, but something about the vision made him sure it was more than typical arcist magic.

He said nothing of this to Jasfer and committed Ekana to the care of the sacred fire. His betrayal was something he could no longer hate, not after his own betrayal. And as he thought of all Bhadrik had told of those impassible mountains, he knew the judgment would come from the fire anyway. Most likely he merely escaped to die another way.

"Good. I'll pass that along to Baram." Spoken so casually, as if he and the high prince had grown up the closest of friends. Maybe that was good, not only for Jasfer, who as far as princes went was a reasonable leader, but also for Jaritta's fate.

Before he could turn the conversation that way, Jasfer continued. "How do you imagine he became a tool of the traitors? How long have they been laying the ground for this?"

"He fell into their hands within the last half a year, *tisrah*. Through the wolf jati, I'm sure, when they captured him for a minor incident involving the silk weavers. The princes may have been planning this for years, but they didn't have someone inside Chaitan's house that long ago."

Jasfer nodded and seemed relieved. Pavresh supposed that Ekana's perfect presence among Rashul's crowd might otherwise imply even deeper plots with other masterminds still undiscovered. It didn't seem likely. There were probably others who'd known parts of the plans, who'd lent a measure of support, but not the key players in the plot, and they would stay quiet now.

"Thank you, Pavresh. You've been a great help to me over the past months." He studied Pavresh, or maybe his eyes were focused beyond the arcist, studying some image in his mind. "You'll be known now. Among the other princes, among their servants and the soldiers. I'd like to offer you a position as a reward. It will no longer be as a spy, though I'll likely have even greater need of that. But as an honored servant, if you'll accept."

Before Pavresh could answer, there was a commotion at the front door and the sounds of many people entering. Kalvandi stuck her head into the room. "*Tisrah*, your lady-wife has arrived."

"Wife?" Pavresh said without thinking.

"Thank you, Kalvandi. I will see to her shortly. Welcome her for me, and see that her servants and items are all installed smoothly."

Kalvandi assented and left, and Jasfer turned to Pavresh with an embarrassed look on his face. "Some relatives arranged it. It will be a good match, I believe. But it does mean you'll be serving in a much larger household. If you accept."

Pavresh tried to imagine what he could possibly do among so many cheetah jati servants. He wouldn't have to pretend he'd been born to it, as he had before, but it would still feel false. He would never be a true part of things. Yet, there was something tempting about accepting the offer for just a few years. It would be easy, a way to rest from all that had happened recently.

He could plan for the journey he still hoped to make among the mumblers, learn what he could from whoever might know more about them.

Tempting, but he knew it was a dangerous comfort, something that would lure him to keep putting the journey off. Just one more month, another season, another twelve-day to learn one final thing or prepare just a bit more.

"Thank you." Pavresh leaned back against the pillow and watched the movement of shadows in the corner of the ceiling. The sun couldn't light them, and even the flickering lamps seemed less powerful than that shadow. That would be him if he stayed, an agent of the fire but powerless. "The offer is a generous one, but I feel I must leave the city again."

"You are sure? I…I would be pleased to have you around, no matter what your role."

It sounded genuine, not simply an offer out of duty, and Pavresh felt another wave of temptation. What hurry was there to flee? But he shrugged it off. "I am sure, *tisrah*. I intend to return someday, and when I do, I may see if your offer stands. But for now, I must travel. I wish to develop my understanding of the magic."

"Your magic. Ah, I see." The whole exchange passed in a sort of haze, as if both of them were grasping at the words, awkward and uncertain, not the easy dialogue they had enjoyed at times in the past. The prince had always been the master and Pavresh the servant, but they'd had a rapport that came as close to camaraderie as their positions allowed. Now it was gone, and they each seemed unsure how to treat the other.

Jasfer repeated, "Your magic. Well, if you return, do check in with me and see." The prince looked about to dismiss Pavresh, so he had to bring up his final concern now.

"What of…Chaitan and Rashul? Will they be blamed for any of this?"

"What? Oh, no. I believe Baram is planning to release

Rashul or ease his imprisonment somehow as a sign for the agitated rabble. And Chaitan remains untouchable, and not in the caste sense."

"And…your sister?"

Jasfer pursed his lips, and wrinkles appeared around his eyes making him look older. "I have no sister. But Jaritta will be… I have no power in such things."

Pavresh leaned forward, almost rising to his feet. "You do now, though. You have the high prince's ear. You've risen in his favor. Use that, and simply banish her. Pay a fine from your own money or sacrifice a bit of your newfound favor to set her free."

"She's a danger now. She tried to overthrow the prince. If I lay my neck out for her, Baram will chop it off and then cast her into the fire just the same."

Pavresh could see that it hurt the prince to say this. He *wanted* to be able to help his sister, even if he couldn't call her that. It was almost enough to make Pavresh take an easier line, even assure him that he did the best he could. Almost, but not quite. He stood, stepped close, and lowered his voice to a confidant's whisper.

"She's no danger. You know that. You know her."

Jasfer rose to his feet at this, a complex series of emotions playing across his face. Anger at Pavresh, fear, anger at himself, frustration, perhaps even anger at Jaritta. "No danger? She attempted to set herself up as high prince. Baram would be foolish to allow her to live, seen as weak."

Pavresh abandoned his calm reasoning. "You kill your own sister."

"Not my sister! And you are dismissed."

Pavresh held his ground a moment, standing kusti to kusti to his caste-superior. Then he turned with a snap, offering none of the expected words as he left.

In the hallway, he passed a number of servants who must

have heard the shouts, but they all looked away, those familiar to him from long-standing service to the prince as well as the new ones. Something nagged at him as he strode out the hallways to the front door, something slightly out of place with the servants he saw, but he didn't pause to consider it.

Only when he was outside on the Avenue of Geysers did he realize what it was. All those he'd passed had been familiar. Not only Jasfer's own servants, but his new servants as well. How did he recognize them? An image rose in his mind of sitting in a room of cheetah jati servants, trying to uncover what he could of the soldiers next door while Indima played kiwan with Datri.

Datri.

He paused as if to return and warn Jasfer about his new wife, but when he looked back at the door, he saw one of her servants watching him. He sped up and left the district of the princely manors behind.

* * *

At Chaitan's house, Pavresh found music. Namrani sat along the wall playing her beautiful, restored instrument, and the memories it evoked brought a lump to his throat. But Chaitan wasn't in the main room, and Kapita told him she wouldn't ask if he would see Pavresh.

"He's very sick, Pavresh. He needs to rest, but I'm afraid even resting won't help for much longer."

Pavresh remembered his own claim when he'd first presented himself to Chaitan. The heir. The image mocked him as he left to wander the streets of Romnai.

He bought a few supplies for his journey. It would be colder than his last journey, colder also than the travels that brought him to Romnai, but he shouldn't have any trouble reaching the ruined city before winter. Then, he went to the last hideout of the rebels to recover anything he might have left behind. After that, he had nowhere to go. He stood in the empty apartment looking at the abandoned rooms, neglected items on the floor. The personal items left behind lent the rooms a heavy sadness. Extra clothing, a few small musical instruments, the ragged ends of the cheap string that had held together some of their food, an empty gourd for tisane.

He didn't think he could spend the night there, though it seemed an obvious solution to his lack of a place to sleep. He feared the walls would reject him or close around him. Or maybe it was simply his own mind that would do that to him if he let himself dwell on the people who'd been here last.

Pavresh was still standing there when the people entered. He hadn't heard footsteps to warn him of their approach. He recognized the two servants just before Datri followed them in and shut the door.

It seemed for a moment that he was back in the Silk City, fearful of others uncovering his identity. But what did he care now if someone knew him? Enough people knew of Prince Jasfer's arcist spy.

Reminding himself of this, he straightened his back and waited for her to speak.

"I've heard something of your discussion with my soon-to-be husband."

Pavresh said nothing. What could she want? Something about her arrival felt less threatening than the times she'd cornered him in the Silk City. But he certainly didn't trust her.

"I wish to help you free the girl."

Jaritta, of course, but his first impulse was to remind Datri that *the girl* was nearly twice her age. All he said was, "Why?"

Datri moved around the room to a high counter and perched on its edge. "I know you don't trust me." Pavresh made no attempt to deny it. "But trust my sense of self-preservation. My husband will be a much more powerful ruler if he's not haunted by being complicit in the execution of his sister."

There was some sense to this, but was that only because she'd found a plausible story?

"Think carefully," Datri continued. "You're leaving the city behind. I won't pretend I wish you would stay because of what you know about me from the Silk City. But I have no reason to betray you." She leaned forward, sliding off the counter edge. "That would be striking against myself. If you were caught trying to free her, then the suspicion would go right back to Jasfer, cutting out the power he has rapidly gained."

Power. That, of course, was what she was after, was what he'd seen in her back in the Silk City. That was his key to deciding whether to accept her help or not. There was no arcist theme that really fit here. Anything he applied oversimplified some part of what was happening. So, what power could she be after? She hadn't married Jasfer yet, so his disgrace could let her marry someone else. But who else had the power? She was exactly right that Jasfer had rapidly become one of the most powerful princes by exposing to High Prince Baram the plot against him. Any other prince besides the married Baram himself would be beneath that, and Jasfer's disgrace would not necessarily raise another prince up. Someone would eventually fill the power void, but Pavresh certainly couldn't predict who.

He could hope that Datri also couldn't predict as much and trust her. As far as this night went anyway. Or he could assume further layers of intrigue beyond what he could even guess and turn away, abandoning Jaritta to her death.

When he put it this way, he was almost certain there were countless layers of intrigue burying Datri's every action, layers impossible to pierce. But at the same time, if there was a chance of rescuing some of the rebels from execution…

"How can we do this?"

Datri smiled, and it didn't reassure him. "I know some people who owe me. Or fear what I know about them."

* * *

The prison that held the surviving rebels was off Tanan Square, where the execution would be. As they neared, Datri went ahead with one servant, and by the time Pavresh entered the open door, no one was in the room. A set of keys lay out in plain sight.

Datri's other servant unlocked the inner door while Pavresh adjusted the travel gear he didn't dare set down, and both went inside to find Jaritta. The prisoners were asleep, and Pavresh realized how late it must be. He unlocked doors as he went, though the first cells didn't have Jaritta inside. Only a handful of cells held anyone, there were so few surviving rebels.

"The *tisrah* said nothing about releasing the other prisoners," the servant whispered, but Pavresh ignored him.

The sound of the key was the only noise in that strange quiet, and Pavresh found it made him move more quickly. When might Datri and the guards return? How long could she possibly keep them away? He couldn't have much longer. But still he opened every door, and the prisoners didn't wake. He found Jaritta, and she woke just before he said anything. Almost strange that her years on the streets hadn't trained her to wake even sooner, but the quick alertness in her gaze spoke of her past.

She followed him out without a word, her eyes were wide in uncertainty, and beneath that, a fierce anger. He could imagine the questions she was asking—how had he come; how would they escape; why would he, their betrayer, rescue them; was it even rescue, or something more sinister—but he couldn't take time to answer. A noise from out in the entrance startled Pavresh. He darted into an open cell and woke the two men there.

They were slower to become alert but followed as soon as they were half-awake. Jaritta had already woken two more, and they moved ahead to wake the rest.

It couldn't have taken long—a hundred flame flickers, a hundred breaths—but it seemed that at any moment, the guards would come running back. Pavresh loosened the knot on his kusti.

At last they were out, and Pavresh paused to speak a few words, even as he wanted only to run, run, run. "I'll be leaving the city, going to the ruins of Eghsal. I think Jaritta should leave, too, or she'll surely be found. If you wish to come with me, you may, or disappear into the streets. Decide now, because once we start running, we won't stop."

He gave them no time to debate or consider but grabbed Jaritta's arm and started running. There were voices from a side room, but they made it out without being seen. Pavresh hardly saw the streets as they made for the bridge. About half the men peeled off into side streets, leaving Pavresh with Jaritta and maybe four or five others. He didn't take the time to count. Across the river, a train appeared ready to pull out, but a commotion near the front delayed its departure. Pavresh guessed that was Datri's doing as well. More of the prisoners must have disappeared into the slums on this side of the river, so it was only two others who climbed into an empty freight car with them.

Almost immediately the argument ceased, and the train gathered speed, pulling them away from the intrigue and dangers, away from Jaritta's home—how must she feel about that?—but what had seemed his home, as well, even in the short and interrupted times he'd been there.

Let them be sad. Accept that emotion, that arcist theme. He allowed his magic to play on it, to swell with the ache of exile. But let them be hopeful, too, for they had other lands and new homes lying ahead to welcome them.

Jaritta leaned her head against the hard wall of the car as far from Pavresh as she could, but Pavresh stood at the open door, watching the darkened land pass by, wondering how he would ever fit everything that had happened into the arcist map of human experience.

Epilogue

Cousin Yatim,

Once again, I send you greetings from my travels. I've been in this eastern city for some time now, learning from the people, getting to know them. Your sister also arrived safely and found former friends. She's now an important part of certain circles here—you would be proud. I don't see her much myself as I move among other groups, and now I prepare to leave.

One thing I wish to tell you about—it will seem silly, so inconsequential for a letter from this distance, and yet I hope you'll forgive my silliness. We played our games of kiwan so many times that I wished to share about a new variation I've learned of, a new type of stone that I've run into in the eastern cities.

Oh, but before I do, I hear you have a new lover? Is this true? In that case, I imagine she will have read this letter by now as well. So, my greetings to you, too.

This new kiwan stone is used in various ways. It is beautiful, and I think those new to it will often mistakenly assume that is its only purpose, beauty. Silky colors and a smooth shine encourage this assumption. But it's a tricky stone that adds much more to the game than some realize. Skilled players are right to be leery of the stone. It is difficult to trust exactly what the stone will do. Given this spin, will it bounce there, skip here, curl around? I can't really capture in words what it does, but of course, if you have the opportunity to find it involved in a game, you'll have to experience its surprises that way.

It can drastically shift an entire game, and not necessarily in favor of the one who played it. Sometimes it favors those who throw it, though, as it did recently when an opponent of mine used it, and I was forced to flee that eastern city. No more of that. I didn't write to tell again of things you know.

But here is the key from those who've come to trust the piece. If they truly understand it, then they speak wildly of the ways it helps them. You almost get the sense that they believe the stone to be a shadow partner, sending out stones on their behalf, even guessing at the intentions of their opponent. It may be tempting to dismiss this as mystical silliness, but I believe there's something to it. If a player learns it can be trusted, the silky piece could be almost as I was to you in some of your games.

Enough rambling of games, I suppose. If you see my mentor—I pray he is still well—send him my love and let him know I am doing as he suggested. The journey will take me far from familiar places, both in geography and in craft. Greet your masters for me.

Your cousin, Parsh.

THE END

DRAMATIS PERSONAE

Assembly of Princes and their attendants

Baram The High Prince
Jasfer a young prince
 Kalvandi Jasfer's steward
 Yatim a trained fighter
 Taurav footman

Apijet Jasfer's mentor
Samatrit Jasfer's cousin
Dartak an eloquent speaker
 Teert head of servants
 Abhish head footman
 Vipak footman

Vedu older member of the ruling 30
Tarak supporter of Dartak in the Assembly
 Sindar his servant

Dhalip friend of Jasfer's father
Arbul friend of Jasfer's father, patron of the railroad
Girmeet former mentee of Apijet
Lakanrik the oldest member of the ruling 30
 Karket his grandson and heir

Shardash member of the ruling 30
Bhainu member of the ruling 30

Chaitan's house

Chaitan	hero of the Mumbler Wars, founder of arcist magic, now infirm
Pavresh	a young wanderer who wants to learn magic from Chaitan
Rashul	charismatic leader of would-be rebels
Ekana	a fisherman and dancer
Indima	a silk weaver and dancer
Namrani	a quiet musician
Jaritta	an outcast with a fire scar on her face
Iksheen	a poet who deliberately obscures his caste
Rilef	also learning arcist magic
Marankaya	former theological prodigy, now disgraced
Tanjali	Chaitan's attendant
Kapita	Chaitan's attendant
Purunrik	supporter of Rashul
Tanmai	supporter of Rashul, brother of Upeng
Upeng	supporter of Rashul, brother of Tanmai

Silk Weavers

Jinsu	Indima's father
Ambal	father to two small children
Kisar	Ambal's wife
Datri	weaver girl, companion of Indima
Malya	weaver girl, friend of Indima in Romani
Charu	weaver girl, friend of Indima in Romani
Juki	weaver girl, friend of Indima in Romani
Raksh	head servant to Indima's family
Shidi	servant woman to Indima's family
Phangun	servant to Datri's family

Soldiers of the Wolf Jati

Karuda   Commander of mountain post
Bhadrik
Surjit
Tugar
Deraj
Hirsha

Timeline of the Valley of Eghsal

Year 0:   People journey from Forgotten South. Details
                 of why and how have been lost (or perhaps
                 intentionally destroyed)
0-300:   Many skirmishes with the mumblers who
                 originally inhabited the valley
300:   First reliable records. Caste structure and
                 system of 30 ruling princes already in place
340-375:   Major warfare with the mumblers
early 400s: Jarnur and Pashun founded (isolated
                 fishermen had previously lived at the mouth
                 of the river, but no actual settlement)
450:   shifting of volcanic activity leads to Eghsal
                 City being abandoned. Romnai founded and
                 declared capital
500-506:   Tensions between cities lead to Pashun and
                 Jarnur both declaring independence from
                 Romnai; army of untouchables becomes a
                 threat to all cities and leads to them re-
                 uniting
575-590:   The Mumbler Wars—nearly disastrous, won
                 in large part because of Chaitan's arcist magic
630:   present day

About the Author

Daniel Ausema is a speculative fiction writer and stay-at-home dad. He's had a number of stories and poems published over the past few years in a variety of venues, including *Strange Horizons, Mythic Delirium, Daily Science Fiction*. His story "Untouched by Fire" was published in *Myriad Lands* also by Guardbridge Books, and it introduces some of the characters in this novel. Prior to moving to Colorado and staying at home with his kids, he worked in experiential education (high ropes courses, team building, climbing walls) and more traditional education as well as freelance writing.

His writing interests are broad and draw from a great variety of sources, but most of the time what he writes falls somewhere in the broad and nebulous regions of fantasy and science fiction, with some touches of horror here and there, and a good deal of deep strangeness, magical realism, and wild surreality. He loves writing that is lyrical and imaginative, writing that touches on social justice and that evokes a sense of wonder, and especially prizes creativity, even for its own sake. He describes *Spire City*, his serial fiction project, as steampunk with touches of New Weird.

www.ingramcontent.com/pod-product-compliance
Lightning Source LLC
Chambersburg PA
CBHW060757210726

48292CB00013B/209